ISBN 978-1-989868-00-3 (Paperback Edition)

ISBN 978-1-989868-01-0 (Electronic Edition)

Editing by: Fox Edits and Cauldron Press

Cover design by Cauldron Press

Cover illustration @2020 by Odette Aurora Bach

Published by Cauldron Press

info@cauldronpress.online

Visit www.ansage.ca

KARTEGA

KARTEGA CHRONICLES, BOOK 1

A. N. SAGE

CAULDRON
PRESS

*"Though my soul may set in darkness,
it will rise in perfect light;
I have loved the stars too fondly
to be fearful of the night."*

-Sarah Williams

ONE

THE AIR TASTED of bitterness and oil. Like week old algae kibble rolled in engine fluid. Sid smacked her dry lips together, trying to wash away the taste but it clung to the roof of her mouth, unwilling to budge.

"WARNING! WARNING! THE EMERGENCY SELF-DESTRUCT MECHANISM IS NOW ACTIVE!"

The ship's high pitched, mechanical voice boomed over the sound system as Sid skidded across the floor of the spacecraft. Sweat beaded down her olive brow, threatening to fall into her large-set eyes. She unzipped the top of her suit without losing momentum, ripped the top layer off her drenched body, and rushed past the med bay doors.

Her legs sliced through the air and she briskly grabbed a toolbox off the dining table without breaking her sprint. The box screeched as she dragged it across the steel tabletop, making Sid's thighs quiver with discomfort. The ship's corridors were a maze of twists and turns, a maze she knew like the back of her hand having spent the majority of her days fixing the never-ending malfunctions of the system. She didn't mind passing all her time fumbling around with wrenches and grips; after all, time is something she had plenty of. The ship was a puzzle that only she knew how to solve and keep together. What did bother her, however, was that lately the ship, *her* ship, seemed to be missing too many pieces. Her puzzle was incomplete.

"DANGER! CARBON DIOXIDE VALVE FAILURE! ALL ON BOARD MUST EVACUATE VIA THE EAST WING ESCAPE PODS!"

"Oh, shut your metal starhole!" She yelled to the ship, hoping it might actually come to life at her words. The Arcturus had been her home for almost thirteen years but at times like this, she wanted nothing more than to hop into an escape pod and watch it drift off into eternity. "I'm almost there, you metal piece of junk!"

Two more rights and a sharp left and Sid slid to a determined stop in front of the greenhouse control room. The normally fogged glass doors were dripping wet and a small puddle was already starting to form at the base of the panes. Air production was failing quickly.

"Starspit!" Sid hissed, immediately regretting her words. Even alone she hated the roughness of the swear rushing from her lips.

She wiped a sweaty palm on the base of her suit and raised it to the keylock. The system beeped maniacally for a brief moment before a green light flashed and the doors slid open. Sid bolted to the control panel, dropping the toolbox with a shattering bang and dug out a set of ratchets. Her fingers fumbled through the sizes, landing quickly on the correct one. Not missing a beat, Sid raised the tool to the faulty valve and began to twist. Her callused palms, red from the pressure, ached immediately. The skin ripping on the unforgiving roughness of the metal.

With each turn, the force of the ratchet slowed as the valve refused to be turned back into its place. "Oh, for the love of the Star! Come on!" She cried and continued to work. She had fixed the faulty part four times in the last month alone, not counting all the other valves rusting around it, waiting to break.

Sid wiped her now soaked brow and tried to remember the date of the next supply shipment. Colton said he would pack a few spare valves to help with air control. The pressure on her head and chest was making her lose track of the dates. When was the shipment? Next week? Or was it the one after next? Whenever it was, it wasn't in the next ten minutes so there was no point figuring it out.

Tightening a fist around the ratchet handle, she offered an annoyed huff and turned the tool again.

"THE SHIP WILL DETONATE IN T MINUS FIVE MINUTES! MANUAL CLIMATE CONTROL OVER-RIDE WILL SHUT DOWN IN TEN, NINE, EIGHT..."

"I thought I told you to keep it down!" She yelled, pushing her entire body weight into each twist.

At her minimal height, Sid was nothing if not resource-ful. If she needed to be stronger, she willed herself to be as strong as a hundred droids. If she needed to reach something off a high shelf, she built a system of pulleys to help her. There were a million ways to die living alone on a dusty, old spaceship and if there was one thing Sid knew for certain, she wasn't dying because of some broken valve.

"SIX, FIVE..."

She dropped the ratchet and twisted the chain until her hands grabbed the largest tool in the set. Her arm stretched behind her, Sid gathered her strength and slammed the ratchet on the valve.

"Not today, you pathetic piece of space garbage!" She screamed, delivering another blow.

"THREE..."

Sid swung again. The blow landing squarely in the middle of the valve, causing it to bounce back into position. She tossed the set of tools to the ground and turned. One twist. Then one more. Turn after turn until she was sure the stardamned thing was secure and no longer leaking gas. Her hands shaking, she stepped back, raising her palms in surrender. Her head swung around, waiting for the next announcement.

She grit her teeth, "come on, come on, come on."

Silence.

"Come on!"

Sid balled her hand and brought it down to the wall with a thud, immediately regretting the decision. The pain hit her as soon as her bones met with the metal. She jerked her hand away, shaking it to bring the feeling back and hissing under her breath.

"Oh, for the love of–"

"CARBON DIOXIDE VALVE SECURE. SELF-DESTRUCT MECHANISM DISENGAGED. ALL SYSTEMS NORMAL."

Sid let out a sigh and leaned against the cold steel next to her, sliding slowly to the floor. She reached for the goggles on her head, stretching the band to wipe the fog from the glass then popped them back on; covering her cat-like grey eyes and the thin vertical pupil that ran across them. Obstructing the one thing that singled out her species from view. "You know, one of these days you're going to kill me, Rusty." She sighed, "and I'm starting to think you might be happy about it."

Silence enveloped her shaking body.

"Rusty?" She raised her grey eyes to the ceiling, searching for the camera lens. She cleared her throat, "Arcturus?"

A red light blinked in the corner of the room and a small lens adjusted until it was centered on her face.

"ALL SYSTEMS CHECKED. DETECTING NO ANOMALIES AT THE PRESENT TIME."

"Muck. Now I have to reprogram your command recognitions, Rusty."

She watched as the camera offered a few more lens twists and returned back to the base. Rolling her eyes, Sid picked up the set of ratchets from the floor and tossed them back into the toolbox. Maybe she could get her metal friend back to normal before dinner. She'd have to remember to ask Colton for a new speech module for the ship's computer. Sid would sooner space herself than spend the rest of her life calling it Arcturus. It sounded like one of the incurable diseases she'd learned about in her history projections. The ones that made Colton's people come to Neostar in the first place. Well, her ship wasn't a disease. Her ship was regal and strong and—

Drip!

Sid wiped the water from her eyes and looked up, tracing the drip to the now leaking ceiling above her.

"Time to get you patched up again!"

With a loud huff, she tugged her suit back on and made her way out of the greenhouse, her fingers running along the lightly yellowing leaves of the plants as she passed.

"How about a nice red leaf broth and a frigger egg for dinner, Rusty?" She asked the ship, "I think we deserve it."

TWO

"STARDAUGHTER!" Sid cursed as air began hissing from the pipe above her. She had been splayed beneath the belly of the ship's engine for hours and every time she had managed to patch something up, another problem reared its head. The Arcturus reminded her of an old man on his deathbed, making bargains with the nurses to help him transition to the afters. Except in this case, she was the nurse and she hated every minute of it.

"SUCH LANGUAGE IS IN DIRECT VIOLATION WITH THE NEOSTAR ORDER'S RULES OF CONDUCT." The ship's voice echoed in response.

"Shut it, Rusty!"

"COMMAND OVERRIDE ACCEPTED."

"Yeah, yeah," Sid sighed. She had managed to restore the voice commands to her preferred settings after yesterday's meltdown and was quickly regretting not deleting Colton's original codes for language control. While she was fully aware that rough language was not something dignified little girls lived by, the occasional slip of the tongue did not strike her as something to be scolded for by a two-hundred-ton metal scrapyard. As soon as she was done patching up the oxygen pipes, she'd have to reprogram the beast to a more acceptable social standard. At least, as social as a standard could get on a ship with a population of one.

Her legs pushed against the metal grid beneath her feet, causing the glider base to slide out from under the engine. Without rising — or looking — Sid's hand found the bracket in the mess of parts next to her and she pulled herself back into position. Her tongue curled up to touch her top lip, "come on, Rusty. Let's get you breathing nice and proper so we can have time to shower before Colton calls."

"IMPROPER USE OF WATER WILL CAUSE A BREAKDOWN OF THE SHIPS ELECTRICAL CIRCUITS. PLEASE ADVISE ON A NEW COMMAND PRIOR TO ENGAGING IN THE UNDE-TERMINED SHOWER PROTOCOL."

"Oh, for the love of the star, Rusty. I didn't mean you! Fine, no showers!" She lifted her arm and inhaled quickly, "On second thoughts, maybe just the one shower for me then."

Sid reached into her suit pocket and popped a few screws into her mouth, readying them for the job. She tightened the first screw, then the next, each one leveling the pipe's angle slightly closer to where it should be. Everything was just a few inches off from where it should be on the ship. On any other day, Sid wouldn't mind playing around with parts until she figured out a way to solve a problem but today was different. Today was the day of her scheduled weekly call from Colton and she had to be on her best behavior. Not that Colton cared much for how she looked. He had seen her at her worst and still took care of her, as much taking care of as someone can do from two hundred thousand klicks away.

A burst of air shot through the crack in the pipe and she jerked her head to the side to avoid it, completely forgetting the trusty goggles that tightened around her eyes. Sid had sported the deteriorating eyewear since as long as she could remember, one of the first gifts Colton had sent to her with a supply delivery. *To protect you,* she remembered him saying. Protect her from what exactly? The only thing she needed saving from was the utter boredom of spending years alone on a ship orbiting a star she was not allowed to step foot on.

Sid did not remember much of her young years before her life on the Arcturus. There were flashes of memory here and there but all of her knowledge of Neostar came from self-led lessons on the ship's database projections. Colton had laid out a strict regimen of lesson plans for her to follow and being the good girl that she was, she ingested the information hungrily — almost as fast as she ingested her dinners each night.

She pressed her palm against the crack, letting the pressure of the cold air pound against her skin until it burnt. Yanking her hand away she reached for a small scrap of metal in her suit pocket and the welding torch resting next to her. Her back arched for leverage as she carefully traced small circles with the flame around the edges of the scrap. The metal bubbled and she let out a soft chuckle, impressed with herself for a brief moment. A very brief moment indeed. As soon as she had patched up the leak, the pipe creaked and groaned, as if upset for her caging it. Sid was just about to attempt a second patch when the scrap of metal shot from the pipe and fired at her eyes.

"Rusty!" She yelped, touching her finger to the now cracked glass of the left goggle. "Get it together!"

She fished out another scrap of metal and forcibly shoved it against the leak, "Fine! If that's how you want to play, that's how we'll do it!"

Her palm heated around the metal, the blood within her bubbling with energy and fire. Sid squeezed her hand tighter around the pipe, unyielding to its screams beneath her fingers. Her entire body shook as she directed all of her energy into the metal in her grip. She could feel the scrap melting, slowly at first, like the slow drip of molasses from a cut tree. Then, within mere seconds, the molecules of the metal bid her command and liquified, unable to contain their solid form. She pulled her hand away and wiped the excess molten metal with a handkerchief, forcing it into the crack. As soon as she was no longer in contact with it, the metal settled and formed a rigid tissue in the pipe.

Sid tapped the pipe in encouragement. "See, Rusty?" She raised her left arm, lining up the scar she got from fixing the last air leak to the shiny metal line now running through the pipe. "Now we're twins!"

There was a light rustle at the end of the corridor and Sid sprang up, her breath catching in her throat. If anyone saw her use her magic, there'd be no escaping Colton's wrath on their call today. She was never to use her magic. No exceptions. That was Colton's only rule and she hated breaking it. But what could she do? It's not like he was here to help her with this mess. Besides, who could possibly even be on the ship? Colton locked her away in the piece of junk and drifted her off. Why did she even need to hide? Why couldn't she live with him on Neostar? Sid knew the answer to that, but it didn't make her resent the notion any less.

Colton was waiting for the right moment to bring her down, waiting until she was older and stronger. But she was strong enough! She wasn't the little kid he had saved from parents who threw her away like a shipment of garbage. She didn't need to hide, why couldn't he see that?

The rustle sounded again, this time louder — more defiant — and Sid instantly recognized it. There were a few sporadic clicking sounds and then a whoosh of air sounded through the pipe above her. Just the air control system kicking back in.

"We don't tell anyone about this, Rusty." She said, raising a threatening fist in the air. "You're no rat, right?"

She watched as the camera lens rearranged gears and focused on her face.

"IN THE FIRST YEAR OF THE NEOSTAR ORDER, ALL THOSE IN SUPPORT OF THE AL'IIL WERE DEAMED AS CONSPIRATORS AGAINST THE QUEEN AND EXECUTED UPON CAPTURE. THEY WERE LABELED AS DOMER RATS BY THE MASS PUBLIC OF NEOSTAR."

"That's what I thought," she winked and lowered her fist. "We're no Domers, you and I."

Even as she said it, Sid's mouth dried. She truly disliked that word. In all of her studies, it was the one thing about the Neostar Order that she didn't support. Something about it didn't sit right, like it was wrong. Worse than all the swear words she whispered under her breath when she was angry. Domer. It was too jagged of a term and even though it described the inhabitants of the domes so perfectly, it tasted sour in her mouth.

She had once asked Colton about it but he simply shrugged it off. According to him, when his people first created the domes to preserve the future of Neostar and everyone's harmonious survival, the term wasn't widely used. *Someone probably just threw it around and it stuck,* he said, *you know how these things are, nothing for you to worry about.* But she had no idea how things really were, all she knew were whatever scraps of information she could stitch together from her lessons; that Colton's people saved the star, and everyone was grateful for their blessings. Without them, the star was on a path of self-destruction and the technology they delivered saved the entire native population from extinction. They had developed the Circulum System as a means of life support for the dying star, using it to work hand in hand with the magic of the Al'iil; though no one called them that anymore. Most of the original inhabitants stayed in the domes with their own kind which led to the name Sid had developed such a distaste for — Domers. It fit but it was too descriptive for her to ever get used to it.

"I don't think I'd like to live in a dome, Rusty." She smirked, "You're a way better home."

She knew, of course, that when she finally got to go to Neostar, Colton would do no such thing as shove her into the domes with the rest of the workers — she was sure of it! She'd get to live with him in the towers. Above them all, in the fresh air. Sid closed her eyes, imagining her future. She would spend her days learning the intricate webs of the technology Colton had told her so much about, the saving grace of the star. Her nights would be spent exploring Tower City and getting to know each and every fine Citizen that crossed her path. Sid was determined to meet them all. "The queen, Rusty!" She yelped with excitement, "I'd get to meet the queen!"

She sucked in a breath of air, picturing the day she

would finally lay eyes upon the beauty of Queen Leona. Not in some projection but in real life, Sid would be so close to her she'd be able to smell her. She would smell like star flowers and power.

Sid stretched the goggles from her eyes and popped them back in place on her messy bangs, rubbing the dent the elastic left on her temples. She took another sharp breath and coughed from the dust that trapped itself in her throat.

Right. Until that day comes, she was still stuck floating around in circles in the belly of the ship's metal grip. Stuck imagining the life she would have and getting glimpses of it from Colton's stories and...

"Stardaughter! Rusty? What time is it?"

"CURRENT TIME IS TWELVE MINUTES TO STARSET."

"Time to go!" Sid yelled out and ran down the corridor towards the ladder leading to her sleeping quarters. She had twelve minutes to make herself look less disheveled before Colton called in.

She was halfway down the corridor when she stopped in her tracks and ran back to the pipe she had just repaired, tossing the stained handkerchief in her pocket over the metal scar and the imprint her fingers made when she melted it. *Better safe than sorry,* she thought and tied a tight knot to bury the evidence of her magic use. Maybe it was alright to hide for just a little bit longer.

THREE

SID TUGGED AT HER FINGER, trying to rip off the dead layer of skin that had formed on top of one of her calluses. She had been sitting in the upper deck of the ship for seven minutes, eagerly awaiting Colton's call. He was late and Colton was never late to anything. In fact, the last time Sid lost track of time and kept him waiting, he'd scolded her on the importance of punctuality. *Your word is the only thing that matters in this world,* he said when she asked why she needed to be punctual in the ghost town that was her home.

"Where's your word now, Colton?" She scoffed and averted her gaze from the blank screen. "I thought your people were all about good timing?"

The ship's manual controls flashed green, red and yellow; casting a kaleidoscope of lights over Sid's small frame. Though she hadn't met anyone of her own species, she assumed that she must have been the smallest of her kind. All the visuals of the Domer population portrayed in the telescreens had been of tall, brute people and Sid was nowhere close to that. At just over a meter sixty, the only thing that showed her resemblance to the native population of the star her ship orbited were her unnaturally large eyes. Her gaze trailed the vast darkness beyond the observation windows, landing immediately on Neostar. The current orbit position of the ship was at such an angle that the star looked like a red ball floating in space. Sid had never seen a beach ball in real life but she imagined it would look exactly like this, covered in red leaf trees and decisively peaceful. She was too far to make out any detail but on particularly dark nights, Sid was certain she was able to make out the star's jungle to the smallest leaf; a lonely imagination was good for finding life where there was none. Within a blink, she saw the Circulum System power up and the ring began to spin around the star. The bright yellow light of energy reflected off the stars surface, coating it in a warm shade of orange as it passed that made Sid wonder how exquisite it must look from the surface. A star-sized energy ring that shone the color of gold would be hard to miss. She wondered if it shone extra bright when it was right above one's head, if it was so bright it obscured the two moons entirely? There were no images of the Circulum System in action from the surface of the star so Sid often had to rely on her own assumptions based on what she could see from her ship's windows. And what she saw was beautiful. Beautiful and so very timely.

The ring's movement could only mean one thing; it was Starset.

There were only two rotations scheduled for the Circulum System daily; one at Starise and the other at Starset. The ring's own movements mirrored those of the white sun and two moons that shared Neostar's orbit, as one slept the other two awakened. When Sid was a kid, Colton once told her that the ring made two passes because it didn't want to miss out on anyone's company. She actually believed the story until she found the common sense to ask for astrology texts. Though to this day, she still had to admit that she liked Colton's version much better. It was poetic somehow and Sid loved a good story!

Something glimmered in her sightline and Sid jerked her head to the opposite side of the observation deck, spotting the bright, white light of the Jericho sun in the distance. *Yep, definitely Starset.*

"Oh, he's definitely late now!" She chirped just as the holographic display flashed on in front of her.

"I'm so sorry, Sid." Colton said, still settling into his chair. "There were some urgent NSO matters that ran longer than anticipated."

"It's fine. Neostar Order always wins out in the end," she shot back with a sigh and slouched into the plush command chair, allowing the fabric to almost swallow her whole.

Colton's face contorted and he brushed back his thin grey hair in defeat. "Don't pout, no one likes a pouter," he joked, raising a bushy white brow in her direction. Why did he always know how to make her smile when she was upset? It was infuriating.

"Fine," she perked up in the chair, "so what happened? Not the droids again?"

"No, no, we repaired those last week." Colton rubbed the bridge of his nose and she traced her eyes along the shape of it. It looked so much like her own. Same slant, same bone structure, even almost the same length. Sid knew he was not her biological father but sometimes she wondered if they were somehow related, at least she had hoped they might be. After all, he was the only family she actually had. An impossible dream since they weren't the same species. Colton was Colton and Sid was Sid. That was the end of it.

"So, what is it? The Starblades? The Magistras?" She guessed, naming every faction she could think of, "Stardaughter! Not the queen?"

"Hey! Language!"

"Sorry."

Static coated the hologram for a moment and Sid sat forward in her chair, her heart beating faster in fear of losing the connection. Their call had only been severed once in the thirteen years they'd been communicating but it was enough to ruin her entire night. She let out a relieved breath when Colton's blue eyes appeared again on the screen.

"Leona is fine. Better than fine, really. She's taken on a new Magistra and the training is progressing splendidly. This girl is quite the bright, little student!"

There was a pang of jealousy settling in the base of Sid's stomach. To be a Magistra had been a lifelong dream for her. As far as she was concerned, the queen's ladies in waiting had the most glamorous job in Neostar. Sure, the guards and Starblades guarded the city and domes, and The Arcane held the keys to the ring and the stars entire existence — but to be that close the queen at all hours? Nothing could be better.

"That's nice," she said and forced a meek smile that barely reached her eyes. "But why are you avoiding my question?"

Sid squinted her eyes and trained her gaze on Colton. Either the static was infringing again or there was sweat pooling at the top of his brow. Was he nervous to tell her what happened? What was he hiding?

"Not at all!" Colton finally said, "There was a disturbance in one of the domes but it is all taken care of now."

"A disturbance? What kind of disturbance?" She yelled.

Colton jumped back in his seat and rubbed his ears, "For the love of the Star, Sid! There's no need to yell. It was nothing and it's handled now."

Her bottom lip quivered and her nostrils flared lightly. She hated being lied to and Colton was most definitely lying. As soon as their call was done, she was going to get to the bottom of this. If something happened in the domes, there'd be coverage of it on the telescreens. Just because he wasn't going to tell her about it, didn't mean she wouldn't still find out. She was nothing if not resourceful.

"I've gotten through all my lessons," she boasted, hoping to change the subject. "I'm all the way through to the end of the Metal Years now. I had no idea how much your people did for the star."

"That's wonderful, Sid! You're really getting through this. I'll make sure to send you extra plans this shipment. And a few small gifts," he winked.

Sid knew exactly what that meant: sweets, her favorite. She was hoping for soy puffs, a combination of a bean paste and sugary molasses. Sid could eat those for the rest of her life without wanting anything else. There was one time when Colton had sent an entire box of them and she managed to gorge herself on the treats for a few hours straight. Needless to say, she was not exactly well the next morning but as far as Sid was concerned, it was worth it! An overdose on soy puffs was a blessing and not to be taken lightly.

"Colton?" She asked sheepishly.

"Yes?"

"When can I come to Neostar?"

He cleared his throat and sat up taller, leaning into the screen slightly. "Sid, we've already talked about this. It's not safe right now."

"I know. But when will it be safe? I'm strong, Colton! I can handle it!"

"Oh darling, I know you're strong. You're the strongest kid I know! It isn't you I'm worried about."

"Then what? The Domers? My parents? You said it yourself, they ran off into the jungles and the Al'iil probably killed them by now. They won't come looking for me. They didn't want me in the first place." She cried.

"The NSO is in the middle of a very intricate situation. I can't say much but let's just say that we have had a few," he paused to think of the right words, "indiscretions within the domes that we are currently investigating."

"What kind of indiscretions?"

"Nothing too serious right now but threats have been made. Threats against the ring."

"The ring? Why? Why would someone threaten the one thing that holds the entire star together?"

"Sid," Colton said in his usual deep voice, "I'm certain you've come across mentions of the Domer resistance in your studies. Not everyone we saved wanted help. Some were quite happy going down with a dying planet. When Leona's mother," he paused to collect himself, "when the queen's mother brought forth the concept of the chips, of using them to power the ring, it didn't exactly go over smoothly with some of the star's native population. Some of the inhabitants were weary of the idea, some were even violent."

Her mind raced through history lessons, landing on the texts she'd read about the creation of the Circulum System.

From what she was able to gather, the queen's mother was part of the original landing that delivered Colton's people to the star. When they arrived, they had realized that the electrical magic the native population possessed was overpowering the star's resources. The queen's mother was a brilliant mind and began to work out the plans for a ring system, a system that could use the magic of the natives as a means of producing power. Power they could use to sustain the technology they brought with them. Power that could save the star and offer a means for both races to live together without putting strain on the star's Eco-system. They developed chips that could access the magic of the native residents and feed into the ring, which then redistributed the power to a generator. That generator powered Tower City, the three towers that housed the Citizens, and the domes; assuring that all of the resources needed for survival were self-sufficient. They took nothing from the star and in return, the star allowed them to live.

"But I thought everyone who was against the chips ran off into the jungles?"

Sid never understood this part. If she could get some dumb chip installed into her neck and have it save the entire star, she'd never dream of saying no. Sid held an immense amount of anger for the deserters. Running off simply because they didn't like being chipped or living in the domes or some other such nonsense. Selfish savages, that's all they were. What was the point of having any magic at all if they wouldn't use it to help bring peace and life to their home? *Idiots.* She was glad they ran, hopeful that the wild jungle swallowed them whole for their cowardliness. Sid would take their place without a question and she wished Colton could see that. She wished he could understand what being un-chipped made her feel like she was the same as the deserters. A coward just like them.

"Ah! Looks like you *have* been doing well in your studies!" Colton yelled, impressed by her ability to retain information. "And yes, you are correct. Most of them did but some of them stayed. Maybe to give the new ways a try or maybe to revolt from within. We're not certain what their reasons were but what we do know without exception is that the Circulum System must be protected at all costs. If it falls, we all fall."

"But it won't fall, right? You and the Starblades will protect it?"

"Of course we will. Queen Leona would never let anyone jeopardize the life she has built here."

Something about the way he emphasized her name made Sid feel uncomfortable. Like he was trying to tell her something without actually saying it. She shrugged the feeling off, convinced that she was probably just hungry and trying to find a mystery where there was none.

"Besides," he continued, "there is no way we'd let anyone near the Arcane and without them, access to the ring is as good as buried."

"So, when can I come down then?"

He sighed, "Not yet, Sid. Soon, I promise, just not yet. Not until we figure out who's making the threats and stabilize the situation."

"But you'll bring me down? Soon?"

"Yes, Sid, soon. As soon as I can."

That didn't sound like very soon at all. He was lying again. She wasn't sure when it happened but lately, Colton had been keeping quite a few things from her. *It's not fair. How come he can lie, and I have to tell him everything?* She wanted to yell at him, to throw something at the screen, to send a wave of her powers all the way down to Neostar to strike him in his seat. "Ok," she said instead and lowered her head.

"I have to go now," Colton announced. Then, as if sensing her turmoil, "What's the number one rule, Sid?"

"Never use your magic. Especially if you're not alone."

"Good girl."

Sid reached to disconnect the screen when she saw Colton shift in his seat.

"Oh, and Sid?" He said, leaning in again. "You need all three."

Then the screen went dark.

"What?" She shouted, "Colton! I need all three what?"

He couldn't hear her, she knew that, but her bewilderment overtook her sense of logic. Sid's breaths grew shallow, the air catching in her throat and tickling her tonsils. She wanted to scream — or to cry — anything but sit here in front of a blank holographic display. Anything but be completely alone again.

"Rusty?" She swiped the tears forming in her eyes and looked up, "Pull up Neostar's telescreens. Look for a disturbance in one of the domes from earlier this evening."

"THERE WAS ONE SOCIAL DISTURBANCE FOUND IN THE SYSTEM'S CATALOGUE. AN ATTEMPT WAS MADE TO DESTROY ONE OF THE WORKER PODS HEADED INTO THE TOWERS. THE SUSPECT HAS BEEN IDENTIFIED BUT NOT YET CAPTURED."

"Pull up the suspect's image please."

She slumped her chin in her hand and stared at the face on the screen, chewing the edges of her fingernails. Something about the green eyes that stared at her seemed so familiar. They looked like hers. Wide set with the same thin pupil. But there was nothing strange about that, all natives of the star had the same eye shape. Colton said they look like feline eyes which led to even more of her questions about what felines were. Turns out they were a sort of animal from Colton's home planet. From everything Colton had told her about felines, they seemed like an entirely useless creature that contributed in no way to a person's life. She supposed people liked them because they were soft and small enough to fit under crevices. A useful trait to have if one was to lose something in a tight space.

So, what was it about this woman that made Sid feel like she had seen her before?

"Rusty, any information on the suspect?"

"THE SUSPECTS NAME OR LOCATION HAVE NOT BEEN DISCOVERED."

"Or announced," she retorted. "We both know the telescreens don't post every detail."

"WOULD YOU LIKE TO RUN A SEARCH ON ALL MISSING DETAILS FROM TODAY'S SCREENINGS?"

"Stars no! I want to eat."

She hopped off the seat and waved her palm to shut off the projection, eager to get some food into her stomach. Whoever this woman was, she was not more important than the steaming bowl of broth waiting for Sid in the diner.

"WHAT DO you think he meant, Rusty?" Sid asked, her hands tenderly massaging the yellowing leaf of a nearby plant. She loved spending time in the greenroom, especially when her mind was racing with thoughts. Something about the soft sound of rustling leaves and the scent of fresh oxygen made her feel like she was safe. Even the loud clanking of the carbon dioxide tanks brought a sense of meditative peace that she could not find anywhere else on the ship.

"PLEASE CLARIFY THE INTENT OF THE QUESTION."

"Ugh! You're really useless sometimes. Isn't he, Beanie?" She patted the spreading leaves of the soybean plant in her palm. "That I need all three. Obviously! Do you even listen to the calls? Aren't you supposed to be recording them? And everything else for that matter."

"I AM UNCERTAIN OF THE NATURE OF THE COMMENT. THERE ARE MANY THINGS THAT COME IN THREES. STAR ATOMS, FRIGGER EGGS, SOYBEAN LEAVES." The ship listed off without pausing. "YOU WILL NEED TO CLARIFY THE INTENT OF YOUR QUESTION SO THAT I CAN CALCULATE THE MOST LOGICAL RESPONSE."

"Forget it. And I obviously know that many things come in threes. Are you going to stand for that, Beanie?" She poked the plant and laughed as it bounced back, hitting the small bush next to it. "Hey! Do I need to separate you two? No fighting in the greenroom!"

She picked up a watering hose and waved it in front of the plants. "If you keep this up, you're going to bed without dinner!"

Sid let a few drops of water pour into the feeding tubes, mesmerized by the trickle of liquid as it pumped into the pipes before being absorbed by the soil at the bottom of the plant trays. The soil darkened from the moisture but turned an ashy grey again within moments. She let out a frustrated sigh; these plants were eating up water by the gallons lately. It wasn't long ago that she used to be able to water them once a week and have new sprouts pop up each month. These days, no matter how much water she gave them, the soil remained dry and inconsistent while the leaves yellowed and dried. Sid hated when her plants suffered. They weren't just a food source; they were the closest thing to friends she had on the ship. And she'd hate to lose her friends to poor air circulation, especially since they were such great listeners.

"Rusty, when is the next shipment due to arrive?"

"THE SHIPMENT DEPARTED FROM NEOSTAR EARLY THIS MORNING AND IS SCHEDULED FOR RECEIVING IN APPROXIMATELY ONE HUNDRED AND EIGHTY-FOUR MINUTES. WOULD YOU LIKE FOR ME TO SET A TIMER FOR ITS ARRIVAL?"

"For a hundred and eighty-four minutes? No, thank you!"

Hopefully, Colton had packed a spare carbon dioxide valve for her this time around. She had asked for one repeatedly and he promised he would send it with this shipment. She wasn't sure how long her makeshift repairs were going to hold and judging by the state of these plants, the entire air pump could be in trouble.

Sid rubbed her dry eyes with fisted hands and walked over to the system control station.

"Run an air control diagnostic report," she commanded, swiping her palm in front of the sensor.

The station buzzed, flashing a projection of codes from the center of the base. Sid watched the numbers roll through until she caught sight of what she was looking for. "Stop there!"

Using the tip of her finger she flicked at the display, scattering the codes she had no interest for in all directions. She squeezed two fingers together to expand the number sequence on the screen. All the saliva in her in her mouth evaporated.

"This can't be right! Five thousand and fifty minutes of air remaining? But that's only one week!" Sid tapped the screen ferociously, "Run it again!"

The code flashed before her eyes and rolled to a stop on the same number sequence. Her heart raced and her head felt lighter than a neutrino in a zero-gravity chamber. "Rusty! How did you miss this in the last systems check?" She yelled, steadying her shaking body on the metal table.

"THE SYSTEMS CHECK INDICATED A CONSIDERABLE DROP IN OXYGEN PRODUCTION BUT IT HAD NOT YET REACHED CATASTROPHIC LEVELS."

"And it didn't occur to you to warn me?" She howled.

"MY COLLECTION OF DATA SHOWS NO SIGNS OF LIFE-THREATENING DAMAGE TO THE SHIP'S ATMOSPHERE."

"Use your head, Rusty!"

"WOULD YOU LIKE FOR ME TO RUN A SYSTEMS CHECK ON THE SHIP'S STARBOARD?"

"Not that head! I meant think, Rusty! Think!"

"I HAVE NO PROGRAMMING FOR THAT COMMAND. SHOULD I RUN THE SYSTEMS CHECK NOW?"

Sid looked over her shoulder, her eyes widening. How did she not notice the state of the greenhouse? How did she let it get this far? She rubbed her eyes again until she could feel the grey in them turn to a frosty pink from the pressure.

The shipment was due to arrive in a few hours and she needed to keep a cool head. Colton would send the valve; she was certain of it. It should only take her twenty minutes to replace it and once that's done, she could forget about this entire ugly turn of events.

Her palms clammed up and she rubbed them on her suit leg to wipe the dirt-caked sweat off. She raised one hand in front of her face and let the energy particles ripple off her skin. They danced in front of her in a harmonious symphony of lights; red and yellow like the blissful shine of the ring itself.

Sid shut her palm, letting the energy of her magic settle back into her body. There was no point getting upset over something as silly as a faulty valve. She straightened her back and petted the dying leaves of the soybean plant. "Don't worry, Beanie. I got this."

Then looking up at the camera lens, "You better hope that valve is on the shipment, Rusty."

The ship did not respond, leaving her in a void of nerves and panic and a feeling she had become much too accustomed to. The feeling of being stranded in the dark — lost, scared and so utterly alone.

FOUR

TUBES OF VACUUM packed frigger eggs spread out across the docking bay as Sid frantically tore apart the Neostar shipment. Her fingers dug through the packages, pushing them out of the way until she had cleared the capsule of all its contents.

"Where is it?" She shouted, rushing over to inspect the mess on the floor. "He said it'll be here!"

Sid had been counting down the minutes to the arrival of the shipment and lunged on it as soon as air control stabilized and it was safe to open the dock doors. She ripped through every piece, hoping to find the valve Colton was supposed to deliver. When she was done going through the contents, she rummaged through them again — and again, and again — until all that was left was an unruly mess of a dock and a breathless Sid on its floor.

"He said," she gasped, "it'll be here! Where is it? Why is it not here?"

Her fist met with the metal grate beneath her and she let out a scream as she continued to pummel the floor. Sid's eyes were stinging from the tears, it had been days since she felt anything but dry discomfort and she swatted at the wetness in between hits. Did Colton forget to pack the valve? Why would he do that? He knew how important it was; she'd asked him for one for weeks now.

"Where is it?" She gasped in between tears, "Where is it?"

Her hands were shaking, red welts already forming from the blows. Unsteadily, she opened her palms and patted the tear stained flooring beneath her. *It's alright, it'll be fine. I'll just call him and ask him to send one right away. Tell him it's urgent.* She pushed herself up to stand and dusted off the debris trapped in her suit. Still breathless, she kicked her way through the remnants of the food and headed for the observatory.

"Rusty! Get a line out to Colton! I need to speak with him immediately!"

"YOUR CALL WITH THE NEOSTAR ORDER GENERAL IS NOT SCHEDULED AS PART OF TODAY'S ACTIVITIES. WOULD YOU LIKE FOR ME TO CHECK THE CALENDAR AND LET YOU KNOW THE EXACT TIME OF YOUR NEXT APPOINTMENT?"

"I don't care if it's not scheduled, Rusty! Get him on the line! Now!"

Sid punted a pack of concentrated fruit paste, splattering the blue substance all over the wall. This was not the time for following rules, too much was at risk. She knew Colton wouldn't be pleased with her interrupting NSO business but he left her no choice. She needed to get a hold of him.

The sound of her footsteps echoed down the corridor as

she made her way to the observatory, slamming doors in her ascent to the top.

The back of her suit was drenched with sweat but whether it was from fear or anger she couldn't be certain. As she sped up her steps, her palms danced against each other, letting the sparks of electricity she created flash against her skin until it looked like she was holding a massive ball of fire. "Don't use your magic, Sid. It's not safe, Sid." She teased, expanding the electrical shots into an even larger mass.

Her fingers tingled from the sparks, each one sending a jolt of energy back into her body. "The only thing that isn't safe is this piece of space garbage you trapped me in, Colton! And you better help me fix it!" She yelled down the corridor before dropping the hold on her magic and taking off in a sprint up the stairs.

"AGAIN, RUSTY." Sid sighed, exasperated from listening to the repetitive sound of the comm trying to connect the line.

"COMM LINK ESTABLISHED. ATTEMPTING SIXTH WAVE OF COMMUNICATION."

The screen blinked rapidly in front of her face as the beeping of the signal intensified before silence enveloped the observatory. Sid stretched out her legs and let her eyes wander to the glow of Neostar in front of her. She used to love having a three sixty view of the star as her ship circled around it; it felt like they were caught in a dance, a moment shared between lovers. What was the name Colton used for slow dancing on his home planet? Waltz? *Another dumb word*, Sid thought. The star's *Waltz* felt excruciating to her, slowly moving in its usual path, as if completely unaware of the danger she was in.

"One more time, please," she huffed.

"COMM LINK ESTABLISHED. ATTEMPTING SEVENTH WAVE OF COMMUNICATION."

"You don't have to count them every single time, Rusty!" She spat.

"I AM SIMPLY NOTING THE CALLS FOR YOUR RECORDS," the ship echoed, "SEVENTH ATTEMPT- NO ANSWER ON THE RECEIVING END."

"If we can't get a hold of Colton, we're as good as dead. Do you get that?"

"I'M SORRY, I DO NOT UNDERSTAND YOUR REQUEST. I HAVE NOT BEEN PROGRAMMED WITH A CODING SEQUENCE FOR DEAD."

"Show off," she said under her breath, "again, please!"

"COMM LINK ESTABLISHED. ATTEMPTING EIGHTH WAV–"

"Shut up, Rusty!" She screamed, throwing her hands forward. A burst of energy shot from her palms and barreled at the small comm on the table in front of her. Before she could stop it, the bolt of lightning cannoned the device. Sid watched as the comm burst into sparks of orange, red and yellow. Fuming for a moment before the screen above it disappeared and the comm device let out a puff of smoke; fried.

Sid looked down at the charred box in front of her. "No!" She cried and leaped forward, her hands reaching for the few wires that seemed to have been left intact. "Rusty! Try again!"

"EIGHTH WAVE OF COMMUNICATION WITH NEOSTAR FAILED DUE TO A COMM LINK

MALFUNCTION. I CANNOT ESTABLISH A CURRENT LINK OF COMMUNICATION WITH THE RECEIVER. ALL COMM SYSTEMS ARE DOWN."

"What have I done, Rusty?" Sid cried.

"I CANNOT BE CERTAIN UNTIL I RUN A FULL DIAGNOSTIC OF THE SYSTEM BUT IF MY PRELIMINARY CALCULATIONS ARE CORRECT, YOU HAVE DISLODGED THE INTERNAL WIRING OF THE INTEGRATED AUDIO SYSTEM."

Sid held up a handful of blackened wires, "You think?"

Her legs buckled. She slowly slipped back into the chair, letting her head hang heavy in her hands. This time, she'd really messed things up. Colton told her not to use her magic. He told how dangerous it could be. And what did she do? The first time she got angry, she fried the only way she had of communicating with him. The only way she had to send him a request for the missing valve. The only chance she had of salvation.

He'll figure out something's wrong. He'll figure out something's wrong when he can't reach me and he'll come here. He'll save me.

"Right, Rusty?"

"RIGHT. SOMETHING THAT IS TRUE OR CORRECT TO THE FACT." The ship ran off the definition of the word, "THE BEST OR MOST APPROPRIATE CHOICE FOR A PARTICULAR SITUATION."

"Let's hope so, Rusty. For the love of the star, let's hope so."

BLUE LIGHT ILLUMINATED the observatory as Sid flipped through the videos on the large projection in the center of the deck. After her outburst with the comm earlier, she'd decided to take a break and get ahead in her studies, hopeful to get her mind off the trouble she was in. Sid spent hours trying to come up with yet another temporary solution for the valve malfunction. The problem with temporary solutions was just that; they were too temporary. A makeshift rotator would not give her enough control over the carbon dioxide production and fusing the valve in place would only render it useless. Sid had run through possible fixes a million times in her head and the answer was always the same; she needed a replacement part. She was furious with Colton for leaving her stranded; even more furious with herself for not reminding him to send it on their last call.

"I'm sorry." She whispered and patted the grate beneath her folded legs, "I really messed things up this time."

Her eyes scanned the videos again, landing on a telescreen recording of a Starblade being attacked in the train dock of one of the domes. She tapped her finger to the projection, shifting it to the front of the video loop. "When was this screened, Rusty?"

"THE RIOT IN THE SOUTH-EASTERN DOME WAS TELESCREENED LAST MONTH."

"What happened?"

"A JUNIOR STARBLADE WAS ATTACKED BY RESIDENTS OF THE DOME WHILE PATROLLING THE TRAINS. THERE WERE SEVEN CASUALTIES TOTAL."

"All Domers?"

"SIX RESIDENTS AND THE PATROLLING STARBLADE."

"They killed him?"

"THE NSO ISSUED A STATEMENT THAT IN ORDER TO PREVENT CIVILIAN CASUALTIES, HE HAD EXERCISED PROTOCOL 207 AND IMPLODED HIS BLADE."

"He killed himself? And the Domers?" Sid yelped.

"THE STARBLADE COMMAND HAS ONLY THREE OBJECTIVES. NUMBER ONE, PROTECT THE ARCANE. NUMBER TWO, PROTECT THE QUEEN. NUMBER THREE, UPHOLD PEACE AND ORDER IN THE DOMES."

"How is suicide and murder peaceful exactly?" She lashed out, unable to understand the reasoning.

"BY TAKING OUT THE OPPOSING FACTORS, THE STARBLADE SUBDUED ANY FURTHER THREAT THAT COULD RESULT IN A HIGHER DEATH COUNT."

"So, kill seven to save thousands?"

"THAT IS A CORRECT ESTIMATION OF THE CALCULATION. ONE THOUSAND THREE HUNDRED AND TWENTY-SEVEN RESIDENTS WERE SAVED FROM POSSIBLE HARM."

"That's the dumbest thing I've ever heard, Rusty. You said he was junior? So he was just a kid!"

"THE STARBLADE ON DUTY IS REPORTED AS BEING SEVENTEEN STAR YEARS OF AGE. THAT IS TWO MILLION SIX HUNDRED AND–"

"I don't need the minutes, Rusty. I get it. He was young." Sid rolled her eyes. "What I don't get is..."

Her eyes widened and she pinched her finger on the corner of the screen. "Stars! Do you see that, Rusty?"

"I DO NOT HAVE A VISUAL FUNCTION

INSTALLED HOWEVER I CAN CALCULATE THE POSSIBILITIES OF A SITUATION BASED ON A SIMPLE EQUATION OF–"

"Never mind! Can you just enlarge the bottom right corner, please!"

Sid squinted as the image parted into countless triangles. Pieces flew off screen, disappearing from view as they hit the borders of the projection. She watched intently as the part of the video that caught her attention reformed in front of her. Piece by piece until she stood, slack jawed, staring at a pair of familiar green eyes. The same green eyes she was drawn to from her last search of the telescreen recordings. The Domer suspect from the so called 'disturbance' Colton was trying to hide from her.

"Run recognition software to the suspect in the recording from three days ago."

The screen split into two, pulling up a still frame of the woman's face from the previous recording. Code flashed across both screens, pausing intermittently to match a sequence of numbers before continuing to run the check. After a few seconds, which to Sid seemed like an actual eternity, the number sequences paused.

"UPON RUNNING A FACIAL ANALYSIS AS WELL AS BODY TEMPERATURE CHECKS, THERE IS A NINETY-NINE POINT FOUR PERCENT CHANCE OF IDENTITY MATCH."

"Why was she here? Has the NSO said anything?"

"THERE HAS BEEN NOTHING TELEVISED ON THE CONNECTION BETWEEN THE TWO ATTACKS."

Sid's head ached. Why was the same woman at both attack sites? And why had the NSO not made the connection? Worse, if they had made the connection, why were they hiding it from the public?

She took a deep breath, trying to calm her rising nerves. She didn't know why she was obsessing over this matter when there were much more important things for her to worry about. Things that posed a danger much closer to home. But something about this woman made her uneasy. What made Sid even more uneasy was her connection to the attacks. She was present at both scenes. Not just present; front and center, watching. But why attack the trains? Or a junior Starblade for that matter? If you're going to be starting some sad, little revolution, just go straight for the queen. You'd get nowhere. Worse, you'd get yourself killed over it but at least you'd get some attention. Who cares about some stupid trains?

None of it made sense to Sid.

Out of the corner of her eye, the ring made its majestic rotation around Neostar, sending rays of shimmering yellow in all directions.

"THE CIRCULUM SYSTEM HAS JUST COMPLETED ITS STARISE ROTATION." The ship announced.

"Right," Sid nodded and jumped to her feet. "Time to feed the plants!"

FIVE

THE GREENROOM WAS nothing more than a graveyard filled with hopelessness and the reeking carcasses of dead plants. One of the Drowsy Vines Sid had spent half her life nurturing slumped across the floor like an exhausted reptile. She stepped over its thick trunk; her chapped lips parted as she took in the state of her once prideful garden. The familiar rustle of leaves was barely audible and the carbon dioxide tanks sounded like they had developed a wheezing cough, struggling to filter air with each pump. Sid could barely manage full breaths herself so she could imagine what the plants must have felt in that terrifying moment. The ones that hadn't already died were in rough shape, their leaves crumpled in batches of brown tones.

She blinked rapidly, trying to wet her eyes without success. Everything on her body felt like it was covered in scorching hot sand. Sid had never set foot on Aria before — one of the twin moons that orbited Jericho alongside Neostar — but she imagined that this is what life must have been like there. Colton had told her that the reason his people never settled on Aria was because of the moon's uninhabitable desert-like atmosphere. It was the exact opposite of Ceon, the second moon, which consisted entirely of water. Sid always said that they should smash the two together; it seemed pointless to have two perfectly good masses taking up space without being at all useful.

"Well, at least you match your name now," she smiled, tugging at the faded yellow stems of the Yellow Tongue bush. "Looks good on you!"

If Sid's eyes weren't so dry, she'd be bawling. She couldn't stand what was happening to her plants. Aside from Colton and the ship, they were her only friends. Losing each one was like losing a limb - painful and crippling.

The valve gave out another rough groan and she shot a slanted glare in its direction. "Trust me," she said to no plant in particular, "I'll stardamn fix this."

With that, Sid turned on her heels and marched out of the greenroom, determined to save everyone on board.

SPARKS the color of fire shot in all directions as Sid twisted the last wires of the comm device together. She jolted back from the shock, quickly recalling that she was immune to the heat of electricity. The perks of having the star's magic coursing through her blood. She pinched the metal coil and stepped back.

"Give it a shot, Rusty."

There was a crinkled sound, like someone had crumpled a piece of paper in the next room, then smoke billowed from the device and the wires ripped in opposite directions; tearing apart the work she had just put into them.

"Oh, for the love of star, Rusty! Just this one time, can something work on this heap? We need this! We all need this!"

Sid fell to her knees, forcing the two wires back together again. She slowly coiled the exposed metal and planted a small kiss on the twist. *For luck,* she thought and crawled away. "Try it now!"

Crinkle, crinkle, crinkle.

Pow!

The wires repelled again, this time almost ripping out from the comm device entirely.

Sid wanted to scream. No, she wanted to chuck the star-damned device out of the dock bay. Why was it so hard to get a comm operational? She had been fixing everything on this floating junkyard for over a decade. There was nothing that Sid couldn't fix. Except, it seemed, a box of wires the size of a water jug that broke by simply being on the wrong side of her anger. "Rusty! That's it!"

Sliding on her knees, she shifted herself closer to the comm, stubbornly coiling the wires back together. "Broken by magic, fixed by magic!" She hollered and continued to twist.

She landed another soft kiss on her masterpiece, "Now, Rusty! Do it now!"

This time, as the ship tried to turn on a fried comm, Sid squeezed the metal coil tightly in her fingers. Her blood shimmered beneath her skin, the vessels electrifying with power. Sid had no idea how the magic within her worked. Colton had refused to teach her anything about it and if it wasn't for a happy accident unloading a shipment when she was eight, she never would have found out. All she knew was that when she let her mind clear, let herself feel the gravitational pull of Neostar, her blood somehow reacted to it. It wanted to be free of her body's vessel, wanted to come home. Once the electrical energy flowed within her, she could direct it anywhere she wanted. And right now, what she wanted was for the stardamned comm to work.

Smoke started to form at the base of the spiral and Sid directed her magic into her clenched fingertips, fusing the coil and sending a wave of electricity into the wires at the same time. She closed her eyes, "Please..."

Sid had never understood what praying was when Colton explained the concept of religion to her. All she could think of was a bunch of people in a room talking to air. It seemed very impractical to her. Though at that moment, floating in an abyss of doubt and counted days, she could do nothing more than ask for help. She had no idea who she was speaking to but if there was anything out there other than her, her ship, and Neostar; now was the time for it to make its mark. "Please, please, please," she repeated in a whisper.

The wires sparked again, this time staying put in their place and Sid yelped with glee as the comm device powered up.

"It worked! Rusty, it worked!" She shouted, hopping in giddy twirls around the observatory's starlit floor. "Connect to Colton!"

The ship was silent.

"Sorry, connect to the NSO general's line please." She corrected herself, biting her lower lip hard enough to draw blood.

The comm's screen projected in front of her. It flickered grey for a brief moment before shutting down.

"I AM UNABLE TO FORM A CONNECTION WITH THE RECEIVER."

"What are you talking about? Try again!" She yelled.

The screen appeared once more and once more it shut down in front of her panicked face.

"I AM UNABLE TO FORM A CONNECTION."

"Rusty! Why can't you connect to him? The comm is working perfectly fine!"

"THE COMMUNICATION DEVICE IS FULLY OPERATIONAL. THE RECEIVERS LINE IS NO LONGER ACTIVE. THE NSO GENERAL'S LINE APPEARS TO HAVE GONE OFFLINE. I AM UNABLE TO FORM THE CONNECTION."

Sid's legs buckled and she found herself sinking into the grated, metal floor beneath her. Her face flushed as small drops of sweat ran down her back, steadily soaking the base of her suit.

"Rusty, I don't want you to panic," she whispered, "but you might want to think about this thing called 'praying'. It's supposed to help in times like this."

SIX

SID WOKE to the sound of the ship's alarm ringing through the corridors. Her back was drenched and pieces of her short, platinum hair clung to her forehead and cheeks. Why was she covered in so much sweat? She opened her mouth to speak but immediately felt her lungs constrict. Her hands clawed at her throat as she managed a few jagged breaths in.

No! Not yet!

She jolted upright, her forehead colliding with a low hanging pipe above her head that knocked her back down. She fell asleep in the engine room again. Sid was known for sleeping anywhere but her nightly quarters — her preferred spot being in the freedom of the observatory — but in the last few days, she had trouble keeping her eyes open and found herself dozing off in the most peculiar places. She wasn't sure if it was the lack of air on the ship or simply exhaustion from trying to fix a problem that didn't seem to have a plausible solution. After the failed attempt to contact Colton, Sid had spent every waking hour trying to repair the valve without progress.

The bruise from the collision with the pipe was already forming into a bump and she shook off the sharp pain before springing to her feet.

Her heart raced and she raced against it, climbing step after step to get to the greenroom.

Running against time she didn't have.

Sid couldn't remember getting to the upper deck. Couldn't remember opening the greenroom door. Couldn't remember when she started screaming and crying. On her knees with her hands fisted around batches of plant stems; lifeless, yellowed and stiff.

"They're dead," she managed to whisper in between small breaths and sobs, "they're all dead."

The greenroom was a shambled mess of destruction and death. The limp carcasses of her plants were strewn across the trays and floor. She didn't understand how it happened or how long she had lost consciousness for this time. It looked as if the plants had died within the last few hours, and soon she would be dying with them. Sid found it ironic that the place that had sustained her for most of her life would be the thing that kills her. "At least we'll all go together," she smiled at a blank spot across the room. "Maybe we should float ourselves? A proper burial and all?"

Suddenly, her eyes brightened, the grays turning to an almost transparent white and the pupils contracted until they were nothing more than thin lines. *Floating! Of course!*

She was on her feet within seconds. "Rusty! Try to connect to the NSO general again! We need the activation codes for the escape pod! There's no time to get my notes!"

Not wasting any time, Sid slid through the sliding doors and ran. Her legs hurt, and her entire body felt like it was turning to mush but she pushed forward. She shifted her stride and made a turn toward the dock bay. She could see it in the distance, just past the connecting vestibule. Sid picked up the pace and bolted forward. Halfway down the vestibule, she caught something in the corner of her eye, just on the edges of the outer layers of the ship. Feet grinding to a screeching halt, Sid pressed her face to the clear panes of the vestibule. The parts of her skin that made contact with the panes froze immediately. There was even less time left than she thought. The ship was leaking oxygen. And fast.

"Rusty! The NSO general!"

"I AM UNABLE TO ESTABLISH A LINK. THE LINE IS NOT OPERATIONAL."

"Keep trying!"

Her hand slid across the vestibule's pane, leaving a streak of droplets behind as she hurried to the doors. Each step was slower, heavier. Sid's heart went from trying to burst through her rib cage to barely stirring. Squeezing two fingers behind her ear, she tried to count the beats. One, then silence. A moment later, a second beat. *Too long of a moment,* Sid thought. Her body was starting to shut down.

She leaned against the doors, using the last of her strength to prop herself up. "Ru–"

Her voice cut out and she heaved over her knees, a sharp pain in her lungs. Slowly, Sid raised the palm of her hand to the door, hoping she was at least in the same general area as the scanner. To her relief, the door offered several beeps of recognition and slid open. Sid collapsed through and tumbled onto the dock bay floor.

Using her arms and the last ounce of muscle strength in her upper body, Sid pulled herself across the bay to the escape pod. She wanted to call out for help but knew it was pointless. No one could help her. No one even knew she was up here except Colton. She needed to preserve whatever air the ship had left and shouting commands or panicking was only going to speed up the failure of her vital functions.

The grated floor tugged at her skin, causing red streaks to run down her forearms but she continued to crawl. Two more tugs and she was at the base of the escape pod. Her lungs felt like they were going to collapse.

Sid raised a shaking finger to the keypad. She was kicking herself for not exchanging it for a proper sensor. Running number combinations in her head she started to work the lock. Seven, four, three. Sid entered her name into the keys and waited. Nothing. Maybe her full name? Seven, four, three, two, seven, four, eight, seven. Still nothing.

She tried to enter in Colton's name, his birthday, her own, even the ship's date of creation. Nothing worked. The keypad blinked infuriatingly, as if mocking her errors, but remained closed.

Her head started to spin. She looked down at her hands that had turned a very dominant shade of blue. The pain in her chest vibrated again her ribs. She tried to take another breath without success.

This is it, she thought. *This is how I end.*

Then, as a last resort, Sid slumped her palm against the keypad, pressing each and every number. She grit her teeth, almost breaking the canines right out of her jaw and pushed a small amount of electricity out of her body. The blue of her skin flashed a brilliant orange as her magic rushed down her arm. It hit the keys with such force that the lock shattered in her hand, blowing bits and pieces across the bay floor.

A tearful smile formed at the edges of her lips as the door of the escape pod screeched and slid open. Sid pulled herself across the threshold and used her magic to manually override the keypad on the other side, shuffling her legs out of the way just in time before the doors slid shut.

"POD AIRLOCK SECURE." The ship's comforting voice sang over the speakers.

Sid's eyes widened and she filled her lungs with air until she was no longer able to contain in. She let out a loud sigh and sank against the doors.

"What now, Rusty?" She asked. "How much time do I have left in here?"

"THERE IS APPROXIMATELY FOURTEEN HUNDRED AND EIGHTY MINUTES OF AIRTIME REMAINING IN THE TANKS."

"So two days, more or less. Where can we go in two days, Rusty?" She asked.

Without waiting for an answer, her eyes drifted to the window behind her. She straightened her back and walked over, placing her hand over the red leaf covered ball floating in front of her. Sid fell back, buckling herself into the control seat and snapping her goggles in place over her eyes.

"Set course direction, Rusty. Destination Neostar."

BY THE TIME Sid opened her eyes again, she was surprised to find that the pod had been traveling for almost a full day. The chaos on The Arcturus drained her entirely and though she didn't remember sleeping, she felt as if she had been out of consciousness for weeks. The ride in the pod was far from comfortable. Every slight change of course sent her rocking from side to side and she had intentionally kept the seatbelt on, only occasionally getting up to stretch her legs and inspect the remnants of her oxygen deprived ship in the window. Despite the way in which it ended; Sid wanted nothing more than to be back in its metal hold. Safe and secure in a space whose crevices she knew inside and out. She most definitely did not want to be tumbling through space in a tin can, hurtling at impressive speeds to the one place Colton told her she could not step foot on.

It's just until I find him, she convinced herself. *I'll find Colton, get the valve and be back on the ship in no time.*

The more she repeated the words, the more finite they became, as though they resonated with her blood somehow, forming a promise that she intended to keep at all costs.

Sid spent the rest of her time on the pod in a tidy state somewhere between lucid and dreaming. Each time she fluttered her dark eyelashes and opened her eyes, Neostar appeared closer in the observation window. And each time her heart sank even more. A mixture of fear and excitement. Mostly fear.

It was within this dream state that Sid felt an unbearable shake take hold of the pod. When she opened her eyes, lights flashed past the window, making her feel like she was being spun through space in a decent that was picking up speed.

Which is exactly what was happening to her.

"Rusty! We've broken through the atmosphere! Initiate landing thrusters!" She screeched, waiting for the creak of the thrust mechanism to take hold.

Her command fell into nothingness. "Rusty! Landing thrusters! Now!"

The pod's silence broke her into pieces. What in the name of the stars was wrong now?

"Rusty!" She commanded, then, "Forget it! I'll do it myself!"

She ripped off her belt and fell onto the navigation pane,

her fingers frantically searching for the manual engage button. Each second it took for her to locate it was one second less she had to correct the landing. She was moving too slow.

Her eyes beaded at Neostar, its landscape coming into focus rapidly. She was so close she could almost make out each tree on the horizon.

Sid tightened her fingers, landing a fisted blow to the button. In the background, somewhere in the heart of the pod she could hear gears clanking in an odd combination. She had gained control of the engine. Without pause, she reached for the landing thrust lever and pulled. Sid pulled until her palms burnt. A grunt escaped her lips as the lever smashed down into place. The pod jerked roughly back and Sid flew forward, using her hands to block her face from colliding with the window.

The pod was slowing down. It was still spinning maniacally but it was slowing down.

She glanced up again. It wasn't slowing down fast enough! She could see the ground clearly, lush red leaf trees and not a mass of water in sight. She was going to crash right into the stardamned jungle!

Sid pushed herself back into the seat and strapped in, snapping her goggles into place and catching a glimpse of herself in the window's reflection.

Is this what I look like with these things on? She laughed, trying to see at least a glimpse of her eyes.

"Next time, warn a girl if she's walking around looking like a stardamned fool, Rusty." Was the last thing she said before the pod crashed through the trees and her world went dark.

SEVEN

IF LIFE WAS anything like the alternate reality projections Colton described from his home planet, Sid would have been seeing stars when she woke up in the escape pod. Then again, she also would have been a two-dimensional creature with a fuzzy exterior and a ridiculous name like Bugs or Mickey. Regardless, her head felt like she had spent an hour hammering in gutter rivets using only her forehead.

She glanced up, quickly realizing that up was down and that she was hanging in the pod suspended at the hips by her seatbelt.

"Muck," she hissed through gritted teeth and reached for the eject button.

Her left shoulder hit the ground with a thud and she rolled over, yelping in pain. Sid's eyes scanned the pod's interior as she tried to determine the extent of the damage. The rough landing had dented one of the convex walls but aside from that and several torn wires, it was surprisingly in decent shape. Sid headed straight for the bay doors but the first step she took left her winded. She leaned against a wall, trying to stop the nausea inducing vertigo from taking hold. That was her first mistake. Her second was to land an angry fist on the metal wall.

Before she could make a run for the seatbelt, the pod shifted its weight and rolled. No, not rolled. It plummeted.

Sid's body crashed from side to side with occasional breaks of being pushed down into the walls as the pod leapt into the air in between landings.

"Aaaahh–" her scream cut short as her back slammed into the control panel.

The seatbelt swung teasingly in front of her and she made no hesitation in tearing her hand toward it. She grabbed hold of the rope, using her own weight to stabilize herself. As the pod rolled, Sid matched its momentum until she was bouncing off the walls with each turn, her hand gripping the seatbelt for support. Dents formed in the pods interior each time it hit a sturdy object outside. She felt like she would be rolling forever.

She wasn't.

As quickly as it had started rolling, the pod slowed to a halt. When she was sure the ground below was flat and stable, Sid let go of the belt. "Well, at least we're upright."

Taking carefully calculated, light steps, she made her way toward the doors again. Without thinking, she reached for the keypad. "Ugh, right," She sighed, remembering that her last interaction with the lock had rendered it useless. Her head was still pounding, a random beat beneath her temples that sent a shiver down her legs with each hit. Pushing the dull ache aside, Sid rubbed her hands together and took a deep breath in. She closed her eyes in concentration, breathing in air and breathing out electricity through her cells. The skin on her palms tingled as her magic made its way to the surface. It was minimal at best, her body still recovering from the crash, but she managed to create a large enough jolt to jump start the lock. The wires flickered franticly and moments later, the pod doors screeched and slid open.

"Stars be damned," she whispered.

Sid stretched the sleeve of her suit and used the worn fabric to wipe the grime off her goggles. Even through the caked film of dirt, the brightness of Neostar was nearly blinding. Unsteadily, her hand gripped the doorframe as she stepped through to the other side. Her heart raced and she tried to contain her attention, focusing on the view ahead.

Sid had never seen anything more beautiful.

Sure, she'd spent endless hours memorizing every detail of Neostar in her lessons but nothing could have prepared her for the sight that unfolded in front of her now. She wasn't certain where the pod crashed initially, but after the endless rolling it had come to a stop in what seemed to be a clearing. Or at least an area laden with rocks and bushy, purple shrubs that fought their way through the gaps in the surface. Star flowers coated the clearing in a rainbow of colors, each one shining brighter than the next. There was a small peep of friggers ahead, their small beaks poking at the ground for lost seeds, feathers ruffling in the light breeze. Sid looked beyond the vast emptiness of her landing pad to the jungle before her. She had no words. For the first time in her life, Sid was speechless. The densely packed jungle of Red Leaf trees with vines as thick as the corridors on her spaceship stretched well beyond her view. Over their bushy tops, she could see protruding rock formations that were so overgrown with shrubbery, they looked like purple puffs of smoke. And beyond them... Sid's pale eyes watered as she saw the light of Jericho reflect off the tips of the towers. The glass construction peered over the jungle's heart like crystal. The bright white of daylight danced over the panes, glistening as though it were dancing to some secret beat of music she wasn't privy to. Three perfectly pointed tips, one for each tower. It was magnificent.

And the sound! Sid felt like she had spent her entire life in a silo when she finally let her heart calm down and listened. The star sounded like her greenroom but amplified, the rustle of the plants drumming its repetitive beat, mixed with screeches and whistles she'd never heard before. It was as if the entire star was breathing. As if it had been sleeping and her less than docile descent had woken it up. Sid crouched, listening to the stirring of the world around her more attentively. Trying to isolate each sound; a task that would have otherwise been easier to accomplish if she knew what she was hearing in the first place.

Sid had no idea what any of it was.

She knew the sounds the plants made, knew most of them by heart in fact. It was everything else she couldn't put her finger on. The shrilling, high pitched yodels that echoed in the distance were nothing like what she was used to on her ship. *Those aren't plants,* she thought and tightened her suit around her. Whatever was beyond the rows of trees at the edge of the clearing was alive. Something whistled in the distance — closer than the previous sounds she heard — and Sid jumped to attention.

"Hello?" She beckoned but received no response.

Instinctively, her hands balled into fists and she took a small step back, fingers so tight they left small imprints in her skin. The whistle sounded again and Sid could have sworn she heard a rustle in the trees in the distance. Something was out there. Something big.

Without hesitation, she turned on her heels and sprinted back into the pod, locking the door briskly behind her. She didn't know what lurked outside but there was one thing she knew without a doubt; she wasn't alone in the jungle.

Sid peered through the dusty, oval viewing pane. The trees were silent, peaceful almost. Maybe she was just imagining things, her fear tugging at her still clouded mind and drawing on nightmares instead of staying rational in the situation at hand. There was no time to waste. It was getting close to Starset and if she waited any longer, she could be trapped in the maze of the jungle in the dark. She definitely did not want that.

Her gaze landed on the navigation pane window. The ring's yellow light was nowhere in sight. The Circulum System had not yet started its Starset rotation. She still had time. How much of it was the real mystery though. Sid had lost track of time and with the pod's system down, she could only guess at when the next rotation would take place. But guessing wasn't good enough right now, she needed to get the pod back online. Maybe being on the star would prove to be useful, she might have a chance of reaching Colton from down here.

Aside from the obvious dents to the pods hull, there didn't seem to be any damage to the mechanism. At least none that she could see. Sid patted the pockets of her suit, eagerly pulling out the first thing she could grab. "Aha!" She yelled out excitedly, twirling a small screwdriver in her fingers.

It only took a few minutes for her to unscrew the latch under the navigation pane.

"Let's see where you're hurting," she whispered and reached in to inspect the wiring.

Her hand pulled out a few wires that looked like someone had chopped them into bits. The mess in Sid's palm resembled one of her dinner preps, a roughly cut mash of random pieces ready for boiling. Except in this case, the outcome wouldn't be quite as delicious. The pod's motherboard was useless. "Well, that can't be good."

She reached into another pocket, pulling out only a loose screw and a rolled-up piece of lint.

"Great, just great," Sid huffed, crawling out from under the platform. "Now what?"

Her eyes scanned the pod's interior in hopes of finding something that could help. Nothing. The pod was as empty as her gurgling stomach. For an escape pod, this thing was incredibly poorly equipped for survival. There was nothing in sight that could aid someone in an actual escape. Sid wondered who'd designed such a useless piece of junk, quickly remembering that she had been picking it apart for scraps to fix the Arcturus for years. She cursed herself under her breath. *Stupid, foolish girl!* How in the star's name was she going to get out of this now? Unless...

Sid slid back down and rested her hands over the pods wiring. The current within her spread in tremors, crackling with electrical waves. She closed her eyes, barely visible beneath the shield of her goggles, and let her magic loose. *Not here, not where someone can see.* The thought barely grazed her mind before she pushed it away, letting her magic flow into the pod's core. Sid could hear the pod rustle as though it was struggling to awake. She closed her eyes, beads of sweat rolling down the back of her exposed, un-chipped neck. Just a few more...

Snap!

Sid jerked away from the pane and jumped to her feet. Something cracked outside. A twig? A rock? Was someone here? Had they found her?

With wild eyes, she inspected the landscape, jolting her gaze from the windows to the doors. The trees swayed lightly but there was nothing in the vicinity that screamed danger. At least nothing outside of being trapped in a dead pod on strange lands she was distinctly instructed to stay away from. Then she saw it. The yellow beam of light slowly rising over the horizon. The ring's Starset rotation had commenced which could only mean one thing; she had a few hours at most before the star completed its rotation around Jericho and she would be covered in night.

Sid kicked the seat behind her in frustration, "This is pointless!"

Tucking the screwdriver back into her pocket, she wiped the sweat from under her goggles and snapped them back on. There was no way she could fix the pod right now and there'd be even less she could do once it gets dark. She needed help. She needed Colton's help.

She closed her eyes and took a deep breath before opening the pod's doors again. The light had already started to fade, painting the jungle in front of her a million different shades. Sid settled her gaze on the glint of the towers which seemed even brighter now. So far, she had only seen the towers rendered on telescreen recordings and televised drone footage. But even the drones never made it out this deep into the jungle. She wondered what they were afraid of and quickly realized that it was probably the same thing she should be afraid of too. If only she knew what it was.

"Stop it!" Sid hissed at herself, "You need to find him. It's the only way out of this now."

With renewed hope, she gripped the screwdriver in her pocket and stepped through the clearing into the jungle's mess of trees, letting the light of the rising ring behind her guide the way.

EIGHT

THE YELLOW GLEAM of the Circulum System ring cast a warm light over the jungle and Sid welcomed the change from Jericho's bright white glow. While she knew the white sun provided the warmth that Neostar needed to survive, Sid was much more used to gentler shades of light. Having grown up hurtling through space in a dimly lit spaceship, her eyes took some time to adjust to Neostar's dazzling views even with her googles on. Her muscles screamed for relief, exhausted and overly used from hours of walking through uneven terrain.

The trail she had been following was wild with hills, forcing her to pitter patter down oily, slick grass the color of night only to then have to climb a wall of rocks in her way. There was no rhyme or reason to how the jungle had taken shape. It reminded her of a puzzle Colton sent once of a three-dimensional reconstruction of the towers. What he'd failed to mention were the seven missing pieces in the game, pieces that made everything make sense and come together. Sid had spent days constructing globes and cubes, trying to force them together; except they never quite fit. No matter what she tried, she ended up with a mess of angles that didn't look anything like the magnificent towers she had seen in her studies. The queen wouldn't have stood for the catastrophic creation Sid had come up with. When she finally figured out that parts were missing, she called Colton, furious and crying over the lost time. He only laughed, telling her that she had learned a good lesson that day; life is full of hills and valleys, what matters is what you do to get across.

As she stepped over a log covered almost entirely in purple star flowers, she smiled remembering Colton's words. They could not have rung truer to her current situation.

Sid's head was starting to spin and her stomach growled from hunger. From a distance, her clunky steps and loud belly noises likely sounded similar to the rest of the jungle creatures and she welcomed the camouflage with a smile. If whatever she'd heard near the pod thought she belonged here, it probably wouldn't try to eat her head.

Smacking her dry lips together, Sid dragged herself forward with a smile. In her last few hours of stumbling through the jungle, the only thing she encountered that even slightly resembled water had been the dew that collected on top of the large, purple leaves of Hickerberry that seemed to crowd the base of every tree in the jungle. She knew there must be water nearby for such a lush environment to flourish and could have sworn she heard the rush of water somewhere in the background of the jungle's cacophony.

She carefully lowered herself down a rocky incline and sat at the base, her feet dangling off the edge and lightly brushing the cool flow of water in the river below.

"Well, I'll be stardamned," she announced, reaching her hand into the chilled river. "This thing goes on forever!"

The river stretched on for as far as Sid could make out. It looped and swerved in the distance, cutting the jungle in half. Over its surface, she could see vines the size of tree trunks growing from one side to the other, forming bridges and passageways that loomed atop the trickling of the water. The trees were denser here, stretching so high that she lost sight of where they ended. She traced their trunks, extending her gaze as far as it would take her, all the way up to the yellow glow of the ring.

It must have been right above her now because the rays from the energy the ring collected from the Domer chips glowed through the treetops, forming glistening pools of light in the river.

"Beautiful," Sid whispered, lazily petting the Needling fern next to her. This was always one of her favorite plants though she'd never been able to sustain one into adulthood in her greenroom; the vitamins it required from the soil did not lend well to the artificial life she was able to provide. Regardless of her failed attempts, Sid would spend days tending to a young Needling, trying to coax it into existence. Something about the green shoots that grew sporadically out of its circular base made her think of a creature from Colton's home planet. The porcupine or something silly like that. *Why porcupine?* She asked Colton once. His response was as useless as ever. *Why not?* Was all he offered and at that, she left the matter alone.

The ring shifted somewhere high above her, causing the rays of light to duck behind an overly thick tree trunk.

"Oh, for the love of!" she yelled, suddenly realizing that if the ring was over her head that meant it was halfway through its rotation. She had no idea how far away she was from the towers, knowing only the general direction towards which she should aim based on her view of them from the crash site. If Sid had to guess, she'd say she walked almost half the way there but there was no way of telling for certain. For all she knew, she'd gotten turned around somewhere and strayed even further off the mark. The last thing Sid wanted was to spend the night in the jungle alone. If the noises were scaring her now, they'd do a lot more damage when she couldn't see a centimeter in front of her face.

She hopped off the rocky edge and splashed her boots into the river. The water was low, just grazing the top of her ankles, and the bottom felt soft, almost like sand but with a sticky base that gave it some form. It was a welcome change from what she'd been climbing over thus far. She jumped up and down, giggling each time the water splashed back and hit her legs. This was nothing like the shower on the Arcturus. Sid laughed hysterically, kicking her boots in every direction, twirling and screaming for joy.

"Grrrrrrr," a low, guttural sound emerged from the trees behind her, followed by a similar screeching, yodel to the one she heard earlier.

Sid's face paled and she froze, each muscle tensing from trying not to quiver. Her eyes turned first, followed by her head moments later. A few very excruciating moments.

"There's nothing there. There's nothing there. There's nothing there," she recited as she stretched herself up to look over the edge of the riverbank.

And how mistaken she was.

She saw its claws first, digging into the rocky terrain just above her. Claws that protruded from massive, muscled paws that looked like they were made for crushing. Her gaze traveled up the creature's legs; although logs would have been a better way to describe them. Its entire body was covered in grey skin that had the pearlescent texture of scales. *Can this thing swim?* She thought. *Oh, who cares! You need to get out of here!*

Sid ripped her attention away from the beast and started to run, turning only once to see it open its wide set jaw to growl. The beast's teeth glistened with saliva; all two rows of them. She could see it dripping down the large patch of dreaded hair that hung from the lower half of its face. The only hair this thing had on all of its body.

"Right, who needs hair when you have ten tons of body muscle to keep you warm!" Sid yelled, still running.

The creature turned down its pointed ears and without hesitation, took off after her.

Sid's legs propelled her forward like she was hooked to a rotator engine. Each turn of the river slowed her down but only by a fraction. She could hear the creature on her tail, steps as loud as the crash of her pod must have been. She didn't get the best look at the stardamned thing before she ran but she would say it was twice her height and that's not counting it standing on its hind legs. Which is exactly what it started doing when she turned around again; getting up as high as it could before growling and charging after her again. It was like it was trying to show her just how big it was. As far as Sid was concerned, that wasn't necessary. She understood the size of the beast. She was doing everything she could to not empty her bladder in her suit because of that understanding.

"Leave me alone!" She yelled and tossed a rock behind her.

The creature swerved right, the rock missing it by a few

centimeters. Its eyes narrowed and it huffed loudly, small puffs of smoke escaping its wrinkled nostrils. *Great, now it's mad.*

Sid jumped out of the river, climbing onto the bank opposite the beast. She caught its gaze. Something wasn't right here. The creature wasn't running at full speed, it was almost galloping next to her. Like it was trying to slow itself down to match her pace.

At the next turn, Sid stomped her heels into the ground. Her body skidded to a stop and she balanced on the tips of her dirt covered boots to stay upright. She turned to the beast, her eyes widening as she watched it do the same. "No way!"

Sid took a few steps back. The beast followed. She hopped forward; the beast hopped after her. Well, attempted to hop. Its muscle-bound body barely left the ground but she got the message. She ran as fast as she could and came to an abrupt stop. The beast took off, grinding down the ground until it skidded to the same mark across the river; its wrinkled half-tail shaking wildly. "Starspit! You're playing!" She yelped and took a light step toward the edge of the river.

One leg at a time, Sid lowered herself into the water. She was almost waist deep when the beast leapt past the edge and plummeted into the cold wet next to her.

Sid wiped beads of river water off her goggles. She was soaked.

Letting out a heart pounding laugh she stepped toward the beast, but it shrank away from her, startled by the sound.

"No, don't be scared!" She yelped, "I won't hurt you."

Sid raised her hand gently and inched it closer to the creature's nose. She closed her eyes, standing as still as she could manage with her palm outstretched in front of her.

Squinting, she opened one lid to a sliver. "Come on," she whispered. "Come on."

Before she could reach her hand further, the beast lowered its weighted head and pressed its grey, wrinkled nose into her palm. *Ew,* she thought, feeling the wet of its nose slobber on her fingers. Sid moved in closer, this time the beast stayed firm, pressing into her hand agreeably. As she moved her palm up the ridges of its malformed nose line, Sid patted what she could only assume was a forehead. It was hard to tell with all the lumps in the way.

The beast wiggled under her touch excitedly.

"You're just a big softy, aren't you? With your stupid teeth and scary growls. You're nothing but a giant pet!" She yelped, petting the beast furiously.

The beast's tail wagged enthusiastically. "You wouldn't know which way leads to the towers, would you?"

Silence.

"You know," she said again, pointing her hands above her head to mimic the shape of the buildings. "The towers!"

The beast hopped back excitedly and shoved its nose as straight as it could get it in the direction opposite the flow of the water.

"It's that way? Really? Wow, I'm really turned around here." She sighed, "I'll never make it before Starset."

Sid slumped over her legs. She was stuck in the jungle. Over night; with no food, no water and no shelter. She wanted Colton. She wanted her ship and she wanted home. Sid straightened up and looked at the beast's questioning stare, its head tilted sideways as if trying to understand her sorrow. At least she had a friend.

She was about to climb out of the water when two large

paws outstretched in front of her. Her lips parted as she watched the creature lower its head and look up at her.

"What do you want now?" She asked.

The beast stomped its paws further into the riverbank and lowered its head so low it was almost close enough to take a sip. It wiggled its tail, then the rest of its body, watching her the entire time.

"Wait, you're not serious? You want me to get up there?"

Sid pointed to the beast's back and it shook its head dramatically. "Climb on you? Really?"

There was a mix of emotions rolling in her. This was by far the most dangerous thing she could ever do and if Colton was here, well, she'd never hear the end of it. Although if Colton was here, he'd likely have killed the creature already and she would never have gotten the chance to meet this spectacular animal.

"What in the stars does Colton know anyway?" She exclaimed and walked around the side of the beasts hunched body.

Sid raised one arm up, patting its back to test it. It was definitely sturdy enough to carry her. Her and possibly even her escape pod with a few weights added for good measure. The animal next to her was the largest thing she'd ever seen! She wrapped a fist around one of the dreads of fur on the beasts chin and hoisted herself up. *Well, this is weird.*

"So, what do we do no—"

Before she could finish asking the question, the beast shot up and Sid tightened her grip on its fur to keep from toppling over. It took a step forward, splashing waterfalls of river from its paws. It was testing her, making sure she held on. "Clever little thing," Sid mused and leaned in.

Her new friend wasn't exactly the best smelling thing

she'd been close to lately but it still beat having to walk the rest of the way.

"To the towers!" Sid yelled and tried to keep yesterday's dinner in her stomach as the beast galloped forward.

THE RIDE WAS FASTER than Sid expected and after a few close calls, she had actually gotten the hang of moving with the beast's jerky strides. She leaned into the fast turns and lowered her body tight against its muscled back when it ran faster. All things considering, aside from the sour smell that came off the animal, this might have been an even smoother ride than the escape pod.

They had long passed the river's outstretched bank, making most of their journey through the dense jungle instead. Sid couldn't see much as they zoomed past the trees but once in a while, when the beast slowed to catch its breath, she had a chance to admire the beauty around her. Wild and untouched, like the bottomless pit of her own heart.

After an hour of riding, the trees began to part, letting the setting light of Jericho glisten over the horizon. She could see the outline of the ring in the distance, its Starset pass coming to an end. The beast halted, digging its taloned paws into the ground.

It was then that Sid saw it.

Not too far off from where they had stopped, the overpowering glitter of the tower panes sprouted before her. They were so much taller than she had imagined. It was as though they were mocking her simply by existing. Light reflected off every perfectly sculpted angle, making the towers look like a kaleidoscope of colors. Kaleidoscope — another word Sid never understood.

"Look at that! Isn't it something?"

She patted the beast's side, urging it to move but it refused to budge. Sid tapped it lightly with the side of her boot but the beast only shook its head and continued to stand still. "You don't want to go in, do you?"

The beast shook its head again and slowly lowered to the ground. Its gaze downward in a melancholy refusal.

"It's alright," Sid smiled. "Don't feel bad. I can go alone."

She climbed off its back and started to walk toward the light, turning back to face her new friend.

"Thank you. Really, thank you!" She said and waved before running to the larger than life steel and glass bridge that stretched out before her.

CROUCHING at the edge of the bridge, Sid was careful to stay out of sight. She could see a few Starblades patrolling along the sides of the bridge with a larger group closer to the entrance arch. She studied them carefully, taking in the glory of their perfectly tailored blue suits that formed seamlessly to every taut muscle. The material reflected in the light. *Chromium*, she thought, remembering that the suits the Starblades wore were more than just a fashion statement. Each piece was designed to offer the best chances in battle and each piece was constructed from a breathable metal that offered not only support, but an impenetrable shield of protection. Colton had once told her that on his home planet, his own people often participated in hand to hand combat and suits — much like the ones on the Starblades before her — prevented injury in immeasurable ways. The nanite-infused fabric acted not only as a safeguard but a lifesaving device, able to repair tissue damage if a Starblade was hurt in battle. Sid could never understand that part; if the two species of Neostar were at peace, why would Colton's people need that much protection?

The Starblades seemed lost in conversation, chattering about their day and laughing heartily at jokes Sid could only imagine were aimed at the Domers. Each held their blade upright, ready for attack. The spear-like blades were over a meter in length fashioned in the same light-blue shade as the Starblades uniforms. The tips of the blades beamed a pulsing blue glow, continuously recharging their power.

Sid had studied the weapons for nights on end, learning everything she could about their mechanics. The spears drew their power from the ring, circulating across the shaft and sending electrical currents into the tips. On impact, the electricity collided with the victim, causing either paralysis or death, depending on the thrust and weight behind it. They were simple weapons that when used correctly, could take down an opponent in the blink of an eye. Sid had no doubt that if any of the Starblades spotted her lurking under the bridge, she'd be dust before she could curse the stars.

There has to be another way in!

Her attention shifted to the arch beyond the bridge. She could maybe climb in? The thought had barely made an imprint before she shook it off. Even if Sid could scale the web-like dome structure, she'd have to drop five stories down to make it into Tower City. And who knew what she'd be falling into, or if she could even survive the drop. Looking up at the entrance arch, that seemed like a very big *if*.

"Pod coming in!" She heard one of the Starblades yell out and turned to follow his gaze.

Just beyond the rail under which she was hiding, an oval shaped pod whooshed past her and came to a stop just meters away. Sid was so busy admiring the Starblades, she completely forgot about the worker trains.

Yes! Sid shouted in her head. She simply needed to wait for the workers to pile out of the train and be led into Tower City. If she could blend in with them, she'd get past the Starblades and into the city without a hitch.

She held her breath and waited. A few moments passed and Sid was almost blue in the face when the pod's doors slid open and a mass of workers piled out. She counted fifty-seven, just enough to hide her in plain sight.

They rushed the pods doors, emptying out onto the bridge and staining it the color of rust and grime. The worker's faces, covered in debris and oil, made them look like they had not bathed in weeks. Sid studied their mannerisms and the casual way in which they interacted with one another. A man slapped the back of a boy next to him and her eyes jerked to the scar on the back of the kid's neck, still fresh from the chip injected in there. Her fingers grazed the back of her own, un-chipped neck and she smiled. Sid was glad she had at least one thing that made her different from her own kind. She was un-chipped and though she knew that having gotten to hold on to her magic was not something a Domer was allowed to do, it made her just that much closer to Colton's people than her own. It seemed odd to her that the only things that made the two races different was the shape of their eyes and magic. She'd give both up in a heartbeat if it meant she could be nothing like the group before her now. As the last of the Domers stepped off the pod's platform, the doors slid shut and the transport pod shot up into the air, leaving behind a windblown mass of workers in filthy clothes. A stark comparison to the group guarding the bridge. The workers attire was nothing like the pristine suits of the Starblades, tunics made of patches and random scraps of fabric — that Sid was certain were just more patches — wrapped around their bodies and tied off at the waist with long belts. While her suit did not look exactly like their ripped cropped pants and belted hoods, all the dirt she had gathered on it from her trip so far should help disguise her in the crowd.

Sid stayed down until half of the workers were off the pod then made a run for it.

The Starblades were so busy ushering in the crowd that no one was paying any attention to her hiding spot beneath the bridge. She might actually have a chance at this!

Her hands were shaking and her goggles started to fog but she ran nonetheless. She swerved past a group of workers who turned to grimace at her. One of them raised a threatening fist and Sid turned, shooting up her hands apologetically. She rushed through the crowd, trying to push her way into the belly of the hoard. To stay as hidden as possible.

Muck! This is going to work!

The smile had no time to reach her lips when Sid turned, crashing face first into a Starblade. Her feet twisted beneath her and before she could stop herself, she pummeled the man to the ground.

Sid's face met his chest plate first. Her hands followed soon after. She squinted her eyes, opening them one by one to face the Starblade, her body splayed directly on top of his. She started to hoist herself up to apologize when he spoke, his voice rough from having the breath knocked out of him.

"Well, this can't be good," the Starblade noted.

Sid followed his eyes to the floor. Her face contorting into a look of horror as she took in the bent, and very broken, light-blue spear laying next to them.

So much for blending in...

NINE

"I'M SO SORRY!" Sid squealed, scrambling to her feet. "It was an accident, I swear! I'll pay for the damages!"

The Starblade jumped to his feet effortlessly, dusting off the back of his perfectly fit suit. He was taller than Sid originally thought, though she couldn't tell much of anything with her chest pressed awkwardly against his moments ago. Taller and a touch more attractive than she would have liked. She bunted her goggles up, straining to look up at him. The Starblade fixed his sky-blue eyes on her and she rapidly looked down at her filthy boots, hiding her flushed cheeks. He felt familiar to her somehow and she got the sense that if their eyes were locked for much longer, she would be in serious trouble.

"Pay for it? With what? Your little Domer dockets? We both know those are useless in the city," he scoffed.

So much for being attractive, Sid thought. *This man is a stardamned fool!*

"I'm not a Domer, you imbecile!" She roared, raising her fist as if to strike him.

The Starblade pointed a blue-gloved finger at her face. "You sure about that?"

"What in the stardamned sky are you talking about?" Sid was furious. Who did this kid think he was to go around pointing fingers and assuming she was some sad, little worker? *Wait 'til Colton hears about this, he's going to rip you into pieces!*

"Oh, my. That's quite some mouth you've got there," the Starblade chuckled, "I meant your eyes. They're, you know, different."

Of course. Sid had forgotten that without her goggles, the only feature that differentiated her from Colton's people was out there for anyone to see. When she first realized that every native of Neostar had the same, dreadful feature, she cried for days. Colton tried to console her, telling her she wasn't like any of the Domers, that she was special. But she didn't care for his words. She didn't want to be special. She wanted to be just like him and his people. Just like Queen Leona and this insufferable Starblade that was standing in front her, judging who she was based on a set of eyes. Colton was wrong, she wasn't special. She didn't want to be anything of the sort. Didn't want the Starblade to look at her like she belonged on that worker train. Didn't want him pointing out that she will never be like him.

"You're either a Citizen or a Domer. Can't really be anything else," the Starblade smirked.

Sid's mind played out a dozen scenarios all ending with him slumped on the floor with a bloody nose from her angered blows. Instead, she snapped the goggles back over her eyes. "Right," she whispered because he *was* right. There was nothing else for her to be down here.

"So, what are you?"

"Someone who's going to help you fix your stupid blade!" She howled and kicked the remnants of the weapon on the ground.

"And how do you plan to do that exactly?" He smirked.

Sid was getting quite tired of this fool's constant smiling. If she saw any more of his teeth, she'd be tempted to knock them right out of his perfectly shaped skull. She picked up the two pieces of the blade, studying the torn edges where it snapped. "I just need replacement wiring and a soldering gun," she finally said through gritted teeth.

"Impressive," the Starblade smiled, "you some kind of mechanic or something?"

"Or something."

"Well, that's not saying much, is it?"

She rolled her eyes, "I'm not here for the conversation. There's somewhere I need to be so either you want your dumb blade fixed or not. Your call."

The Starblade raised his hands in defeat, "You're really feisty for someone who just broke NSO law."

"Wait, what?" Sid's eyebrows raised so high you could almost see them over the rim of her goggles. "What law?"

"I mean, you technically attacked an officer of the queen's guard. And broke his weapon. Sounds like an act of rebellion to me."

"Attacked? What are you even talking about? *You* were in *my* way! And I didn't break anything. I'm trying to help you fix it, mister officer of the guard!" She hissed. Annoyed that a mere Starblade would dare consider himself a member of the queen's own guard. Starblades were the last on the chain of command. Well under the guards that held such high status in the NSO regimen.

The Starblade crossed his arms and Sid tried not to be

impressed by the bulge of muscle tightening against his suit. "I'm just saying that you could probably stand to be a little nicer to me. Considering the fact that I haven't had you detained yet."

"Yet?"

"Exactly," he smiled forcibly, "I'm not having the best week here so my judgement is likely not great."

"Oh, what happened? Your perfect little life giving you trouble?" Sid offered sarcastically, "I don't have time for this! Either take me in or get out of my way."

"Well, that's one way to make friends, I guess." The Starblade grabbed for his blade, yanking it out of her hands abruptly.

"I'm not trying to make friends," Sid said defensively.

"Yeah, no kidding. What's your business in the city again?"

Muck.

Sid had to come up with a story, something believable and simple. She couldn't very well ask where Colton is; the Starblade assumed she was a Domer and a Domer would have no business with the NSO general. She could tell him she's there to see the queen, perhaps pretend she's an apprenticing Magistra; she could be a lady in waiting, right? Sid looked down at her dirt stained boots and fingernails blackened by motor oil. *Well, that won't work.*

The Starblade cleared his throat, jerking Sid's attention back to him. *Muck, muck, muck!* How long has she been quiet for? *Long enough to look suspicious,* she reckoned.

"I'm here because..." Sid felt the tip of the screwdriver in her pocket, wishing she could stab the pointy end into the Starblade's broad shoulder and make a run for it.

"Because?"

Her fingers tightened as her thoughts rushed to formulate a lie. "The droids!" She yelled suddenly, loud enough to cause a commotion in a group of workers ahead of them. Some turned to see who the high-pitched wail belonged to, losing their interest quickly once their eyes found Sid. "I was asked to check the droids.'

"You?" The Starblade ran his gaze up and down her small build, "Really?"

"Yes, me, really! I happen to be a very skilled technician. Those droids will never know what hit them when I get over there!" She raised the screwdriver in the air, "I will fix them so good they'll be begging me to move in!"

The Starblade pressed his hand to her forearm and slowly lowered it down, "Alright, alright, let's not be pointing sharp things around a dozen armed guards. Not unless you're looking to get fried."

Sid blushed and tucked the tool back into her suit. "Not like you could fry me with that bent little stick of yours," she muttered under her breath.

"Let me guess, it's your first time in the city."

She said nothing, instead taking the chance to grunt annoyingly and roll her eyes away from the Starblade. She was growing tired of his incessant questions and pointless attempts at conversation. It was like he was purposefully trying to prevent her from finding Colton.

"I'll take that as a yes."

"Look, no offense but I really need to get going." Sid eyed the group of workers that was almost at the end of the bridge now. She couldn't miss her shot at getting into Tower City, especially not for some junior blade that wanted to waste her time talking.

"Do you even know where you're going? That place is a

maze, unless you have someone to show you around, you'll never figure it out." He pointed to the retreating group of workers in the distance, their backs a wall of stone-grey tunics. "Doesn't look like you have a lot of friends in there."

Sid wanted to punch his teeth out. *The nerve of the mucking fool!* She looked in the direction of the group and slumped her shoulders, he wasn't exactly wrong. Whatever she'd seen of Tower City, it was the kind of place she did not want to get lost in. Not that she had many options at the moment. She looked back at the Starblade but said nothing. *Starspitting jerk.*

"How about I make you a deal? You fix my blade and I'll take you to the droid station," he said and straightened his stance.

Great, Sid thought. *He's even taller now.* "Why can't you just take it in for repairs?"

"And risk the ridicule of having to explain that I let the star's smallest Domer run me down? No, thank you!"

"Hey! Watch it!"

"What?" He scratched his head and looked at her alarmingly.

"I'm not that small!"

"Sure, you're huge. Anyway, what do you say? You help me and I help you. Sound good?"

Nothing about this sounded good. Colton told her it's not safe and here she was, heading into Tower City with a fake identity and a Starblade as her escort. The amount of trouble she was going to be in when she finds him was not something she wanted to even think about right now. She should say no, take her chances in the city without the Starblade. She shouldn't risk any more than she had to. On the other hand, she had a much better chance of blending in with him by her side. And if she played her cards right, she could even get him to tell her where Colton is without having to scurry in the shadows of the city.

"I fix the blade and you take me to the droids?" She confirmed, knowing full well she'd be gone long before they got anywhere near the droid station.

"That's the deal," he reached a hand towards her and she cringed at the irritating strength of his handshake. "I'm Ashlan, by the way. And you are?"

She hesitated, briefly considering giving him a fake name but decided against it. More lies were not going to help the situation. "Sid," she said defiantly, squeezing his hand firmer.

"Sid. I like it, it suits you. Short and odd," he chuckled.

"It's a nickname so you can shut up now."

"Oh?" Ashlan raised an eyebrow, "What's your full name?"

"Sidarius," she scoffed. "Long and complicated. Happy now?"

She started to walk but Ashlan stopped short behind her. "Hmm."

"Hmm, what?" She asked, gesturing for him to move.

"Nothing, I guess," he smiled. "That was my grandpa's name too. Kind of a weird name for a girl. And a Domer."

"Not as weird as Ashlan," she bellowed and stuck out her tongue. "We going to walk or do I have to break something else?"

"Whoa! You sure you're a girl? You don't act like any other girls I know," Ashlan said.

Sid looked him up and down. If she moved quick enough, she could probably run a jolt of electricity through thick skull without anyone noticing. Sid growled and let the magic reach just below the surface of her skin. *Not so tough without your stupid blade, are you?*

"Relax, I'm just kidding." He motioned her toward the gates, "Welcome to Tower City, Sid. Try to keep up!"

TEN

BY THE TIME they made their way into the heart of Tower City, Jericho had set and night engulfed their world in deep shades of blues and golds. "Oh. My. Star." Sid took in the masterful construction of Tower City, slack jawed.

The layout of the entrance arch spanned so wide around the city's perimeter that it was difficult to see the size of what lay beyond the arch's protective walls. And it was magnificent! The central street they walked through was at least ten times wider than the entire span of the Arcturus with tall glass panes running parallel to one another, creating passageways for people and traffic pods; which zoomed by them in each and every direction, leaving traces of blue light in their wake. Even in the late hours of the evening there was a steady pace of movement all around them, muffled by circular glass buildings jutting out like tree trunks from the floors. Each building was connected to the one next to it with a series of tube-like passageways which stretched so high up that Sid wondered how anyone felt safe enough to walk across them. She could see a scurry of activity running through a passage in her peripheral and her breath caught in worry for the travelers. They made it across without a care and Sid let herself relax, the tension in her shoulders pulsing a steady beat behind her ears. A pod flew by them and landed a few meters away at one of the street's many intersections. The clear doors slid open and a family of Citizens rushed out into the street, a man and woman, followed by four small children. Sid's eyes widened at the sight of them, she'd only seen children in her lesson projections thus far — they were so much smaller in person. *Like little pets,* she thought, studying the family. Despite the gleeful hops of the children, they looked regal. Sid peeked further out from behind Ashlan's shoulder, taking in the Citizens around them. All of them dressed in varying fabrics in shades of blue and white and all of them walking about like royalty. She couldn't even imagine what the queen must look like if this was the general population of Tower City. It was as if they were weightless, gliding down the labyrinth of metal and glass. The city was full of life but serene at the same time; frozen in a constant state of activity.

Sid made sure to stay behind Ashlan to avoid drawing too much attention to herself, only occasionally popping her head out to scan the new environment. Each time she glanced around, she felt like she had shrunk to half her size — small in comparison to the vastness of the architecture around her. It was as though she was swallowed by glass and telescreens and light. Pure, all-encompassing light that shone so bright from each live screen that she could feel her pupils shrink to accommodate its presence. She thanked the star for her goggles, adjusting her sight to the glare around her, her thoughts immediately landing on Colton. How could she find him in this place? The task seemed nearly impossible now. They had been walking a straight line down the central passage but she still felt like she had been turned around a million times over. Everything was different and new and absolutely petrifying. Sid was completely lost. And with reason, she hadn't the slightest idea where she was and where Ashlan was taking her.

"You weren't kidding when you said this place was a maze," she noted, pointing up to trace the ten-story high building to her right. "How do you even know where to go?"

"You get used to it," Ashlan answered with a laugh. "It's really quite simple once you orient yourself."

"Doesn't seem simple enough to me."

He laughed again and she tried to push the warmth that rose to her neck away, she still hated the stardamned jerk.

Ashlan stopped at an intersection and nudged her to look up at the blue projection running atop a pillar in the middle of the road. Bright blue holographic numbers spilled into the air above, circling around an invisible center. "See that?" He pointed to it, "There's one of these at every corner to mark the district number."

She scanned the projection to note a flashing number scroll across the screen: thirty-seven.

"So we're in district thirty-seven?"

"Uh huh. The districts are all numbered based on their proximity to the Queen's Tower. So, we're thirty-seven districts away from it, putting us about halfway in."

"There are seventy-four districts in the city?" Sid yelped a little too excitedly. Despite the years she'd spent studying the nuances of the city, there was still so much she didn't know. Every new piece of information shattered her and left her giddy with excitement. Minus the present company,

Tower City was everything Sid imagined it to be; an absolute wonder.

"Seventy-six, not counting the gardens." Ashlan said.

"There are gardens?"

Ashlan chuckled and threw his arms up, "Of course! Tower City has the most beautiful outdoor spaces!"

"Isn't it all one big outdoor space?" She asked, pointing to the dark, night sky above them.

"Sort of. The entire city is atmosphere controlled. You can't see it but the shield is there. Always."

She took a breath in, realizing that she had not felt the coolness of air since they stepped foot through the arch. With Jericho's light out, it must have been freezing at this time of the evening but she felt completely content. She guessed the shield spanned across the city in a dome and functioned like the climate control breakers on her ship. Invisible to the eye but continuously running code to maintain the most optimal temperature. *Brilliant!*

"Wow, you really are new here!" Ashlan said, noting her open-mouthed stare.

Sid tightened her lips into a thin line and let the embarrassment wash over her. "Not all of us get to live in this perfect little oasis, you know! Why don't we just get to wherever it is you're taking me? And let's make it a silent trip, alright?" *He is unbearable, the fool.*

"Hey, I didn't mean anything by it. Just most Domers have been here at least once in their life. Haven't you ever had to work or get supplies for your family?"

Sid raised a finger to her lips and shot him a glowered gaze, "I thought I said silent?"

"Seriously? Fine, suit yourself. I was going to take you through the falls but no matter."

"The falls? As in *the* waterfalls?" She grinned, hopping from foot to foot. She had spent hours on end replaying drone footage of the falls in Tower City. Huge masses of water that cascaded down from the rooftops of two of the tallest buildings at heart-wrenching speeds. Colton told her that there were Citizens brave enough to propel down the falls and dive effortlessly into the pools beneath but she never believed him. A drop like that would kill anyone who tried, she was sure of it.

"Oh, no, no. You said silent. They're much too loud. Let's just keep going quietly. As you wished."

"You're honestly the most annoying person I have met in my entire life!" She exclaimed, keeping the part that he's only the second person she's met to herself. "Which way to the falls?"

"Not sure. You'll figure it out. You seem to know every-thing, no?"

She punched him in the shoulder, knocking the remnants of his blade from his grip and laughed sheepishly when it rolled on the ground a few steps away from them. Ashlan reached down to pick it up, shaking his head.

"I'm sorry. You don't have to be quiet just please can we see the falls?" She said, hoping that he'd let it go.

"Who's the annoying one now?" He huffed, then, "They're in district twelve. We should hurry it up if we want to make it there and to the blade cells before dinner."

"You're taking me to the blade cells?" She exclaimed.

"Well, obviously. You said you'll fix my blade, remem-ber? That was the bargain!"

The glass pane next to them suddenly felt so much closer than before. The wide, open-aired street they were on seemed to shrink in size before her eyes. Sid felt sick, she felt like she was suffocating. Her mind was a blurry mess and she felt sick to her stomach. She couldn't go to the blade cells! The cells, used for charging and repairing the Starblade weapons, were located on the bottom level of the queen's own tower and from what Colton had told her, it was guarded to the rims. Someone could figure out she didn't belong here, that she wasn't some Domer Ashlan found. If she was found out, she'd be in so much trouble! Worse, they could trace her back to Colton. As much as she wanted to find him, she didn't want him to jeopardize his position because of her stupid decision to follow this daft Starblade into the city. What in the name of the star was she going to do now?

"Hello?" Ashlan waved a palm in front of her face aggressively, "Is Sid somewhere in there?"

"Sorry, I just got dizzy for a second. I'm probably just hungry."

As if on command, her stomach growled loud enough to spark the attention of a Citizen next to her. The tall woman looked her up and down, shook her head with a sour expression and turned away, rearranging the folds of her sheer blue skirt and continuing on her way. Sid wanted to ram her fist right into her smug face. How dare she act like Sid was lesser than her? What gave this mucking woman the right to...

Sid stared wide-eyed as the woman was greeted by two Starblades, each bowing their heads to her until she waved for them to stand up. The first Starblade flicked his wrist and within moments, a pod descended next to them with a sudden whoosh that sent Sid toppling backwards. She looked up frantically to see that three more pods were idling above them, waiting for the woman to board the airy carriage. The woman lifted a few layers of skirt off the ground and stepped through the pod's glass door. Without hesitation, the two Starblades followed suit and settled in seats next to her. She shot Sid a sideways glance through the pod's clear walls before being shot up into the air and disappearing from sight. The other pods followed suit, leaving Sid staring blankly into the blue-lit trails of their take off.

Was that a Magistra? Did I just see a stardamned Magistra?

Sid tried to brush the dirt off her suit sleeve unsuccessfully. *Of course she looks at me like I'm nothing. Look at her and look at me! As far as this place is concerned, I am nothing.* Sid's head ached and she wanted to push her way out of this stardamned place. She wanted to go home. To be alone again where she didn't feel like she wasn't worth the air she was breathing. As much as she wanted to live here, it felt empty without Colton. She wished it was him that was taking her on this tour. That it was him that she was on her way to see the falls with. Not this annoying Starblade with his self-assured smile and perfect row of teeth.

"We can stop for food on the way if you'd like?"

Muck. He's still here.

"I'm fine. Let's just get going, it's getting late." Sid pointed to the projection above them. The time read eight thirty-four, well past her usual dinner time. She needed to get rid of this kid and find Colton before she passed out from hunger. If she could only get him to take her close enough to the general's quarters. But how?

"You sure? You don't look great. No offense."

She scowled but quickly perked up as an idea sparked her attention. "Actually, you're right."

"I am? Wow, that's a change coming from you!"

"Don't get used to it. But I am hungry and need to clean up a bit."

"Why?"

"Because not all of us can be all prim and put together all the time, Starblade! Some of us don't have little blue suits to keep us safe and clean!"

Ashlan raised his arms defensively, "I just meant that you don't look terrible. Just like you could eat. Star help me, you're something else, aren't you?"

"Listen, you going to take me somewhere I can clean up, or not?"

He dropped his arms to his side and sighed, "Fine. Let's go."

Perfect! Now she simply needed to lose him and she'd be free to search for Colton. Hopefully he'd take her somewhere with a crowd so she could disappear with ease. They weren't that far off from the towers and once she was alone, she'd have a better chance of hiding herself. She was wrong to think that walking with the Starblade would help camouflage her from the Citizens, all it did was draw more attention to them. A Starblade and a Domer walking together like they were pals. It must look even more out of place than it felt. Sid had never heard of such a thing in all of her studies. Starblades were Starblades and Domers were Domers. The two didn't mix.

"Shouldn't you get back now? It's getting late. Don't you have to be somewhere about now? Dinner or something? With your perfect little family?" She teased, hoping he'd take the bait.

Ashlan said nothing. His gaze drifting off past the edges of her white hair and into an unknown distance beyond them. *What's wrong with him? Did I break him?*

"Hello?" She howled, "Mister Flawless? You thinking about your ideal life, huh? Yeah, I get it. You should definitely get back to it though. I'll be completely fine on my own. And come find me tomorrow! I'll fix that blade of yours then."

"Actually, my father was killed this week." He lowered his gaze and stepped aside, "so my ideal life is not exactly welcoming right now. And don't try to get out of fixing my blade. We made a deal and you're stuck with me until it's handled."

Wait, what? His father died? I am an actual mucking idiot. Sid felt foolish and rude and utterly selfish. This entire time, Ashlan had been trying to talk to her and she never once asked him about his life. Maybe if she did, he would have told her sooner about his father and she wouldn't be feeling like a jerk right now. Yes, she needed to find Colton. And yes, Ashlan was an annoying Starblade that she had to get rid of to do that. But she couldn't shrug him off, at least not until she knew he wasn't upset. *People who are upset do stupid things;* Colton once told her. What if the stupid thing Ashlan did was to turn her in before she found him?

"I'm sorry about your dad. Really. What happened to him?"

"Nothing I shouldn't have been ready for. He was the NSO general so it's not like his job was all that safe."

The Starblade tried to smile but Sid's head spun before she could focus on the row of bright, white teeth lining his grin. "NSO general? Your father? He was..."

She couldn't finish the words. *No, no, no! It can't be!*

"Yes. The one and only. He gave up his entire life for the queen, now he died for her," the Starblade shrugged. "He's a hero. I guess."

Sid could barely form the words that she was aching to shout. "What... what was his name?"

"General Colton Tirian Mandelev. Why?"

In seconds, Sid's entire world collapsed. She felt like she was on the pod again, barreling at full speed into an incoming object that was sure to either kill her or render her entirely useless. Her mouth was dry. Her knees weaker than the pathetic carbon monoxide valve she'd spent months trying to fix. Colton was dead. He was the only one in this stardamned world that she cared about and he was dead! She was in Tower City looking for a dead man. The only person who could help her get off this star was a dead man! Dead. Colton. Dead.

Her gaze drifted to Ashlan's olive skinned face. This was Colton's son. She didn't even know Colton had a son. He never spoke of his family and Sid naturally assumed he didn't have one, aside from her, of course. Yet there he was, standing in front of her. All muscle and grins and self-assuredness. She hated him. She hated that he got to spend his life with Colton. Really spend a life with him. Not on some weekly scheduled calls, not on a rusty ship wishing he was closer. He was close. As close as one could get to a father. As close as Sid wished she was.

Sid shook her head, realizing she'd been silent for what must have seemed like forever.

"No reason," she finally uttered, "so your father, how much did you know about him?"

"What?"

"The general, did he tell you anything? About a ship perhaps?"

The Starblade tilted his head, "That's a really weird

question. You alright? You didn't hit your head when you fell on the bridge, did you?"

Sid grimaced. She must sound pretty crazy but if he thought she was insane, that could only mean that he didn't know about the Arcturus. He didn't know about her. Colton had always told her that she had to stay away, stay hidden. It never occurred to her that he might have been keeping her just as hidden as her ship was. Far off where no one could find her. She was some filthy little secret he had and it made her furious. The anger rushed through her like a tidal wave, her hands shook. In fact, her entire body vibrated. Fury mixing with sadness and grief until she didn't know which one was which. She could feel the magic within her awaken, threatening to surface. She should let it. She should melt the entire city to the ground. The electricity crackled in her palms, readying to explode.

"Anyway, we should go. You'll have to see the falls on your next trip in. I need to get this blade fixed before someone realizes what happened. It won't be good for either of us if I don't turn it in tonight."

The blade? How could he think about his dumb blade right now? Colton was dead! Her thoughts screamed, pummeling through her but not reaching her lips. Of course that was all he could think about. He was selfish and arrogant and he didn't care about Colton. Not the way she had. She had to get out of this place as soon as possible. Away from the city, the Citizens and Colton's selfish son. With him gone, she needed to get the valve on her own no matter what it took.

Based on her vague knowledge of the towers schematics, the blade cells were a few floors above the rings control booth. The entire system ran on a symbiotic current of power being fed by the electricity generated by the Circulum System. There had to be a mechanics station nearby, close enough for regular maintenance of the system. If her valve was anywhere, that's where it would be held.

"How long will it take us to get to the cells?" She asked, straightening her stance.

"On foot? Too long." Ashlan looked her way, smiling. "But we don't need to waste time walking."

"You don't mean..."

He looked past her and she followed his gaze to a row of docked transit pods at the end of the street.

"Let's take a ride, shall we?"

ELEVEN

THE VIBRATION of the transit pod on take-off would have made Sid nauseous if it wasn't for the absolute emptiness of her stomach. She probably should have taken Ashlan up on his offer to eat but there was no time to waste. She wanted to get off this star immediately. The stench of Colton's death seemed to coat the city in waves only she could see. She wondered if Ashlan felt the same when he first heard of his father's passing. Could he be mourning his loss as much as her? Sid doubted that was possible. No one loved Colton like she did. No one owed him their life like her.

A projection zipped into sight on the pod's windowed wall. The words trickled over the glass, sliding in from one side to hover in the center for a brief moment before sliding away. A trail of blue light skidded across the surface and stayed on the screen like a ghostly reminder of the announcement.

"Now passing district twelve," Sid read aloud.

She pressed her hands against the glass, careful not to seem bewildered by the rush of the city below them. The other passengers in the pod seemed oblivious to the beauty stretched beneath their feet. All Citizens with the exception of a Starblade, two Starblades if she counted Ashlan. She didn't. Sid glanced back at him, noting the nonchalant way he inspected his fingernails while reclining on the squeaky white lounge seat. Pointing his chiseled jaw upward in an air of superiority. This is who Colton made? This brilliantly self-adoring sack of skin? He's lucky they're surrounded by watchful eyes and Sid was on a mission, otherwise she would have thrown him off the pod already. She rubbed a finger against the screwdriver in her pocket and gave a sigh of relief. Soon, she'll use it soon.

A hush fell over the pod as even the least interested of passengers looked down. The sound of water falling reached her ears and Sid let her hatred for Ashlan dissipate to take in the awe-inspiring view of the falls below. Water pounded from a building rooftop, threatening to collapse it beneath its weight before plummeting off the edge and into the abyss below. She watched the waterfalls, mesmerized. From their current viewpoint, it looked limitless and Sid wondered how anyone could brave hurdling off the edge and into the dark stream of water. *Colton must have lied,* she thought. *He must have!*

"Beautiful, aren't they?" Ashlan's voice rang in her ear, closer than she would have liked. She jerked herself away from him, tearing her gaze briefly from the falls.

"They're alright."

"Alright? They're magnificent! You know, it took them about five years to get the layout just right. I heard that they almost wiped out the entire district during the construction."

"So why keep going?"

"You really need to ask?" He said, gesturing to the view.

"So that's all they are? Something pretty to look at?"

"Yeah. Why?"

"Because it's a waste. That's why. That water could be used to grow things. To feed people."

He cocked his head in confusion. *Stardaughter! So dumb!* She cursed herself. Of course, he had no idea what she meant. No one starved in Neostar, at least no one important. The ring made sure of it. A limitless energy source meant an unlimited supply of food harvesting. She had better be careful with her remarks or else she'd be trapped in a rapid fire of questions from him that would all lead to her truth being found out.

"I mean, you could grow more plants. For your gardens and stuff."

"Trust me, they don't need more plants." He said, confusion still coating his eyes.

"So how long have you been a Starblade?" She asked in hopes of changing the subject. Relieved when she saw a glimmer of excitement in his gaze. Her relief faded as soon as he spoke again.

"Since I was a kid. My dad insisted on it."

His dad. Colton. She hated hearing the word on his lips. *He's not just your dad!* She wanted to yell. *He's my everything! He saved me!* "You were a kid Starblade? Isn't that dangerous? And dumb?" She said instead.

"Well, I obviously wasn't in the guard when I was a kid. I just started preparing for it, training and such. Every day for as long as I can remember. Until I was big enough to hold the blade. Then every day after that."

"That sounds-" she faltered, "really boring."

"It wasn't all bad. Not more boring than anything else really."

Not more boring than being trapped in a rotting spaceship without anyone to talk to for days?

"So, you like it? Being a Starblade?"

"It is what it is. I'm not sure what else I could be."

"You'd make a lovely Magistra, I think. I can see it right now! Flowing, billowing skirts and laces the color of stars! They'd really bring out the blue in your eyes."

Ashlan bolstered a laugh loud enough to knock the pod off course if it hadn't been following the invisible transit rail system. "So, you noticed my eyes, huh?"

"What? No! I'm telling you you'd make a fine lady!"

"Sure. Whatever you need to tell yourself to get your mind off me," he chuckled.

"Believe me when I tell, *you're* the last thing on my mind!"

"So what's the first thing? On your mind that is."

Your dad. My ship. My magic. Death.

"Nothing. Just thinking of how we can fix your blade so the queen doesn't throw you off the guard."

"That won't happen." His eyes narrowed and he looked down to inspect his shoes. "I'm a Starblade for life."

"Isn't that a good thing? To serve the queen?"

His voice lowered to a hush, "It would be a good thing to have a choice."

"Why don't you have a choice?" Sid asked, bringing her own voice down a few octaves to match his.

"No one has choices in Neostar. Me most of all."

Blue illuminated his face and Sid looked up to see another projection scroll across the wall. They were in district six, close enough to the towers that she could make out their base through the buildings ahead. *Almost there,* she hummed.

"Right. Your life is just so awful. It must be terrible to get everything you want whenever you want it. To see the queen every day. To never run out of food. Or air. You're right. Your life is starspit. You should probably just end it all."

"Run out of air?" He asked, "What?"

Muck.

"Nothing. It's just annoying that you seem to hate your life when you have it so good," she recovered quickly.

"*I* have it good? Are you joking?" He flailed his arms in shock, "I get told what to do all day, every day. My entire life has been decided for me since I was born. I have to clock in on the hour and never have any privacy and my dad just died! How great could I possibly have it? At this point, I wish I was born to a random Citizen or even a Domer. Anything could be better than this!"

Sid placed her hand on his shoulder then quickly jerked it back. "You don't mean that."

"Which part?"

"All of it. That part about being born to someone else. Your dad was-" she paused, "your dad was probably great. And trust me, you don't want to be some worker. You get to serve the queen! That's pretty amazing! *She's* amazing!"

"Oh, yeah. You're definitely new."

Sid's eyes narrowed, "What does that mean?"

"You idolize her. Why, I don't understand. You're a Domer. You should hate her, want to kill her in fact. Not drool over her like she's some savior."

"She is a savior! She saved this entire star!"

Ashlan looked at her, really looked at her, dumbfounded. "Her mother built the ring. She doomed your entire race. Are you serious?"

"What the muck are you talking about? Without the ring, the entire star would die."

"Without your chips, there would be no ring. And without her mother, there would have been no chips," his eyes narrowed again, this time to slits so thin she doubted he could see her at all. "Don't tell me you're happy you're chipped?"

Sid felt the back of her neck and pulled up the collar of her suit to cover a non-existent scar. "Of course. I help power the ring. I'm helping keep the star alive. You should probably thank me, you know."

"Thank you..." Ashlan said in more of a question.

Another projection flashed in front of them. District three.

"We're close," Sid noted. "Remember that silence we talked about before? How about we try it out now?"

"Fine by me," Ashlan scoffed and returned to the lounge seat.

The way he crossed his legs made Sid furious but she couldn't help but notice the bulge of muscle in his legs nonetheless. The thought made her anger rise to new heights and she looked away, training her sight on the towers ahead. They were clearer now and so much taller than they seemed from her first impression in the jungle. Three clear spikes spanning all the way into the sky, almost into eternity.

I made it, Colton, she thought and hoped that, wherever he was now, he could hear her. And that he was proud.

TWELVE

DON'T MOVE. Don't move. Don't move. Sid recited melodically as the Droidhound sniffed at her neck. Even with her balancing on her tip toes, the metal hound reached an arm's length over her head. She'd seen the robotic creatures in projections but the idea of meeting one in person terrified her, and with good reason. The Droidhounds were originally developed by the queen's lead scientists to act as bodyguards for the Starblades but now that Sid was up close and personal with one, she was sure the hounds were more weapon than guardian. The one now standing in front of her looked to be almost half a ton of pure steel, shaped to mimic the muscle toned build of a canine creature from Colton's home world. He called them Dobermans and as Sid looked up at the hound's large face, she decided she hated Dobermans. The hound's chest plate split in two, revealing a complex system of wires behind an acrylic wall that glowed a faint blue.

"What is it doing?" Sid whispered between clenched

teeth. Her eyes stayed fixated on the Droidhound as it rammed its hard-shelled nose into her collarbone.

"He's scanning you. To check your DNA. Aren't you, boy?" Ashlan said enthusiastically. "You've never seen one do that?"

The hound turned to Ashlan, twisting the sharp points of its silvery ears to the side. The sound of metal rubbing metal made Sid cringe but she was relieved to have the droid's attention off her. "I've never had one scan me before. What's it doing with my DNA anyway?"

"Seriously?"

She didn't answer, hoping he would read into her annoyed look instead. Luckily, he did.

"It can't see you. It's a droid."

"And?"

"And it needs to know which side you're-" he paused, "if you're a Citizen or not."

Her eyes rolled before she could stop herself, "And if I'm not? Then what? It eats me?"

"What? No!" Ashlan reached up to pet the hound's head though she doubted it made a difference to the droid. "It gives you clearance accordingly. You know, the droid hive mentality? So you don't get zapped for being somewhere you're not supposed to be?"

Sid had no idea what he was talking about. The only thing she knew about the droids Colton's people built was their internal functions. When she was ten years old, she asked him to send her one for her birthday but when he refused — stating that it was too difficult to transport one in a supply pod — she settled for a three-dimensional hologram. She tinkered with the droid imposter for months, digitally taking it apart and putting it back together until she could assemble a droid with her eyes closed. Sid was even able to redirect the holograms API to her ship's mainframe to make her false droid take on code commands the same way a real machine would. But a hive mentality? She had no idea that something of that caliber was programmed into the functions of the droids. Of course, she never had more than one hologram to work with. She snuck another glance at the Droidhound in front of her and added seeing the information processing unit to her mental bucket list.

"Which district did you say you're from again?" Ashlan asked, looking her over.

Son of a Domer! Sid tried to think of an answer that could explain her pathetic lack of knowledge about the towers and the culture on the star. If she named a district that was far enough away from the city, he might be swayed to believe her ignorance.

"Uhm, one twenty-eight?" She said, shrinking with the words. "We don't leave the dome that often."

"Right."

A relieved breath exploded from her lips, making the Droidhound rip its glare away from Ashlan and return its snout to her neck. *Great! This again!* "So how long does he need to, you know, scan me or something?"

"What? That? Oh, he's already done. I think he just likes you!"

"How can a droid *like* anything? That's actually the dumbest thing I've heard you say so far and that's quite the statement."

Ashlan turned his back to her and pressed his palms against the hounds puffed, metal cheeks. "Don't worry, buddy. It's not you. She's this way with everyone. What's that? Oh, I know! Tell me about it! She's a handful!"

"Very funny, Ashlan. I know you can't talk to him," she rolled her eyes.

"Can't I, though?" He smirked back, "And Ash is fine. Ashlan is what the queen calls me. And you are definitely not her."

"Whatever do you mean?" She cooed and twirled before offering an exaggerated bow, "And here I was getting ready for the next ball!"

His laugh was infuriating. Or intoxicating, Sid wasn't certain yet. "We don't have balls. This isn't some fairytale."

Turning away, she hiked up her suit's collar to hide her red cheeks and stormed away from him down the main hall of the tower's entrance.

"Where are you running to? You don't know where you're going, remember?" He shouted after her.

"Then you better catch up!" She yelled back and turned the corner, hoping this was her chance to lose him. While the serene layout of the Queen's Tower held many passageways and doorways, it also gave her a chance to duck away from him and be rid of the Starblade for good. This may have been her first time outside the ship but if there was one thing Sid knew well, it was how to find her way in confusing spaces. After all, the Arcturus was one big maze and she could walk end to end blindfolded.

Sid skidded to slow her pace and made a sharp left past a large painting of the queen's mother holding a miniature replica of the Circulum System in her palms, finding herself in a fork of corridors. *Who in the name of the star built this thing?* She cursed and looked up at the painting.

Oh, she gulped. *Right.*

The woman towering above her was beautiful — not in the same sovereign way Queen Leona was — but beautiful nonetheless. Unlike her daughter, the queen's mother had light features; blue eyes and long blonde hair that seemed to mimic the lightness of the glass tower's interior. And while the reigning queen's black eyes pierced with purpose, her mother seemed serene and lost in thought; as if she was dreaming of a world beyond this one. Perhaps she was. Perhaps she was dreaming of the world her raven-haired daughter would soon inherit. Sid wondered what it must have been like for Queen Leona to find out her mother had been stricken with Amperfuge. She didn't learn much about the disease in her studies, mostly because lessons of biology and medicine bored her to tears, but from what she had gathered, Amperfuge was a deadly disease that affected Colton's people who had come into prolonged contact to direct sources of the star's magic. Sid always assumed the late queen contracted it while experimenting with procedures to create the ring and was filled with respect and pride. Anyone willing to die for two races to survive and live in peace was the type of ruler she could get behind. Too bad she'd never get to meet her. Sid was willing to bet the late queen was someone you could carry a proper conversation with. *Not like that dumb Starblade,* she thought, her thoughts rushing back to the present. *Right or left? Which way, Sid? Oh, who cares!*

She ran left at full speed and regretted the decision instantaneously.

A man's heavy back collided with her forehead, knocking her to the ground so fast that she slid back on her rear. Sid was still rubbing the spot that was bound to bruise by morning when she heard a familiar — and very annoying — voice behind her.

"Pardon the girl, general! It's her first time in the towers.

I swear, I took my eyes off her for one minute and... Well, you know how these Domers can get."

Sid was about to rebut the insult but an inconspicuous wave of Ashlan's hand made her rethink it. It's not that she trusted the fool but right now, she trusted him a lot more than a general in the queen's army. At least he'd been moderately helpful so far.

"Ash! What a pleasant surprise! And please, Abbot is fine. Or do you forget who used to bathe you when your father was busy tending to army matters?" The general laughed, his breath catching in the grey strands of his overflowing mustache.

"For the love of the star, Abbot. What did we say about that story? It sounds alarming when you phrase it that way!"

The general let out another hearty chuckle and patted Ashlan on the shoulder. Sid could tell the attention was making him embarrassed in the way one would feel if their parents were telling stories of their childhood in front of their friends. Not that she would know. No one ever told stories about her and even if they did, there'd be no one to tell them to.

"So you picked up a Domer, did you?"

Sid wasn't sure how she felt about this Abbot. She knew she didn't trust him but beyond that, he was nearly impossible to read. *The same way Colton was,* she realized. *It must be a general thing.*

She watched as Ashlan took a step forward, positioning himself in front of her. "Just showing her the way."

"The way to what then?"

"The cells?"

"The cells?!?" Abbot bellowed, "What on the star would

a Domer be doing in the cells? Most of them can't tell right from left, you know!"

It was decided — Sid hated him.

"This one is pretty useful. A Domer is a Domer, I know, but she was sent for a job so the least I could do is get her to it."

Pure power rushed below the thin surface of Sid's skin. Why would Colton spend his time with these horrid creatures? They were nothing like him! He was kind and good and caring and this general was — she took a breath in — a monster! A real life monster! And so was Colton's son! The two of them, standing around snickering about how stupid Domers were. They were the dumb ones! Him and his stupid mustache and bald head. Who died and made this guy feel so important?

Her stomach twisted into a knot so tight, she thought her entire body would convulse. *Colton. That's who. When he died.*

"So, Domer girl, what's this special job they have for you?"

A full breath later and Sid was able to tuck her magic back into hiding. She stepped out from behind Ashlan and raised her chin high to stare into the general's brown eyes. "The droid malfunction two weeks ago, they think it might affect the blade battery circuit. Wanted me to check it out."

"And you're the best man, sorry, woman for the job?"

"Looks like it," she scoffed, trying to sound as assuring as possible. Her ankles trembled in her boots.

"Where did you learn this very intricate task? There aren't many technicians in the domes."

Why was he asking so many questions? She needed to

get out of there right away. "My dad was a technician. Taught me everything he knew."

"Was?"

"He died a few years ago."

The general reached his wrinkled hand to twirl his moustache, "What happened?"

Wow. Not even an 'I'm sorry' or something. What a jerk!

"Got too close to a live wire. Died on impact."

"Hmm," the general sighed.

"What?" Sid asked before she had a chance to stop herself. She should probably show more respect to this Abbot to pass as a real Domer. Workers would never be allowed to speak to an NSO general in that tone. To her relief, Abbot did not seem to notice.

"You don't hear too many cases of Domers getting fried, with your connection to electricity and all."

Sid thought about his comment for a moment, straightening her back and stepping closer to give him full view of her. "Everyone can die," she said defiantly.

"That is very true, Domer girl."

"My name is Sid."

"Wonderful. And which dome are you from, Sid? You and your mother, I take it? Or is there a mister Sid in the picture? You seem quite young but I never know with you people?"

Sid's fists raised and she took an aggressive stance but Ashlan veered in front of her, spinning her on her heels and away from the general.

"Will you look at that?" He exclaimed, "I didn't even notice the time! I have dinner plans soon and we still need to get to the cells! So sorry, Abbot! We'll have to catch up later,

I cannot miss this dinner. You know how those Magistra girls get when you keep them waiting!"

He turned back and winked at the dumbfounded general before pushing her away toward the hall with the painting, and away from the general's intrigue and Sid's growing anger. This man was supposed to set an example for the rest of them. He wasn't supposed to go around treating the workers like they were worth less than him. Sid didn't feel like a Domer but she was offended on their behalf regardless. Colton would have never spoken to her that way, or anyone for that matter. *He* was a true general, not this grumbling old fool she just met.

"Well, that was a close call!" He yelped when they were out of Abbot's earshot. "What were you going to do? Punch an army general on your first trip to the city?"

"Yes! I stardamned was but you interrupted! What is your problem, anyway?"

"*My* problem?" He sneered then raised his voice, "MY problem?!? You are not even supposed to be here! If anyone finds out that I brought you back here so you can fix the blade YOU broke, I'd be suspended for weeks!"

Her arms raised in mock defeat, "Oh, I'm so sorry! I wouldn't want you to miss your special little dinner with the Magistra!" She wrapped her arms across her chest and mimicked a kissing motion, hoping she got it right since she'd never actually been kissed.

"There is no dinner. I just said that to get you out of there before you got both of us in mucking trouble!" He slapped her hands away from her chest, "Grow up."

"Did you just curse?" She asked, a smile forming on her lips.

"No, I-"

"Oh, my star! The proper, perfect specimen just cursed! I can't believe it!" She slapped her thighs and laughed harder than she had in weeks, "Careful now! We wouldn't want your face to crack from the profanity!"

A smile twirled at the edges of Ashlan's full lips, "So you think I'm perfect, huh?"

"What? No! I didn't say that!"

"Yeah, you did. Proper and perfect, in fact," he grinned and she immediately stopped laughing.

"Forget it, just take me to the cells so I can fix that blade and be free of you already. Just in case you have some other fictitious dinner to attend to, you dumb liar."

"Ha! You're one to talk!"

"Excuse me?"

"You know what I'm talking about. Your little story about being asked to look at the cells? Pretty believable."

"Would you have preferred if I told him the truth? About your little blade and our fun run in?"

Ashlan shook his head furiously. "No! Obviously not! But you're lucky I got you out of there before you started blabbing about going to the cells."

"And what if I did?" She shrieked. "Why can't I go wherever I stardamned please in this place? I'm here to work, aren't I?"

"Because," Ashlan said with caution, "only Domers with special clearance get into the cells and you don't have one."

"So how do I even get in there to fix your blade?"

He cleared his throat and threw her a salute, "With me! I thought that was obvious?"

"Fine. Let's just get on with it. And I'm not that good of a liar, the general didn't seem to believe a word I said."

"Who? Abbot? Oh, don't mind him! He's that way with

everyone. Domer, Citizen, droid, plant, you name it! Abbot hasn't trusted anyone in his life except-" his voice caught in his throat.

"Your father?" She asked.

"Yeah."

The melancholy covered his face in an almost physical sheathe, and for a brief moment Sid let her heart sink for the Starblade. His loss was her loss. They had lost the same person and they shared that grief even if only one of them knew it. What if Ashlan was just as lost without Colton as she was? What if he missed him just the same? Like his own leg had been torn off. What if they could be friends after all?

"You going to keep staring or do you want to actually fix what you broke?" He said from behind her.

Not friends. Not ever.

Sid followed him down the brightly lit hall to the cells. Soon she would be free of him and back to her mission. Finding the valve and getting the muck off this star and back to her ship. She glanced once more at the painting and let her eyes lock with the old queen's gaze. Something about the way they shone made her feel like she was watching her. Laughing at her from behind ten coats of paint.

THIRTEEN

BLADES FILLED the story-high holsters of the clear, concave walls in the charging cells and Sid found it impossible to look anywhere else. She barely heard Ashlan when he left her to her own devices, promising to return in a few hours for his blade. Did she really agree to repair it by that time? Glaring at the rotating, perforated steel shelves as they charged the off-duty weapons, Sid was finding it difficult to focus, let alone figure out where anything was located. The shelves stretched all the way from floor to ceiling in neverending rows. An uncountable number of blades pulsed their bright blue lights at different intervals as they recharged to be ready for use. She always found it odd that the ring's glowing power field that shone in the brightest shade of gold dulled to a steel-cold blue when recycled into the power needed to sustain the technology Colton's people invented. So far, everything in the towers had felt sterile and cool to the touch. Such a complete opposite to the star's magic coursing through her veins every waking moment. *Would I be blue and frozen if I lived here?* She wondered, realizing the foolishness of her question. The chipped Domers had been powering Neostar for over a decade and none of them changed color. If you didn't count their dull and bland attire, of course.

Not that she had any intention of actually fixing Ashlan's weapon. The first part of her plan was already underway; he had left her alone. All she needed now was to sneak away and find a technician's dock; from there, locating her valve should be a spacewalk in the stars. A robotic arm locked a blade into a charging dock next to her and sent it off into rotation, spinning the charging shelf in unison with the rest of the docked blades. Maybe she could fix his blade before she looked for the tech dock?

Just forget about that guy!

A lock mechanism hissed and a door slid open at the end of the hall in front of her. Sid curved her body tightly to the wall and inched away from the walkway. A moot point since the only thing separating her from whoever was heading her way was two panes of glass.

Sid squinted, peering out from the edge of the thick glass, careful not to show her face. A harder task than it seemed and she was quickly starting to realize that flattening herself out to the thinness of a leaf was not a talent she was born with. She edged closer, studying the stranger walking toward her down the corridor.

A short, stout man stumbled in her direction, his fingers tapping maniacally at the projected screen in his hands. His wide-set nose was scrunched in frustration and Sid could see beads of sweat forming at the top of his brow. He wiped the wetness off with the edge of his lab coat and continued to tap.

Her eyes scanned the area, trying desperately to find an

exit without success. She had hidden herself in a dead end and the man's brisk walk was rapidly closing the distance between them. Sid had to be quick and come up with a convincing enough story for her being here. If she could fool a Starblade and the NSO general, she sure as the stars could fool this man. Judging from his lab coat, he was likely one of the scientists working on the droids and ring operations. She could say she's a junior scientist that got turned around? No, too obvious and her filthy suit did not match the story. A student? That wouldn't work either. She didn't even know the first thing about how students behaved in the city.

Think, Sid! Think! She urged herself as the man walked close enough for her to feel a breeze from his steps. In a moment, her mind cleared and she landed on a solution. *I got it!*

But before she had a chance to practice her lines, the man turned the corner and stopped right in front of her.

She wasn't certain if he even knew she was there, his fingers still gliding over the projection screen. Sid watched the rows of data code flash across the screen as the man concentrated to find whatever it was he was looking for.

Maybe he's blind? She wandered.

As if reading her mind, the scientist paused his finger and pointed it in her direction instead.

"Can I help you?" He asked, looking her up and down with a frown.

"Actually," Sid answered without pause, "I think I'm here to help you."

The scientist pressed a button and the screen of the projection shut down. He tucked the interface box into his pocket and burned his gaze into Sid's eyes. She wasn't wearing her goggles so there was no point pretending to be anyone other than a Domer. Even with the goggles on, she had a feeling this man was much too intelligent to fall for it. She was starting to feel foolish. The longer she stood here with her jaw slack, the more doubt she put into her story.

"I was asked to assist you. With the-" she gulped, "the droid malfunction."

The scientist narrowed his eyes and Sid's heart sank. He didn't believe her. It was over. Her first instinct was to cry. Her second to run. Neither seemed like a good idea at that moment. Before she could make a choice one way or the other, the scientist spoke again.

"Ah! Of course. I hadn't realized they had called someone in. Typical, I've had twenty-four hours to resolve this and they are already panicking. The nerve of some people!" He scoffed. "I am perfectly capable of fixing the stardamned droid myself!"

Sid sighed in relief. *How many droids were breaking down in this place?*

"No matter now," the scientist said. "You're already here so we may as well get to it."

"Get to what, exactly?" She asked, genuinely curious.

"Please tell me they briefed you on the problem at hand?"

Sid shook her head.

"Oh, my. They're just completely incompetent, aren't they?"

Sid tried to figure out who the 'they' were that he was constantly referring to but her memory went blank. Whoever 'they' were, the scientist was not a fan. She offered a shy smile and shrugged her shoulders, hoping to say as little as possible.

"Very well," he pulled up the code he was studying

before and handed Sid the screen, "see if you can make sense of any of this."

Rows of numbers flashed before her and Sid studied each sequence, trying to understand what malfunction might be plaguing the poor droid in question. "What are the droid's symptoms?"

"Symptoms?" The scientist scoffed, "It's a droid, not a patient."

"Right. Of course," she agreed, her cheeks reddening. "I meant the anomalies it's displaying."

"Well, it's gone completely bonkers!" The scientist flayed his arms in exaggeration. "When it's not spinning in circles, it's freezing everything in sight. The stardamned thing is entirely off its sequence! We had to seclude it in a solitary wing just to make sure it doesn't cause any damage to its owner."

Sid scanned the code again. It sounded like an issue with the axel but the freezing threw her off. She rolled her eyes over the flashing sequences, pausing abruptly and using her finger to scroll up a few pages. *Of course! Just like Rusty!* She thought excitedly, remembering a time she got the ship's nitro tubes tangled up and almost froze the entire engine room. She tapped her finger to a random sequence, "Here! See?"

The scientist squeezed closer to the screen and squinted. From this angle, he looked more like a child than someone who was likely four times Sid's age. "Hmm," was all he said while examining her findings.

"He's just all turned around. His nitro tubes are scrambled."

"And how do you explain the spinning?" He asked, though to Sid, it seemed more like a test than a question.

She turned the screen back and scrolled until she found what she was looking for. Sid pushed the projection back to the scientist. "Because they're not just scrambled. They're looped around his axel. If he was a person, he'd be dead right about now."

"If he was a person, he wouldn't have an axel or nitro tubes," the scientist chuckled and she was surprised that a man this serious had something resembling a sense of humor. "Not bad, Domer," he added approvingly.

Sid wanted to reach down and slap the man but thought better off it. She couldn't keep acting offended every time someone thought she was one of the workers. If anything, it only meant her acting skills were improving. She held out the interface box to the scientist and waited until he grabbed it and tossed it back into his lab pocket.

"We should probably get going."

"We?" Sid raised an eyebrow.

"Of course. It's why you're here, isn't it? Besides, I'm happy for the company and you're the one that found the anomaly. You should get the honor of getting the droid functional again."

"The great honor of being a technician," Sid sneered under her breath.

"What was that?"

"Oh, nothing, just talking to myself. Happy to help in any way, of course!" She almost saluted the man but stopped herself from yet another embarrassment.

"You should be! It's not every day you get to fix a Magistra's personal droid. I'd assume this is a very big deal for someone like you."

Sid's eyes bulged so far out that she was sure she was

about to lose one to gravity. "I'm sorry, did you say a Magistra's personal droid?"

"Of course. Why else would we waste this much time on a machine? You think they'd employ the queen's lead scientist for just any droid?" He shook his head, "I recommended we wipe the foolish thing but the Magistra insisted on repairing it. Something about having built a rapport with the piece of junk. I'll never understand it but here we are."

Her head was spinning. She was about to help fix a droid that belonged to the queen's lady in waiting. Sid felt like she had won the prize of a lifetime. She had always been jealous of the Magistras and their proximity to Queen Leona and now she could solve a problem for one of them. She had something they didn't and it felt good. It felt better than good. It felt like she was someone.

She was still smiling from ear to ear when a frail and potmarked hand poked into her peripheral.

"I'm Professor Cevil," the scientist said with an outstretched hand.

Sid reached down and shook his palm lightly, surprised at the coldness of his skin. "Nice to meet you. I'm Sid."

"Well, Sid. Are you ready to get started?" He asked and motioned her back to the doors he came in through.

Sid nodded and followed the short, little man obediently. She'd never been more ready for anything in her life.

FOURTEEN

"THIS IS JUST A MESS!" Sid groaned in frustration as she stared at the droid's open, metal chest cavity.

Professor Cevil set her up to work in his private lab while he went to check on the satellite projections from the Circulum System. He didn't seem too pleased with the task, complaining endlessly about the remedial notion of it and that a much more junior scientist could have been fitted for the job. Apparently, checking the feeds that made sure the correct energy amounts were collected from the chips of the worker population and distributed into the towers' generators was something any fool could do, at least according to Cevil. She let him drone on, using the chance to gather any information she could on the ring and its mechanics that may have been missing from her studies. But after a few minutes of cuss-infested complaining she couldn't help but shut out the professor's voice and focus on the task at hand. Maybe if she could actually fix the Magistra's droid, he'd take her with him to the ring's control room and she could finally get closer to the ring's mechanics station. And closer to getting the muck off this star but Sid didn't let that thought linger. No point getting distracted now.

She brushed her fingers over the tubes protruding from the droid's chest, trying her best to avoid making eye contact with its glassy stare. The droids were manufactured to resemble enough of the human form to make them feel approachable but different enough not to get mistaken for one. To Sid, they looked like a reflection of a person. It was like staring at a human through a shattered mirror. Everything was where it should be but just a little off. It made her feel uneasy and she didn't understand why the scientists who made them couldn't at least add a few more touches to make the droids less harrowing.

For starters, the lack of lids on their eyes made them look like they had ill intentions when she knew full-well that droids could not think for themselves. It was as if every time one looked at you, it was trying to peer right through you. Or plot your very untimely demise. Sid wasn't sure which one. Then there was the lack of artificial skin. Not everywhere, just in certain areas around the back of the head, sides of the arms and parts of the thighs and legs. Sid always found this to be the most bizarre part of the droids. She knew the skin-like covering that had been installed on them was used to house sensors in order to facilitate realistic movement and human interaction but could they not have covered them up entirely? Did they run out of the material or something? The blue glow of the star's energy that ran though the fiberoptic makeup of their bodies shone through the fleshy pieces brightly enough to light a dark room. If the scientists were aiming to make these things look different from themselves, they sure did succeed. No one in their right mind could confuse a partially skinned, blue glowing droid with no eyelids for a person.

Sid tugged at one of the droid's nitro tubes and yanked it out from under the robot's axel. There was some damage to the tube's casing but she should be able to patch it up fairly quickly and with enough luck, have this thing up and operational before the professor returned. The sooner she got away from this droid and the professor the better. Professor Cevil was a downright grouch. Sid was almost entirely certain that he was too preoccupied with his work and position in the towers to have any time to worry about the likes of her. And while this suited her plan just fine, she couldn't help but feel slighted by his lack of attention. The more time she spent in the towers, the more she realized how wonderful Colton was compared to the rest of his people. For all she knew, he was the only one on the star worth talking to. Except for Queen Leona, of course. As far as Sid was concerned, she was nothing if not pure magic formed into the shape of a queen.

Sid carefully laid the tubes back into their casing, managing to arrange them in a similar pattern to what she had seen on her droid anatomy projections back on the ship. They looked like a bowl of silver intestines, and the thought alone made Sid want to throw up her stomach's contents. As if to mock her, her belly groaned and growled and she made a mental note to ask the professor for some food when he returned.

Her arm muscles strained to lift the chest plate back onto the droid's front cavity but she had it positioned and screwed into place faster than anticipated. She gave the droid a final glance before pulling out the interface box from the side table next to the gurney.

"Here we go," Sid said, gritting her teeth as she entered a command code to wake up the droid. "You better work!"

The droid's blank eyes lit a pale yellow and she could see the fiberoptic wiring of the interior begin to glow its familiar blue.

"Please work," she whispered, watching the droid turn its head as if to look at her then bolt straight up to stand.

It was at least a full head taller than her, if not two, and it made her take a step back to put a safe distance between them. She had seen a few droids walking around with their owners on her trip through the city with Ashlan but standing next to one in person was mildly intimidating. The thing could crush her skull in moments if it wanted to. Sid knew it was a foolish thought, this thing didn't have wants or needs, but she moved back regardless. Better safe than sorry, as Colton always said.

The droid's head tilted right then left, its gaze continuously locked on Sid.

"What in the name of the star do you want?" She asked.

The droid tilted right again.

"Oh, right!" She laughed, "I'm supposed to tell you that!"

Sid entered a code sequence and watched as the droid came to life before her. Its hunched body straightened, making it even taller than it was before. She let her fingers enter a few more numbers and it leaped in the air in a fierce and calculated jump, landing back on its metal feet with a loud thud. Sid laughed and entered the numbers again, smiling as the droid continued to bounce in front of her like a kid waiting for a present.

"How about a dance?" She asked.

Tap, tap, tap. Her fingers ran over a long sequence and

she let one side of her lips twirl into a smirk before she pressed enter. The droid straightened again, then raised its hands in front with folded elbows — one pointing up and one to the side. Like it was holding an invisible dance partner. Sid let a few more lines of code escape her before settling back cross-legged on the gurney to watch the droid twirl around the room.

Its steps were clunky at best but there was no mistaking what it was doing. The droid was dancing the Waltz.

Sid fell over laughing and her thoughts immediately landed on Colton. How he would have loved to see this. Tears formed behind her lids, threatening to pool but before they could burst out, a light shuffle of feet entered the room.

"Well, this is something else," Professor Cevil said sternly from behind the dancing droid.

"I'm so sorry!" Sid jumped up and fumbled for the projection screen. Her fingers moved quickly to power down the droid and she had it slouched in the corner in no time. "I was just testing it! To make sure it worked."

"It seems it works just fine, then?" The professor said and Sid could swear she saw a smile form on his lips.

"It was exactly what we thought it was. The nitro tubes and the axel. Nothing more complicated than that."

"Very well."

The professor paid her no mind and walked over to inspect the droid. He pulled an interface box out of his coat pocket and connected it to the droid's system. The few minutes that passed while the professor read over the code sequences were excruciating. What if she didn't do a good enough job? What if the professor finds a mistake and starts asking her questions? What if he finds out she doesn't belong here? What if...

"This is a job well done, Sid. I see the internal speakers are still out of order but that can be looked at another time." The professor nodded in approval before she could continue to spiral out of control. "Magistra Kelyn will be most impressed. In fact, I am quite impressed myself. Not bad for a Domer at all. Maybe after you've delivered the droid back to her quarters, we can discuss extending your stay for a few more days. I could certainly use the help around here."

Sid almost choked on her own words. "You want me to deliver the droid back to the Magistra?"

"Who else would do it? You honestly expect the queen's lead scientist to run deliveries?" He scoffed.

"Uhm, no, of course not. It's just that I wasn't told that I'd be delivering the droid back, only fixing it. When I was called for, that is."

"Do you have somewhere else to be right now?" The professor lifted an eyebrow and Sid swallowed audibly.

"No, not at all. I will, of course, deliver this droid, sir."

"Please don't call me sir. Save that for those brainless Starblades. I am perfectly comfortable with Cevil."

Sid stifled a giggle. She knew the professor was trying to be friendly but she found it hard to believe the act. Anyone who wants to be friends with you doesn't ask you to call them by their last name. "Of course, Cevil," she said and hid her smile.

The door slid open and the professor was out of the room before Sid could ask where Magistra Kelyn's quarters were located. Or where any quarters were located for that matter.

She grabbed her screen and powered up the droid again, watching as it beamed with light next to her.

"You don't know the way to go, do you?" She asked.

The droid's blank expression was more answer than she needed.

"Muck. Fine, let's figure it out together. But keep your head low and don't attract attention," she scowled.

The droid nodded in her direction and walked out of the room, banging its metal forehead against the top of the doorway.

Oh, this will definitely go smoothly.

Sid rolled her eyes and followed her new friend into the corridor, hopeful that they'd find their way to the Magistra quarters without getting noticed. Or as unnoticed as one can be while walking hand in hand with a two-meter-tall, blue-glowing droid that liked to dance.

FIFTEEN

SHE WASN'T LOST; at least not exactly. One couldn't really be lost in a place where most of the walls were made of glass, even if there were about fifty floors of those walls spanning high into the sky. Sid knew the Magistra quarters must be on one of the higher floors, as close to the queen as possible. The layout of the Queen's Tower was fairly simple. The top floor was occupied by the Arcane, the most highly regarded creatures on the star due to their connection to the ring. The queen's floor was right below them, with her ladies in waiting just beneath. Everything under the main three floors were dedicated to the weaponry, droid stations and the mechanical rooms of the Circulum System. What the two towers that housed the Citizens looked like was beyond Sid but she had this one memorized in fair detail. Her admiration for the queen extended even to her living quarters. Which is why it surprised her when she turned a corner and found herself in utter confusion as to her location in proximity to the top three floors.

The elevators from the labs took her and the droid as far

as the dining hall just below the throne room which she assumed had put her roughly three quarters of the way there. Though when she glanced out of the clear side panel on the staircase she was climbing, she realized they couldn't have been higher than the twentieth floor. What was the queen storing between here and her own floors? And why had Sid not seen any of these layouts in the disclosed tower schematics?

She searched for another elevator but when she couldn't find one, opted for the large glass staircase that seemed to lead all the way to the top. The stairs spiraled triumphantly with large steps that could fit three Sids lengthwise lying down. Everything in the Queen's Tower was larger than life and Sid found herself shrinking with each step she climbed.

It was eerily quiet on the staircase, the only thing jarring her back to reality were the obnoxiously loud footsteps of the droid — or Fred, named by Sid after one of the famous dancers from Colton's home planet. Each one of Fred's steps made the breath caught in her throat tremble and she insisted on holding onto the handrail despite there not being any real danger in sight.

After climbing a few floors, Sid stopped, motioning for Fred to join her on the bottom step for a break.

"Are you excited to be back with your Magistra, Fred? What was her name? Kelyn? It's a beautiful name, don't you think?"

The droid stared blankly at her and she tapped her fingers on the projection screen, making him nod furiously in response. Satisfied, she rested her chin in her hands and stared out over the railing at the bird's eye view of Tower City below them. "Everything is beautiful here, Fred, just everything." She cooed at the vast city lit up by nightly activity. The lights that shone bright blue in the early evening had now been transformed into a mélange of rainbow colors, all forming intricate patterns above the streets below. Telescreens projected videos and images of things Sid had never experienced on the ship. Beauty products and foods and living quarters that felt false in their perfection. A few of the screens played pre-recorded messages from the queen herself. Sid watched in awe and admiration. "That must look pretty amazing from down there, huh?"

Fred was silent, still shaking his head from her last command and she felt silly for not coding him to stop after the first few nods. She was about to enter in a sequence when the sound of light footsteps coming from the floor above them stopped her.

Sid had a good story in place and with Fred by her side, she had no reason to come off as an outsider but she still would have preferred making it to her destination with as little interaction as possible.

Hopping to her feet, she readied herself for the encounter. Her eyes watched the tall, silver boots descend down the stairs toward her until she was face to face with the stranger on the stairs.

"Well, hello again. I see you made a friend." The stranger, who was no stranger at all, said.

"Ash. I should have known that'd be you. Shouldn't you be somewhere else right now?"

"Not really, I usually spend the evenings alone and," Ashlan paused and looked past her shoulder, "why is he nodding like that?"

Sid looked back to the droid that was still shaking his head maniacally. "Who? Fred? He's fine. Just have to turn him off."

She entered the code into her screen and the droid relaxed his stance, resting his head to the side which Sid was certain looked even odder than the nodding. She'd really have to figure out these commands before handing him over to the Magistra.

"You named your droid?"

"He's not my droid!" She exclaimed. "I was fixing him for Professor Cevil. He's Magistra Kelyn's droid."

"So what exactly are you doing with Kelyn's droid in the middle of the night in a stairwell? Please tell me this isn't some weird little date."

"What? Ew! No! I am returning him to his owner but I got turned around somewhere and was just taking a break when you showed up."

"Thank the stars. I thought I'd have to bring you in for improper droid use." He chuckled and she stuck her tongue out in response.

"Well, you don't. So move along to wherever it is you were going."

"How do you even get lost in a stairwell? Don't you just go up or down?"

Sid scrunched her nose, annoyed with the petty jabs at her expense. "I didn't say I got lost. I said I was turned around. I got off the elevators and though I was right under the throne room but then it seemed there were all these other floors I didn't know about and now I have no idea how long it'll take to get there. And I'm starving so how about we cut this conversation down and go our own way?"

"Wow. You sure know a lot about the towers for a Domer," Ashlan said curiously.

"I like to read."

"Right. So do you need some help getting there maybe?"

"I'll be fine. Like you said, it's just up!"

He laughed and she hated that her lips twirled into a smile at the sound of his cheer. "It's not exactly just up. I really don't mind showing you. Come on! Let's go!"

Before she could object, he grabbed her hand and pulled her behind him on the stairs. When she met his steps with her own, he let her hand go and she could feel the warmth of his fingers linger for a few moments. Sid shoved her hands in her pockets and marched after Ashlan with furious but obedient steps.

"So what's on all these floors? I don't remember seeing them in the tower plans."

"Here? Oh, nothing really. Just empty rooms." Ashlan bit the bottom of his lip and she wondered if he was lying. Why would there be almost twenty empty floors in the Queen's Tower?

"Really? Nothing? That's odd. Why wouldn't they just give the Arcane or Magistras more space?"

"Oh, they wouldn't want that."

"That's crazy. Why not?"

"The queen's ladies are very close. Unnaturally close, really. They're like sisters but even closer if that's possible. It's impossible to keep them separated."

"And the Arcane?"

"Kind of the same except the sister part. They have to stay close for the Circulum System."

"Because each holds one of the keys?" Sid asked, remembering her studies of the ring system. The three women of the Arcane were chosen from the native population of the star. Picked for their loyalty to the queen's mother and her plans for their collective future. Each woman was given a key, a chip like the rest of the Domers but much more powerful. Instead of syphoning the magic into the ring, the Arcane's chips were coded to give their inner magic control; a connection to the ring's control panel. It was one of the main reasons Sid had always dreamed of working with the Circulum System; she found it entirely fascinating how one small chip could have such an impact on magic. The things Colton's people technology could do was stardamned amazing! On their own, the keys are useless but when the three women that form the Arcane are together and can intertwine their magic, the keys come alive and can be used to turn the Circulum System on and off. From what she'd read, Sid understood that when the queen's mother developed the ring, she needed to make sure it could be shut down for maintenance but due to the sensitive nature of its existence, allowing just anyone in her ranks to have access to it would be too dangerous. To further show her support for the native people of Neostar, she offered them the honor of joining the Arcane — a means of giving them control over the ring. It was this act alone that allowed for the chipping to be instated and for the Circulum System to become the life-saving machine that it had become. The population of the domes may be giving up their magic to help sustain the technologies of the towers, but it is the chosen three that have full control. The honor of being chosen had always fascinated Sid and she wondered how many Domers stood in line to be considered for the roles when the keys exchanged hands every two decades. She assumed it was a lot.

"Yep. Each has a key so they need to stay close together."

Again, something about the way his words trailed off made her think he was lying. She wanted to push the point further but her stomach growled loud enough shake the walls and suddenly, she was unable to think of anything but her hunger.

"Please tell me that you've had a chance to eat something tonight?" Ashlan asked.

She shook her head and tried to smile proudly but her lips barely made a move and she looked instead like she was trying to digest a frigger egg too big to be swallowed whole. Muck. She really *was* hungry!

"Come on, we're only a few floors away from the Magistra floors. There's a dining hall there we can get some food in. Just make sure that thing stays put and in the corner," he said and pointed to the droid.

"Don't worry about Fred. He's the silent, brooding type." She smirked, winking at the droid playfully. She took two stairs at a time, jaunting behind Ashlan excitedly, her stomach cheering with every step they took. "So," she asked, "do tell, what mouth-filling magic are we about to consume?"

"Also, that. Don't say things like that," Ashlan frowned.

"Fine. Let's just get something to eat already!" She yelled and passed him running up the stairs.

SIXTEEN

MAGISTRA KELYN'S living quarters looked the complete opposite to the rest of the tower. The sweeping ceiling murals in shades of burgundy and gold were only slightly shadowed by the lush, velvet drapery pooling across each of the full-wall windows on the South side of the room. Each detail was covered in glittering bronze, shaded to mimic the gold from Colton's home planet. He had once told her that the rich metal was ultimately what led to the destruction of his home, that and the planet's inability to sustain the pollution his people's technology created. Sid couldn't imagine poisoning your planet to the point of red rains and dead soils but somehow they had managed to do it. And for what? This gold? Sounded like a fool's error to her, why not just pick a different metal to obsess over?

Sid tried to count the tassels in the room, losing track after twenty. Everything in sight had a tassel, it seemed.

She felt uncomfortable in the space. Not just uncomfortable but lost. Like she was trapped in one of Colton's bedtime stories. A curious girl falling down a rabbit hole to find herself in a land that was as bizarre as it was mystical. Except there was no rabbit in this reality and the only other person in the room looked like he was just as uncomfortable as she was.

One glance at Ashlan and she almost burst out laughing. He had been bouncing from boot to boot since the guard told them to come inside to wait for Magistra Kelyn to get ready to greet them. His eyes were nervous wrecks and he was fidgeting enough to make Sid want to smack him.

"Do you need to use the bathroom or something?" She whispered out of one side of her mouth.

"What?"

"You keep moving around. It's annoying."

"Oh, sorry. Just hate being up here. I never come up this way and it's just so over the top!" He gestured to the large painting of Neostar's jungle nestled in an ornamental brass frame. "I mean, is this really necessary? It looks so dumb in this place."

Something about the fact that Ashlan didn't make it a habit to spend time in the sleeping quarters of the Magistras made her feel more relaxed. She convinced herself it was because she could trust in him more now that she knew he wasn't as high up in the food chain as she originally thought. She was about to ask him when the last time was that he came up here when someone cleared their throat behind her. Sid turned around to find one of the most beautiful women she'd ever seen standing behind them with her arms crossed impatiently. The woman's long, black locks fell almost to the top of her curvy bottom in perfect tendrils. The light bounced off her hair, drawing even more attention to her very tall and very fit body. She looked as if she had been created in a lab, perfectly taught cheekbones, large eyes with even larger lashes, and a small but pointed nose that was turned up proudly.

"How can I help you?" Magistra Kelyn asked, her tone changing melodically when she spotted Ashlan. "Oh, Ash, how lovely to see you. I apologize for the wait; they hadn't told me it was *you* waiting."

"Us," Sid corrected under her breath but Kelyn paid her no mind.

The Magistra straightened her sheer, layered skirts, draping them out of the way of the flesh-colored, skin-tight suit she was wearing beneath. As she walked, Sid could see her long legs stretch from under the magenta fabrics of the skirts in an evocative manner. Whatever this show was, it was definitely put on for Ashlan. She couldn't help but roll her eyes as Kelyn made her way past Sid, pushing her aside lightly as she moved closer to Ashlan.

"Have you gotten taller, Ash?" She asked playfully, "I swear on the star, you just keep growing!"

Kelyn ran a red-nailed finger across his bicep and Sid made a vomiting motion with her mouth. She was glad when Ashlan pulled away and came to stand beside her.

"Sid here has brought you something."

"Oh, of course! Where are my manners?" Kelyn looked in Sid's general direction and loosely extended a hand. She held it just above Sid's lips, dangling the glass charms on her bracelet lightly.

Is she thinking I'm going to kiss her hand? Sid fumed and took a step back.

Kelyn frowned in disappointment, "Oh, Ash. Looks like you found the only one of these things that doesn't want to play. How dull."

"Excuse me!" Sid hollered, "I am not a thing!"

She plopped her goggles over her eyes and raised her fists, ready to knock the girl out. Magistra or not, no one spoke to her that way. Ashlan took a step forward and positioned himself between her and Kelyn.

"Come on, Kelyn. Loosen up. You don't need to prove a point every time we get a Domer in here."

"For the stars, Ash. How many times do I have to tell you that Lyn is just fine? I mean, after everything, you'd think we'd be on more casual terms." She winked and Sid choked on the bile in her stomach. The girl was insufferable.

"Let's keep it professional," Ashlan said and straightened his shoulders. "Let the girl deliver her package and we'll be on our way."

"Shame. I was quite restless this evening," her pointed finger traced the inseam of her plunging neckline suggestively, "perhaps you'll stay behind?"

"No can do. I'm responsible for the Domer," he sneered and motioned for Sid to speak.

"Right," she shook her head to try and erase Kelyn and her voluptuous body from her mind, "I was sent to deliver your droid to you."

Kelyn looked over to the corner of the room, only now noticing the large metal droid glowing in the background. She clapped her hands together in glee, "Finally! He's back!"

She rushed to Sid, waving her palm in front of her face. It took Sid a moment to understand that Kelyn was obnoxiously asking for the droid's interface box. She reached into her suit pocket and slammed the device into the Magistra's cold and clammy hand, rolling her eyes dramatically as she did so. Kelyn fumbled with the device before eagerly typing in a series of numbers. The droid's stiff body jerked to action, rushing to the Magistra's side and crouching in front of her with its head bowed.

"Would you look at that?" She cooed and placed a perfectly pointed shoe on the droids back. She reached down to retie the lace of her heels, "He's back to normal again!"

"You're using him for a footstool?" Sid asked, her eyes wide.

"Sometimes a seat," Kelyn answered dryly, "and sometimes..."

Her fingers tapped the screen, demanding the droid to stand up and walk to the opposite end of the room. He spread his feet and hands wide, like he was trying to mimic the shape of a star. Kelyn waited until his body steadied and reached to brush one of her skirts away from her thigh. The lack of fabrics revealed a holster, tight on her leg, filled with a variety of knives. Her blood-red nails tapped around the edges of the knives until she landed on the one she liked most. Before Sid could object, she shot the knife through the air, her eyes squinting on her target. The sharp edge of the blade rushed across the room, impaling the droid in its open palm and nailing it to the wall behind.

Kelyn grinned, "Sometimes target practice."

The room spun and Sid tried to focus on anything but the droid's impaled metal hand and the glisten of Kelyn's knife protruding from its body. Was he in pain? Could he be in pain? Did it matter? She rushed to the droid's side and pulled at the knife. It was lodged so deep inside the wall that she had to use her feet for leverage just to slide it out.

"Why? Why would you do this?" She asked, tears forming behind her lids. "He didn't do anything!"

"He?" Kelyn laughed, "It's not a 'he'. It's a thing. And it's *my* thing."

"You're," Sid trembled, "you're-"

Before she could finish the thought, Ashlan tugged at the back of her suit, urging her to stand down. Her fingers shook and she glanced down to see the electricity in her blood rushing to the tips, tiny bursts of lightning coming to the surface. Each flash of memory of the knife piercing the droid made her magic boil. Her lungs were tight and her heart felt like it was going to explode. Heat rose within her with each furious breath she took. Flashes of electricity jumped between her fingers as she caught Kelyn's gaze travelled down her body, almost to her sparking hands. She told herself to breathe, to relax. There was another way out of this. Another way to save Fred — her friend.

Caging her magic for a moment, she shoved her hands behind her back, backing away to stand behind the droid.

"So what else can it do?" She asked grimly, hoping Kelyn would take the bait.

The Magistra smiled giddily at the invitation, her fingers pumping out code sequences to show off. As the droid started to move to assume whatever position Kelyn had programmed it to perform, Sid let her magic flow from the tip of her finger to the back of the droid's arm. The electricity rushed from her to the droid, zapping the Magistra in the shoulder and knocking her back.

"What in the name of-" she shrieked, rubbing the spot where the magic touched her. The fabric of her bodysuit was charred and Sid could see red spreading across her skin from the burn. "Ash! Help!"

Ashlan rushed to her side to inspect the wound.

"Looks like a flesh wound, you'll live." He said and patted Kelyn on the back while Sid stifled a laugh.

She put on her most convincing look of concern and ran

towards the Magistra. "I am so sorry, ma'am! He seems to still be glitching. I'll make sure to have him fully repaired for you as soon as possible. Again, many apologies for this!" Sid grabbed the interface box from Kelyn's hand before she could protest and gestured for the droid to follow her.

Without waiting to hear back from the Magistra, she turned on her heels and stormed out of the room. Her grin was spreading so fast that it was best to get out of there before she was laughing in her face. In the background, she could hear Ashlan bidding his goodbyes to follow her out and her smile broadened from his loyalty.

"Hey! Wait up!" He yelled from behind her.

She slowed her stride but didn't stop.

"Hello? Sid?"

"What?" She scowled, still riled from her encounter with Kelyn.

"Where are you going?" He gestured to the empty corridor ahead.

"Anywhere but here," she said. The thought made her remember her ship and the reason she was on this star-damned rock in the first place. She looked Ashlan up and down and grinned. "How about we fix your blade now?"

"At this hour? Don't you sleep?"

"I'd like to get started tonight. Who knows how long it'll take me to fix it?"

He nodded but still looked unsure. "I guess. What do you need from me?"

"Not much," she smiled coyly, "just the blade. And the directions to the mechanics room. For parts."

SEVENTEEN

A WILD SCREAM sat just below Sid's ribs and she tried her best not to let it escape. She had spent an hour dragging Ashlan from room to room — under the guise of fixing his blade — in an attempt to locate a spare valve for her ship. How was it possible that there was not one pathetic little valve in all of Neostar? The Citizens must have ships and means of transportation other than the pods she'd seen thus far. She simply needed to find them and take what she required without being caught. Sid felt hopeless, lost and entirely defeated. What was the plan now? She couldn't very well stay on the star and continue lying to everyone. Sooner or later, someone was bound to catch on and what would happen then? If she was lucky, she'd be detained, chipped and thrown into the domes. She didn't want to think about what would happen to her if she wasn't lucky. Sitting on the floor of the blade charging docks, surrounded by an endless amount of weaponry, she tried hard not to imagine what the new general would do to a liar like her.

"So now what? You can't fix it?" Ashlan whined.

He'd been so quiet that she almost forgot he was there. Sid crouched and turned to look at him, taken aback by how tall he looked from her low vantage point. His shoulders broader somehow and the bulge in his biceps intensified with each squeeze he gave to his broken blade as he slammed the pieces together.

"No, I can fix it," she sighed.

"What was the treasure hunt about then?" His blue eyes narrowed.

"I was just," she tried to think of a convincing lie, "looking for something to maybe make it better. Give it more kick, you know?"

Ashlan let out a bolstering laugh, his eyes still teary when he looked at her. "You thought," he said breathlessly, "you thought that *you* could do better than all the scientists here?"

"First of all, that is incredibly rude and for all you know I *can* do better. Second of all," she crossed her arms, "you might want to reconsider insulting someone that is trying to help you."

"You're right, you're right. I'm sorry. It's been a long night," he knelt beside her and she turned away defiantly, "what do you say we get out of here? Get some food and call it a night? You can fix the blade tomorrow, right?"

She thought about it for a moment before nodding and following him out of the room. It might be good for her to get her mind off things anyhow.

"SO LET ME GET THIS STRAIGHT," Sid laughed, her mouth full of bean dumplings, "you actually kicked the general in front of everyone?"

"Not everyone. Just the queen, and the Magistras, and most of her guard. What can I say? I was a handful as a child." Ashlan smiled as if to imply he wasn't sorry about it at all.

"And what did he do?"

"He just kind of stared for a moment. Like he couldn't believe I'd actually do that. Then he laughed and sent me home. Said mom would deal with me."

His face scrunched at the memory and though Sid knew better, she still couldn't help but ask. "She's not around anymore, is she?"

"My mom? No, not for years."

"What happened to her?"

"Amperfuge. When I was still young."

Sid thought about the horror he must have endured as a child watching the disease take his mother. The worst part about the illness was the slow speed with which it attacked. Once exposed to enough of the star's magic, the human heart didn't give out immediately. The disease attacked the eyes first, then moved to the muscle tissue, and only after the person was unable to move or see, a process that could take years to complete, did it shut the lungs down. For all the years that Colton's people worked with the star's magic, no one had ever been able to reverse the effects or find a cure. It was as if the disease was targeting them. Sid sometimes wondered if the Al'iil created the illness just to punish Colton's people but she knew that was a foolish thought. In the end, there was no explaining magic.

"I'm sorry," she finally said. "That must have been awful. It's horrible what all that electricity can do to your people."

Ashlan raised an eyebrow, "Not just mine."

"What do you mean?"

"The chips? The ring?" He gestured, waiting for her to clue in.

"Yes, I know. But it's not like it can hurt us."

"Unless you don't check in at Starise and Starset. Then," he shook his hands like he had been electrocuted, "zaaaaaapppp!"

Sid shrank back in her seat. Starise and Starset? What was he talking about? She tried to remember anything from her lessons or vague conversations with Colton but nothing came to mind. "Zap?"

"I'm sorry. That was insensitive. The entire concept of the check-ins is barbaric if you ask me. To have to come back to your own domes before the ring makes a pass or you get electrocuted? It's disgusting!"

There was darkness everywhere. Sid couldn't focus on his face no matter how hard she tried. All she saw was tears and dark. This couldn't be right. *He* couldn't be right. Colton's people, they weren't monsters. They didn't force people to stay in the domes like caged beasts! They couldn't! And they wouldn't kill any of the workers, not in that horrible way. Not by turning their own magic against them! None of this made sense. Neostar was at peace. It had to be. It just had to be!

"But-" she stumbled on her words, "but Queen Leona-"

"You're right. I guess we do have her to thank for all of it," he rolled his eyes and stuffed a piece of boiled frigger leg in his mouth. "Again, sorry. I get really worked up about this stuff."

Sid fisted her hands and relaxed them again, willing the tears away. She couldn't let him see her cry. Not over this. Not over something that was supposed to be common knowledge. Is this why the Domers rebelled? She wouldn't blame them if it was. Could the queen really be capable of such cruelty? Sid had too many questions and no opportunities to ask them. Colton should have told her about this instead of protecting her like she was some foolish child. Why had he kept so much from her? How did keeping her in the dark help? It certainly didn't help her. She bet he thought that hiding the ugly truth was going to make her hate him and his people. Little did he know, the only thing she hated at that moment was how foolish he made her feel.

Taking small, weak bites of her food she tried to will herself to relax. Maybe Ashlan's wrong, maybe he's just confused.

"Can we talk about something else, please? I feel like I'm making you upset."

You think?

"No, it's fine. I'm just not used to talking about this with a Starblade," she said, finally not lying. "We can talk about whatever-"

"Well, lucky me, Ash!" Abbot barged in behind them and smacked Ashlan on the back hard enough to knock the food out of his mouth. "Twice in one night!"

Sid used the distraction to wipe the tears from her eyes with the sleeve of her suit and fixed an assured glare in Abbot's direction. His fiery stare never left hers, even as Ashlan spoke.

"Abbot! Nice surprise! What are you doing out this late?"

"You know the drill, son. The queen's business never

rests." Abbot answered, his gaze traveling between her and the droid at her side. He looked like he was about to ask her about it, but instead pursed his lips and straightened his shoulders, his hand casually grazing the powered-down blade at his side.

Sid made a mental note of the familiarity between the two. Abbot had been brave enough to refer to Ashlan as 'son', and so soon after his real father's death. She watched them attentively, studying their interaction with each other. How comfortable it felt, how accustomed. Ashlan must have known this man his entire life and she wondered how he felt to see Abbot wearing his father's title. Colton's title. *Her* Colton.

"Anything I should be worried about?" Ashlan asked.

"Not at the moment. You stay here. Enjoy your date!" He winked but she could swear she heard a growl when he glanced in her direction.

Red coated Ashlan's skin all the way past his collar. "It's not a date!" He protested, a little too eagerly. Sid wanted to defend herself but decided it was best to stay quiet and under the radar. She shoved an oversized dumpling into her mouth and chewed loudly. Good, this will keep her mouth shut for a while.

"Whatever you say, son," Abbot laughed. "Well, I'll let you get to it. I've got an early morning so I should get to bed before Silva sends a search party."

He turned to walk out, pausing to squint in Sid's direction. "Goodnight, Domer girl," He mused with poison on his tongue.

"Goodnight," she growled under her breath and threw half of an uneaten dumpling back onto her plate. "I should probably go too. It's pretty late."

"Do you have a place to stay tonight?"

"Of course!" She lied, "They set me up with a bed near the labs. I'll be fine. *We'll* be fine, that is." She knocked on the metal arm of the droid.

"Are you sure?"

"Am I sure about having a bed? Yes, I'm sure. What? You think I'm going to be sleeping on the floor of some corridor? Stardaughter! We've definitely spent too much time together as it is." She gestured for the droid and shoving a final piece of dumpling in her mouth, turned to leave. "Thank you for the dinner, really. And I'll see you back in Professor Cevil's lab in the morning."

She could hear Ashlan grumble something which she assumed were complaints about her leaving but didn't bother turning back. She wanted to make her way back to the professor's lab before he could see her sneak in there for the night and wonder why she was lying about having a place to stay. As she made her way down the glass stairwell, she stared at the deep dark beyond, a dark that seemed to swallow the star whole. The type of dark that made hearts stop beating.

The droid's loud footsteps scraped against the stairs, pulling her thoughts back. At least she didn't have to face it on her own.

EIGHTEEN

IMAGES OF QUEEN Leona flashed beneath Sid's trembling, closed lids as she tossed and turned on the lab's floor.

The queen was climbing, her golden skirts flaring behind her, and each step reverberated against the growing mountain under her feet. She tried to reach out, to pull at the gilded chains that trailed over the rock, to stop the queen from going further. Something was wrong. Sid couldn't quite put her finger on it but the fear that paralyzed her was unmistakable. She scrambled, taking large strides to climb but each time her foot landed, it only pushed her further behind. It was as if something was holding her back from reaching Leona.

With quick steps, the queen reached the top of the mountain and turned, her fierce eyes trained on Sid. She gave a soft bow and her lips curled into a smile that was more sinister than welcoming. The tip of her pointed nose lifting as she raised her arms to the side in welcome. Behind her, the ring grew over the horizon. Its yellow glow deepening as it rose until Sid could barely see ahead of her.

She sheltered her eyes with the palm of her hand, squinting to make eye contact with the queen.

It was then that she saw it.

The light of the ring's energy shone brightly over Leona, the jewels in her raven hair sparkling playfully in the glow. Her smile was fixed and relentless but her gaze drifted down. Sid followed it, her eyes widening in horror as she realized that the mountain was no mountain at all.

Every rock was a Domer skull.

Leona was standing on a pile of corpses. Freshly killed by the ring rising behind her.

SID WOKE up covered in sweat and scrambled around in the dark, blue glow of the lab. For security purposes, none of the labs had windows facing out and it was hard to tell what time of day it was but she estimated it couldn't have been past Starise. It was simply too quiet in the corridors.

She shook her head and rubbed the sleep from her eyes, glancing quickly to the droid slouched against the wall next to her. Sid knew it was just a dream, a nightmare brought on by the information she'd found out at dinner but even knowing so, she was shaken to her very core. She tried to erase the image of the bodies but it refused to budge. A nightmare permanently etched into her bones.

"Great, Fred. Because that's just what I need right now," she sighed and got up, quickly tidying up her makeshift bed of lab coats to avoid suspicion. "How about we figure out another way to get off this star?"

The droid tilted its head and stared blankly at her.

"Well, I don't know how, Fred!" She exclaimed. "But we can't just sit here until someone catches us."

Sid paused to listen to words that didn't exist.

"Well, of course you're coming with me!" Her hands shot up in protest, "And I don't want to hear any more about it!"

Grasping the interface box, she entered a series of codes that propelled the droid to follow her out. With her lack of success in finding a replacement valve, she needed a new plan to escape the increasingly tormenting hold of Neostar. Sure, there wasn't anything in the mechanical rooms and sure, she hadn't seen any ships resembling the Arcturus so far. Come to think of it, with the exception of the pods, there were no other means of transportation in all of Neostar. The thought tugged in annoyance in the back of her mind but she brushed it off.

Colton's people arrived on this star somehow. There had to be ships around. She simply had to find them! And she knew the perfect person to help her with that.

"Come on, Fred! Let's find Ash and get to work!"

THEY WALKED in silence along the edges of the garden, following the rock laden walkway that curved in and out to mimic the landscape outside. Ashlan was not kidding when he said they had mesmerizing gardens in the city. This place was the size of a small jungle! Sid found it hard to concentrate on anything other than the sounds of animal life playing in the speakers above them and the pure whiffs of oxygen pouring off the leaves of the luscious fronds that spanned the area. She ducked her head under a fallen vine and took the next left at a fork in the walkway.

"Have you ever gone out?" She asked and pointed to the far edge of the jungle beyond the city's barriers.

"Out where?" Ashlan raised an eyebrow in concern.

"Out there. Past the domes."

"To the *jungle?*" The way he emphasized the word made Sid wonder if it was fear she could hear in his voice. "Why would I go there?"

"I don't know. To see what else is out there. It's a pretty big star."

She gestured dramatically to the sprawling landscape of Neostar. From her years spent on the ship, it was nearly impossible to see the detail of Tower City and the domes that lay in a circle around it. Even when she'd tried to piggyback off the ring's satellite, she could only make out patches of white and grey where the bulging constructs lay before the feed gave out. Down here, everything looked different. The domes were so much larger than she imagined, of course, they had to be to house nearly a thousand workers each. They looked like massive, polished rocks that jutted out of the ground and towered over the landscape. Trees that had been growing for decades took root around the convex walls of the domes and she could even make out vines that whipped around some of the exteriors, reaching almost as high as the windows that encased the top edges. The same vines spread and twirled in every direction, squeezing all their weight over the tubes that connected the domes to the city. She wondered if it was dangerous to have plant life so close to the power supply that delivered the collected energy from the workers but assumed that someone much brighter than her had likely already thought of it.

"A pretty dangerous star too," Ashlan said.

"Everything is dangerous until you figure it out."

"Yes, but not everything could kill you."

"The jungle can't kill you, Ash. You're being ridiculous! It's just a place." She rolled her eyes and remembered how scared she was when she first entered into the green abyss. "You adapt. Like you did when you first came to Neostar."

"We didn't adapt," he whispered, "we took over. There's a difference."

"Either way, everyone is doing great and we're all alive. So what's the problem with a little adventure and exploring?"

His nose scrunched in a way she was starting to find endearing, "Not that I expect you to know your history, but we already tried that. And it didn't work out that great."

She took offense to his comment. Sid knew her history very well. "Meaning what?"

"Well, I obviously wasn't around then but my dad used to tell me stories."

"I like stories. Do you like stories, Fred?" She yelled back to the droid on their tail. "See? He likes stories too!"

"He can't actually talk to you, Sid."

"Not the point. Tell your story," she crossed her arms and huffed.

"Fine, fine. Basically, after the first year of the Circulum System's operation, the queen's mother sent some of her guard into the jungle. To scout the surrounding areas and find resources. She knew that the Domers that didn't agree with her methods of using their energy abandoned the rest and left for the jungle but assumed they would stay away. Keep to themselves, you know?"

"But they didn't?"

He shook his head. "No, they most definitely didn't."

"What happened?"

"No one knows for sure. According to my dad, only one guard returned. Well, barely. I guess they hurt him pretty bad but left him alive long enough to deliver a message."

Sid's voice trembled and caught in her throat, "What was the message?"

"That the star didn't belong to my people and its magic was not for our use. That anyone who dares come after them and any other Domer that defects would suffer the consequences. The guard that came back died soon after he delivered the message but before he did, he said these Domers were something different entirely. Like they had changed somehow. They ripped out their chips and it turned them. Made them more," he paused, "Al'iil."

The Al'iil; a word Colton had sworn her not to utter out loud. It was what the native population of Neostar called themselves before the peace treaty between their peoples. She had never associated it with something horrible until just that moment. How could one word mean so much? Change someone so greatly? But it could. One word could do many things. Colton taught her that when he was pronounced 'dead'.

"But ripping out their chips, that would kill them, right?"

"In theory. But no one had ever tried before, most of the Domers chose to be chipped. To be given the technology my people brought, homes, work — a future. But a prison is still a prison no matter what you call it."

"Did that guard say anything else? About the jungle people?" She was still too afraid to use the word.

"The Al'iil? Not that I know. Just that they changed. Mutated. Became savage in a way that was violent and cruel.

I was still a kid when my dad told me this story but from what I remember, he said the guard came back not really whole."

"You mean emotionally?"

"No, I mean his arms were missing. They had been sliced clean off his body."

Sid gasped and raised a hand to cover her mouth to keep from retching. The droid behind them, coded to emulate her every move, slapped himself in the mouth. The sound of metal on metal echoed through the otherwise serene garden and even Ashlan jumped in surprise. She stopped in her tracks and bent over, her hands resting on her thighs to catch a breath. "Your dad told you this? When you were a kid?" She couldn't imagine Colton telling *her* stories like that when she was little. It felt so careless and she never knew Colton to be anything but calculated and calm.

"Of course. We all know the history here. Everyone who was born on Neostar knows it. We even cover it in school. I guess they keep it alive as a warning, for us not to go wandering off. And it sure does work! So to answer your original question, no, I haven't ever gone out. I like my arms just fine, thank you."

She didn't understand any of it. Why did the Al'iil become so cruel? Why did the queen's mother not try to repair the relationship? Why did everyone refer to her as the queen's mother? Didn't the woman have a name?

She was still racing through countless questions when a low beeping sound interrupted the nature calls on the speakers.

"What in the name of the star is that?" She yelped and covered her ears.

"Shhh," Ashlan commanded, "it's a special announcement from the queen."

Sid's eyes widened and she followed his gaze to the three large telescreens projecting in the center of the garden above their heads. There was white noise and the regular snow of the screen as the satellite connected to the feed, before Queen Leona's perfectly porcelain face appeared. She was even more beautiful enlarged and magnified by three but what struck Sid as most interesting were the gold jewels woven intricately into the dozens of braids that fell down her straight back. They were identical to the ones she had been wearing in her dream last night.

"My loyal Citizens," the queen said in a serene and haunting voice, "I regret to inform you that recently, the number of incidents of rebellion has increased substantially. While I understand that fear may be building within you, and that fearful minds must talk, I urge you not to give in to the fruitless conversations that may be carrying on in our common areas. You are safe here in the city. You are safe here with me. You are simply, perfectly safe."

Leona shifted in the camera view slightly and Sid noticed her checking something off screen. Her eyes narrowed and she shook off the distraction and collected herself once more. This time, a smile tugged at the edges of her lips as she spoke. "Earlier this morning, there was yet another act of revolt taken against one of my trusted Starblades in the docking station of dome number nine." From where she was standing, Sid could hear a low gasp escape Ashlan's lips, likely worried for one of his friends. "I am pleased to tell you that no one was hurt. The Starblade is safe; aside from a few minor bruises."

Ashlan's shoulders relaxed but Sid squeezed every muscle taut. Where was this speech going?

"I am even more pleased to tell you," Leona continued, "that we have apprehended the Domer responsible for this act and believe they were connected to the revolts in Domes fourteen and eighty-seven earlier this week."

The camera began to tilt and Sid found herself shifting her weight from foot to foot. Something about this seemed wrong. There was no way that one Domer could be responsible for all of that chaos, at least not from what she'd seen on her telescreen recordings back on the ship. These were organized attacks and whoever planned them had help. Her thoughts landed on the woman's face she had been attempting to find more information on after the first two attacks. She knew her somehow, from some other life before this one. Could she be who the queen had in custody?

Don't be her, don't be her, don't be her. Sid whispered as the camera swung around and landed on the blurry shape of a very large, very muscular man. She breathed out in relief though why she was relieved for the safety of one particular Domer she'd never met was beyond her.

"This man will pay!" Leona's voice boomed over the speakers and Sid wondered if the volume had been turned to the maximum. "He will be held responsible for his doings and for endangering all of you! I will not let one bad seed destroy the life we have built here. The life my mother has died to protect."

A single tear rolled down Leona's cheek as she continued, "As I speak to you now, my most beloved Citizens, a message is being screened in all the domes, with incentive for anyone who steps forward with information in regard to the accomplices of this terrorist. We will not be broken!" Leona raised a fist in the air, "We will not be derailed! And anyone who tries, will answer to me!"

With that, the telescreen shut off.

Sid stared at the empty space that was once filled with the queen's magnificent presence in awe while her droid slumped foolishly next to her. If she thought she had questions before, she definitely had more of them now. There was so much she still didn't understand about the intricate balances between the Domers and Citizens. Her ever-explorative mind wanted to know but the rational part of her, the part vaguely raised by Colton, told her to concentrate on what mattered. She had to find information on the original landing ships of his people. There was time to learn all about Neostar's politics when she was safe and sound aboard the Arcturus.

"Hey, Ash? Do you know if– "

Another procession of beeps interrupted her, this one higher pitched and coming from Ashlan's comm device. He raised the device to his eyes and as soon as it recognized his retina, the low mumble of a voice sounded in his earpiece. It was too quiet for Sid to hear but she could make out the words 'immediately' and 'order'.

"What was that about?" She asked.

"The queen wants to see me. Let's go."

"I'm sorry, what? Why do you need me?"

"Because you still haven't fixed my blade and if I show up without it and the stardamned queen notices, I'll need to explain a few things."

"But I-"

"I'm not arguing over this. You made a deal. I held up my end but you haven't held up yours. You don't strike me as the type of person that would back out of a deal or am I wrong?"

He looked at her and she shook her head. "Good, thank you. Now let's go before she sends guards to come find me. Leona is not exactly the patient type."

Ashlan reached for her sleeve and tugged her along. Away from the peacefulness of the gardens and the comfort of a conversation with him that felt almost like home. Sid let her eyes meet the fog settling over the jungle on the horizon and smiled, her thoughts rushing to one small detail that she had almost ignored in the chaos. For the first time since she'd met him, Ashlan called her a person instead of a Domer and stars help her, she liked how it sounded. If he could see past her eyes, maybe others could too. Maybe Colton was wrong to protect her. His own son was starting to come around and it gave her some hope. Sid still wanted to get off the star as soon as possible but at least the time she would need to spend here might be worth her while. She could experience life on Neostar instead of reading about. Spend time in the city, take more walks in the gardens; she could dive off the falls if she chose to!

Her lips parted and she smiled so wide that her face started to ache.

I'm going to meet the mucking queen!

NINETEEN

HIDING in the shadows of the throne room, or as much shadow as she could find in the colossal room, Sid tried to stay quiet and inconspicuous. Per Ashlan's instruction, she had left the droid outside, but standing here in the circular room with nothing separating her from Queen Leona but air and uncertainty, she wished she had someone metal and strong to lean on. There was a lull in conversation and Sid held her breath, worried that even a gasp of air might catch the queen's attention. The guards at Leona's side stood motionless, their eyes drifting to survey the throne with piercing concentration. When their collective gazes turned, Sid drifted her eyes in their direction, taking note of each detail of their appearance. Unlike the Starblades, the queen's guards dressed moderately. Their suits — though made of the same material as those of the Starblades — were as dark as a black hole, a blue so deep it was almost void of color. Each suit glimmered as the guard's chests rose and fell and Sid felt mesmerized by their shine. She searched for their blades but quickly realized that not one of the guards possessed one. Instead, strapped to their backs like second skin lay large, curved swords with glass hilts. Squinting, Sid noted the energy that sparked across the handles, flowing all the way down the razor-sharp edges. No wonder they hide these guys, she thought. The guards were the scariest thing she'd seen in Neostar thus far.

Leona straightened her back on the throne, burying her weight deep into the thick glass backing and carefully flipped one of her gilded braids behind her. She looked every bit the picture of royalty: perched high above the rest of them. The glass of the throne reflected each speck of light and at times, when Leona shifted her weight, Sid had to squint her eyes from the glare. The queen rearranged her legs, sending the slit of her gold colored skirt higher than Sid felt comfortable with. Everything that Leona had on looked uncomfortable to her. From the dragging skirt to the bronze corset, all the way to the metal collar that grazed just beneath her ears. Sid had no idea how the queen managed to move in the attire but if she was in any discomfort, she did not let it show. There was no doubt that Leona was the most powerful person in the room. On the entire star, really.

"The situation has gotten out of hand, general." Leona addressed Abbot calmly, "You have given me your personal guarantee that these incidents in the domes were nothing more than acts of frustration from the workers. It seems to me that their frustration is growing, wouldn't you agree?" Her lips pursed into a thin line and she dug her gold nails into the edges of the throne.

"Yes, my queen. I assure you; we are doing all we can to stop it once and for all. We have increased security in the domes and I have men scouring the streets to find the ones responsible." Abbot explained with more pride than Sid imagined him having. "We will find them."

"And yet you haven't found them yet? That's disappointing, to say the least."

"My queen, we are working on this day and night. There have not been any signs that show an organized group effort."

Sid chewed on her bottom lip, remembering the face of the woman she saw in the telescreen footage. That woman was a clue that could help the queen capture the rest. Or at least get some answers. Sid was almost giddy at the thought that information she had might be of use to Leona. *She* could be of use to Leona. She took in a deep breath and a small step forward and opened her mouth to speak.

"Bring in the traitor!" Leona shouted before Sid had a chance to utter a word. "Bring him to me now!"

Panes of glass slid apart next to her and four Starblades entered the room. Behind them, tied at the wrists and neck, the Domer who was captured was dragged forward by a lightline. One of the younger Starblades yanked at the chain and the Domers skin hissed at the touch, a burn mark forming immediately on his neck. Sid could see tears forming in his hazel eyes from the pain but he shook them off and stood tall again. His tanned skin was riddled with scars, the likes of which Sid had never seen. He looked like a warrior. Like a wild thing she had only read about in stories as a child. He was tall and muscular and proud. The belt of his tunic was tied loosely and she could see the scars that ran up his arms crept along his chest and stomach. Although the more she studied them, the more she realized they weren't scars at all. Scars didn't take on the shapes of stars. He was marked from head to toe with symbols; circles and lines that Sid didn't understand. It was beautiful and comforting and so familiar. Sid could almost remember touching those symbols and giggling from how they felt at the edges of her fingers. Rough but soft at the same time. She could see it so clearly, the chubby little fingers of a child scratching across this man's arms. Her chubby little fingers. She snapped her attention back into the room and pushed the image away.

Sid's eyes raced between him and the queen in fear and anticipation.

"Who are you working with?" Leona demanded.

The Domer stood silent yet his gaze was fixed on Leona defiantly. He shuffled his feet and raised his chest, appearing to be even taller now.

"I suggest you answer, young man." Abbot nodded at one of the Starblades that yanked on the lightline again in response. "Your queen demands the truth."

The Domer took a step forward, cocked his head, and spat at the base of the throne. "She is no queen of mine."

Sid nearly collapsed from stifling a shocked gasp. She expected Leona to rise from her throne and slap the prisoner across the face. It's what she would have done if someone had shown her such an adamant lack of respect. Instead, the queen chuckled quietly, her lips curling into the same smile Sid saw in her dreams.

"Foolish, stubborn creature. If you think you're protecting the rest of your group, I must tell you that you're highly mistaken," she drew lazy circles with her nails across the throne's glass. "I will not stop until I find out everyone who is responsible and make them pay for disrupting our peace."

"You call this peace?" The Domer yelled back. "This is not peace! This is enslavement! You take what isn't yours and expect us to kneel at your feet. Well, we're done kneeling!"

A gold nail pointed to the ceiling and a Starblade pulled on the lightline so fast that the prisoner fell to his knees. His hands wrapped around his throat and he rubbed at the burn furiously.

"Looks like you are not quite as done with kneeling as you may believe," she laughed. "Tell me who you're working with. I won't ask again."

On shaking legs, the Domer pushed himself up to stand. His eyes travelled past Leona to Abbot, then to Ashlan, finally landing on Sid. Her knees buckled and she begged him to look away, to draw attention to anything but her. But his gaze stayed trained on her, as if he was magnetized to her presence.

"She is not your queen," he said, "she is your death."

The queen's calm demeanor faltered and Sid took note as her lips tightened into a thin line. Though she tried to hide it, Leona let the Domer's words pierce her with their intensity, cracking the all-powerful facade she had earlier displayed. Sid felt for her. The woman was only trying to do what's best for the star and this man was acting like she was a murderer. If Sid wasn't frozen in her spot in the room, she'd have rushed over to hug the stoic ruler in front of her.

Before another word could escape the Domer's lips, Leona tapped her raised finger to the throne and all four Starblades raised their weapons. They pointed the tips of their blades at the back of the Domer's neck and lunged. The blades barely grazed his skin but Sid could see the electricity in them humming and itching to get out as they reached the edges of the chip in his neck. Light burst on impact, driving the Domer to the ground, his body convulsing as a dark burn spread across the back of his neck and down his shoulder blades. The room smelled of burnt skin and hopelessness. Sid wanted to look away, she wanted to scream, run out of the room and keep running until she was nowhere near this place. But she stayed put. Her eyes wide and staring at one spot only. The charred remnants of raised markings on the Domer's back.

Leona got up from her throne and brushed invisible dirt from her skirts. "It seems we have a guest with us tonight!" Her fierce eyes locked onto Sid who was still gasping for air and staring at the body of the prisoner. "Would someone like to tell me who this is and why she's here?"

"I'm sorry, my queen," Ashlan jumped in front of Sid as if to shield her. "This is Sid, she's from dome one twenty-eight, here to help Professor Cevil. She's quite a gifted mechanic from what I gather. I'm just showing her around."

Was he nervous? She hadn't heard Ashlan stumble over his words like that before. He was either nervous or scared and she didn't like either of those options. They both meant she could be found out and end up just like the prisoner laying dead in front of her.

"Pleasure to make your acquaintance, Sid." The queen cooed and Sid wondered what the protocol was for this.

Should she curtsy? Do they curtsy here? She cursed Colton for not teaching her more about the customs of the city. It was then that she realized it, he never taught her the customs because he had no intention of bringing her down here. Her heart felt larger in her chest and every beat was like a building pressure that threatened to. Her eyes stayed down, steering clear of the dead body in her peripheral. Did he keep her away from here because he was afraid she'd suffer the same fate? Her breaths were short and shallow and hurt like a punch to the chest. Everything was wrong and everything was broken. She was completely alone. More alone than she had been on the ship. At least there she had Rusty. Sure, he wasn't a real person but she never wondered if he wanted her or not. And she definitely never wondered if he was going to shoot thousands of watts of electricity into her neck and kill her.

"Sid," Ashlan whispered back to her and she blinked her eyes wildly. "Say something."

"Right. Of course. My apologies, my queen."

Leona paused for a moment and Sid instinctively covered the back of her neck for protection. A foolish notion since there was no chip there for the queen to destroy but something about it made her feel slightly comforted. After another excruciating second of silence, Leona broke into a laugh.

"Oh, my. You're absolutely adorable! And helping the professor? That must be quite the challenge in itself. He's a bit of handful, isn't he?"

Sid nodded which seemed to satisfy the queen for the moment.

"Abbot!" She howled and the general was at attention by her side before Sid had a chance to blink. "I want another group sent into the domes. As soon as possible. In fact, sooner than that."

"Yes, my queen. Of course, my queen. I will put my team together and have them-"

Leona put a finger to his mouth and pursed her lips. "No, you will not." Her gaze turned to Ashlan. "I want him to lead this."

"Me?"

"Him?"

Abbot and Ashlan's shocked faces looked like mirror reflections. Neither man seemed to be able to understand the order.

"Yes, him. You." Leona specified and pointed to Ashlan as if she wasn't clear before. "You will pick your team and leave immediately. Abbot's had enough time on this and we are nowhere closer to finding the rest of these vile creatures. We need new eyes on this and what better than the eyes of the son of our most accomplished general!"

Sid turned to Abbot to see if he was remotely offended by the queen's words but he did not seem to mind. Instead, the look in his eyes was more fearful than angry.

"Are you certain, my queen?" He asked.

"You're questioning my decision?" Leona roared over him.

"No. Of course not, not at all. Forgive me, my queen."

The tight smile returned to Leona's lips and she turned to look at Sid over Ashlan's broad shoulders. "And you will take the Domer with you."

Muck.

"Sid? Why?"

"Because she may prove to be useful in getting the rest of the population to trust you," she said confidently, "and because she can help fix your blade. Should it happen to break again."

Ashlan's cheeks reddened and he rubbed the spot on his back where his blade would usually be holstered. Sid had no idea how the queen knew his blade was broken or why she hadn't bothered to punish him for mishandling his weapon but she was relieved nonetheless. At least she didn't have to explain how it broke in the first place.

She expected Ashlan to retort with one of the annoying,

self-assured comments she was used to but he simply nodded and looked down.

"Wonderful. It's settled then," Leona clapped her hands in front of her chest and turned back to the throne. When she was just about to climb onto the glass encasement, her head turned partially, revealing the intoxicatingly perfect shape of her profile.

"And clean this mess up, the smell is unbearable."

Sid didn't stay to watch the body get dragged out of the throne room. She had enough nightmares as it was to deal with.

TWENTY

STOPPING her mouth from gaping open as she walked through the dark streets of dome nine was a more difficult task than Sid originally imagined. With Ashlan walking next to her and Abbot watching her every move, she needed to act the part more than ever now. A Domer wouldn't be impressed by a dome. No matter how unbelievable it was.

She expected the same dark and solid environment she had on the Arcturus but this place was something else entirely. For starters, it was taller than she expected. The circular structure spanned about ten stories up with a large, gaping opening at its core. The windows that ran along the top floor were there for decoration — some almost entirely overgrown with vines — more than to provide any real light, not that the dome needed it. There were neon-lit signs of every size and color surrounding the shops that littered the base of the dome in no distinguishable pattern. Each shop was housed in a tent, some small and some large enough to fill a transit pod. Around her, voices rose in alternating decibels as patrons shouted over each other. Some bargained for goods while others yelled out orders and directions. The dome was the most chaotic place Sid had ever stepped foot in and she tried to settle her racing mind. Her eyes caught sight of a row of tents that boasted long, floating table tops full to the brim with puff pastry, bowls of broth and a million other foods that Sid couldn't name. Her stomach growled loud enough to catch Ashlan's attention but she waved him off and sped up. Her shoulder hit the heavy fabric of a tent beside them and it sent a whiff of fried pastry through the air, making Sid's stomach sing with anticipation. A light flashed from further within the web of shops and Sid glanced around to try and find some semblance of organisation. Though without street signs, or streets for that matter, it was nearly impossible to tell which way was which. The only thing she knew with certainty were the small flats that stacked back to back along the top floors of the dome.

So they live up there and socialize down here. That makes sense.

Sid stretched her gaze to the dome's ceiling and admired the bright blue sky above her. The clouds drifted slowly, forming and reforming unintelligible shapes with their puffs. Every once in a while, the screen that projected the sky glitched and she found herself disappointed in the mirage.

Unlike Tower City, there were no timers counting down the hours and the only thing that alluded to the time of day was the projection of the ring across the clouds above her. She listened intently, trying to find another sound that might allude to wildlife inside the dome. There was nothing of the sort. No sound of waters in the background, no rustle of winds. Just the projection of the sky, a gazillion signs, and an automated trash disposal every ten steps. Which surprised

Sid because dome nine was likely the filthiest place she'd ever stepped foot inside.

Garbage lined the streets as though it was put out on display and she had to watch her step to avoid stepping in disposed frigger stew that someone just tossed on the street. Coupled with the nearly unbearable heat, the smell that wafted past her periodically was enough to make her gag. Though she wanted to like the domes, this place wasn't really giving her the best impression of the residents. Sid coughed as she almost tripped over a pile of papers covered in what she hoped was mud.

Ashlan yanked her out of the way just in time. "Watch your step. Or you'll be covered in street junk before Starset," he said and shook a loose piece of paper from the bottom of his shoe. His eyebrows danced as if he'd just proved a theory he'd been working on for years. "I don't know how you live like this, to be honest."

"Hey! I don't live like this!" She slapped him on the shoulder and the droid behind them mimicked her action. Ashlan winced from the second slap and rubbed the pained spot.

"You're telling me your dome, is what? Clean? I thought they were all like this."

"Well, you thought wrong." She said. Time to deflect the subject. "Wait, you haven't been to all the domes?"

He rubbed the back of his neck, "Not really. Don't get me wrong, I'd love to see them all but most of the NSO's patrols are closer to the city."

"But what if something happens further away? Shouldn't you be there to help?"

"We really should be. But the queen is in the city. And she comes first."

Sid scrunched her nose and motioned for the droid to come around her other side, putting a distance between herself and Abbot. She could see him sneak glances at her every few minutes and it was beginning to annoy the stars out of her. "So if something happens in say, my dome, there's no one there to help?" She whispered.

"Not really."

"That's disgusting."

"I agree," Ashlan said, his voice coarse in a way that made her actually believe him.

A group of Domer kids who were walking in their path caught sight of their group and turned away, making their way down a darkened alley created by the tents of shops. The Starblades laughed and carried on their conversation, walking with their chests bulked even more than Sid thought was humanly possible. She tried to see who the Domers were that ran off to avoid them but they had either hidden in one of the shops or disappeared entirely. When she looked into the eyes of the Domers around them, she realized it wasn't just the groups of kids that wanted to avoid them. Everyone they passed either looked down, looked away or pretended to be busy with something else that required their immediate attention. Hands exchanged Domer dockets for goods, mothers straightened their children's clothing; anything to stay otherwise engaged and out of sight.

Sid watched one of the Starblades knock something off a display shelf in front of a tent shop selling glass sculptures. The sculpture shattered on the floor at his boots and he laughed, stomping over the pieces as he walked past.

"That's enough, Connor!" Abbot yelled from behind her and smacked the Starblade across the back of his head. "If you can't behave, you're off the team."

"I thought this was Ash's team," Connor huffed in an arrogant tone that made Sid dislike him immediately.

Abbot glanced back at Ashlan who nodded. "Looks like he agrees. Now keep it moving and keep your hands to yourself."

As they passed by the shop, Sid peeked in and saw a young girl half her age scrambling to pick up the remnants of the sculpture from the floor. Her eyes narrowed in Connor's direction and turned back to the girl.

"I'm sorry for that," she said and bent down to help her pick up the shards of glass.

The girl was startled, but her shoulders relaxed when her gaze finally reached Sid's eyes. "Oh, it's alright, you know how they are."

Sid wanted to say that she didn't. That she had no idea how they are and why they were like that. She wanted to ask this girl so many questions that she had trouble pinpointing even one of them. More than anything, she wanted to wipe the tears that were creeping to the edges of the girl's lids and tell her that Connor will pay for breaking her things. That she will make sure of it. Instead, she nodded silently and scraped the rest of the broken glass into the sleeve of her suit and tossed it on the display counter.

"Thank you," the girl said. "You really didn't have to help."

Sid looked around at the tents that lined the center of the dome, forming a maze of shops and street vendors that yelled at everyone that passed to get their attention. Her gaze drifted up to the rows of flats above her, their residents hanging out of the windows that faced the marketplace to talk to each other. She watched a family of Domers fussing around a newborn that was louder than any alarm her ship had ever screeched, and the shop owner that came out with a bottle of warm soy-milk to calm him. She noted the delectable smells of foods and the sounds of laughter coming from the hub of activity that was the center of dome nine and smiled.

"Yes," she said calmly and patted the girl on the shoulder, "I really did. I really, *really* did."

CONNOR'S GRIP loosened around the Domer he was holding over the railing and she held furiously to the metal. Her fingers clutched at the edge as her back twisted over the metal balcony until she looked like she was almost bent in half. The Domer's wild hair, half loose and half braided, hung over the rail and the gravity made it look like a heavy anchor pulling her down. With a smirk, Connor poked a fat finger to the woman's shoulder and she tumbled back further. Another poke, and she would fly over the railing and splatter the ground five stories down. The beads of sweat that had gathered on her brow dripped to the street below, a crowd already starting to form at the bottom. Some outstretched hands, hoping to catch the woman when she fell but Sid knew it would be no use. From this height, she was as good as dead.

"Tell us who you're working with!" Connor shouted over the screams of the Domers below.

The woman shook her head, fear so sewn into her being that Sid could see it crawl over her skin. She was made of fear entirely it seemed. Connor raised his finger again, readying to shove the Domer to her death. Before he could make contact, Sid took a step toward them. She didn't care if

Abbot was watching, she didn't care if it would blow her cover. There was no stardamned way she was going to stand by while this self-righteous imbecile murder someone in cold blood. The queen demanded they collect rebellion members and bring them in for a trial. As far as she could tell, Connor was not one who should be deemed fit to pass judgement.

She walked faster, the droid keeping up with her at her side but before she could grab for Connor's arm and twist him around, Ashlan stepped in. His muscled chest rigid with power as he lunged himself between Connor and the Domer, one hand latching onto the woman to keep her from falling and one palm shoving the Starblade away.

"Enough, Connor!" He hissed, "This is not what we are here to do."

"She is one of them! How are you protecting her right now?" Connor yelled, his face red with fury, making him look like a bowl of mashed pot-belly fruit.

"We were tasked with securing the members and returning them to the queen. Nothing less, nothing more. You are not to kill this woman or anyone else in your misguided solution for interrogation."

Ashlan's voice was calm, though Sid could sense a touch of anger beneath his words. Each syllable was cut a little too short when he spoke which made his words slice through the air like flying knives. She glanced in Abbot's direction who looked to be neither impressed nor amused. Instead, the brawny man watched Sid with trained eyes and she felt her cheeks redden from the attention. She looked back to Connor and Ashlan but the general's gaze was still searing through her back. *Stardaughter! This guy just won't give up, will he?*

"We should be taking them out as we find them! Before

one of these animals plots another attack." Connor's eyes were full of more hate than Sid could ever imagine a person being able to possess. How could someone so young have so much animosity toward an entire race? It was such a ridiculous notion to her, to decide you know someone even though you've never truly met them. Connor had never spoken to this woman before today. Had never gone to school with her. Never asked her to a dance. Never had her break his heart into pieces and leave him for another man. He never had so much as shared a portion of a life with her, let alone enough time to make him despise her so.

"And then what? What will that accomplish, Connor? Please enlighten me on your brilliant idea!" Ashlan pushed him further away from the railing and the Domer who cowered behind him. "You're going to go around killing people in front of everyone and you think that's going to what? Help the situation? Right. Because if the rebellion is building, murdering a Domer in cold blood is what's going to make them stop."

"I," Connor gasped, trying to rebut his point, "I just think we should do something."

Ashlan patted the Starblade on the back and walked him away from the crowd. "We *are* doing something. We're doing what the queen has requested us to do. And we're going to do it so stardamned well, she'll promote the whole lot of us! Right?"

He looked at Connor who nodded and scuttled away, his eyes refusing to meet anyones in his hurry to leave. Sid couldn't be sure but from where she was standing, it almost looked like the general was smiling. He caught her staring and if there was a smile on his face before, it was definitely nowhere to be seen now. In fact, he looked like he was scowling at her. She rolled her eyes and motioned for the droid to follow.

The Domer was still huddled on the floor of the small balcony in front of a flat. Sid wondered if it was her own but as she looked down the long corridor, she realized each and every flat looked exactly the same. The woman could have lived anywhere. When she asked Colton about the design of the domes, he said it was made to mimic the living spaces of motels on his home planet. He didn't do much in ways of explaining to her what a motel was, stating only that it was a collection of living quarters that people paid for to spend the night. The explanation did not exactly help Sid make sense of the architecture but it was all she had to go by. And she liked having small bits of information on Colton's home planet; it made her feel closer to him somehow. How she wished he was here right now. He would know what to do and what to say to this petrified mess of a woman on the floor. Sid, on the other hand, was completely lost.

She could see people start to pile out of their flats, eager to take a look at the disruption and decided the added attention was not going to make the woman feel better. She crouched next to her, blocking the view from the onlookers and gestured for the droid to do the same on the opposite side. Together, they formed small walls around the Domer's shaking body and she had hoped it was enough for now.

"Are you alright?" She asked. A stupid question, all things considering.

The woman nodded, looking up at Sid's eyes. "You're-"

"A Domer? Sure am!" She rubbed the back of her neck, "You're probably wondering what I'm doing with this lot, huh?"

Another nod.

"It's a really long story. Let's just say they have something I need and I can't get it until all of this over."

The Domer laughed, "Well, it's about time someone used them for a change!"

"Why didn't you tell them what they wanted to know? To save yourself, I mean. If Ash hadn't come through, you would have..." she couldn't finish the sentence.

"Died?" The woman said it for her, "I know. But I would have died knowing I protected the ones that matter. The ones that will save us all from this."

"I thought Neostar was at peace."

"Darling, what Neostar do *you* live on? The one the rest of us are on has us being sucked dry of our magic so the Citizens can continue their reign on the star! They even make us speak their stardamned language!" Her voice raised, words defiant and strong and Sid slinked back, shadowed by the power in them. Something about her felt so familiar, not the same as she felt with the woman on the telescreens or the man that was executed by Leona yesterday. Yet something about the way she moved her mouth when she spoke, the dialect of her language. Sid was certain she'd heard it before. The way the word 'magic' fell off the lips of a Domer. It was as if she had dreamt about it before — the domes, the Domers, magic.

"What Dome are you from?" The woman asked.

Sid readied herself to lie but a strong hand gripped her shoulder and she spun around to see Ashlan next to her. The woman's shoulders tensed and she went back to cowering as soon as her gaze met Ashlan's blue-suited form.

Sid put a palm on the woman's knee, "Don't worry. He's alright, surprisingly. What do you want, Ash?"

"We need to go. It's almost Starset. We should get back

to our accommodations for the night, let everyone here get some rest." He gestured to the heads bobbing out from their flat doors.

"*Our* accommodations? Where exactly?"

"We have some tents set up in the center of the dome. The Starblades usually stay there if they've been patrolling too long and are too tired to make the journey back to the city. Don't worry, it's safe. You'll be sharing a tent with me."

"You're joking, right?" She scoffed, "You think I'm going to share a tent with you? All night? How convenient, Ash! How long have you been planning this little scheme, huh?"

"Calm down. You're a last-minute addition to the team. No one planned anything." He looked back to the group, "If you'd prefer, you can bunk with Connor. Or Abbot."

She sighed loudly and rolled her eyes. She'd never be able to get away with him around. Not that she knew where she would try to get away to but it was still nice to have options. *Great! Just great.*

"Don't worry, if it makes you feel better, you can code your droid to kill me if I try anything funny."

"His name is Fred. And don't think I won't."

The group marched in unison, the Starblades' boots shaking the ground each time they landed. As they passed by the flats, people peered out of the doors and small, circular windows to see what the commotion was about. As soon as they caught glimpse of the Starblades, they went back inside, sheltering their children as they did. Fear and anger drenched the walls of the dome and she could see it drip down the metal panels. There was no peace here. Whatever story Colton had sold her was a lie. These people were afraid and they were afraid of *his* people. And of her now that she was walking alongside them, about to spend the night bunking with one of them. She didn't know what to believe anymore. On the one hand, she was on the side she wanted to be for so long, finally walking amongst the Starblades like she belonged. Sure, they didn't trust her yet but she was still near them. Close enough to listen to their conversations and not just watch them from telescreen recordings on her ship. On the other hand, they were nothing like what she thought they would be. They were cruel, and heartless, and driven by power and control. What did that make Colton? What did that make her now?

The Starblades dragged the Domer woman behind them and Sid slowed her pace to walk alongside her. With the Domer on one side, a Starblade on the other and the droid right behind them — Sid had no idea who she was anymore.

TWENTY-ONE

"THAT WAS GOOD," Abbot said, chewing on a piece of fried frigger, "what you did back there. Connor is a good fighter but he wouldn't know political tactics if they hit him on the head."

"Thanks," Ashlan nodded agreeably.

"If he's so daft, why take him on these missions?" The words slipped out before Sid could stop herself and she readied for one of Abbot's negative comments, surprised when his lips curled into a smile instead.

"Because sometimes, it's better to build an army that you can control. One that doesn't do much thinking outside of orders."

"An army of fools," she mumbled under her breath and took a bite off the frigger leg on her plate. The meat was still moist, despite the cool temperature and she pretended it was steaming hot when she bit into it. "He could have killed her back there."

Ashlan scooted closer, closing the space between them

almost entirely. His gaze met hers. "That might be a better option than what she's heading for," he whispered.

"What do you mean? Doesn't she get a trial?"

"Everyone gets a trial," Ashlan said. "But no one comes out of their trial alive."

"What?"

"The trials are just a way for the queen to be seen as a fair ruler. At the end of the day, she'll do anything to protect Tower City and its Citizens. Anything."

"What about the Domers? Who protects them?"

Her voice started to rise and she could feel the whites of her eyes begin to radiate with magic, blending into the thin line of her pupil. Sid gripped the metal bitesticks in her hand, hoping the pressure would prevent her from shaking. She was fuming. Angry with the queen for her treatment of the workers, with Ashlan for his following of rules that he so blatantly didn't agree with; with herself. Because she had risked so much to come to this star only to find out everything she knew about it was a lie. There was no peace here. Not unless you were one of Colton's people; the chosen Citizens. One look at the eyes she hid behind her goggles and it was clear as starday that she was nothing like them. Even if Colton was alive, there would be no place for her here. No wonder he tried to keep her away as long as possible. Who knows what would have happened to her if he'd never put her on that ship? Would she have joined this group of rebels? Would it have been her hanging off the side of the railing with Connor's fat finger threatening to push her over?

Sid's fingers tightened against the metal sticks and she could feel the energy shift within her. Crawling from its secret depth under her skin closer to the surface. Closer to the Starblades. To their beating hearts and skin that begged to be scorched. She let the magic reach her fingers, directing it to the metal in wisps of electricity. Tears streamed down her face, catching on the rim of her goggles and forming small pools of saline at the ridge of her nose.

"Sid? You alright?" Ashlan asked.

She took a deep breath and looked down at the bitesticks in her hands. The once straight metal sticks were misshapen, tailored perfectly to the indents of her fists. All twisted and broken, wrong somehow. Just like her. She shoved the sticks into her suit pocket before anyone could see them and got up. "I'm fine. I'm done eating."

Grabbing her plate, she walked out of the tent, letting the flaps of the entrance dance wildly behind her. She could feel Abbot's squinted eyes on her as she passed but didn't bother to look back. She wanted to get away from him and from Ashlan; even Fred was a constant reminder of everything that was rotten on this star. She couldn't take it anymore. Forget getting information from Ashlan, she'd have to find another way to get off Neostar. Nothing was worth sticking around to see more people tortured or killed for something she didn't even understand. It was too dangerous for her to stay here longer. What if someone found out she has magic? She couldn't trust anyone. Not anymore.

The tents in the dome's marketplace seemed to get more confusing the deeper she got into the center. Some jutted further out, causing the shops to form alleys and passageways that filled with people well into the night. Workers crowded every free space, bartering for services and goods with one another. She spun around when she heard a loud yell behind her only to spot a woman arguing with a man over a grey shawl. Sid wasn't sure why the woman needed it; she was already covered in at least ten different pieces of fabric that twirled around her as she swayed her plump body from side to side. Next to them, a couple sipped two cups of red leaf broth over an intense conversation. She watched as the man brought the woman's hand to his lips and kissed it lightly and her cheeks burned hot at the touch.

Sid's eyes jumped from one neon-lit sign to another, trying to figure out where she was in the space. Her lips sounded the words as she read the signs one by one: dinner here, all night games, girls girls girls. She shook her head, trying to erase the lights flickering before her. There were too many options and none of them leading to any place she wanted to be.

"Magic," Sid read aloud, gawking at the bright red arrow on the sign. "Now we're getting somewhere."

Hot air whipped past her as she made her way through the tight alleyways, following the sign's direction. She saw another arrow and turned to pursue it further into the core. A few more arrows and she found herself in front of a dark tent entrance that didn't look to have a beginning or end. The circular tent stood in the center of the dome, its strangeness burdening the street. Something about the place made her feel more lost than found and she wondered why she felt relieved to have ended up here.

Sid took another deep breath and parted the tent's curtains.

The heavy fabric scratched against her skin as she passed through to the other side. Her breath caught in her throat for a brief moment, the new surroundings stopping her dead in her tracks.

What is this place?

Running a clammy palm against the tent's curtained walls, she couldn't help but notice the way the fabric — that looked like a dull sack from the outside — changed colors against her touch. It resembled the feel of the Starblade uniforms except this material glowed shades of orange and red. It looked like it was on fire.

Signs in a rainbow of colors shone above her head that led all the way down the oppressively dark corridor she found herself in. Each read the same message: Magic Here.

"At least I'm in the right place," she turned around, half expecting to see Fred on her heels but quickly remembered she'd come there alone.

Sid followed the signs that got brighter as she passed them to another large curtain, this one a deep shade of gold. When she reached out to touch the fabric, the magic in her stirred and the electricity jumped from her fingers and sparked along the edges of the curtain. She watched, wide-eyed, as the sparks twirled in circles before flashing out of existence. *Seriously, what is this place?*

Before she could take a step back and consider her options, the curtain yanked to the side and a tall, lanky Domer stepped in front of her. She stumbled back awkwardly and landed on her behind. The man was at least four heads taller than Sid and his bony shoulders blocked the entrance just enough that she couldn't see through to the other side. He surveyed her from head to toe, crossing his scrawny arms with some unease. Sid looked over his tunic, draping endlessly long to the bottom of his fitted pants but it was what covered his face that took her breath away. His entire face was concealed in a metal, sheath-like mask shaped like one of the winged creatures that were rumored to live in the jungles of Neostar. A pointed beak ran down the face of the mask all the way to his neckline. The mask covered every feature of the man's face except his eerily red eyes that shone brightly from the two large openings on either side of the beak.

"Dome number, name, and purpose of visit." The man grunted when Sid finally managed to get back up. He projected a screen from the interface box attached to his sleeve and started typing.

"Uhm, one twenty eight. Sid." She answered. Purpose? She didn't even know where she was let alone her purpose here. "Magic?"

The man glanced up from the screen then entered the information slowly. She was sure she messed it up somehow; that he would either throw her out or return her to the Starblade tents and ruin her cover. Sid got ready to flee, her back hunched down, eyes darting between the man and the exit curtain behind her. Instead, the man unfolded his arms and stepped aside, holding the curtain open for her to pass.

"Enjoy," he said lightly and closed the fabric behind her.

Sid wasn't sure how she was supposed to enjoy this place. The tent was like something out of a bad dream, bigger and darker on the inside. It was sectioned into small compartments, all closed off by dark, heavy fabrics. Behind each, she could see lights flickering that reminded her of the electricity she saw rush from her fingers when she first entered this place.

A curtain to her left flung open and Sid ducked into the shadows to avoid being seen.

A man walked out of the room, waving to someone with a grin on his face.

"Until next time, Gamon." A woman's small hand waved from inside the compartment and she heard a few more female giggles follow.

The man wavered towards her, tripping over something

on the floor and falling right into Sid. His clumsy hands reached in front to steady himself and the two of them barreled backward, crashing through the curtained wall of the compartment behind them. Sid's back hit something hard and she cried out in pain. Her hands reached back to grab hold of anything to keep from falling down to the floor with this fool of a man on top of her.

When Sid regained her balance, she looked down at the man whose hands were cupped perfectly around her breasts. Flushed, she shook with anger, stretching out her arm and pushing him off so abruptly that he slid across the floor before knocking into a large chair, losing his balance and falling to the floor.

His grin met her face before his eyes did. "Are you one of Serryl's girls?" He asked, teeth barred. "Make sure you're in my box next time, I like them full of fire like you."

Sid stepped forward, her fists ready to slam into the man's pointed chin, each hand already glowing with the magic rusting within her. His eyes widened in awe and he trembled, reaching for her with a shaky hand. She stepped back and shoved her hands in her pockets.

"You're," he said in disbelief, "you're-"

"You're burnt up, Gamon. Too much magic in one day. You saw nothing." A coy voice rang from the shadows next to her. "I suggest you leave before I have you thrown out."

Sid turned swiftly and focused on the shape of a woman in front of her who sat perched in a chair, wearing nothing but a translucent, skin-tight, red body suit. The woman's eyes were a beautiful shade of yellow and her long, white hair was parted harshly to the side to reveal the side of her head which was shaved down to the skin and covered in intricate drawings. Sid tried to make out the markings but the woman flipped her hair over before Sid had a chance to inspect them.

Lights shined through, backlighting the woman as she shifted her weight in her seat and four large projection screens came to life, glowing a bright pink with the word 'Magic" pulsing across them in white. The woman uncrossed her legs and Sid looked down shyly to prevent herself from seeing up her long, smooth legs. Above her curvy figure draped hundreds of wires that stretched from the center of the compartment in each and every direction.

"Energy tubes. For the boxes," the woman said as if in answer to Sid's silent question.

"Boxes?"

"All the little rooms in here. It's where," she paused, "where the magic happens."

"The magic in the tubes?"

"Exactly."

Sid's eyes narrowed and she followed the trail of tubes along the tent's ceiling. The lights flashing behind the curtains of the boxed rooms, the man's confused walk, his bewildered eyes when he saw her magic escape.

"You're stealing the ring's energy." She whispered.

"Can't steal what's already yours, kid." The woman got up and stretched out her hand, "I'm Serryl. The proud owner of this fine establishment."

"Sid," she reached out, carefully offering her hand in return. "You're stealing the ring's-"

"Yes, yes. You got it. We're stealing the ring's energy to use for our own entertainment. Very good, you're all caught up."

Sid stared, dumbfounded. "But that's not allowed. The queen-"

"The queen has no idea what happens in these domes. She's never even set foot in one herself. This place belongs to us and our magic belongs to us. All we're doing is taking some back and reusing it."

"For what?"

Serryl flipped her head back and laughed, "Oh, kid. For fun of course! There's nothing quite like a good jolt of magic when you've been left dry your whole life." She walked closer to Sid, grazing her exposed shoulder against Sid's suit. "Not that you have that problem, of course."

"What? What are you talking about? Look, I don't know what you think you saw but I have no idea what you're implying."

"Relax, kid. Your secret is safe with me. Although, one of these days, I'll definitely want to hear your story. And don't worry about Gamon either."

"I can trust *that* guy?"

"Oh, stars no." Serryl laughed again, her teeth a bright white against the pink glow of the box. "But he's much too addicted to the magic and to my girls to risk getting kicked out."

"Your girls?"

"And boys. The *other* reason people come to see me. There's a Magic in every dome. Because sometimes you need magic, but sometimes you just need someone to talk to. And enjoy." Serryl flipped her hair again and walked past Sid out of the box, her bare feet high on tip toes, making her full hips sway in exaggeration from side to side. "You coming?" She called over her shoulder and winked.

Reluctantly, Sid followed the barely clad woman out of the box and back into the tent's hallway.

She stayed close enough to Serryl to be able to latch on

in case someone attacked her from the back but far enough that she could run if the woman decided to turn on her. Her hands stayed at her sides, ready to electrocute anyone who came too close.

"Relax, kid. No one is going to hurt you here. We're all friends in Magic."

"Where are you taking me?"

"I'm not taking you anywhere. You're really all mucked up inside, aren't you? I might need to hear your story sooner rather than later," she winked again.

"Can you please tell me where we're going?" Sid asked, her voice shaking.

"Like I said, we're all friends here. But there's someone I think might be a better friend to you than others."

With that, Serryl swung open the curtain of one of the boxes, revealing a woman with her tunic half open, straddling a bare-chested man in a chair with an energy tube wrapped around his neck. The woman tugged at the tube and the man groaned in pleasure as she let the sparks of star magic fly across his chest. Breathless, the man turned his head and Sid noticed that he wore a similar mask to the tall man at the entrance, though his was more intricate in design with laces of metal running through it. A staggering waterfall projected on the curtain behind them with water so real, she could almost smell it. When the woman heard the sound of the curtain opening, she jumped back, tugging her tunic across her chest.

"For star's sake, Serryl! Ask to come in next time!" The woman waved a hand in front of a projection screen and the waterfall disappeared. She stepped back to tighten the belt of her tunic and that's when Sid saw her.

The woman from the telescreen reports. It was her.

Sid glared into her green eyes, hoping to find some form of recognition, a semblance of a memory but nothing came to mind. Something about this very short woman, with sharp green eyes and red hair shaved almost down to her scalp was familiar. Sid just didn't know how.

"Relax, Nyala. I brought someone to see you."

So that's your name. Nyala. Sid rolled it around in her mouth. So familiar.

The woman stepped forward, her eyes meeting Sid's. "It can't be!" She reached for her but Sid jumped back.

"Forgot to mention, this one's a little jumpy."

"Stars. Where have you been this whole time?"

Her voice was soft. So soft that Sid could hear it in her ears as she closed her eyes. Could see her green eyes watch over her before sleep took her. Could feel her strong arms reach around and tug her closer, into comfort and safety.

"Stars help us. You don't remember anything, do you?"

Sid shook her head and took another step back. "Remember what? Who are you? Who's *that* guy?" She pointed to the man with the bare chest still reclining on a chair behind Nyala. "Who are all of you people?"

"That one's mine, and he was just leaving." Serryl nodded to the curtain and the man picked up his discarded tunic and walked out without a word.

"And you?" She pointed a finger in Nyala's direction. The magic in her warmed the tip until it beamed a brilliant yellow.

"My name is Nyala," she said, then pointing to her hand, "well, at least he wasn't lying when he said he'll protect you from the chipping."

"Who? Colton? You knew Colton?"

"I knew the general quite well. Most of us Freedom Runners did. Most of all your parents."

The tears in her eyes clung to her lashes for only a moment before she blinked and let them rush down her cheeks. "You knew my parents?"

"Oh, darling, your parents were the greatest people I've ever met. They're the reason we're still fighting. Them and the promise of you coming back to us."

"What are you talking about? What's a Freedom Runner? Who are you people and how do you know anything about me? Or Colton?"

Nyala rested a cold hand on Sid's shoulder and she let it stay, hoping the touch would bring forth another memory but her thoughts remained bare. She was as blank as she had been before and even more confused now. How did this woman know Colton or her parents? What if she was lying and this was just a trap set by Queen Leona to bring her out of hiding? Sid didn't think the queen suspected her of dishonesty but perhaps her act wasn't as convincing as she thought it was? What if Ashlan betrayed her? From what she'd seen, the NSO would not protect her as Colton would have. The queen pulled all the strings and there was a good chance that if she knew about Sid, it would be her on the end of a lightline on her next visit to the throne room. She'd be the one waiting to be put down.

"This isn't the place to talk of these things." Serryl said and nodded to the curtain next to them. Light shone through the bottom slit as the session next to them commenced.

"She's right," Nyala agreed. "Irin, I don't know how you got here and why the general did not tell you anything about us or your past. What matters is that you're here, where you belong. You're home, Irin. And now we can finish what your parents started all those years ago. This place isn't safe to speak-"

Serryl cleared her throat, clearly offended by the comment but Nyala didn't seem to notice.

"Come to this flat tomorrow morning. We can speak there. I promise to tell you everything but for now you have to go. It isn't safe for you to be seen with me." She reached for an interface box in her tunic pocket and pulled up a projection of the dome. Her fingers swiped the screen and the dome's walls shattered to reveal the floor-plan of the flats. Pinching her index and thumb, Nyala zoomed in on a flat and tapped the screen. "You'll remember?"

Sid nodded. "Nyala?" She asked shakily.

"Yes?"

"Who's Irin?"

"That stardamned fool!" She hissed and her eyes turned a deeper shade of green, a sadder shade. "That's you, child. Irin is the name your parents gave you when you took your first breath."

Her head felt hollow and lighter, like it was in danger of drifting off her body and into the skies above. She tried to stay as still as possible, certain that one step would send her tumbling face first to the floor. More lies, more secrets, more reasons to get the muck off this star and away from these people. Her once clammy hands were dripping with sweat now and she tried to wipe off the moisture on her suit's pant leg. More of everything bad. But also more reasons to stay. To find out what they knew about her. To find out about the parts of her she never knew existed. They couldn't be that bad; Serryl saw her magic and hadn't called the Starblades. Yet. She could stay, meet Nyala tomorrow and find out everything she could. Between her and Serryl, one of them was bound to know where the original ships were kept, or at least know someone who might. She could press them for information, threaten to expose their little thieving exploits if they refused. Yes, that could work. It had to.

"I'll be there. As soon as I can get away."

"Where are you staying?"

"In the Starblades' tents. With Colton's son."

Nyala's eyes went blank.

"Don't worry, he doesn't know who I am. *I* don't even know who I am. And I can handle him."

"I'm hoping you'll have all the answers you need tomorrow," Nyala smiled.

That makes two of us!

She gave the woman a small nod and followed Serryl out of the box and back to the exit. She had one night to come up with an excuse to get away from Ashlan tomorrow. Her eyes traced the brightly lit letters above her head as she walked away and she couldn't help but laugh.

She sure could use some magic right about now.

TWENTY-TWO

GETTING AWAY from Ashlan and the Starblades was easier than Sid had anticipated. When she returned back to the tent they were sharing, he was already asleep. After a restless night with Ashlan snoring at the foot of the bed, she had enough time to come up with a plausible excuse not to join the group on their patrol today. It was more of a hunt than a simple patrol, and Sid used that to her advantage. She had told Ashlan that the incident with Connor and the Domer was more than she signed up for. Which wasn't quite a lie since everything thus far had been much more than she signed up. Sid put quite the show on, telling him she simply had to get away last night. That she spent all night walking around the shops and trying to clear her head, even adding a few tears for good measure. He seemed unsure at first but once she started bawling and shaking uncontrollably, he was more than glad to give her the day off the patrol. Going as far as offering to accompany her for the day. Before he pressed the matter, she assured him that all she needed was a day to herself. Domers did not get tangled up in the queen's business and she just wanted to make sure that she could return to her family unharmed and continue being the good little Domer she was. The lie slid off her lips like wild tree sap and by the time she was done, Ashlan was almost running out the door.

Which led her right to that moment, standing at the door of a flat on the seventh floor and debating her life choices.

Sid must have raised her white knuckled fist to the metal a dozen times before she actually mustered up enough courage to knock.

A small slit appeared at eye level and though she couldn't see through, she was certain Nyala was on the other side, inspecting to make sure Sid came alone. And she did. Sort of. She wasn't counting the droid that stood solemnly next to her like a dumbfounded bodyguard.

There was a ruffle behind the door and the slit disappeared as quickly as it came. Mere seconds later, the metal creaked and slid halfway open, letting Sid and the droid enter.

"And who's this?" Nyala asked, pointing to the droid.

"This is Fred. He's fine. Say hello, Fred. Don't be rude," she tapped on the screen and Fred raised his hand to wave. Slowly, so slowly Sid cringed from the discomfort of the interaction. She looked past Nyala, avoiding her questioning eyebrows and pushed her way inside. "So this place is safe then?"

"As safe as anything can be right now."

Nyala gestured for Sid to come in and she scanned the living quarters, though quarters was far more grandiose a word than Sid would have used to describe the space. The entire flat was no bigger than one of the boxes in Magic. There was almost no furniture except for two cots that looked very much unused in the corner, a table full of discarded food packages and another door that she hoped led to a bathing area.

"It's very," she said, "straight forward."

Nyala chuckled, "The one who lives here doesn't spend much time inside. It makes sense to move around when you're one of us."

"A Freedom Runner?"

"That's right. You remember."

"What exactly *is* a Freedom Runner?" She asked.

"It's kind of like those little Starblades you're surrounding yourself with." A gruff voice sounded behind her, "Except without the queen in their ear and living on the right side of the truth."

Sid nearly tripped over the droid's metal foot when she twirled to face the other person in the room. She thought Nyala would be alone and now not only did she bring another Domer in, but one that knew things about Sid. This was unacceptable. This was absolutely not what they agreed on. This was...

Stardaughter! He's beautiful.

Her mouth gaped and she was hoping in the name of the star that she wasn't salivating. She tried to keep her focus on the man's uncannily dark eyes and not let her gaze travel down past his full lips to his unfairly chiseled chest. Tried but failed. Sid noticed herself staring and looked down at her nails, suddenly finding them incredibly interesting. Anything not to notice the way the pale of his skin accentuated the deepness of his eyes and thick eyelashes.

"Tann," Nyala said, "this is our Irin."

"Who? Oh, right, that's me. I kind of go by Sid now. Hope that's alright. You can call me Irin if that's better but no guarantee I'll answer you. It's just, you know, not what my name is." *Mucking stars, stop babbling.*

Tann extended a strong arm, "Nice to meet you, Sid. I'll call you whatever you like."

How about 'darling'?

"Great, thank you." She shook his hand, holding it a little longer than was necessary, and backed away when she caught Nyala staring. "So this is *your* place?"

"Mine and my fathers. But we barely stay here. Him even less than me."

"Why?"

"I think Nyala will be filling you in on that part. I'm just here because I wasn't sure I believed it."

"Believed what?"

"That you're actually alive. That you came back."

"You knew me?" Her mouth was open again. Why couldn't she just keep her stardamned lips shut around this guy?

"Of course. We basically grew up together. I'm sorry, this must be a lot. We can talk about that some other time."

"No, no. It's alright, I don't mind. I'd like to know about both of you," she hesitated. "And about my parents. And Colton."

"The general?"

"Yes, the general, Tann," Nyala added sharply. "The man who saved and raised her."

"Right. Him."

She wasn't sure why, but Tann did not seem to like Colton much. By the end of the day, Sid was determined to find out more about what happened to her and how she came to live on a ship orbiting the star and not down here in the domes with this stunning specimen who was apparently one of her close childhood friends.

"So me and you were friends and you knew my parents?" She asked, hoping to steer the conversation back to Nyala.

"I more than knew your parents, child. I grew up in the same flat as your father. He was like a brother to me and your mother, well she was just the most amazing woman I've ever met. It's no wonder they ended up together. Greatness carries greatness."

"So what happened? If they were so great, why did they throw me away?"

"Throw you away? What on the star are you talking about?" Nyala looked genuinely shocked at Sid's question which made her head hurt and spin.

"Colton said they didn't want me. That he took me away so they wouldn't hurt me. That they wanted nothing to do with me."

"That stardamned brute fool! Of all the crazy things that man ever said, this has to be the worst of them all!" Nyala screeched.

"So he lied?"

"Well, of course he lied, child. Your parents loved you more than anything on the entire star. That's why when the chipping started, they fought to protect you. So you wouldn't end up like the rest of us."

"But why? Why give me away? Why throw me on some ship and never talk to me? I want to see them! I don't care if they don't want to see me, I want to see *them*!" She screamed. She was finally going to confront the people that left her alone and scared and living a pointless life on some rotting ship.

Nyala went silent and Tann only lowered his gaze and bit his bottom lip. *That lip!* She swooned. *Get it together, Sid! Now is not the time!*

It was a few moments before Nyala spoke again, her hands coming to grip Sid's in a fierce hold. "You cannot speak to them, Sid." She whispered, "You cannot see them because they're dead."

Sid's vision blurred and her stomach turned in so many rapid flips that she was sure she'd lose her breakfast any moment. She pulled away from Nyala's grasp and reached her hand back to find Fred's sturdy arm. As the familiar cool of his exterior reached her, she squeezed with all her might, careful not to fall over on the rigid floor beneath her.

"How?" She asked shakily.

"Right after Colton took you. He saved you but he couldn't save them. The queen's guards were too fast, too strong, and too many. And that was before she sent the Starblades in. Many of us died that day; your parents among them. I'm so sorry, Sid." She dropped to her knees in front of Sid, wrapping her arms around her legs. "They loved you so much! Everything they did was to protect you. To protect this star so you would have a future worth fighting for!"

Sid reached down and pulled Nyala to her feet. She wiped the tears from her cheeks and snapped her goggles over her eyes. "It's alright. Let's sit. Tell me how they died," she said, her breath hitched. "And tell me how they lived."

THE STORIES SID let Colton tell her on their calls were nothing like what she learned that day. Her parents weren't just Domers. They weren't just people that showed up and gave up their magic for the ring's grip. They didn't believe in the Circulum System, didn't believe it was the only way for them to share the star with Colton's people. They wanted a better life and they loved their magic too much to give it up. Sid still wasn't sure if that made them heroes or fools but it did make them one thing in the eyes of the queen's mother. They were rebels; Freedom Runners.

The Freedom Runners were a group of resistance fighters organized across several domes that had been trying to restore the equilibrium to the star's habitat. They did not believe in the chipping, thought it was a foul practice and one that made sure they could never leave the confines of the domes.

Nyala said that when the ring was first put in place, the Al'iil had no choice in the matter. Colton's people brought with them a technology that they couldn't fight. Arms and weapons that were stronger than all their magic combined and to stay alive, they had to agree to the queen's mother's plans for the star. To give up their magic for the sake of improving life for everyone. Or so they thought. It wasn't until years after the chipping that they realized the queen's mother had no intention of sharing the magic they had poured into her ring. She did it all to better the life of her own people, of her Citizens, and they were left in the dust. Forced to live in the cages of the domes and do her bidding. After a while, the conditions in the domes were lowered so greatly that the queen offered another exchange. A way for them to earn back some of their magic to help provide more adequate living solutions. To give more energy to the domes so they would have heat and running water, basic needs to survive. They could work for her, on a tightly timed schedule, helping her manufacture more technology and more machines. Help her grow her precious Neostar into the place it is today.

When the queen had a child, the Al'iil — who now had all but forgotten that name — prayed to the star that the girl would grow up to be a better leader. A better queen than her mother and someone they could reason with. Upon the queen's mother's untimely passing, Sid's parents went to her, begging for the chance to work together and a way for the Domers and the Citizens to live side by side.

"And what did she say?" Sid asked as Nyala told the story, though she had the notion she already knew what the answer would be.

"She all but laughed in their face. I'll never forget the way your parents looked when they returned that day. A young couple, in love, about to have a child. A child that would be chipped and live her life bound and shackled like the rest of us. Their hopes were shattered in a matter of one conversation. Leona had no plans to rule in any other way than her mother's. In fact, from what your parents could gather, she was going to be a much worse leader in the end."

"And they weren't wrong," Tann added.

"No, no they were not." Nyala continued, "It was that day, right there in their small flat in dome forty-eight that the Freedom Runners started. It was just a small group of us at first. Young kids trying to come up with schemes and plans to start a revolution. Your parents hid you from the queen and her guard, your mother gave birth to you in Magic; off the records and away from watchful eyes. You spent your entire young life hiding in a flat and we all made sure you stayed hidden. We were young and stupid then, thinking one child could save the star but that's what you do when you are young and have people you love depending on you. You make up tales and stories to stay strong. You stay alive. We called ourselves the runners because we would spend our days running from dome to dome before the ring made its turns to pass messages to one another. Spreading the word of better days to come. We had no idea what our feeble words would turn into."

"And my parents? What happened to them?"

"One day, a few years after you were born, we were close to getting more information on the Arcane. Information that could help us shut down the ring, once and for all. Your parents were so sure that this was it, the thing that would change everything. They didn't know Leona had been watching them for weeks, figuring out their every move. Where they ate, where they slept, who they talked to; who they loved. She planted false information for anyone who crossed their path, leading right into a trap. We were ambushed. So many died. I remember crawling through bodies to find them and when I did, I was horrified. The general himself was standing over them as your mother clutched you to her chest. I crept closer, trying to hear what they were saying but all I could see was your father dragging you out of your mother's arms and handing you to Colton. I screamed for them to stop, not to give you up when your mother reached out her hand to stop me. She told me it will be alright. That the general will save you and that one day, you'll save us all."

"And then what happened?"

"Then," Nyala sighed, "your mother asked him to kill them. To keep the secret of your whereabouts from the queen and anyone else that might do you harm."

"And?"

Nyala let a loose tear fall down her face and hit the top of her torn tunic. "And he did."

ONCE AGAIN, everything Sid knew was a lie. Another lie in an endless loop of misdirection. Can a lie that was a lie that was another lie still even be a lie? Or is there somewhere along the lines that it simply becomes the truth? Could this be *her* truth now?

An orphan that let the man who killed her parents raise her. A helpless fool stuck on a ship for years. These people thought she had come to save them, how was she supposed to tell them that it was her that needed saving?

Tann rested a hand on her shoulder and she remembered he was in the room. She was suddenly all too aware of it. How long had she sat there, stunned and silent? How long had she let him see her as the broken piece of scrap metal she felt like?

She shook off his hand and stood up. For a moment, she considered telling Ashlan everything. He was a Starblade and she shouldn't trust him but he was Colton's son. Her parents trusted Colton with her life and with their death.

Someone coughed behind her — Tann again — and she spun around to face him.

"You," she said with as much bravado as she could muster, "you're never here, right?"

"Uhm, yes, why?"

"That means you're out there? Doing that running thing?"

"Passing messages and building the army, you mean?"

"Yes, sure, that." She cleared her throat and looked

between him and Nyala. "Between the two of you, you must know quite a lot about where things are hidden here in the domes and in the city. And if not, you could find out, right?"

Tann looked at Nyala with worry.

"Why, child? What are you looking for?" Nyala asked.

"I want to know where the queen keeps the original ships. The ones that Colton's people came here on."

"Why do you need that?" Tann asked gruffly.

"Because I want an out."

"Sid, please. You can't."

"I'm not leaving, not yet. I will help you with this revolution of yours. As much as I can, though trust me when I say, it won't be much. But after that, I'm gone. I want nothing to do with this."

"You're kidding?" Tann roared, "After everything you've just heard, you're gone? Really, Nyala, let's go. This kid is a waste of time."

Excuse him? Sid's fire screamed within her. *Who the muck does this guy think he is? I'm a waste of time? I'll show you a waste of time!*

Before she could stop herself, her hands sprung in front of her and the magic in them propelled from her body in a ray of bright yellow light. The energy materialized as it left her body, picking up speed and looking for a target. Like all energy, it needed to ground itself to something. Sid watched horrified as the ball of energy shot straight at Tann, grazing his shoulder and missing him by a millimeter before burning a fist-sized hole through a cot and crashing into the floor tile. His body jerked to the side, whipping around from the hit. His arms went instinctively to the burn wound on his shoulder.

"Ow!" He yelled, then turned to her, eyes wider than the engine core on her ship. "How did you do that?"

"She's not chipped, Tann." Nyala said and nodded to Sid's neck.

"Yes, Tann, I'm not chipped. Keep up." She stuck her tongue out and looked at the gap in the cot. "Sorry about that."

"You should be, I sleep there. Sometimes."

"So do we have a deal?" Sid asked. She was so tired of making deals with people.

"You help us shut down the ring and we help you track down the original human ships?"

Human. So that's what they're called. Good to know.

"Yep," she nodded.

Tann's eyes found Nyala, who looked down and stayed quiet. He turned back to Sid, a brightness in his dark eyes she hadn't seen before. "Yes, magic girl. We have a deal."

TWENTY-THREE

THAT NIGHT, Sid dreamed of the queen.

Her triumphant smile with all teeth bared as she strolled down the core of dome nine in all her finery. Each tent she passed crumpled and fell, deteriorating in Leona's path and rotting before her eyes. She tossed and turned, sweat pooling on her brow as she saw small children run after the queen — eager to meet her — only to be met with the same hostile glare that Sid had seen in the throne room. When the children laughed giddily, the queen bent over, her smile unfazed. She whispered something to the young Domers and chuckled when they stood in line at her command. One by one, Leona tapped their foreheads and one by one they fell. Small bodies limp on the ground, disintegrating in moments like they had never existed. Sid screamed but no sound escaped her, her words a silent cry of agony that no one else could hear. She ran to the queen, her hands fisted and ready to strike. Two more steps and she would have her. Two more steps and...

Sid awoke to Ashlan slurping broth noisily at the edge of her cot, his eyes dancing with excitement when she opened hers and he pushed a bowl her way. The liquid was hot and burned going down but she was parched, her throat parched from silently screaming in her sleep.

"So how was yesterday?" Ashlan asked, arching his eyebrows so high she thought they'd tickle his hair line.

"Yesterday?"

Muck! Does he know? Who told him?

"Your day alone? To clear your head?"

Thank the stars.

"Oh, it was fine. Nothing spectacular. It was good to walk around and see another dome in action. I'm happy to be back though," she lied. She wasn't sure how she felt about being back in the Starblade tents but happy was not a word she'd use to describe it. Uncomfortable and itchy were a closer match.

Ashlan scratched the back of his head and peered up at her, eyes vivacious and bright. "Good, that you're happy that is. Not sure I've seen that yet," he grinned. "If you like it here, I'm about to make you even more ecstatic!"

"Oh?"

"We got a lead on the location of three more rebels. Two here and one in dome eighty three. I'm sending Connor and three more Starblades there and the rest of us will handle the two in this dome."

Two rebels. Two Freedom Runners. In this dome. The panic rose in her chest, her heart constricting like a light-line around her neck. They found out about Nyala and Tann and if they did, it could be all her fault. Perhaps she wasn't careful enough and he had her followed. Or Abbot had, she wouldn't put it past the general to distrust her enough to have her tailed. Her eyes felt like they started to sweat almost as much as her underarms. She tried to keep them focused on Ashlan's face, to decipher what he might know. Was he trying to trick her? Get her to say something to put holes in her story about yesterday and trap her into telling him what happened? She should just tell him the truth. Maybe if she did, he'd go easy on her. Though he wasn't the one she should be worried about. If news got back to the queen about her betrayal, the feeling of a lightline around her would become a lot more real than she'd like.

"We still don't know much. Just that there's at least two in this dome so we might be stuck here for a few more days."

Sid sighed in relief. It wasn't Nyala and Tann, at least not as far as they knew. "How many more days?"

"Like I said, we don't have much. There's some club in the center of the dome we need to check out. I'd rather not but it might lead us to their identities."

Magic. No! They can't go there!

"I'll come with you!" The words escaped her mouth like gas hissing through a leaky pipe.

"You? To the club? Didn't take you for the dancing type."

"Oh, keep quiet, Starblade! I'm not going for the dancing."

Ashlan puffed out his chest and winked her way, "Just for me then?"

"You wish!"

She rolled her eyes and punched him lightly on the shoulder. Why *was* she going with him? He was basically giving her an out, a reason to make up an excuse and to disappear from his sights forever. Instead, she did the exact opposite and made sure she was stuck with him for another few days.

Wait, do I want to be stuck with him? Stardaughter, please no! Not this guy!

Sid took a moment to look him over one more time. Her attention moving from his ruffled blonde hair, to his blue eyes and sharp nose — Colton's nose — down to the defined bulges of muscle under his perfectly prim Starblade uniform. When her gaze paused at the edge of his belt she had to shake herself back to attention. She couldn't possibly like this guy! He was obnoxious and rude and she didn't even know if she could trust him. If she should like anyone, it's Tann. Tann with his beautifully mysterious dark features. Tann who was like her and who was fighting for their people. Whether Sid felt like she belonged in the domes or not, this was her home. The home her parents died to protect.

So why is it that right now she wanted nothing more than to hold Ashlan's hand and tell him everything she learned about herself yesterday? Share with him the entire story of her life and spend hours on end finding out about his.

No! She couldn't like him! She couldn't trust him and that should be enough. And if Colton wanted her to trust his son, he would have told her about him. Though thinking about it now, Colton didn't even seem to trust her enough to tell her much at all.

"You sure you don't want to stay here?" Ashlan asked and she realized she had been staring at the stardamned edge of his belt this entire time.

Her gaze snapped up to meet his eyes, cheeks as red as an electrical fire. "I'm sure. And not for you, in case you're getting any ideas!"

She reached up for her goggles, ready to flap them back

over her eyes and end the conversation but Ashlan pressed his hand on her arm to stop her.

"Don't do that," he said in a voice so tender she wasn't sure he was himself anymore.

"Do what?"

"Hide those. Your eyes. You shouldn't hide them."

"I'm not hiding them!" She snapped back.

"Sure you are. And you shouldn't."

"Oh, and why the muck not?" She asked, noting the way he cringed at her cursing.

"Because they're beautiful. And they're who you are. You should never have to hide who you are."

Stars help me.

Sid blushed. No, Sid burnt and exploded from the inside out. At least that's what it felt like. Her hands instinctively reached back for the goggles but she stopped herself, choosing instead to fumble around in her pocket for her interface box. She aimlessly entered code sequences into the screen and somewhere behind her, Fred came alive in a jerky motion.

Sounds of metal feet trampling the floor rose from the back of the tent and Ashlan let out a belly laugh.

"Wow! You're really quite terrible at accepting compliments," he chuckled, looking past her shoulder.

She turned back to see the droid balancing his very heavy body on one arm with his legs outstretched in either direction. "Stardaughter! Fred! I'm so sorry!" She entered another code sequence and the droid flipped back to stand, oblivious to his recent gymnastics.

"Look, I didn't mean anything by it. It makes you uncomfortable. I'll stop."

"No," she blushed. "I mean, yes. It does make me uncomfortable but no, don't stop. If we're going to be friends, we should learn to be nice to each other."

"So we're friends now?"

Tann's dark eyes flashed in her vision.

"Yes, friends. And as a friend, I have to tell you, that outfit," she ran her finger up and down his body, "is not going to get you into Magic."

"So you're an expert on clubs now, are you?"

She mock flipped a lock of hair off her shoulders, "I'm an expert on Magic."

Ashlan laughed and the warmth of his cheer made her knees buckle.

"And what title should we give you, miss expert?"

A tiny electric current ran from her index finger to her thumb as she thought about his question. She made sure his eyes were locked on hers before she let her magic loose and felt the heat of it rush from her hands straight into her fast beating heart.

"Magic girl," she smiled, all teeth bared. "You can call me magic girl."

TWENTY-FOUR

SINCE MAGIC CLOSED its doors during the daytime hours, it was decided by the group that they would pay a visit to the club's owner after Starset, giving them the entire day to themselves. Ashlan had retired to the tents, eager to catch a few hours of sleep before the evening. According to him, one never knew what could be waiting for them on the other side of the club's curtains. But Sid knew and she had every intention of warning Serryl before the queen found out that she'd been siphoning magic right under her nose.

When she was convinced Ashlan was fast asleep, she decided to make her way to Tann's flat, relieved she didn't need to lie again to get away. She was even more relieved to be away from Ashlan and the confusing thoughts she had about him throughout the day. This was the wrong time to be confused. Sid still had no clues as to where the original ships might be and having feelings for some boy, a Starblade even, was not helping matters one bit.

She took one last glance at his sleeping form and

frowned at the warmth spreading over her legs from just looking at him.

Stupid, dumb, Starblade!

With ardent, silent steps she pitter pattered her way out of the tent and into the confined freedom of the dome.

It took Sid the better half of an hour to find her way back to Tann's flat. She got turned around between the shop tents so many times that she actually ended up right back where she started. Twice. Asking for directions was out of the question so she had to trust that somehow, she would figure it out on her own. Her feet had swelled to twice their size by the time she reached the flat's door, the skin rubbing against the plastic of her boots and causing unbearable blisters to form.

Tann opened the door with a smile and stars help her, he wasn't wearing his tunic. What was going on in this dome? Was every man in her life dead set on distracting her today?

Eyes to the floor, she pushed her way into the flat.

"You need to get me in touch with Serryl. It's important!" She shrieked before noticing the four other people in the room.

"Important how?" The man standing in the far corner of the flat asked. He had the same dark skin and eyes as Tann though he was definitely older. Somewhere in his forties Sid reckoned.

Tann stood beside her and gestured to the man. "Sid, this is Edek, my father. Father, this is the girl I told you about. The one with magic."

The man took a few steps forward and Sid shrank, hiding her hands in her pockets. She was furious with Tann for telling his father about her magic. It wasn't his secret to tell and he should have asked her first. Though she was starting to think that perhaps everyone in the domes knew about her and it enraged her. First it was Abbot watching her every move, then Ashlan asking her what she's doing each minute he was near her, now Tann disregarding her opinion about her own magic! It was as if everyone in Neostar thought they knew what was best for her even though none of them knew her at all. She was fed up with all of it.

"Why are you telling your dad and the rest of these people about my magic?" She snapped. "I never agreed to this, Tann!"

"Edek is the lead command for the Freedom Runners. He's our leader. Mannar," he pointed to a short, stout man with yellow eyes and a bald head, "is his second in command. The redhead on the cot is Lexia. She's one of our top runners. And you already know Nyala. Everyone in this room is integral to our success in taking out the ring and they all knew you since you were born; whether you like it or not."

She rolled her eyes and crossed her arms. "I *don't* like it."

"I know. But it is what it is."

There was a long moment of silence before Edek finally spoke and Sid let out the breath she'd been holding. "So you're Kiril and Gaya's daughter? You've gotten big."

Kiril and Gaya. The names rolled off his lips so easily that she could almost see them taking shape. Her heart felt bigger somehow just by hearing him say them out loud. Kiril and Gaya: her parents. The people who died to keep her from being chipped. Who died for her magic. She wished she could go back in time. Tell them it isn't worth it, that their lives are not worth her magic, that she's not worth it. Instead, she settled for the comfort of knowing their names and that they didn't throw her away. They loved her enough to die for her and she owed it to them to at least help the people continuing to fight for their cause.

"I grew up," she noted sternly.

"Quite the looker too, just like your mother." Lexia sang, "She was always the prettiest girl around. Eyes just like yours, could see straight through you." She picked up a bright green berry from a bowl and tossed it into the air, snapping her jaw shut around it as it fell.

"You helped my parents too?"

"We all did." Mannar said, "Owe them our lives."

"And our futures," Edek added.

Another uncomfortable silence fell over the flat and Sid decided to break this one herself. "So you knew my parents and you know about my magic. I'm assuming Tann also filled you in on what I want in return for helping you take care of the ring?" She shot Tann a nasty glare and he looked away sheepishly.

"He did. Though I'm still not sure why you'd want to leave after we destroy the ring and free the domes."

"Because I just do."

"That's not really an answer, child," Nyala noted, speaking for the first time since Sid arrived.

"Well, it's the only answer I've got. Those are my terms. Tann agreed to them and I'm hoping you will as well."

She looked from face to face and waited for each of them to nod. "Good, So where do we start?"

"First, we need to know how much magic you have without the chip."

"Sure."

"So what is it you can do?"

The stability she was just starting to gain back shattered into pieces inside her. She felt like she had swallowed a bag of broken glass. Sid had no idea what she could do, in fact, she'd spent her entire life trying not to do it at all. She knew if she was going to help the Freedom Runners, she'd have to use her magic eventually but the idea was so vague in her mind that it barely sank in. Sometime, and soon, she'd need to use her magic against anyone that tried to get in her way. The queen's guard, the Starblades, maybe even the queen herself. Horror pinched at the lining of her stomach.

Ash.

She couldn't hurt him herself, though she imagined simply knowing that she had magic in the first place might do enough damage. For some reason unbeknownst to Sid, he seemed to trust her. The idea of breaking that trust hurt her more than she expected. There had to be a way to help the Freedom Runners and still keep him safe. Keep everyone safe that didn't deserve it. And as far as Sid was concerned, no one deserved to be hurt. At least not by her, not by some imposter that crash landed on their star in a pathetic attempt to find Colton. A girl who had no idea what they've been through. A kid that spent her entire life wishing she could live in a misguided dream amongst the humans. She had no right passing judgment, she didn't even know which side she was on.

"How much magic do you have?" Edek asked again.

She thought about his question, "You tell me."

"You don't know what you can do?"

"I wasn't allowed to use my magic. Ever."

Edek's eyes found Nyala's who shrugged casually. "Colton kept her in the dark about all of this. He thought he was protecting her."

"That foolish, stubborn son of a– "

"That's enough, father!" Tann interfered. "We're not

here to judge how Sid was raised. He kept her safe, that's what matters."

She whispered a quiet thank you his way and could see him nod in her peripheral.

"Fine. I'll keep my opinions to myself but if we have any shot at winning this, we need to figure out how much she can do. And fast."

"Well, I'm still here for a few more days at least. I can try to sneak out as much as I can and we can test me out. We'll need to find a secluded place. Like I said before, I haven't really used my magic so I'd want to keep a safe distance from people. Just in case."

"In case you fry us all to bits?"

"She'd be more at risk of frying herself if she doesn't have control over it," Mannar said.

"What? How?" Sid's head jerked to him in shock.

"You have to learn to control the electric current running through your body. Know how to ground it. Too much of it can burn you from the inside out. It's kind of like our version of-"

"Amperfuge," she whispered.

"So you do know some things about this place."

"I kept up to date. But I knew about Amperfuge from Ash. His mom-" she stopped, eyes as wide as Jericho. "Oh, stardaughter! Ash!"

"The Starblade?" Tann asked and she tried not to smile at the bitterness in his tone.

"Yes, the Starblade! That's why I came here in the first place! They have a lead. Someone tipped them off to Magic and they're going to be raiding it tonight. They think they'll find Freedom Runners there. We need to warn Serryl! Now!"

Their calm expressions confused her. Here she was, almost breathless with worry and the five of them stood around like it was any other day of the week. Was Lexia grinning? What was wrong with these people? Magic was about to get raided and they didn't have a care in the stars!

"Did you hear me? They're raiding the club!"

"We heard you, child." Nyala said calmly and rested a hand on her shoulder. "I wouldn't worry about it. Serryl has plenty of measures in place for moments just like this."

"She does?"

"Of course! How do you think she's been able to keep these places hidden from the queen for so long? The club will be fine. Serryl too."

"I'd be more worried about your magic than hers," Edek said.

Sid sat down on the cot, resting her chin in her hands. She started to reach for her goggles but held back, remembering what Ashlan said that morning. *Don't hide who you are.* If only it was that easy! The only thing Sid knew how to do was hide. She wished she could be hiding right now instead of sitting here in the flat of a Freedom Runner about to help mastermind a plan that might get them all killed.

She ran her fingers through her short hair, hiding her face away from the group.

Hiding for just a little while longer.

TWENTY-FIVE

"HEY, SID! WAIT UP!" Tann ran to catch up with her down the winding steps leading to the floor below. "You want some company?"

Not really, she thought. All she wanted was a break from everyone to get food and clear her head.

"Or I can just mind my mucking business and leave you alone," he smiled and she melted.

"No, it's fine. I'm going to try and find some food if you want to join."

"I can always eat! Come on, I know a pretty good spot!"

His hand reached out and she reluctantly wrapped her fingers around his and let him pull her faster down the steps. His grip was strong and she could feel each callous bump on his palms brush up against her own. Unlike Ashlan, his hands were rough and strong and permanent somehow. She squeezed her palm tighter, testing the distance between them and flushed when he squeezed back. Maybe this is what home was supposed to feel like. Strong and pushy and warm.

They were already down to the second floor when Tann stopped in his tracks and turned to face her. His fingers still looped around hers. His dark eyes gazed down, as though she could read his mind and this was the best way to shield himself.

Sid let him brood for another brief moment, then snatched her hand back and slapped him across his chest. Even beneath his thick tunic, she could feel a wall of muscle meet her palm.

"For star's sake! Out with it! What's going on?"

"Nothing bad," he said, eyes still on the floor. "I was thinking about what you said. About leaving."

"What about it?"

"I don't get it." He shrugged.

"Don't get what? We find the ships, I take some parts, fix my pod, shoot up out of here and that's the end of it." She hoisted her fist in the air to sign the motion in case he still wasn't getting it.

"That's not the part I don't get. I know how ships work."

"So what's the problem?"

"The problem is that I don't understand how you can just abandon us like that. Your own people."

Sid scrunched her nose in annoyance. "Uhm, until a few days ago, I didn't even know I had my own people."

"Well, now you do."

"Doesn't change anything."

"How could it not change *everything*?"

She wanted to make him understand it, how confused she felt all the time. Every minute of every day was like a waking dream. She was here but she wasn't. He couldn't possibly know what that could feel like. He knew who he was and who he was supposed to be. He knew which side he was on. Knew his own family. How could he even imagine what she was going through? She wanted to scream at him. To tear at his skin and beat at his annoyingly strong chest. She wanted to tell him that she's scared and that she can't stay because if she did, she wasn't sure which side she'd pick to fight for. That she's not the girl they all thought she was and that if he knew her, *really* knew her, he might not like her so much. She wasn't even sure she liked herself these days.

"I just can't stay. You need to accept that."

"And if I can't?" He demanded, his eyes a dark well of fury and probing.

"Why?" She shouted, her fists beating at his chest, tears pooling beneath her lids. "Why can't you accept it? Why can't everything go back to how it was? I just want to go home! Stardaughter! Just let me go home!"

He grabbed her shoulders and squeezed, the warmth of his touch spreading across her body and making her legs numb. "You *are* home, Sid. Here, with us; it's where you belong."

"With you?"

"Yes, with me," he smiled, teeth whiter than Jericho's glow.

Sid finally blinked and the tears sitting in wait behind the cages of her eyelids ran freely down her cheeks, leaving lines of clean on her dust-covered face.

And then she did it.

Pushing herself to her tip toes, she wrapped her arms around his neck and pulled him closer. Her face reached up and she closed her eyes, bringing her lips to his.

Sid had never kissed anyone, unless she counted the time she tried to practice with her own reflection in the shiny doors of her ship's dock. This was nothing like that time. For starters, when she opened her eyes just a smidge, it wasn't her own grey eyes that stared back at her. Another notable difference for Sid was the taste. Tann's plump lips had none of the metallic flavor that her first kiss carried. A taste Sid couldn't wash off for days after; the drawbacks of locking lips with an aluminum doorframe. His lips tasted like a mixture of heat and salt and she couldn't get enough of them.

Sid was so absorbed in the moment that she didn't even notice the stiffness of his back or the way his hands didn't move to wrap around her waist. By the time she realized she was kissing a statue, it was too late. Tann's face had already taken on a state of shock, his arms so rigid at his sides that it was a wonder he didn't pull a muscle from the strain.

She let go of his neck and slowly placed her full weight back on her heels. *What's wrong with him? Did he break? Did I do it wrong?*

"I'm sorry, I didn't mean to surprise you like that. I thought that... Well, I don't know what I thought."

"It's fine, Sid. It's not you. It's-"

"Please don't say anything else. I misread the situation. You don't need to explain."

"I really feel like I should," Tann rubbed the back of his neck like he was trying to get rid of a dirt patch. "You caught me off guard and I wasn't expecting-"

"Stop," she commanded. "I don't need an explanation. Let's move on and pretend this never happened."

"Are you sure?"

"Very, very sure. Listen, I should probably get back to the Starblade tents. I've been gone for a while. Can't have them wondering where I'm off to all the time. Make sure you tell Serryl about tonight if you see her. Just in case."

"Sid!" Tann called after her but she was already running.

Cheeks hotter than the rush of magic surging through her veins. She felt like a fool. No, worse than a fool — she felt like a complete, mucking idiot. Why did she do that? Out of all the things she could have done in that situation, why did she think kissing him was the best idea?

Electricity buzzed within her, rising from the balls of her feet to her thighs as she ran, taking two steps at a time until she reached the ground floor of the dome. She couldn't breathe, couldn't think, couldn't anything. Her blood bubbled under her skin, pumping massive bouts of energy all through her. It was as though her body wasn't hers anymore. She was running but she couldn't feel her limbs. Something else had control now.

Sid rushed past the shop tents, signs flickering on and off in her wake. Her body moved instinctively, like a creature held back for too many years that finally got a taste of open air. She breathed in, pulling the energy from the lights around her into her body. Sucking them dry.

People clamored out of the shops, their eyes dazed and confused, watching as sign after sign flickered and died. Their gazes followed the maddening ball of fury with short white hair and glowing grey eyes barreling through their Dome.

She could hear the whispers but words did nothing to stop her. Nothing could stop her now.

A man grunted somewhere in the distance and a few seconds later, a large metal chest slid into her path. She looked around and found the one responsible, hoping it would be Tann so she could show him exactly how he made her feel. Rejected. Pathetic. Alone.

It wasn't Tann. Just a shop owner that had more fear in his eyes than someone readying for an execution. He was scared of her. They were all scared of her.

Muck them!

Sid pooled her magic into a single, linear thought and directed it at the chest resting in her way. She stretched her arms toward it, pushing the concentrated electrical current forward with everything she had. The current ripped through her body, glowing a pulsing yellow when it broke free of her skin. It flew at the chest, hitting it head on and shattering the metal casing like it was nothing more than air.

Wide eyed, she watched as the current levitated in front of the wreckage for a moment before altering its projection and slicing back in her direction. She started to duck out of the way but it was too late, the current she created smashed into her body, knocking her flat on her back. Sid patted her stomach where she was hit, convinced there'd be a current-sized hole right in the center of her. But she was fine. She was better than fine; she felt energized. Like the current had powered her up somehow.

She jumped to her feet and looked over the marketplace. The tents that still had lights on were closing their curtains, hiding from her like she had come delivering death itself to their doorstep. A child cried to her right and she spun around to see a young girl of no more than five crouching behind a table full of dumpling samples.

"It's alright," she whispered, hands outstretched in surrender, "I won't hurt you."

The girl looked up at her through teary eyes. "*What* are you?" She asked with a trembling voice full of fear and confusion.

"I don't know," Sid answered. "I really don't know."

She turned away from the girl, snapped her goggles over her eyes and ran in the direction of the Starblade tents. She wanted nothing more to do with the Domers, or Tann, or even her own magic. There was a reason Colton told her not to use it. Magic was bad. Magic hurt people. Magic made you a monster. Sid didn't want to be a monster. What she wanted was to be normal, like Colton was. She wanted to be human.

Running faster, she made her way past the judging eyes of the people around her. Away from everyone that made her feel like she was different, like she didn't belong. Tears collected in puddles on the inseam of her goggles and she lifted them off her face to let the saline drain down. She couldn't breathe, she couldn't think, but she could run.

Sid ran faster than she'd ever had to, lights buzzing and dying as she flew by them.

Until every bit of the dome's core was dark.

TWENTY-SIX

ASHLAN'S EYES narrowed to near slits and she strained to
see the blue in them shine through. He sat on the cot in the
tent with arms crossed tightly over his chest, enraged. She
started to inch towards him but stopped short. It was best to
leave a bit of distance in case she needed to make a run for it.
Behind her, her index finger tested the slit in the opening of
the tent's curtains, gauging how fast it would take her to
barrel through it.

"I can't believe you! I trusted you, Sid! And what? You're
meeting with the enemy this entire time. How could you?"

By the time she made it back, he was already awake and
waiting for her impatiently. Outrage coated his face in a
steady shield while he tinkered with the droid's visual
recordings on the screen. As it turned out, she wasn't as good
at sneaking out as she thought and when he couldn't find her,
he pulled up the droid's recordings from the last few days to
get an idea on her location. What he found was a lot more
than just her GPS coordinates. The droid's cameras recorded
her first interaction with Tann and Nyala, capturing every-

thing to the last gritty detail. She looked over the footage with a frown, noting how friendly she seemed with the people Ashlan resented to the core. The only thing saving her were the broken internal speakers that she never got a chance to tinker with. Ashlan could see her but he couldn't hear a word. At least the secret of her magic was still safe.

Thanks for the help, Fred.

If he didn't know about her magic, she might still have a chance of persuading him to stay quiet about this. Though even if he didn't detain her, she had no idea what he might do with the Freedom Runners. Colton's son or not, he was still a Starblade.

"Oh, now you're finally quiet? No smart retorts?" He scoffed, "Why are you meeting the rebels? Are you a part of all of this somehow?"

"I'm not a part of anything!" She yelled back. "And how do you even know they're rebels? That's quite a judgement call to make."

"Because this one right here," his finger tapped at Nyala's frozen face on the footage reel, "has been linked to every attack on the trains so far. You want to tell me I'm wrong? Lie some more?"

She kept quiet. *So they have clued in.*

"Fine. They're rebels," she slouched and rolled her eyes, "but it's not what you think."

"And what is it that I think, Sid? Please enlighten me!"

"You think I've been helping them this entire time and lying to you and that's just not true."

Technically, not a lie. All good.

"So what is true?"

"I met them, yes. But only because I was curious. I

wanted to know why. You know how I feel about us Domers helping to save the star, helping the queen. I only wanted to know what would make someone change their mind. Make someone want to hurt people. I just don't understand it. I thought if I could listen to their point of view, I could talk them out of it somehow."

"Talk them out of it? They're rebels, Sid! You can't talk them out of anything!" His voice boomed over the fine folds of the tent's fabrics and she wondered how many people were outside and close enough to hear him. Was Abbot there? Did he know about this too?

"Stop yelling at me, Starblade! I haven't done anything wrong!"

Yet.

"You haven't done anything wrong?" He shouted, "Are you kidding? You did literally everything wrong, Sid! I should report you! I should have you detained!"

A knot twisted in her stomach. He really should do all those things — so why wasn't he? Something about all of this felt different. If he wanted to have her detained, she'd already be on her knees with a lightline tight against her throat. Maybe he hadn't made up his mind and if that was the case, she still had a chance to get out of the situation.

"Ash, please, listen to me. I didn't mean anything by it. I'm not on their side, you know me."

"I don't know anything about you!"

"Yes, You do. You know that I'm the girl that put her entire job on the line to help you fix your blade."

"After you broke it," he scoffed under his breath.

"Yes, after I broke it. But if I was really a rebel like you're saying, what would I care about your stardamned blade?"

She dared to glance his way. "I'm also the girl that came here with you in case you needed help."

"At the order of the queen!"

"Again, if I was a Freed-" she stopped herself quickly, "a rebel, why would I care what the queen wanted?"

"I don't know. To trick me, to get closer to me so you can plan your little schemes."

She stifled a laugh, "To get closer to you? Really"

"Not like *that*! You know what I mean."

"I do and it still wouldn't add up. If I was truly a rebel, don't you think that the minute I got into the throne room and saw Queen Leona I would at least *attempt* to assassinate her? The last thing I'd do, if I *was* a real rebel, is come here to help you hunt down the rest of my supposed team. I mean, it's so farfetched it's actually funny!"

His gaze shifted, eyes deepening to a shade of blue that reminded Sid of a night sky on a warm day. Dark and endless.

This is not the time, Sid!

"So you're actually expecting me to believe that while you snuck away to spend time with the exact rebels we are trying to hunt down, you were simply trying to understand their point of view so you could change it?"

"Well, when you say it that way, it does sound really foolish."

"It is really foolish and probably a lie."

"It's not a lie. I wanted to get to know them."

Again, technically not a lie.

"And did you? Get to know them?"

"Sort of."

"And?"

The next thing she said could make or break everything.

She could lie and tell him that she managed to sway their opinion and stop their rebellion but that would only put him in danger. She could tell him that they didn't listen to her or that she didn't get enough information about the next hit. She could, of course, always tell him the truth. About all of it. The Freedom Runners, her parents, Colton, her magic.

Sid's heart ached to talk to him. Despite being a Starblade and a tremendous pain in her behind, Ashlan was also kind-hearted and more than that, he was Colton's son. There might be a chance that he would be sympathetic to the Freedom Runners' cause if he knew his father had been. That he had saved her to help them. There was also the chance that she didn't know anything at all and he would betray her before she could part the tent's screens to escape. She couldn't take that chance, no matter how slim she thought it might be. There were too many lives on the line. Not just hers and Tann's — but everyone else on Neostar. All of them would be at risk if the queen knew she still had magic.

Whether or not she trusted Ashlan was not the problem at hand. She didn't trust herself enough to know which side she'd choose if it came down to it.

"They're not who I thought they were," she said finally. "I never should have gone."

"You need to tell me exactly where you met them. I want every detail. Names, facial features. Stars, I want to know what their favorite food is if you know it!"

"I can't tell you that."

"Excuse me?" His eyebrows arched and the look of distain on his face was enough to make her want to hurl.

"They're not who I thought they were but they are still

people. They're *my* people. I can't sentence someone to death just because you need answers!"

"*Your* people? You can't be serious! You want to know what *your* people were doing while you were off on your little rendezvous?"

What was he talking about? The Freedom Runners weren't doing anything. If something was planned they would have let her know at the flat. She shook her head in confusion, a dull ache forming behind her eyes.

"There was an attack in this dome's core. Someone had tampered with the power in the shop tents. Every business in the dome is shut down for repairs indefinitely and the first four floors of the flats are down too. It seems *your* people care more about hurting the queen than their own kind. If we can't get the power back up, half the dome's population could freeze to death overnight."

Sid's head wailed. That wasn't the Freedom Runners! She wanted to shout, that was all her! She was the one that killed the power in the dome. She was the one that caused the businesses to shut down. She was the one that put the people of those flats in danger. The pudgy face of the little girl flashed before her eyes. Children; she put children in danger.

"Will they be alright?" She asked, voice trembling enough that she barely formed the words.

"I've called for more Starblades to come in and bring supplies. We're setting up temporary tents on the upper floors. It won't be comfortable but we can keep everyone warm until the ring's next rotation. We'll redirect the power to the dome once it passes and kick the power back in."

"Thank you."

"You don't have to thank me, Sid. Just open your stardamned eyes and figure out what you're dealing with here. These people need to be stopped before they destroy Neostar."

"I thought you weren't a fan of the queen's way of ruling?" She asked.

"I'm also not a fan of kids dying of hypothermia. The queen isn't my biggest worry right now."

"What would you do if you were me?"

He turned away from her, eyes still darker than death. "I would tell the truth."

"Even if it got people killed?"

"Only those that deserve it."

"And who decides who deserves it, Ash? You? Me? Leona?"

He stilled for a moment before walking past her to exit the tent. "Those of us who aren't willing to kill to get our way." He said quietly and walked out.

The tents taut curtained walls felt like they had crept in on her, their fabrics slowly moving closer to her body until she was sure they were grazing the dirty edges of her boots. She couldn't breathe. Struggling to unzip the top of her suit she slouched over her knees, taking shallow gasps of air. How did she get here? To this point where the survival of so many people rested on her small shoulders. She wasn't cut out for this. No one could be, let alone someone that was a complete stranger to this world.

In that moment, Sid hated Colton. Hated his lies for all those years. Hated that he had kept the truth about who she was from her. Hated that the reason she was in this mess was because of him.

Neostar was by far the worst place she'd set foot on —

and she'd once set foot in a puddle of her own excrement when the ship's sewage pipes exploded in the engine room.

She needed to get out of here. Leave Ashlan and Tann and the Freedom Runners behind. Leave the stardamned queen to do her bidding as she pleases. This wasn't her home; it hadn't been for years and she was a fool to think it could ever be anything of the sort. Her home was in the stars, orbiting around this sad place, safe and very far away.

Sid didn't care about the deals she made; not with Ashlan and not with Tann. The only thing she cared about was getting her life back to normal. She could figure out where the ships were kept on her own, without having to worry about which side of the war she was on. It wasn't even her war to fight in the first place! Let them have their star. Let them kill each other over it. She was done!

Parting the flap carefully, she peered outside, surprised that Ashlan didn't have someone watching her. There were two Starblades in one of the tents to her right but they seemed to be busy with a game of some sort, neither looking in her direction. This was her chance to get away for good.

With a quick glance at Fred, slumped in the corner of Ashlan's tent, she parted the curtains and made her way out. The darkness she had wreaked upon the dome was a perfect cover for her escape.

There was only one thought on her mind as Sid made her way out of the dome and back into the jungle. *Muck this place and everything that came with it.*

TWENTY-SEVEN

DARKNESS SET ON THE POD, bringing with it a night's chill that dug its claws through Sid's bones until she found herself curled in the control seat with chattering teeth. She had already started to miss the climate controls in the domes and towers when her stomach gurgled and growled. Looking for food was pointless, there was nothing in the pod that could keep her alive for long periods of time. Why didn't she think to bring supplies with her? She was so eager to get out of the dome that she didn't even consider what spending the night in a powered down aluminum capsule would mean. If she didn't freeze to death by Starise, she'd likely pass out from starvation. Then freeze to death in her sleep.

There was no way to tell this story that didn't end with her freezing to death.

Great, just perfect.

With Jericho's light tucked away for the evening, the jungle around her was dark and menacing. Light from the two moons above cast shadows from the surrounding trees in jagged angles and patterns which made Sid feel like she was encased in a prison of pure darkness. Locked away behind shadowed bars for crimes she was yet to commit, if she hadn't already. According to the queen, the stunt she pulled in the dome was a crime punishable by, well, Sid had no idea what but she was certain that whatever it was, it couldn't be all that pleasant.

The cold air bit at her skin, taking chunks out of her will to keep her eyes open. She tried to focus on the jungle outside, tried to stay awake as long as possible for fear of not waking up again. But her thoughts pulled her inward. Toward Ashlan and Tann, toward the Freedom Runners and the domes, toward Leona.

Sid could all but see the rancid smile on her face. The same smile she wore when she killed the Domer in her throne room; a Domer Sid was convinced she must have known as a child. It seemed there were many people that knew her and her parents and she wished for nothing more than to find them. To get at least one step closer to finding out who she was and who her parents were.

"Stardamned, foolish Colton," she cursed under her breath.

Was it really necessary to hide the truth from her? What would she do if she found out? Hop in a pod and barrel her way down here at the first chance she got?

Sid could almost laugh at the irony. In the end, truth or not, that is exactly what she did.

"Way to do everyone zero good at all, Colton." She shook a fist in the air, noticing the dull, blueish tone her skin had taken on. "I'm down here anyway and somehow in the middle of the nonsense you and your Freedom Runners started. You should have warned me!"

Tears froze on her lashes and she rubbed at their edges

furiously to keep her face warm. The heat from her hands burnt but the sharp pain was welcome just to keep from freezing. Sid clapped her hands together and watched as her magic snapped in response. The tiny sparks of electricity surged at the edges of her skin and flew in bursts of light as they clashed with one another.

She kept clapping; lips curled into a smile to inspect the light show she was putting on.

"Hang on..."

An idea sparked in her. The lights and electricity she was creating, she could use that. Her magic was finally going to be helpful for a change!

She remembered the way she was able to collect the energy from the lights in the shop tents, all she had to do was redirect her own energy to flow outward. She's done it before, just enough to heat metal but maybe if there was no receiving end, the magic would flow out of her. Enough energy around her could keep the pod warm and keep her alive. It was worth a shot in the least.

Rubbing her palms together speedily, she let the energy leave her body. The warm, yellow glow surrounded her and she could already feel herself warming up. Her skin tingled when rogue electric sparks made contact with it but she kept going, kept letting the magic spread out in a cocoon of energy and heat.

Before long, Sid had the entire pod glowing and emanating heat that rolled off her skin and into the metal casing of the pod. The trick was to warm the metal just enough to provide the comfort of a hot pod but not so much that it melted the exterior. The last thing she needed was her only home melting in the middle of the jungle.

After practicing with a few controls of her inner electrical current, she had the magic and the pod's temperature perfectly tuned. She was even starting to sweat a little.

She wished Ashlan and Tann could see her. Wished they could be here with her so she could have someone to talk to. Even Fred would be good company at the moment. Sid felt a pang of guilt tug at her heart that she hadn't once wished that she was back on her ship. It wasn't that she didn't miss the familiarity of the Arcturus but something about the idea of being completely alone again felt dirty and wrong. How could she walk away from everything she'd learnt in the last few days? She couldn't. No matter how much she may have thought she wanted to, Neostar was important to her now. Not in the same way it was when she worshipped it from afar and memorized its customs through holographic lesson plans. It was important because it was a part of her. It always had been and it simply took her a bit of time to get here. To get back to herself.

As she recounted the events of the past days, she let herself stretch out in the seat. Her feet dangled off the edge and her goggles fogged from the magic around her.

Within moments of closing her eyes, Sid slept.

And as she slept, the pod glowed a bright yellow in the midst of the dark jungle, a beacon in the night.

SOMETHING POKED at her ribs and Sid jolted awake. For a moment, she had forgotten where she was, and opening her eyes to see only the fogged glass of her goggles did not help orient her in the slightest.

She tried to reach up to take them off but something was holding her down. Sid wrestled against the restraints, shuffling in the seat and kicking her feet in every direction. Whatever had a hold on her was strong, too strong. *The beast she met before? No, not even close.*

"Let me go!" She screamed.

The fear that rushed through her made her lose control of her magic and she could already feel the cold air return into the pod. Sid didn't mind, she didn't need it to be warm right now. What she needed was to get loose from whatever had her trapped.

She bucked and shouted and kicked but nothing worked. Her heart raced and she could feel sweat soaking the curve of her lower back but she couldn't stop trying. As the heat left the pod, droplets of water ran down the front of her goggles, slowly bringing the space back into focus.

Rapidly shaking her head, she tried to coat as much of the glass in wetness to get a good look at what else was in the pod with her, at what it was that had her strapped down and unable to get away. When she could make out the shapes around her, Sid stopped squirming and dared to look around.

There weren't any holdings on her arms, no beast beside her. Her silent hope that the first friend she made on the star had come back for her died instantly.

As Sid's eyes took in the intruders, her heart dropped and splatted at the bottom of her stomach.

She stared, slack-jawed, at the seven large warriors standing in front of her, each holding a knife larger than half her body. There was a man on either side of her that held her arms with such brutal strength that she wondered why she even tried getting away in the first place. Their eyes were like hers so she knew they had to be natives of the star but they didn't look like the Domers she'd met so far. They weren't covered in the standard Domer tunics that she knew were a prerequisite for the workers. In fact, most of them were barely covered at all.

Sid felt flushed looking over the strips of hide that barely grazed enough skin to conceal anything of value. But it wasn't their near nudity that had her flustered; each one of the warriors was covered from head to toe in the same markings she saw on the Domer the queen had executed. Shapes and patterns she couldn't discern no matter how much she tried to remember her lessons. Their faces held no expression, strong noses and prominent cheekbones; muscled necks that led to even more muscled shoulders.

"Who are you people?" Sid whispered.

There was a guttural grunt from one of the warriors in front of her and a few words exchanged in a language she didn't understand. The words sounded like they were being swallowed instead of spoken and she couldn't make out any familiar sounds.

"Look, I don't know who you are but there are Starblades on their way here," she bluffed. "You better let me go or you'll have to deal with the queen."

She saw the two warriors exchange a look and could have sworn a smile formed on the face of the one closest to her. It was the last thing she saw before something hard and wooden hit the back of her neck and she lost herself to sleep.

TWENTY-EIGHT

THE POUNDING in Sid's head was loud enough to wake her, she wrestled her eyes open, confusing the knocking in her head for someone banging on a nearby door. The realization that there was not one door in sight hit her shortly after the reality that she was no longer in the pod. She looked around through the unfocused lens of her eyes and tried to make sense of where she might be. The room she found herself in was circular with heavy, mismatched fabrics cascading over the walls and ceiling. It resembled a deliberately chaotic shack with roughly strewn jungle remnants and animal hides on the floors. There were no openings to the outside and the minimal number of furnishings looked to be constructed crudely by hand and arranged without any recognizable pattern.

Sid threw her legs over the edge of the bed, which she quickly recognized to be endless layers of blankets tucked around one another, and rested her feet on the ground. The soft hide beneath her feet tickled her toes and she let them swoop across its hairs for mild relief. Her head was still a mess of tangles and though her eyesight was starting to sharpen, she could still see glimmers of light dancing in her fore vision when she turned her head too fast. With added pressure, Sid breathed in deeply and tried to stand. Her legs shook from having to carry the weight of her body but she managed to straighten out, enough that the edge of her goggles hit one of the fabrics swooning across the ceiling.

She ducked out of the way, swatting at the fabric and sending dust flying in all directions.

It took her a few moments to locate her boots in the midst of rugs and fabrics and tree stumps. The place reminded her of the forts she used to build in the observation deck as a child when she refused to sleep in the lodgings below. Except unlike her own fort that was full of nuts and bolts, this one looked like a strong wind blew in jungle garbage and no one bothered to clean up.

Careful not to make a noise, she managed to make it to the spot where her boots lay with only a few toe stubs. She laced up speedily, making note of the fact that the vinyl exterior was cleaner and in much better shape than it had been before. Someone had even taken the time to mend the scrapes on the soles and heels.

What in the name of the star is happening right now?

Sid felt the wall, trying to locate some crevice that would imply there was an actual exit point in this strange construction. She nearly squealed with excitement when her fingers fell through and a cold breeze rushed over them. Sid was already stepping forward when a hand wrapped around her arm and yanked her out.

Fabrics and leaves whipped around her, scratching her face as she was pulled through to the other side. Sid landed on her feet and looked up at one of the warriors she had seen in her pod before she was knocked unconscious. The man was large enough to eclipse all of Jericho. Sid cringed as her eyes swept over a freshly carved symbol on his forearm, the pale lines swollen against his dark skin. The warrior's long, dark hair was braided into a delicate pattern that fell over his shoulders and she couldn't help but smile at the stark contrast of the hairstyle to his otherwise rough appearance. When her eyes traveled past his naked chest and landed on the small strip of hide that covered his manhood, Sid forced herself to look away. *How can he just stand there all exposed like that? Cover up for stars sake!* Sid looked herself over to make sure her suit was still intact, relieved when she felt the tip of the screwdriver still in her pocket.

"What do you want from me?" She screamed, "And what is this place?"

Her hand twirled behind her, gesturing to the circular hut she woke up in. The exterior of the hut was made entirely from large chunks of tree and vine and when Sid looked around, she noted at least thirty more of the same constructs all around her. Most of them were much smaller than the one she found herself in but their basic shape and design looked to be identical. The same amount of mashed up nonsense that somehow created an upright shape.

"Il keltic cal sen," the warrior said in a gruff voice, "il sen teck ni sum."

"What?" Her face scrunched trying to understand.

"Il keltic cal sen," he repeated and pointed to her eyes.

"My eyes? What about them?"

"He's saying you are like us, but different," A voice sounded behind her and Sid turned to see a tall young woman, a few years older than her but twice as confident.

Sid tried not to stare but it was hard to look away from

the curves that were so prominently displayed on the woman. Her body, dark and glistening in the light that covered her like a sheet. Most of her glowing skin was exposed with the exception of a few parts covered discretely by dark hides. Her arms and legs were covered entirely in carefully positioned raised skin, markings that Sid had become quite familiar with. The woman walked past her and stood beside the warrior. Long, straight blonde hair flowed down her back, perfectly complementing the yellow glow that swallowed her body. As Sid adjusted her eyes, she realized the warrior was also glowing faintly. Not as brightly as the scantily clad woman in front of her but there was a hint of light on his skin as well. She wondered if they were related perhaps, though their features looked nothing alike. While the woman's face looked stretched, everything from her brow to her nose elongated and slender; the warrior was compact in his appearance, with stacks of muscle that made up his body pushed their way to his face.

"Like you?" Sid asked.

"El selten kun niten," the warrior answered.

She furrowed her brow and tilted an arched eyebrow in his direction, "I don't know what that means. I'm sorry."

"We are the escaped," the woman spoke softly, "the ones free of the domes."

Sid's thoughts raced. *The escaped? Here in the jungle?* That could only make them one thing. "You're Al'iil," she whispered as the realization hit her.

"Yes, we are the Al'iil. And *you* are something very different, aren't you?"

"I'm just a Domer, no one special. You should probably just let me go, no point keeping a useless thing like me around," she chuckled but the fear seeped off her like wet sewage.

"You are not a Domer," the woman said, her voice louder and less lenient now. As she spoke, Sid heard rustling from the nearby huts and when she turned to face the sound, she had to shield her eyes from the brightness that encircled her. Dozens of the Al'iil gathered near them, each with questioning eyes and radiating skin. Sid spotted two children hiding behind Al'iil that must have been their parents; their young skin fresh of markings and glowing only in a light white hue.

"Of course I am. I got lost and-"

The woman raised a hand to shush Sid and she obliged. "Domers do not have magic. You are no Domer. But you are not Al'iil. So what are you?"

There was no point lying now. They'd either kill her or cut her arms off and send her back.

"My name is Sid. And you're right, I don't belong here, not anymore at least. I was born in the domes but my parents saved me from the chipping. They had the queen's general put me on a ship that orbited Neostar for years that I sort of crashed in the jungle looking for him. And to answer your question, I don't have a clue what I am."

Her eyes met the woman's gaze and it felt good to say the truth for once. Even if that truth was about to get her killed, or worse.

"So you are the Stardaughter," the woman said tentatively and the crowd took a step inward, closing in the space between them.

"Stardaughter? Like the curse word?"

The woman looked confused.

"Why did you call me that?" Sid quickly added.

"There have been whisperings about you on the star. A girl of magic that has not been chipped; the true daughter of the star."

"Ha! Well, I'm not anyone's daughter. Trust me. At least not anyone I actually know or remember. You might as well kill me now and get it over with," she straightened her back to look prideful and brave but the sweat running down her neck betrayed her. Sid didn't want to die, but she more importantly didn't want to die a coward.

Do your best!

"Kill you? Why would we kill you?" The woman laughed.

"Because you're the Al'iil and that's what you do."

"Kes tek sum toomkan!" The warrior beside the woman roared, knife raised in the air.

Good job, Sid, now he's angry.

The woman squeezed the warrior's shoulder and he lowered his weapon. "We do not kill without reason. And there is no reason to kill you. We've been waiting for you for a very long time, Stardaughter."

She was never going to get used to being cursed at as a positive sentiment.

"Waiting for me? For what?"

"Come with me," the woman outstretched a hand and Sid took it instinctively. "We have many things to discuss."

The crowd parted and Sid spotted familiar eyes in the distance. Her lips widened into a smile as the beast ran toward her, barreling through the parted sea of Al'iil and stopping short just in front of her.

"You!" She yelled out and reached over to pat the beasts massive head. "I've missed you!"

The beast jogged a circle around Sid, tail wagging with

excitement. Behind it, she could see a few more of its kind approach her slowly, each one with large, curious eyes that were eager to inspect every part of her. She patted them one by one and they ran in circles around her in return. "I see you brought some friends," she nodded.

"Good, you are already familiar with the Tecken. You'd make an excellent Al'iil, Stardaughter."

"Tecken?"

"The animals. Trustworthy creatures that have proven to be an asset in hunts and battles. We found only the most skilled of warriors are able to form a bond with them. They must sense your magic."

"Or they just like me."

The woman smiled, "Or that." She patted one of the beast's large snouts and nodded to the hut Sid came out of. At her command, the beasts ran, tumbling over one another and piling into the hut.

Are they serious? They put me in the creature hut? Ew!

She felt a tug and the woman's eyes met hers, beckoning her to follow. Sid started to walk but stopped in her tracks. "So who are you?" She asked, wondering why she didn't bother finding out earlier.

The woman dropped Sid's hand and brought the back of her palm to her neck. The markings on her skin pulsed as the pent-up magic flowed beneath them, making the markings look like they were slithering over her skin. The glow around her intensified, casting a yellow shade over their surroundings and illuminating the huts in its brightness.

"I am Tazmin," she said and lowered her palm, "High Priestess of the Al'iil."

TWENTY-NINE

IT HAD SEEMED the queen's stories of the Al'iil were nothing but exaggerated tales to bend the truth to her will. From what Sid could gather in the days she had spent with them thus far, the Al'iil were a strong and kind people that devoted their life to following the old ways of the star. She couldn't imagine anyone from the group she'd met thus far being able to rise to anger that would result in the kind of horror she'd heard Ashlan describe. Whoever these residents of the jungle were, she liked them quite a bit.

Was it possible that ripping out the chips had created an entire new species of star natives? Ones that didn't fit into any of the molds the humans brought with them when they landed on the star? Sid's stomach fluttered at the thought of fitting in with them, of spending her days with a group that didn't carry the heavy burden of the domes and towers. Things were black and white out in the jungle, you either survive and pay respect to the star or you don't. There were none of the grey areas that troubled the Citizens and

Domers, no one or the other. If you were Al'iil, then that is all you were. There was no going back once a chip was removed and the magic flooded the system again. Sid could see the effects as clear as day in every Al'iil she met; their bodies glowing with the pulsing of the magic's current. Even the children, un-chipped like her, had some magic in them. Though too young to be of any real use, the glow around them suggested a future generation of powerful people. A generation not unlike the one that greeted the queen's mother when she first stepped foot on the star's native soil.

Sid had spent most of her time shadowing Tazmin in visiting the surrounding huts and caring for the children. The high priestess made several rounds throughout the day, walking from hut to hut with two warriors at her side. When Sid asked her why a ruler would need to be so accessible, Tazmin only shrugged, saying she had no intent to rule — only to lead.

The differences between her and Leona were immeasurable.

Aside from their general appearance, Sid found that the high priestess showed no need to command her people. In fact, she spent most of her time hearing their requests and entertaining their questions. Though Sid couldn't understand most of the conversations, she started to pick up a few words in the old tongue; most of which had something to do with food, her favorite topic since landing on the star.

Though the variety of foods the Al'iil foraged in the jungle was not nearly as complex as the meals she'd had in the domes and city, Sid much preferred their manner of eating and preparing those meals. Each night, contributions were brought in from every hut and after a blessing from the high priestess, the Al'iil joined in casting their energy into a communal fire before commencing to cook. Sid was lost when she first saw the ritual take place, asking Tazmin about it but the high priestess only nudged her closer to the fire and nodded. Taking this as a sign to join, Sid let her own magic escape into the bright yellow phosphoresce that hovered above the ground.

There were no words to describe it. Nothing in her entire life had ever centered Sid more than throwing her magic in with others like her. It was as if everything she had that was unique flowed out of her veins, mingled and then returned to her. Changed. She felt like a more complete version of herself, a stronger version.

"We are one but we are many," Tazmin whispered behind her with a smile. And Sid nodded back because she truly understood. The Al'iil were united. Not just by the markings they shared — the etchings on their skin that paid respect to the star they lived on — but by so much more. They worked as a united front; a community that would sacrifice for one another if needed.

On the days when Tazmin left her to her own devices, Sid filled her schedule by helping with hut maintenance and tending to the herds of Tecken that passed through the camp. She quickly realized that her years of fixing the ship came in handy and the Al'iil seemed grateful for the help. Some of the women snuck gifts into the hut she shared with the beasts; intricately woven tunics and jewels carved from tree bark. She thanked them, collecting the pieces under the blankets she used for a bed but never took to changing from her suit. She felt grateful for the simple act of having given it a good wash, refusing to part with an article of clothing that felt like second skin to her.

After five days with the Al'iil, Sid was surprised when

the high priestess called for her to join them in their training, a private ritual she had not yet been privy to. She had assumed that a hut would be set up for just this instance but Tazmin and the four warriors called for the Tecken, climbing onto their backs with ease. Despite her last ride, Sid was not as graceful as the rest at mounting her beast. A few failed attempts and arm flails later, she was atop the animal's back and following closely behind the group.

They rode through the jungle for hours, until Sid could barely feel her behind from the bumpy terrain. When Tazmin finally raised her hand to signal the group to stop, she nearly plummeted from the beast's back, eager for the feeling of using her legs again.

"This is it," Tazmin said, effortlessly dismounting from her Tecken.

"Where exactly is 'it'?" Sid asked.

She hadn't seen much of the jungle aside from her initial trip into the city and the tear-stained run back to her pod. This part was something different entirely. If you glanced over it, the river's adjacent hillside didn't look much different from the rest of the wilderness. The same trees covered in the same vines overbearing the same mossy ground. But if you looked closely, really looked, you'd notice the glow of each leaf as it rustled in the wind. You'd see the sparks dancing between the outstretched tree branches when they grazed the purple grass below. You'd hear the low electrical hum of the water.

"*What* is it?"

"This," Tazmin stretched out her arms, "is Kartega."

"Kartega?" Sid asked, the multicolored glimmer of the jungle reflecting in her eyes. "What's a Kartega?"

The warriors chuckled gruffly and started to unload the packs resting on their beasts' backs.

"Kartega is not a what, Stardaughter. It is more of a where."

"And where is it, exactly?" She looked around, trying to find something to help her pinpoint the location. The ring was right above their heads so she had an estimated time of day, just past noon, but that was about it.

"It is everywhere, it is in everything."

"What does that mean?" Sid was even more confused now than before, the continuous laughter from the warriors as they unpacked did not help. She shot them an acidic glare but that only made them laugh harder.

Tazmin stood beside her and rested a strong hand on her shoulder. "Before the humans came to this star and polluted it with their machinery and toys, we lived in tune with the star's magic. It gave to us and we gave to it. After the arrival of the human race, everything changed. They couldn't use the star's magic so they used us instead. We helped them power their ring with our magic; magic stolen from the star. Most of the jungle has been drained dry by now but there are still parts that lay untouched. The parts that we, the Al'iil, feed with our abilities as best we can. Parts like this one here. It is where our magic is strongest."

"So Kartega is a part of the jungle?"

"No, Stardaughter, Kartega *is* the jungle. It is the river and the trees. Kartega *is* the star."

Sid replayed the history lessons in her mind, but not one mentioned anything about the star being renamed. Though why would that be mentioned in history texts written by the humans? It made sense if she thought about it. Neostar.

New. As in built over something old. Something that already had a name and a way of existing. *One more lie! Good going, Colton!*

Sid spotted a pair of glowing green eyes shining behind one of the trees.

"What do you call that?" She asked, pointing to the small creature with a skinny tail longer than its body and a head covered in red fur and brown spots. The creature blinked once and cocked its head to look at her.

"That is a Qualin, very harmless."

"Kel tok manna selitek," one of the warriors added and the rest of them laughed.

"What did he say?"

"He said they're not so harmless when they bite through your leg."

"Wait, what?" She looked back at the creature and wondered how something that small could hurt anyone the size of the warrior. As the thought tickled the edges of her mind, one of the warriors tossed a boiled frigger egg in the creature's direction. The small animal leaped from its hiding spot and twisted in the air, its tail wrapping around the egg to catch it before it hit the ground again. When it landed, it stretched its already long snout and opened its mouth to reveal three rows of sharp, pointed teeth all the same green color as its eyes. Sid watch in horror as the creature bit down on the egg, snapping it in half before swallowing the pieces whole. "Stardamn! That thing is running on full blast."

"Why don't you try calling it over?" Tazmin said, her lips curled at the edges.

"That thing? No, thank you. I'd like to keep my limbs intact."

Maybe this is what got that guard's arms back in the day.

"Trust in me," Tazmin said and lowered her palm to the ground, "like this."

With hesitation, Sid lowered to her knees and placed her palm on the ground next to the high priestess. "That's it?"

"Now, give it your magic."

"Give what my magic?" Sid was getting annoyed with the high priestess. She was trying to understand but it was difficult to do when the woman was adamant about speaking in code.

"Kartega," Tazmin said and closed her eyes.

Sid looked down at her hand and noticed the glow around her intensify. Her markings slithered again and Sid could see the priestess's magic begin to flow, crawling through her arm in the direction of the ground. Finally understanding, Sid willed her own magic to respond, directing it into the ground to mimic the high priestess. She felt a prickle on her skin when the energy collided with the solid surface. Slowly, the star caught the strands of electricity she was projecting and pulled. Lightly, at first, then hungrily, like a starving child at a mother's bosom. Sid wanted to pull her hand back but Tazmin steadied her with a comforting palm.

So she stayed.

Stayed until the star drank what it needed. Stayed until the ground around her glowed and sparked. Stayed until she herself starting to glow in return and the small creature crawled to her with inquisitive eyes. It hovered low to the ground at first, then as it reached the circle of magic she had electrified, it stood up on its hind legs and hopped onto her shoulder. Its nose nestled into her neck and she could feel the wetness of it cover her skin.

Sid laughed, tripping over her own legs and falling to the

ground. The creature, startled, hopped onto her chest and glared. She stretched her palm out and it opened its jaw slightly. For a moment, Sid wanted to pull back, worried she'd end up being the next meal it had. Her worry cut short when the creature shoved its small face in hers and licked her cheek.

She was still laughing when Tazmin stood over her and shooed the Qualin away. The animal hesitantly climbed off Sid's chest and scurried back into the abyss of the jungle.

"What was that?" She asked, brushing remnants of jungle off her back and legs. "It felt incredible!"

"That was your own magic, nothing more."

"It felt like much more than just my magic. I've never felt that much power before!"

"Your power comes from Kartega and Kartega's gifts are plentiful," Tazmin said and Sid nodded, coming to terms with the vague information she'd learned to expect from the high priestess.

"So what else can it do?"

"Well, Stardaughter, that is exactly what we are here to show you."

Tazmin stepped aside and gestured to the warriors who had gathered in a circle around a large tree. They knelt, connecting their own magic to the ground beneath and chanted words Sid could not make out. She tried to unravel a few of the words she'd learned but gave up quickly, choosing to concentrate on the wonder that formed before her.

As the warriors chanted louder, their magic moved through their bodies, ripening the markings on their skin into fire hot veins. She could see the glowing circle surrounding them grow and rise, larger and brighter until it encapsulated them in a bubble of electrical sparks. Their magic soared through the air, pushing its way to the tree in their center. Once their forces met, the sparks flew sharply in all directions and Sid had to duck as bolt of lightning rushed by her, nearly slicing her neck.

"What are they doing?" She whispered but Tazmin shook her head, urging her to stay silent.

Her heart beat sporadically and she gasped as the warriors stood tall, raising their arms high and with them, the tree.

It shook and rumbled, the heavy trunk ripping from the ground, its massive roots wriggling in midair. Each root was electrified with the warriors' magic and each one moved as if it had life of its own.

In her peripheral, she could see sets of eyes glowing in the jungle. First one pair, then two, then more than she could count from where she was standing. Her hand covered her mouth to stifle a scream as the roots shot out into the depths of the jungle, further than her eyes could follow. Screeches echoed in the distance, followed by the scuffling of small feet. The warriors chanted louder, their voices overpowering the chaos that ensued around them.

She didn't know what was happening but whatever it was, it didn't sound good.

Before she could scream for them to stop, the roots shot back into the circle's center, each end wrapped around a different Qualin's neck.

"No!" Sid yelled but it was too late.

The tree's roots slithered back under ground, carrying the creatures with them. The warriors chanting slowed and the tree thudded back into the space it once occupied.

Silence followed.

The jungle was so quiet that even the river seemed to have stopped flowing.

Sid ran to the warriors, picking the one closest to her as she drove her small fists into his chest. "Why? Why did you do that?" She screamed, beating his chest over and over again. Tears covered her face and she could barely see but she continued to pummel him. Every hit getting weaker until she was slouched at the warrior's feet, unable to breathe.

"It is the way of the star," Tazmin knelt next to her. "Do not shed tears for the Qualin. Their sacrifice feeds the thing that gives them life. Their magic feeds our magic."

"That is disgusting! How can you allow that? *You* who are so against what Leona is doing to our people? You're exactly like her!"

The high priestess raised her hand and Sid shielded herself from an oncoming slap but it never came. When she opened her eyes, Tazmin was pointing up to the tree. She followed her finger, her sight still blurry from the cries and gasps.

The tree, that was dry and barren before, was covered in small, red fruit. And on its branches, tearing at the fruit and eating it faster than was likely healthy, were dozens of Qualin.

"If it was not for the sacrifice of the few, the many would go hungry and die."

A sob caught in her throat but she didn't let it escape.

"Do you understand now, Stardaughter?"

She nodded but her teeth grit against each other because she didn't understand at all. What the Al'iil were doing wasn't any different than the ring or the domes or anything else that plagued her dreams at night. Everything on this star was a sacrifice. Sid had felt the magic of Kartega in her blood, felt its power. How can something so powerful let itself be used as an excuse for such violence? She doubted Kartega craved the lives of the Qualin or any other creature the Al'iil served up. Stars weren't ruthless and blood-thirsty. Stars weren't anything at all. Whatever beliefs Tazmin and her people followed, it was nothing more than close-minded opinions. Just one side of a story no one bothered to question.

The Qualin above her chittered in excitement, their sharp teeth tearing into fruit after fruit. Some were gathering batches and carrying them off into the distance, to feed others in their flock she assumed. She looked to the high priestess, the satisfaction in her eyes turning her stomach to knots. She was not like her. She couldn't be. There were no answers for her here, the Al'iil were just another group she didn't belong to.

"Would you like to learn?" Tazmin asked with pride. As though killing was a skill that Sid should be grateful for.

"No. Not that."

The high priestess frowned, "What would you like us to teach you?"

"Teach me how to be strong. Teach me how to control my power."

A hand stretched her way, one of the warriors offering to help her up. She instantly recognized him as the warrior guarding the beast hut when she awoke. She took his hand and stood with them. Her legs wanted to flee. To feel the weight shift from leg to leg as she took her body and her mind away from the Al'iil and their sacrifices. But they had power that she did not and she wanted to know what this energy locked within her could be capable of. Because if she could learn that, she might be able to find a way to help all of them. To help right the wrongs of all the people she was nothing like.

So she stayed and let them teach her their ways. Despite her aching heart and her tear-stained face. She stayed because sometimes, a heart that broke was the strongest heart of all.

THIRTY

TIME SWALLOWED Sid whole as the days turned into nights and into days again. She had begun to develop a habit of counting off the hours to the minutes, a small nod to the Arcturus. It amused her that the things that bothered her most about the ship were now the things she missed the most.

Her hesitation about the jungle's residents grew daily and she found herself second guessing every small thing the Al'iil did in her presence. The meals no longer felt like a peaceful gathering and instead, she questioned each ingredient as she turned it over in her bowl. How was the meal in her lap prepared? Which creature died for her to eat? Questions ran through her head until she ended up throwing out the contents of the bowls when no one else was looking. What Sid noticed the most, was the lack of animal life in the camp. There was not even a peep of friggers in sight. The only jungle creatures she saw daily were the Tecken and even they looked worse for wear on days of being driven too hard to transport Tazmin and a few chosen warriors to and from camp. The high priestess came and went on regular intervals and each time, a set of tin boxes were taken out of the camp never to return again. Sid once had the notion of following her out to see where she was headed. The thought passed as briefly as it came. Charging through the jungle without the help of a beast in her condition was not going to prove useful, no matter how much she wanted to see what was inside the boxes. The lack of food and sleep was taking its toll, weakening her already tired body.

By Sid's calculations, she had spent exactly two weeks, four days, seven hours and thirty-eight minutes in the camp. She mostly kept to herself, staying away from the other Al'iil and spending the majority of her time with the warriors. Her ability to pick away at their knowledge of magic grew daily and she was pleased with the control she had learned to harness over her own power. There were a few more attempts to persuade her to take a jungle creature's life — mostly by the high priestess — but Sid denied them at every turn, concentrating instead on intermingling her magic with that of Kartega.

Out of all the warriors, which she soon learned was the majority of the camp, she found the closest relationship with the man she initially encountered — Dalrak, who unlike the others, treated her with respect and solidarity. He even started to teach her more words in the native tongue when they weren't training and Sid could almost form complete sentences. Almost.

Dalrak was the smallest out of all the warriors that circled the high priestess like a hive, though even with that, he was still more than twice as large as Sid in height and weight. In every way, he was her opposite. His features broader and darker than Sid's, his hair longer and more lush, and the way he carried himself — unashamed and prideful — was nothing compared to Sid's constant slouch. An opposite to her in all but one thing; magic.

Something about Dalrak's magic and his use of it complimented her own. While his was brutish and fast, Sid's magic flowed like a hushed breath of air. Each day, as she shadowed him in the jungle, she found herself mesmerized by the way he moved the electricity in his body. Her own powers, though stronger and more raw than the Al'iil's, still depended on concentration and the ability to direct the energy to the parts of her she wanted to send it to. For Dalrak, it seemed to be only a matter of moving. It was as though his energy responded to his very essence without much thought at all.

Once, when he was showing her how to track an opponent by sending electrical vibrations into the ground, she caught sight of the dark scar on the back of his neck from where his chip must have been. Perhaps his power wasn't controlled because he *couldn't* control it. It would explain why the Al'iil glowed without interruption while Sid's magic only manifested visibly when it was in use. It never crossed her mind before that Dalrak's magic was always in use, always on like a broken switch. She couldn't imagine how it must feel to have all that power running through you day in and day out. Sid got exhausted after only a few hours.

"Un dukti kan, sonkotir," Dalrak said after a long day in the jungle. Which Sid roughly translated to 'time to go, stop dragging your behind so slow. I'm hungry, Stardaughter.'

"For the millionth time, Dee! It's Sid! Sid!" She stabbed a finger into her chest to prove her point but the warrior only rolled his eyes, grabbed her by the waist and tossed her onto a beast's back. "Hey! I can get my own stardamned ride, thank you!"

They rode in silence as they often did, the ring's glow setting behind them. Sid turned to look back into the light and she could swear that for a moment, she saw Leona's face reflect in the rings surface. Impossible, of course, as she hadn't so much as thought about the queen in her time here. Aside from the occasional attempt to find a way to unite her and the Freedom Runners, followed by a guessing game of where the queen might have hidden the original ships. Sid tried not to dwell on any of those thoughts as they always either led her to Ashlan or Tann, both of whom she missed fiercely.

On this particular day, the track they were on grew less obstructed and Sid started to make out the camp in the far distance. A dark, heavy smoke lifted from the center of the camp and wild screams could be heard over the whistles and stirs of jungle creatures. Sid pressed her boot into her beast's side, encouraging it to jog forward but stopped when Dalrak raised a large, muscled arm.

She studied his markings, checking for movement but the symbols stayed still and dormant under his skin. They weren't in danger; if they were, his magic would be going berserk. But something was different and she wanted to know what.

"What's happening, Dee? What's that?" She pointed to the smoke that was now at least a story high.

"Kuntosita," he grumbled.

"Celebration? What celebration?"

Dalrak stayed quiet, his eyes locked on the camp.

"What are they celebrating?" She asked, flailing her arms in the air and pointing to the camp again. "Kon kuntosita?"

There was no response from the man of many words riding by her side. Turning his back to her, he pulled on his own beast and started the decent down the hill into the river. Sid huffed in frustration but followed his lead into the cool water rushing below, and all the way to the place she refused to call home.

ᐯᐯᔑ

"SO WHAT ARE YOU CELEBRATING?" She asked Tazmin when they'd finally made their way back.

The camp was littered with burning fires, the smells of foods cooking, and the shrieks of children running amok. Everyone was out. Looking around at the cheer that erupted from the camp's center, Sid let herself smile for the first time since she made the decision to stay with the Al'iil. Truly smile until her cheeks hurt and she felt like she must have looked like a complete fool to anyone who passed. Perhaps she went overboard with her suspicions; there might have still been a chance that the Al'iil were not the killers she had built them up to be in her mind. What did she know of Kartega anyhow? What could she possibly understand about what it wanted? She hadn't lived amongst its wildness for as long as these people had, so who was she to judge what sacrifices were worth making?

"It is finally the night of the Ferteki," the high priestess said in a manner that implied Sid should understand the term. When she noticed her furrowed brow, she added, "The turning of the tide."

"There's a tide? Near here? You're telling me we've been near a water mass this entire time and no one bothered to show me?" She was indignant. *Such an important sight to have missed.*

"Not physical tide, Stardaughter," Tazmin said.

Sid's gaze dropped and she crossed her arms. *There goes another dream.*

"So what kind of tide then? What's turning, exactly?"

Tazmin outstretched her arm to the crowd gathering near the fires. Sid spotted Dalrak at the far end and tried to wave him over but when his gaze met hers, he looked away. *Strange little thing. Big thing. All the same.*

"Come, Stardaughter. Walk with me."

She followed the high priestess to the outer edges of the camp. The wails and screams of the Al'iil could still be heard from where they stood but they were muffled, carrying over the sporadic shrieks occasionally. Almost like a melody playing awkwardly in the background - if anyone had ever composed a melody to be performed entirely in shrieks, that is.

"It has been a long time since we chose to leave our people behind. A long time since we came here. Became this," the priestess gestured to the scar on her neck. "And all that time, we have been preparing. Biding our time until our tide turned and waiting for Kartega to show us the way. We stayed quiet, minded only ourselves, protected only each other and the star. Day by day, we grew stronger. Something I am certain you are learning much about."

The high priestess turned her back to Sid, gazing up at the moons that sat comfortably above them. Her face was more relaxed than Sid had seen it, like a tree trunk had just rolled off her after years of staying still. There were so many things the priestess condoned and encouraged that Sid didn't agree with but she couldn't argue with the fact that she held her people strong.

"Our strength and our magic fed Kartega," she continued and Sid cringed at the memory of the Qualin's horrifying death at her hands, "and now it has found a way to help us free our people."

Sid shook her head, "Who? The Domers? You know how to free them?" She couldn't believe it, this entire time she'd been looking for a solution and it was right under her nose! "Have you made contact with the Freedom Runners? Have you spoken to Tann? To Nyala?"

"No, Stardaughter. We do not need to run from our freedom. Kartega has delivered us our salvation as we had hoped it would."

"Wha-" Sid started to ask when she realized that the high priestess's gaze was burning into her own. "You mean me?"

"Yes, Stardaughter. You are the answer we have been seeking. The reason we have waited so long."

"But what can I do? I can't make Leona or the Freedom Runners see reason. I'm just some girl that got lucky and didn't get chipped. What in the stars can I possibly do?"

"That is where you are mistaken. You are not some girl, Stardaughter. You are the ghost that walks among us. No chip, no name, no life. You are both here and not."

"No offense but I really don't understand any of that. How can me not being chipped help you?"

"It can help because you will not be seen, by any of them."

"So what? You have kids here that aren't chipped, use them!"

"Our children have no useable magic."

"I'm not following," she noted in frustration.

"For us to take back Kartega, we need magic that cannot be detected by the naked eye."

Sid looked at Tazmin's glowing skin, finally understanding. So this is why they stayed away all these years, anything else would be suicide. Unlike her, the Al'iil wore their magic like a mask, always on and visible. If they wanted to infiltrate the towers for whatever crazy plan Tazmin had in mind, they'd never survive on their own. The Starblades would see them coming and attack before they even had a chance to retaliate and, magic or not, even the Al'iil couldn't fight off all the Starblades in Tower City.

"So I can get in and out, so what?"

"You will not be seen when you burn the towers to the ground, destroy the ring and obliterate every human that has brought destruction to Kartega."

Sid's fire roared and she straightened to meet the priestess's sharp gaze. "And why would I do that?"

"Because you will have no choice."

The high priestess took a step back and before Sid could object, something hit her from behind. Her vision blurred and her legs started to give way. Strong arms caught her as she started to fall down, not Dalrak, another warrior that she couldn't place. She tried to stay focused but the light of the moons was suddenly blinding, beckoning her to shut her eyes. She let the arms scoop her up and her body go limp.

Muck, not this again.

THIRTY-ONE

"SO WHAT'S YOUR PLAN? Tie me to a Tecken and send me in? Because *that* won't draw any attention!"

Her hands struggled against the restraints behind her back as she spat the words at Tazmin. She had come to on the floor of the high priestess's own hut with her hands and feet bound by ropes. Sid was getting really tired of the charades the Al'iil wanted to play. She wasn't going to help them, no matter what they threatened to do to her.

"You will help us one way or the other, Stardaughter. I am certain of that," Tazmin cooed from the hide covered bed on the opposite end of the hut. Her legs draped over the edge where a young Al'iil girl was rubbing oils into her skin. Sid averted her gaze, disgusted that the priestess could relax at a time like this.

She strained harder, twisting her wrists in opposite directions. For a moment, she felt as if the rope might give way but the hope was short-lived; no matter how hard she tried, the restraints stayed strong and true. There was no way out, at least not on her own. Behind the loosely drawn fabrics that covered the entrance to the hut, she could see Dalrak's back turned to her. Another warrior stood beside him, both of them watching for something in the far beyond; guarding her. Escape was a futile task, even if she could manage to get rid of the ropes, she couldn't get rid of the two warriors outside. Let alone the high priestess herself and who knows how many more on guard beyond the hut's walls.

"Dee," she whispered in his direction, "Dalrak! Help!"

If he heard her, he chose not to acknowledge it.

"Dee, please," she begged.

The muscles in his back tensed but he refused to budge.

"He will not answer you, Stardaughter. Dalrak is a loyal servant of Kartega."

"Don't you mean a loyal servant of *you?*"

"I," the priestess said, "am by extension Kartega itself."

Sid rolled her eyes and pulled her arms apart again, "Who decided that? Let me guess, *you?*"

"These conversations will lead you nowhere. All you are doing is postponing the inevitable. I know you, Stardaughter. You want to help your people; this is how you do that."

"You don't know the first thing about me!" Sid spat. Literally. As far out as she could to make a point. "You said it yourself, I'm a ghost. Neither here nor there. I want nothing to do with this star or anyone on it."

"Lies will also lead you nowhere," Tazmin noted and popped a fresh green berry into her plump mouth. "We will wait until you make your choice, the *right* choice."

"Dalrak," she cried again. When the warrior did nothing to respond again so Sid did the only thing she could think of, she planted her palms to the ground and sent a wave of electricity in his direction. The jolt zapped at his bare feet and he jumped from the shock. "Got you."

The warrior grumbled something under his breath, gave her a nasty side glance and returned to his statuesque form.

Stardamned stubborn fool!

"You're wasting your breath," Tazmin chirped.

Hope drained from her pores like liquid escaping a cracked glass and she pressed her back into the wall behind her. She wasn't just wasting her breath; she was wasting time that she no longer thought she had.

"AAAAAH!" Sid clenched her teeth to keep the pain from spreading to the rest of her body.

The high priestess dug her knees into her chest, pressing her charged palms to Sid's temples. She shot a pulse of magic into Sid's temporal lobes and sent her into yet another spiral of pain. Sid could feel the energy push its way into her cortex. Her head felt like it was lit on fire as the magic scratched its way into every crevice. She didn't want to cry, didn't want to give Tazmin the satisfaction, but the electricity must have hit a nerve and tears ran down her cheeks uncontrollably.

Above her, the priestess moved her lips but all Sid could hear were jumbled sounds. It sounded like someone had shoved an engine cleaning rag in both her ears. She shook her head, urging for Tazmin's magic to leave her system but it was of no use. It would be hours before she felt strong enough to even move, let alone gain her hearing back. This she had gathered from experience.

Tazmin eased off her chest and said something else Sid couldn't hear before leaving her alone in the hut.

Her eyes burned and for the first time since the torture started, she was grateful that her hands were bound. Otherwise, Sid might be tempted to pull her eyes right out of her skull. When she was sure that the priestess was gone, she let herself take her first full breath that morning. The air filled her, relaxing every muscle until her body curled into a ball on the rough floor.

The sobs came shortly after. They always did.

The high priestess had been using her magic on Sid for two days and one night, taking only short breaks in between to let her gain a small amount of strength. Enough so that she didn't die, but not enough that she could use her own magic to fight back. Sid tried at first but those attempts left her even more drained and she settled on taking the beatings to her system without confrontation. Tazmin wanted her to fight, she could see it in her eyes when she unleashed the jolts of electricity into Sid. Each time it was as though she was begging her to get angry. Which was exactly the reason Sid chose to stay calm instead.

The high priestess wanted to break her, make her so angry and afraid that she would have no choice but to do as the priestess bid. Sid wasn't going to let that happen. She needed to stay strong long enough. Long enough for what, she didn't know. There was no chance of escaping, she was too weak and her only ally had turned his back on her. Quite literally, in fact.

A loud ringing sounded in her ears and she breathed through it knowing that soon her ears would pop and she'd be able to hear again. At this point, her pain was systematic. An organized process of symptoms that she checked off until the magic left her body and she felt semi-normal again. Then, like clockwork, Tazmin would return and the process started all over again.

"What do you think, Dee? Think I should just do it?" She slurred in the warrior's direction. "I know you're there. You're always there, aren't you?"

She listened until she heard the slight rustle of his muscled legs digging into the ground beneath.

"Why won't you help me? I thought we were friends."

Every day was like this now. Tazmin trying to break her, her resisting, begging Dalrak for help, then silence. She hated how repetitive it was, it was enough to drive her completely mad, if she hadn't gotten there already. There were moments when Sid wondered if Tazmin had succeeded; if she had actually lost touch with reality and was on her way into the city to destroy the ring and kill everyone in sight. Or worse, if she had already gone through with it.

In those dark moments, she would try to remember Colton's face, trace every crinkled line of his eyes when he smiled until her heart started beating again. She tried to picture what her parents must have looked like, kicking herself for not asking more about them when she had a chance. She thought she had so much more time to find out the details of their life before her, so much more time to get to know them; to get to know herself. The girl that landed on the star was long gone, if she even existed in the first place.

Sid didn't know that girl anymore; didn't understand her wants and needs. Her childish dreams that seemed so far away now that she couldn't even remember what they meant.

This girl, the girl tied on the floor of a cold hut with a million volts of electricity running through her veins is who she was now. The girl that refused to choose who lives and who dies. The girl who wouldn't pick a side even if it killed her. This was the girl that she wanted to be if not simply for the fact that she was real. No one invented her from lies and deceptions. She wasn't hidden from view or used for her power. This girl was the only truth Sid knew.

"I'm not giving up on you, Dee. You hear me?" She whispered. Her tongue was starting to gain mobility but she could still feel saliva dripping from the side of her lips when she spoke. "I'm not giving up on any of you."

The warrior shifted his weight outside and grunted. It was faint and likely nothing more than a guttural reaction to tell her to keep quiet but Sid could swear it meant something more. For a moment, she thought she heard him say something.

"What? Dee, what?" She beckoned, raising her voice with a desperate plea.

Another low growl followed by a grunt and then a deafening silence.

"Dee! Please! Dee, talk to me!" She cried.

She could hear light footsteps outside that seemed to be getting closer. The heavy fabrics that covered the hut's entrance whooshed and parted. Her heart leaped into her throat and she kicked her feet furiously to turn her sweat soaked body toward the sound. He'd listened! He'd listened and he'd come to free her!

She tried to sit up, sliding her back against the wall to find a suitable position. Her head still felt like it might explode and her hearing had not yet fully returned to but she could move. She could move and she could run. She could fight.

Fists tightened, she waited as the figure emerged from

behind the fabrics one slow step at a time and her world crashed around her.

"Are you ready to stand by us, Stardaughter?" Tazmin asked.

Sid shook her head and looked away, stifling a cry.

"Very well, let's try this again."

THIRTY-TWO

DAYS AND NIGHTS overlapped until Sid could no longer tell the difference between them. A few days ago, she was able to get glimpses of the outside when Tazmin came in for her usual tormenting rituals. Now, Sid found herself unable to see anything but the flashes of electricity that sparked behind her eyelids. Her body vibrated, magic fueled blood rushing just under her skin. It was as though she had been swallowing all of Tazmin's magic, getting fuller and fatter with it without any way of letting it out. She wished she could release the energy, wished she could vomit the magic right out of her system but she couldn't even move her legs.

Her shoulders had long given up on her from having her hands tied behind her back for days on end. When it came to movement, Sid had become as useless as a rock buried underground. Stationary, static, and very, very heavy.

A flash of light sparked in her peripheral and she snapped her teeth, trying to catch it on her tongue. The light levitated before her face, multiplying until she was surrounded by the glow of magic. Her dry eyes blinked rapidly as she tried to make sense of the scene unfolding before her.

"What is this?" She whispered; her voice hoarse from screaming.

The sparks twirled in a hurricane of light, trailing one after the other like a flock. They moved up and down and side to side and Sid jerked her head in each direction as fast as she could to keep up. "Come closer," she beckoned and the lights obeyed. They floated majestically in her direction, changing shapes and sizes the closer they got.

When they were right in front of her, they flickered faster and brighter and she had to narrow her eyes to keep the glare out. They spun one more full turn before changing shape again. This time, the lights banded together into a form, one that didn't look like much at first. At least not until Sid stopped squinting and let her eyes focus.

The more she stared, the more she realized the lights weren't random at all. In fact, with all of them crumbled together, they looked a little bit like her — if she was made entirely of electricity. Sid watched in awe, the same way she used to watch the hologram lessons Colton sent for her. She followed the shape as it floated from one side of the hut to the other and landed back in front of her. As if it was trying to get her attention.

"I see you," she said and the light paused.

A few sparks separated and started to form another shape nearby. This one spread out as high as the ceiling in three sharp points. The towers.

Sid watched her twin of light float to the towers, slowly at first then faster and faster until she was barreling toward them at an unbearable speed. She wanted to reach out and grab it before the two collided but her twin only moved faster and Sid still had no use of her arms.

"Wait! Stop!" She shouted.

Screaming was a futile point. Her electric twin crashed into the towers before she even finished yelling. Sparks of light exploded, covering the hut in brilliant flashes of magic. Sid shut her eyes tightly. When she opened her eyes again, the lights were gone and the hut was as still as ever. There was not one sign of magic in the air and some of her sight had started to return.

"What was that?" She asked the empty hut. "Was that real?" Grounding her legs, she pushed herself to roll over until she was flat on her back. Every small movement made her body cry out as the magic pressed into her very cells. "Was that a sign?"

Maybe the high priestess was right and Sid should stop trying to help the humans. She still wasn't sure why she wanted to protect the people that created the domes and had kept so many of the Al'iil chipped and trapped in their own bodies. And Leona was the reason her parents were dead so maybe taking her out of the equation wasn't such a bad idea.

Sid could be in and out without anyone noticing. She could sneak in just as she did before, find the Arcane, reason with them to shut down the ring then use her magic to destroy the towers. In and out. No problem.

Except there was one problem she couldn't quite get out of her head. Ashlan and the other Citizens; they didn't deserve to die for this.

She closed her eyes and pictured his face. His blue eyes locked on hers, teasing her about something completely unimportant. In the dream, she teased him back, punched his shoulder and furrowed her brow as though she was as mad as ever. But she wasn't mad at him, not now. She would trade anything to get teased by him in that moment. To feel his strong shoulder push against her small fist in an assuring way, like he was a mountain she tried to tip over.

But what could she do? A few more sessions with Tazmin and she'd be so full of magic that she worried her entire body might explode into a billion pieces and she'd be nothing more than a light show, similar to the one she'd just witnessed. Although she still wasn't sure if that was even real.

She wondered if perhaps that was the priestess's plan all along; fill her up to the brim and point her straight for the towers. A Sid-shaped magic bomb ready to obliterate everyone in sight. And if it was, what could Sid do to stop her? Her body was not her own anymore and she couldn't trust her mind to be honest. She was falling fast and reckless into a pit she couldn't crawl out of.

She was falling and no one was there to catch her.

Another spark flashed over her head and illuminated the fabric covered ceiling of the hut. "Not again. Stop! Please!" She begged, not ready to see more visions of what might come to pass. The spark hovered for a moment then shot out in the direction of the hut's entrance. Groggily, Sid's eyes followed its bright trail to the rustle of the fabrics.

She expected Tazmin. She expected pain. She expected death.

Instead, three figures entered the hut. Sid squinted her eyes, trying to make out who was there with her when one of them ran to her side.

"Sid! Stars help us! What did they do to you?"

"Ash?" She asked, confused. "Is this a trick? If this is a trick, I-" Her words faltered. What could she possibly do if it was a trick? She couldn't even move.

Before she could say anything else, the figure reached behind her and she could feel the cold point of a blade across her wrists. *This is it. I die now,* she thought as the blade sliced across.

The ropes holding her fell to the ground and the figure was already at her feet, cutting off those restraints as well. She wanted to yank her arms forward but the second figure reached for her, helping her sit up slowly. "Careful, move slow," he said and she cried out in relief.

Tann — she would know his voice anywhere.

"You came. You both came," she whispered. Her words more of a question than she meant them to be.

"Of course we came," Ashlan said, his finger parting the fabrics to inspect outside the hut. "You've been gone weeks, Sid. What did these monsters do to you?" He was almost shouting, yet careful to keep his voice low enough so they didn't get spotted.

"They're not monsters. It's Tazmin."

"Who is Tazmin?" Tann asked.

"The high priestess, she has some," her mind raced for an adequate word, "drastic ideas." She said finally. Then her gaze shifted between Ashlan and Tann, eyebrows arched and mouth wide open. She pointed a weak, frail finger between the boys. "Wait, what is going on here? Why are you two here together? *How* are you two here together?"

Her eyes swam, "It's not real. You're not here. I'm imagining things again!"

A strong hand squeezed her shoulder. Tight enough that she could feel the warmth of real skin on hers but light enough that it didn't send quivers of pain through her body.

"You're not imaging anything. We're here. Both of us," Ashlan said.

"But how?"

"We have a lot to tell you."

"Not right now. Right now, we have to get you as far away from this place as we can. Can you walk?" Tann asked.

She nodded though she wasn't sure she could. "I might need some help."

Ashlan tapped his fingers on something beyond her sightline and the sound of metal grinding filled the hut. She didn't need to look to know who came with them. "Fred! You brought Fred!" She yelled, stretching her arms to the droid. It dropped down, cradled its glowing forearms beneath her body and hoisted her into the air. The quick rise made her slightly nauseous but she would put up with much more if it meant she could finally be free of Tazmin's hold.

They slowly stepped through the fabrics. Ashlan went first, followed by Tann, then the droid with her draped in its arms.

"How did you know where to find me?" She asked quietly when they were outside.

It was dark and there was a chill in the air that wasn't there a few weeks ago. Sid trailed her gaze over the nearby huts and the jet black that coated them. Night had swallowed the camp and she wondered exactly how many nights she'd missed so far. More importantly, if it was this late, where was Tazmin?

Ashlan pointed to his right, "This one here sent Tann a message."

She followed his finger and, for the first time since they walked out, noticed another person in the group. Dalrak puffed out his chest but his dark eyes looked away from her, as though she could burn through him with a stare alone. "A message? How? He doesn't even speak your language," she prodded, never taking her eyes off the warrior.

"He didn't have to. Serryl found me, panicking. Looks like someone messed with one of her shipments," Tann shot Dalrak a sideways grin, "needless to say, she was after blood until she found your interface box in the wreckage."

"Oh, wait, what shipments?"

"Serryl doesn't exactly just deal in magic," Tann said as if that explained everything.

She shrugged her shoulders, "What was supposed to be in the box, Tann?"

"Fruit, water, weapons. Serryl and the priestess have an," he sighed, "understanding. Have for years."

"Years? Why didn't I know about this?"

"Because you knew us all of five minutes. Everyone gets to have secrets."

The way he looked at her made her uneasy. He knew *all* of her secrets. Well, almost all of her secrets, except now that Ashlan was also here and they were working together who knew. Why were they were working together? It couldn't be just to save her. "And why are you two here? Together?" No point dancing around the topic now.

"When I realized the box was yours, I knew the Al'iil had you. Nothing good can come out of being around them. No offense." He looked at Dalrak again who only shrugged in response. "There was no way for me to get out of the dome to get you out. At least not on my own."

"So you went to Ash for help? Seriously? Do you have a death wish or something?"

"Ha! If you think I can be bested by one Starblade, you don't know me at all!" He laughed. Ashlan rolled his eyes next to him. "I needed help, and I was hoping he cared enough about you to offer it."

"And you did?"

To say Sid was shocked was an understatement. She didn't know how Ashlan felt about her, but she never would have guessed that he cared enough to work with a Domer. Especially not a Domer that was one of the Freedom Runners. Did he know about them? All of them?

"Like I said before, we have a lot to tell you later. Right now we have to get out of here before the priestess comes back."

"Where is Tazmin anyway?"

"Your large friend here sent her off, told her to take a break. Guess she trusts him."

"You don't say," she sighed deeply and let herself relax into the droid's stoic embrace. "Let's go then."

They were already halfway to the next hut over when she realized that Dalrak wasn't moving from the entrance. His chest still strong and stiff but his gazed was on her now, watching her be carried away. She held her hand up in protest, "Wait! We can't leave without him!"

"He won't go, Sid," Tann said. "He won't leave his people."

"I'm his people," she answered stiffly and climbed out of the droid's metal arms. Her back screamed and her legs were so wobbly she thought she'd fall right over but step by step, she made her way back to the warrior. "Come with us, Dee."

He was quiet but when his eyes met hers, she knew there was so much they still had to say to each other.

"I'm not asking again. Let's go!" She tugged at his arms. It was useless. She had better luck dragging a mountain. "Dee, what the muck!"

"Ken sunto kira," he said, eyes trained on her.

"No, you fool. This is not your home. The whole mucking star is your home! Let's go!"

The warrior stood still but she would not give up. She wasn't leaving here without him. Once Tazmin found out that he was behind her escape, he was as good as dead. She'd probably feed him to Kartega like a Qualin. There was no way Sid was going to let that happen.

"Please, Dee. I need you!" Her heart felt like a crack had started to form right down the middle of it. Another tug and the whole thing would shatter into so many pieces she would never be able to be whole again. He was her friend. Even when she thought he'd deserted her; he found a way to get her out of this place. He was always on her side and now she had to be on his. "I need you!" She pleaded, looking for the right words. "Il runtok sum."

She stretched a hand and nodded, her eyes swimming as she begged him to choose her. Begged him not to stay behind. When his own hand reached back she grabbed hold so tight she thought she might rip his fingers off. Without waiting for him to change his mind, she pulled him behind her to the others. The magic that threatened to tear her into pieces bumbled at her fingertips and she let a bit of it escape into him. He gave her hand a squeeze to let her know that it's alright. Little by little, jolt by jolt, she fed him the excess energy that was stifling her for days. This wouldn't be enough to heal her; they both knew it. But as they walked hand in hand through the deathly quiet of the camp, she felt her body cool down, her hearing become clearer, and her body become lighter.

They weren't out of danger yet and maybe they never would be. The important part was that there was a 'they' for her to hold on to.

THIRTY-THREE

PANIC SHOT through each one of Sid's bones as they huddled behind the beast hut. Unlike the rest of the camp, the place was far from quiet but it wasn't the usual growling of the sleeping animals that worried her. Dalrak raised an arm and the rest of them stopped in their tracks on command. They fell silent, even Fred's low buzz of energy quieted down though she wasn't sure if it was a response to danger or his battery slowly diminishing. They pressed their backs against the hut's walls and listened.

Voices shattered the silence. Three low tones from what Sid could make out — warriors. What were they doing in there? Were they checking on the beasts? That couldn't be it, no one checked in on the herd this late in the night. Something else had brought them there. Something that might blow their escape plan into pieces.

Sid listened in, keeping her breathing to a steady tone that matched the howls of the wind around them. It was then that she heard it. A fourth voice; lighter than the rest, more melodic and much more commanding. Tazmin.

Stardaughter! What now?

She took a step forward but Dalrak held her back, his magic wrapped around hers in the spot where their arms touched and she could feel the panic in him as if it were her own. This was out of the ordinary for the priestess and he knew it too. She met his eyes and he shook his head, ordering her not to move further.

They couldn't just stand there. Sooner or later, the priestess and her warriors would exit the hut and even if they could somehow manage to stay hidden, there was nothing to stop her from setting the entire Al'iil camp after them. Sid crawled around the side of the hut, shooing off Dalrak's attempts to stop her, and flattened out on her belly near its entrance. Lifting only a sliver of a limb at a time, she raised her fingers to the heavy fabric and parted it just enough to get a good look.

Tazmin stood in the center of the hut with three warriors at her side. Behind her, Sid counted seven more warriors waiting diligently at attention. Beasts lounged across the hides on the floor, most were asleep but some stared blankly at Tazmin and the warriors as if they were following along with the conversation. The group was whispering, pointing to a large aluminum capsule next to the high priestess. *The trade for Serryl. Nothing stops business, I guess.* Sid rolled her eyes and lowered herself back down, trying to stay as flat as she could while crawling back to the others.

She waved them over and they creeped into a tight circle around her. Sid pointed to the hut then ran off the number of warriors on her fingers, waiting until they nodded that they understood. Ashlan shrugged and she took that to mean that he had no idea what her plan was. She didn't have much of an idea either. The only thing Sid knew was that they couldn't leave with Tazmin awake and on guard.

A plan started to form in her mind, not a fool-proof plan, not even a well thought-out one really, but it was the only idea she had and they couldn't keep standing there all night. Signing, she tried to explain what she had in mind. When she was satisfied that her point got across, she glanced at each of them and smiled. A gesture she thought was reassuring but ended up being peculiar instead. She didn't let that bother her and directed each member of their small group into position.

Ashlan had the first move. He worked fast, entering sequences of code into the droid's commands. Fred didn't wait long to respond and Sid hoped it was because he understood the urgency of the situation and not because he was a mindless machine that did as it was told. He moved surprisingly quietly, his legs taking long strides and landing perfectly still on the balls of his feet. He was at the other side of the camp in moments. Looking back, Ashlan winked and entered more numbers into the projection. At his command, the droid's body whirred, the blue of its energy core pulsating brighter. The group watched as Fred stood tall and let out a blood-curdling scream.

Warriors rushed from the hut in his direction, their muscle-bound bodies trampling dust in their wake. Ashlan's fingers tapped on the projection from the shadows. His lips curled into a smirk as he forced the droid to loop right then left. Pushing it into a mess of movement that made the warriors run around like excited children. They hadn't spotted Ashlan. Not yet. Which meant they still had time.

With the warriors distracted in a pointless feat to protect their priestess, she watched as Tann crept to the back of the hut. A flick of his knife was all it took to slice through the wall paneling. He pulled at the opening, stretching it wide enough to peer through and waited.

"I know you're in there, Tazmin!" Sid yelled.

She was sure that from Tann's position he could see the priestess's face turn; her lips a straight line and her eyes fierce with the heat of anger. He waited until she took the bait and stepped outside before his attention turned to the beasts in the hut. The creatures were wide awake now, their growls piercing through the hut and reaching Sid where she stood. Tann had never seen the Tecken in real life and she was hoping that he would not waste time with fear or intrigue, they needed him to get the beasts out if they had any chance of escape.

A shuffle of massive feet sounded from behind the hut and Sid sighed in relief, turning her attention back to the priestess. Her blonde hair shone silver in the light of the moons overhead and Sid hated noting how specific Tazmin's beauty was. Her wild hair and muscle-toned body made her look like she was made of jungle; a child of Kartega through and through.

"I should have known better than to put my trust in you, Dalrak," the priestess said calmly as she stepped out of the hut.

The warrior tensed and Sid stepped in front him, "You should have known better than to underestimate his kindness."

"It is a shame his kindness will be the thing that kills him."

"You're a monster," Sid said and took another step forward. She could feel Dalrak's magic rise to the surface behind her, "And you will not touch him."

The high priestess let out a laugh that sent shivers down the back of Sid's legs.

"You are not leaving us tonight, Stardaughter. Not until you have done what you are meant to do."

"For the last time, my name is Sid!" She yelled. "And I am not meant to do anything. Least of all for you!"

She raised her hands and started to free her magic from her very bones but before she could direct it at the priestess, Dalrak leaped from behind her, his heavy body knocking her out of the way as he flew at Tazmin.

It took the high priestess less than a second to blast him in the gut with enough energy to send him barreling back onto the ground. He groaned and tried to sit up but Sid could see he was gravely injured, his side charred black from where Tazmin's magic hit. Blood had started to pool from his wound and she ran to his side, pressing her hands firmly into his abdomen. His eyes met hers and, in that moment, Sid knew she was on her own.

"Stay down," she whispered and cupped his hands over his wound before getting up.

Tazmin faced her, strong and regal, her hands back at her sides. The faint glow of her body bright in the darkness of the night around them. "This is what happens when we disobey Kartega."

"He didn't disobey anyone but you and you don't speak for the star! You don't speak for anyone!"

Sid jumped to her feet. The energy pushed itself through her body, flowing from her feet to her face and bouncing off every blood cell. She wanted to scream so loud she might explode. She was full of magic that wasn't hers. Magic she didn't want anything to do with. She felt like an overheating engine ready to combust. Her breath was fast but she managed to keep herself from sounding breathless when she spoke.

"You gave me something," she said and forced the magic to the surface. Her body vibrated, hard enough that everything around her started to shake. She grounded her feet and when she looked down at her hands, she could she was glowing. "I think it's time you took it back."

Tazmin's face contorted as she started to discern Sid's words. By the time she understood, it was too late. The energy that Sid sent her way was large enough to level an entire Dome to the ground. All the magic the priestess spent days feeding into her, torturing her with, soared through the air and back into Tazmin. Back into the vessel it wanted to return to.

Sid's legs shook and she landed on one knee as her strength gave way. She continued to push the power out of her. A scream left her mouth as the last of Tazmin's magic escaped from her body and made a final blow to the priestess's limp form on the ground. She tried to stand but she couldn't hold herself up and she fell back, collapsing on top of Dalrak's shoulder. He wrapped an arm under her and nodded in Tazmin's direction.

She couldn't tell for sure, but she thought she could see the priestess's chest rise and fall. Sid breathed out, relieved that Tazmin was still alive, that her death would not be something to be haunted by. Even more relieved that her body was her own again.

"We need to leave. Now!" Ashlan yelled from behind them and she turned to see warriors running in their direction on Fred's heels.

Before she could start to run, a hand grabbed her by the back of her suit and hoisted her onto a Tecken's sturdy back.

Dalrak, still bleeding, smiled and hopped onto a second beast that stood nearby. She looked around to make sure everyone was ready to ride and charged forward.

They stormed through the camp, evading the thrusts of warriors and jolts of magic zooming past them. Sid didn't look back, not once, not until they broke through the camps barrier and were so deep in the jungle that she couldn't hear the wild screams of the Al'iil in the distance. When she could see nothing but the darkness of sleeping trees, she loosened her grip on her Tecken's matted fur, motioning it to slow its stride. The others rode beside her, with the exception of the droid that jogged alongside Ashlan.

"You did good, Fred," she smiled. "You all did good."

"Not good enough," Ashlan said, his eyes full of grief.

She followed his gaze to Dalrak who was hunched over, his breathing loud and labored. "Who? Him? He'll be alright. He's stronger than he looks, just needs to rest for a bit. We all do."

"That's not what I meant," he said and raised an eyebrow.

"Then what?"

"You missed a lot," Tann answered quietly.

"What in the stars are you two talking about? We got away and they're not following. We're safe."

Ashlan smiled sheepishly. "The Al'iil aren't the only ones on our trail."

"What?"

"The queen, Sid. Before I left, she gave orders to bring you in. Alive, at least as far as I last heard."

"Me? Why me?"

"I think Abbot found out about you meeting with the rebels."

"Freedom Runners," Tann corrected.

"Right, Freedom Runners."

She shook her head, still uneasy about their sudden alliance. "So she wants to what? Have me arrested?"

"I think it might be more than that. She sent every Starblade after you. They're probably scouring the domes right now. There were attacks in four different domes before we came after you. She's bringing people in without questioning. Anyone that might know where you are. And those that don't oblige..." he lowered his gaze.

"What, Ash? What did she say to do to those that don't give me up?"

He fell silent. It was Tann who spoke next.

"They're taking them in. No questions asked."

Her eyes pooled and she ran her fingers through the Tecken's fur beneath her. She knew exactly what happened to those the Starblades took in, she'd seen it with her own eyes. "And what lesson is Leona hoping to teach them here?" She asked through gritted teeth.

"That if they're with you, they're not with her. And anyone not with her dies."

"How many?"

"Several hundred before we left," Ashlan said, "probably more than that now. I just don't understand why she cares so much about one Freedom Runner. If that's even what you are."

He didn't know. Tann hadn't told him who she was. Why? Why was he keeping it a secret? She wanted to tell Ashlan everything. About her magic. About Colton. She thought he would have known by now, that she could be herself — be free. But he was as clueless as ever and for some reason, Tann was helping it stay that way. Was he worried about the rest of the Freedom Runners? Did he not trust Ashlan because he was a Starblade? He trusted him enough to bring him in to save her but not enough to tell him the entire truth. It didn't make sense!

"I don't know what I am," she said and felt Tann tense at her words. "But I know I can't let her hurt innocent people just to get to me."

"Well, you're not going to turn yourself in if that's what you're thinking!" Ashlan protested.

"I'm not thinking that," she said, defeated.

"So what's your plan?" Tann asked.

"I don't know," she said truthfully. "Right now, I just want to get far enough away from the Al'iil and make sure Dalrak is alright. We can discuss everything when we're not being hunted down. Tazmin is not a threat right now but she'll come to and when she does, she'll come after us."

"Why, Sid?" Ashlan asked. "Why are the Al'iil after you? And how did you even take down the high priestess?"

He was confused. She couldn't blame him. As far as Ashlan was concerned, the Al'iil were a force not to be reckoned with. "I didn't," she lied. "Dalrak used his magic and overpowered her."

"Magic. I still can't believe they have magic." Ashlan sighed.

She could feel Tann's eyes on her but chose to ignore him.

"Magic they want to use against Leona and every other human on Kartega."

"Kartega?" They asked in unison.

"Looks like you were right. We *do* have a lot to discuss, later."

They rode on in silence, taking turns sleeping on the

backs of their beasts throughout the night. Sid stayed awake, checking on Dalrak periodically to make sure he was still breathing. His wound was healing slowly but it was healing nonetheless, his magic running though his blood and speeding his recovery. *He'll be alright,* she thought, *they'll all be alright.*

She recited the words like a mantra as they rode into the depths of the jungle. Into the dark unknown that led them away from the high priestess and the Al'iil and into the wilderness of the star. Into the wilderness of danger that Sid knew was yet to come; danger that she had no idea how to protect them from.

THIRTY-FOUR

THE MEAT TASTED burnt and chewy and Sid tried not to think about which part of the insect she was munching on — she tried not to think about the insect altogether but every prolonged crunch sent her imagination spiraling. They left the survival portion of their escape up to Dalrak, trusting that he would have the best means and knowledge to carry them through the dense jungle. Meals like the one they were having at that very moment made her question that decision.

She looked over the burning fire, surveying the warrior. He didn't look bothered by the taste. Instead, he was already reaching for seconds. Sid twisted her mouth and continued to nibble at whatever she had in her mouth. It's not like she could exactly ask to see a meal card out in the jungle.

Sid swallowed audibly and downed a large gulp of river water from a makeshift cup Dalrak had carved for her from loosened tree bark. Careful not to get any splinters on her tongue, she licked the droplets covering the edges. She wasn't going to make that mistake twice. Her tongue still felt sore after pulling out dozens of red tree fragments from her swollen mouth.

"Il torrik sumpto kundrik," Dalrak said quietly in between bites.

Ashlan looked at her, eyes wide and eyebrows arched. "What did he say?"

"He says I need to eat more." She reached hesitantly into the charred mess of insect limbs at the edge of the fire, pulled out a piece then tossed it back in. "I'm alright for right now, Dee."

The warrior turned his nose up and grunted something under his breath before continuing to stuff his face.

"I still can't believe you speak Al'iil now," Ashlan noted.

"I don't. Not really. I can pick up some words and say a few sentences, that's all."

"You seem to do fine with him," he pointed to the warrior who was still busy with his meal.

"I don't think it's about words with Dee. I just understand him somehow. It's odd, right?"

He considered the notion then beamed a smile in her direction. "Considering everything I've seen lately, that's the least odd thing on the list."

"What's the most odd thing?"

She looked up from her cup to follow his gaze past the fire to where the beasts were spread out for the night. Tann was tending to the herd, bringing them water and patting each one on the snout. He had taken to the creatures during their days on the run, his connection to them stronger than Sid's and Dalrak's put together. From her conversations with Tazmin, she thought it was magic that pulled the Tecken to her but Tann had no magic at all and it suited him just fine.

More than fine, she thought as one of the beasts licked his face enthusiastically.

"So you're what? A Freedom Runner too now?" She asked jokingly.

"I don't think that's how it works, Sid. But after what I've seen Leona do, I'd choose them over her any day."

"Even over the humans?"

He fell silent and averted his gaze.

"It's alright if the answer is no. They're your people. You have to do what's best for them."

"Is that what you're doing? What's best for your people?"

A loaded question if there ever was one. Sid had no idea who her people were but there was no chance of explaining it to Ashlan without telling him everything about her and his father. As far as he was concerned, even after all of this, she was just another Domer that got in over her head. It's what she needed him to believe until she found the right time to tell him her story. "I'm doing what's best for everyone."

"That's pretty heroic. I didn't take you for the brave type," he smirked.

There it is. The Starblade returns.

"I'm kidding. To be honest, you're the only reason I'm out here in the first place. When Tann found me and asked for my help, I was going to have him arrested. I was *this* close!" He pinched the air in front of his face.

"So why didn't you?"

"I started thinking about that thing you said, about having pride in helping the planet. That's the reason I let my father push me into the Starblades. To do what's best for everyone in Neostar. Letting the Al'iil take you would go against everything the Starblades stand for."

"Don't you just stand for whatever the queen wants?"

"No, no we do not." She noted a sense of melancholy in his voice but let it go. "When I was little, my father told me that there was great honor in making the guard because we get to be the peacekeepers between the city and the domes. He told me we are the quiet, silent rope that binds the two together. I didn't understand it before. Not until Tann found me and begged for my help. I almost killed him, you know."

Her eyes widened, "You did?"

"Not my finest moment. Peacekeepers keep the peace. I just kept saying that to myself even when all I wanted to do was throw him in a lightline and bring him in."

"So that's why you didn't?"

"That, and the fact I couldn't get the image of the Al'iil doing star knows what to you out of my head."

"I was fine. Nothing I can't handle." She tried to force a laugh but her quivering bottom lip betrayed her. Just thinking of her days and nights in Tazmin's hut made her want to throw up every piece of insect part she'd consumed. Although, if she was being honest, she wanted to throw them up with or without the fear.

"But you almost weren't fine. If I didn't listen to Tann, if I left you here," he shook his head, "I don't even want to think about what they would have done to you."

"They wouldn't have done anything to me. Trust me. They needed me alive."

He reached for her hand and squeezed and every thought she had before this disappeared into a fog. She looked around to see if anyone was looking. Tann was still a way off and if Dalrak could hear or see them, he made no movement to show it. She squeezed back and tried not to smile at the curl of his lips at her touch.

"So they actually thought you'd carry some implosion device into the city for them?"

"Yes," she lied because that's all she could do. It was the story she told him and Tann to avoid further questions. Dalrak played along without saying otherwise and for the first time since she'd met the warrior, she was glad they didn't speak the same language. The less he said, the more chance she had of keeping the truth about her magic from Ashlan. She didn't know why she lied to Tann too, but it seemed easier to tell one lie than try to keep her stories straight between the two of them.

"Well, that's pretty foolish of them. Guess they don't know you at all, huh?"

"What do you mean?" She asked.

He pointed to her goggles and barred his teeth. "You're the girl that doesn't follow orders."

"I HATE THIS PLACE!" Sid screamed and dodged out of the way of an incoming ice pellet.

The storm hit them without warning. One second she was helping Tann feed the Tecken and the next they were running after Dalrak for shelter with angry shards of ice raining down around them. Ashlan raced past her with the droid on his heels and she couldn't help but laugh despite the situation they now found themselves in. It looked like the droid took a few hits, specifically in its behind, and it now zoomed by her with two large, circular dents on each butt cheek.

Sid sped up before she herself met the same fate.

A pellet hit the trees on her right, the sound sharp and

penetrating like the racket of a ship landing. There was another sound immediately after and she barely had time to look before Tann grabbed the back of her suit and pulled her into his chest. His arms wrapped tightly around her and they fell back, their bodies slamming to the wet ground. The hit tree hurled through the air, landing just ahead of their feet with a ground-shaking thud. She opened her tightened eyes and peered over her own chest, rising and falling so fast she wasn't sure if she was even breathing anymore. Tann's heart beat senselessly at her back, the shock of the fall engulfing both of them.

Her eyes were wider than the moons when she finally unhooked his arms and got up. One more moment and she would have been under that tree.

"Tann! Sid!" Ashlan's voice carried over the tree trunk in echoes. "Is everyone alright?"

"We're fine!" She yelled back.

"We're trapped!" Tann added.

The hail was getting stronger and the pieces that fell from the sky were as large as her arm. She looked up, searching for some hint of Jericho's light pushing its way through the clouds but it was hopeless. They were blanketed in the anger of the storm and if they stayed there, the chances of getting hit by hail were not in their favor.

"We need to climb over!" She yelled at Tann who was already on one knee with his hands crossed and ready to hike her up onto the wood.

As she readied herself for the climb, a glowing lightline flung over the curve of the trunk and landed next to her face. "Grab hold!" Ashlan shouted from the other side and she noted the dash of fear in his voice. "We'll pull you over!"

Tann plucked the line from her hands and wrapped it

twice around her waist. "You go first," he tightened the line one more time and stepped back. There was a light tug at the other end and soon she was hoisted in the air, legs dangling and body scraping against the tree bark.

"Use your legs, Sid!" She heard Tann yell from below.

Turning on her side, she pressed her boots into the trunk and tried to match the pace of her ascent with steps. After a few twirls and tumbles, she got the hang of it and was at the top of the fallen tree in no time. She looked down to Ashlan, Dalrak and the droid, noting the end of the lightline at its waist.

"Now what?" She yelled.

"Now, you jump!" Ashlan answered and elbowed Dalrak in the ribs. The warrior took a step forward until he was right under her feet and held out his arms. "Aim for his chest!"

"Are you serious?"

Of course he's serious. He's insane!

She didn't bother arguing, at this point, the only place for her to go was down. Sid unwrapped the lightline and tossed it back down to Tann who started getting a grip on it immediately. Sid looked over the edge, regurgitating the morning's meal. It was high. Not high enough to kill her, but enough to do some serious damage if she missed Dalrak's arms. *This better work,* she told herself and stepped forward.

Air rushed past her and she felt like she was flying. The shrapnel of the ice ricocheted off her shoulders, pushing her through the air even faster. Sid wanted to scream but the words caught in her throat, replaced only by a pathetic whimper. When she landed on Dalrak, she felt like she had hit a wall. In fact, landing on an actual rock wall might have been more comfortable. The warrior's chest contracted with muscle as if she was trying to escape, and Sid had to pat him on the shoulder just to let him know she was alright. Unenthusiastically, he lowered her to the ground, brushing tree bark off her back.

Tann landed in a regal crouch at her side a minute later.

"Show off," she huffed and looked to Ashlan.

"We need to find shelter before we get ripped to shreds."

"Already on it," he said and pointed in the direction of a dark cave entrance barely visible behind the large mass of shrubbery that covered it. "Dalrak found it so I'm guessing it's safe."

"Good, let's go." Sid looked back, "I see you've been busy with Fred."

Ashlan grinned before following Dalrak and Tann into the cave. "I may have made some improvements while you were gone."

"Didn't take you for a mechanic."

"I'm not just a Starblade, you know."

"I know," she said and sped up her pace to shelter. Maybe everyone could be more than one thing after all.

THEY HUDDLED close to the fire and listened to the hail intensify outside, all four of them still shivering from the cold. It would be a while before they could warm their bones from the chilling wet of the storm. Dalrak grunted something under his breath and kicked a nearby rock in frustration. Something wasn't going his way. She glanced at Ashlan and laughed which irritated the warrior even more. With another grunt, he pushed up from his seat and stormed off.

"Dee! Come back! We're just kidding!" She yelled after him but he barely heard her.

"He'll be back," Ashlan said.

She looked at the warrior's disappearing bare back and sighed. Something about his absence made her magic curl at the tips of her toes and fingers; like her energy was reaching for his when he wasn't nearby. Until now, she hadn't realized how connected their magic had become, how dependent on one another. Back in the camp, she thought it was because he was the only one that was truly kind to her but out here, in the middle of nowhere with nothing left to lose, she knew it was something else entirely. They were bound somehow and, stars help her, she was afraid of what that might mean.

"You alright?" Ashlan asked when she didn't respond.

"Sure, why?"

"You're shivering."

"Well, it's freezing in here. Don't act like you're not cold!"

He looked at the small bumps on his arm. "I guess it is a little chilly. Doesn't seem to bother some people though."

She looked at Tann who was not bothered in the least by the drop-in temperature. His tunic had come undone at the belt and he was struggling with barricading the cave's entrance with broken branches from outside. Her eyes slid over the bulges of his chest. *Is that sweat? Is he sweating right now? Seriously?* Her gaze moved over his body and she felt herself flush with an oncoming wave of heat. Speedily, she looked down at her boots before Ashlan could notice. Had he seen her gawking at Tann? She started to say something to distract him in case he caught her but stopped. When she looked at the Starblade, his face was just as red as she assumed hers must have been. She followed his gaze to

Tann's chest and look away uncomfortably, like she had interrupted some private moment that she had no business partaking in. Like she had stolen something from Ashlan.

As though he could hear her thoughts, he shook off his leering eyes and met her gaze. "I," he stumbled, "I was just-"

"Stardaughter! You like Tann!" She yelped.

"Shh! Quiet!" He snapped, "I don't like anyone. I don't know what you're talking about!"

Sid couldn't keep her mouth closed. Ashlan and Tann? How? When? Why? Every question she could ask lingered on the tip of her tongue which started to feel too large for her mouth. All the jokes and banter she shared with Ashlan, did that mean nothing? How could he not tell her that he had no feelings for her? Sid wasn't sure how she felt about him and if the attraction she felt had less to do with him and more to do with finding someone she felt comfortable with but that didn't matter. Ashlan should have told her that the feelings she didn't know she had weren't reciprocated. Sid felt foolish thinking about it, embarrassed and torn. On the one hand, she wanted Ashlan to be happy but on the other... *The fool should have told me!* She had no idea that Ashlan felt this way about Tann, about anyone for that matter. Like her own people, the humans were fluid when it came to choosing a partner but it wasn't the fact that Tann was a man that bothered her. Ashlan liked a Domer. A Starblade liked a Domer. She didn't even think that was possible on the star. What would Colton do if he was here? Would he understand? Or would he condemn his only son for his choices? She wondered if Ashlan thought of the same things when he first started having feelings for Tann. Did Tann know? Did he feel the same? How had she completely misread this situation? There were so many things she wanted to ask him, the thoughts rushed through her like someone was chasing them. But this wasn't the time to bombard Ashlan with her starved need for information. He technically never told her anything and if she was truly his friend, she'd keep her mouth shut.

"I won't tell him. I won't tell anyone," she whispered.

"Good, because there's nothing to tell!" He spat and looked away from her.

"Right. Of course," she smiled and reached over to squeeze his hand.

To her surprise, he didn't yank out of her grip but simply sat there in silence, his eyes trained on the fire. Though if she looked closely, she could see that his eyes were slightly tilted to the right where Tann's body worked idly with the barricade.

It was starting to look like the jungle didn't just change *her*. They were all different now. Better and so much stronger.

THIRTY-FIVE

THE WEATHER CLEARED by morning and the temperature in the jungle spiked by midday. No matter how much time she had spent in the lush mess of it, Sid would never understand the intricacies of Kartegan weather. One moment, Jericho's light beamed bright above them, casting a net of scorching heat and making her pant with dehydration. The next they were running from the rapid fire of ice pellets falling from the sky. No wonder the humans built weatherproof shields over their city, who could live like this?

Sid wiped sweat off the back of her neck, careful not to expose the nakedness and purity of it. Her hair had grown out quite a bit since she landed on Kartega but she still worried that Ashlan might catch a glimpse of her non-chipped skin and ask questions. She'd tell him eventually, she had already decided that, but each moment seemed worse than the next. She couldn't give him more to worry about, not when they were being chased by the Al'iil and the queen, and not so soon after Colton's death. Her muscles tensed thinking of Colton's face and she swatted at her wet eyes. *I'll tell him soon, I promise.*

A sharp cold gripped her side, jarring her enough to jump. Fred's metal hand pulled away abruptly as if she'd slapped it off and she turned to see Ashlan smiling from behind his screen.

"Hey! What was that for?" She yelled.

"You seemed out of it."

"So that's how you bring me back into it?"

"Worked didn't it?" He smirked and went back to fussing around with the droid's sequencing.

Despite herself, Sid was trying to be nice to him. After the exchange in the cave and finding out about his feelings for Tann, she was trying to be diplomatic and kind. She even offered to help him with Fred for a bit, which was truly more for herself than him since she missed the metal fool. But Ashlan seemed to be intent on driving her away. He refused her help, chose to walk as far away from her as possible and now he was tormenting her with her own droid. *That's it! I'm over it!*

She marched toward him, kicking up dust in her wake. Ashlan didn't bother looking up and she picked up her pace, almost jogging in his direction. Without warning, Dalrak swooped into her path and she ran face first into his chest. Sid yelped and rubbed her forehead, the hit already starting to redden from impact. Running into Dalrak's chest felt a little like running headfirst into a rock.

"What the muck, Dee!" She yelled, eyes squinting in pain. "You don't just ram yourself into people like that!"

The warrior pointed to the yellow glow of her shaking hands. She hadn't even realized her magic had kicked in and the thought worried her. Having control of her power had not been an issue before, although Sid was quickly learning that most things that weren't an issue before were becoming liabilities. Dalrak looked down at her then raised a finger to a small parting between two large trees. "Sum kalim todo set," he grunted.

"You're right," she sighed. "Guys! Let's take a break. We've been walking forever."

"Your little legs getting tired?" Ashlan joked and she made a note to knock his teeth out later.

"Just settle in. We'll be back."

She followed Dalrak through the trees, careful to hide the growing electricity on her skin. She could hear water on the other side of the tree lined hill and, as she listened in, realized it wasn't the same as the rapid flow of the jungle rivers. This stream sounded more like a hard pounding descent. Pulling a low hanging vine out of the way, the warrior led her through to the other side. Sid's eyes jutted out as she took in the waterfall before her. She let her fingers tap against each other as she trailed her gaze over the heavy stream. The ones she saw in Tower City didn't begin to compare to the wonder before her. The waterfall was easily twice as tall, reaching so far up that its starting point was lost behind fat, fluffy clouds that floated across it. The water splashed as it hit the rocky surface of the edge and she noticed a few aerial beasts circling above it.

"Turtuk," the warrior said when he noticed her staring. Then pointed a finger at the flying creatures, "Turtuk."

"That's what they're called?" She asked. "They're beautiful!"

And they were. The Turtuk's wingspan was bigger than Sid's entire body and they were covered in a pearlescent fur that changed color as Jericho's light hit them. Some of them flew so high she was worried they might hit the ring and catch ablaze. A foolish worry as the ring was well above the star's atmosphere but it was something Sid thought about nonetheless. She couldn't make out the exact features of the Turtuk from where they stood but there was a distinct red beak protruding from their faces and what looked to be very sharp, very pointed horns in between their ears. Sid thought about the masks the men and women wore at Magic and wondered if Serryl drew her inspiration from the winged creatures flying above her head.

"Wow," she whispered and walked closer to the edge of the water.

There was little time to indulge in the wonderment around her. Dalrak spun around to face her, grabbed for her hands and punted them into his chest.

"Ow! What was that?" She yelped.

He picked up her hands and did it again.

"Seriously, Dee, what are you doing? You like being hit or something?"

The warrior raised an eyebrow and smiled. The subtle glow of his body intensified and she noticed him burrow his heavy legs into the ground. Electricity danced on his skin, calling to the magic inside her.

"Oh! I get it!" She whooped and mimicked his stance. "Well, if it's my magic you want, why didn't you just ask nicely?"

Sid closed her eyes and reached for the power that had already started to wake up. She felt the magic of Kartega rise in her, a steady pull through her legs all the way to her charged up hands. With a quick flip of the wrists, she pushed the energy that was threatening to escape into the small space between them where Dalrak had already readied his own magic to meet hers. Their energies collided, fiercely and without apology. It swirled in a ball of blazing power, growing into a towering electrical surge. Her hands mirrored the warrior's movement as they raised the ball higher and higher until it was levitating just above their heads. Briskly and without pause, they slammed their fists into the ground, landing in a low crouch. The ball followed and pushed its way into the earth below them. Sparks flew around them, encircling them in a blazing wall of electrical fire. The energy swirled and shifted until Kartega was ready to accept it, swallowing it whole.

When the earth cooled, Sid stood up and patted the warrior's broad shoulder. "Really, Dee, is it that hard to just talk to me next time?"

The warrior glanced up at her, eyebrows raised.

"Fine, be that way," she said and started to walk away.

"You don't listen."

Sid spun back around, her eyes wider than wormholes. "What did you just say?"

"You don't listen," Dalrak repeated in perfect human words.

"Dee! Are you joking? You knew how to speak human this entire time and made me fumble around with sign language and pathetic gestures?"

"I don't talk that good," he sighed, "and you speak Kartega now. Sort of."

She laughed. He had a point. She could hear the struggle to form the words when he spoke and she couldn't deny that she quite liked the way the old language rolled off her tongue at times. "Don't be so hard on yourself. You sound just fine to me. Just need a little practice. Which you would have gotten if you just came out and told me that you understood everything I've been saying. You could have saved us a lot of time, you know."

"You talk too fast," the warrior shook his head and got up. "You always talk too fast."

"Yes, well, keep up!" She smirked. "And thanks, for helping me release. Kuntara," She added in his language.

"Il terko," he said back. "Let's go."

"Go? Where?"

Dalrak ran to the edge of the water. "Swim!" He shouted back, "You swim!"

"Oh, I don't think so!" She yelled back. "I definitely do not swim!"

The warrior ran faster, ripping off layers of hide from his body until he was nearly fully bare. *Like you're not naked enough, Dee,* she thought and tried not to look at the exposed dark skin of his back and legs. His legs pushed off the edge and he cannonballed into the water, causing a rip tide of waves to roll and splash at the edges of the falls. For a moment, Sid was worried he wouldn't come back up. She wasn't sure how swimming worked, having never done it herself, but she assumed one was supposed to come up after a while. When the warrior still hadn't emerged, she ran to the edge and tried to peer through the dark, reflective surface. Before she could call out his name, a hand reached out from below, wrapped around her ankle and pulled her in.

Her backside hit the water first, followed by the rest of her body and finally her head. Sid tried to see around her but the water was too dark, too heavy. It had swallowed her whole. She splashed and kicked, forcing her way to the surface. When she finally reached the top, she realized her feet could just graze the bottom while still keeping her head above water. Dalrak stood in front of her, waist deep, laughing uncontrollably.

It was the first time she had heard the warrior laugh. Until then, she didn't even think he was capable of laughter and even though it was at her expense, it was nice to see him happy. She raked her fingers through her soaked hair and rearranged her goggles.

"Thanks for that, glad you're getting a laugh out of it." She sniped.

The warrior splashed water in her face and she growled in frustration. *Water. Time to get you back, Dee!* Sid let her lips curl into a smile and sent a jolt of electricity into the water toward Dalrak. He jumped from the impact, rubbing his hands over the hair that stood up on his arms; singed from the shock.

"Not so brave now, are you?" She laughed.

"That was bad," he said gruffly.

She chuckled again and started to dredge through the water back to shore. "Come on! Let's dry off and get back to the others."

They made their way back through the trees to where the group had settled in for rest. Sid's boots sloshed with water and she was barely able to get the wet out of her hair. Ashlan and Tann were definitely going to wonder what happened to them. She ran through a few excuses for why they were both soaking wet, none of which sounded as believable as the truth. In the end, she decided it best to tell them that Dalrak thought it would be funny to push her into the water and leave the magic part out of it.

"Hey guys! Guess what?" She yelled as they stepped through the trees, "Looks like Dee here knows how to speak human!"

Her boots sloshed to a halt as they stepped over the barrier of trees. There, in the middle of the jungle where they had left the group, stood over two dozen Starblades.

Ashlan and Tann were both on their knees, their arms bound by lightlines behind their back. The Tecken were nowhere to be seen and Fred was slouched against a tree trunk, immobile.

She started to run for them, anger fueling her every move, but stopped as a Starblade pointed his blade at Tann's throat.

"One more step and he dies."

THIRTY-SIX

HER WRISTS BLED from trying to rip through the light-line, each pull was like a cut made with jagged glass. Sid tried to count how many times she'd been bound and dragged against her will since she landed on the star. Too many. Someone slammed a knee into the back of her legs and she fell onto the cold, stone floor of the throne room. The Starblade that did it would heed her wrath first when she got free. But she wasn't getting free, at least not in the near future. Sid couldn't see a way out of the situation. With Ashlan and Tann bound and on their knees, and Dalrak not even in the room, there was not a grasp of hope left in her.

Slow, precise footsteps entered the room followed by the scraping drag of metal on stone; the queen. Sid could tell that self-assured walk without having to look up. It was the same footsteps that plagued her sleepless nights. She glanced up anyway, locking eyes with Leona, refusing to bow down.

"Why are we here?" She demanded. "Isn't there a better use for your guards? You've sent a small army after me, terrorized innocent people, and for what? For one little part of a rebellion?"

The queen didn't budge but the hint of a smile reached her eyes.

"Let them go! They have nothing to do with this!"

"Well, that's not entirely true, now is it?"

She looked at Tann whose eyes begged for her to stay quiet. "Fine, then let Ashlan go at least. He's a Starblade! The son of a general! He didn't do anything wrong. He was just trying to help me. It's my fault!"

"Hmm, at least we agree on something. Sid, was it?"

She nodded.

"It seems we find ourselves in quite the situation, Sid." Leona walked to the throne. She didn't sit, instead she let her weight rest lightly on the side, like an unwelcome guest that wasn't planning on staying long. "You are right, of course. All of this *is* your fault. You and that filthy creature over there," She pointed a red-lacquered finger at Tann, "but my dear Ashlan knew the consequences of his actions and chose to disobey me regardless. I wonder what his father would have said about that. Don't you, Ash?"

"My father would have done what's right!" Ashlan shouted.

A Starblade raised his blade and brought it down on Ashlan's back, knocking him further to the floor. He raised his blade again but the queen waved him off before he could strike. The look of disappointment on his face made Sid's stomach turn. She immediately recognized Connor, likely glad he was getting his revenge on Ashlan.

"That is quite true," Leona continued, "your father did always do what he thought was right."

"What?" Ashlan asked.

Sid lowered her eyes. *Shut up! Don't tell him about Colton. Not now. Not like this!*

"It looks as though my dear departed general has been doing what he thought was right for years. And right under my nose. Needless to say, I'm highly disappointed," she purred.

"What are you talking about? He was loyal to a fault! He was the best man you had on your guard!"

The queen tisked, her attention back on Sid. "I couldn't agree more! He was so great he had kept something hidden from me without worrying about the consequences. Or should I say 'someone'?"

"Leave him out of this!" Sid yelled. Her magic rose to the surface and started to break free but as soon as the electricity left her skin, it bounced off something, some invisible shield trapping it in place. She felt breathless and dizzy, like her blood was rushing into all the wrong body parts.

"Careful now, you don't want to do that. That lightline will fry you to the bone if you try. I had it specifically tailored for just this occasion; when I realized what it was I was dealing with here."

"What are you talking about? Sid, what is she talking about?" Ashlan cried. "Tann?" He begged the Domer tied next to him for answers but Tann only shook his head and averted his gaze.

"She didn't tell you, did she?" Leona mused. "Why of course she didn't! Why would you help her if you knew the truth!"

"No! Ash, don't listen to her! She's lying!"

"Am I? Am I lying, Sid?" Leona walked over to Ashlan and dragged a sharpened nail under his chin. "Such a pretty thing, isn't he? I can see why you'd want him around."

"Just stop. You have me! You wanted me and now you have me! Let them go!"

A howl left the queen's blood-red lips and she moved so fast that the metal of her skirts almost left an indent in the floor. She was at Sid's side, crouched in front of her. Not low enough to equal their height but enough that she was looking directly at her. Her eyes burning through Sid's glare.

"I don't have to do anything you ask," she smiled. A vicious smile that made Sid's hair stand on end. "Once I tell him who you are, he'll be right where he belongs. At my side."

"Tell me what? What is going on right now?"

"Silence!" Leona screamed and the room vibrated. "Don't you want to know why your father died, Starblade? Why you're an orphan at such a young age?"

"Sid," he begged but she couldn't talk. She couldn't even look at him.

With slow, calculated steps, the queen walked back a few paces. She stopped just in front of the throne and motioned for someone beyond Sid's vision. In seconds, Abbot emerged from the shadows of the room followed by two Magistras. One Sid had not seen before and Kelyn, taking small strides with a grin from ear to ear. The two girls looked pleased, like they were enjoying the show but something about the way Abbot moved made her wonder if he was uncomfortable with the situation — angered even. Despite the look on his face, the general walked over to the queen and bowed once before standing next to her.

"Give me your blade, general."

"Pardon me, my queen?"

"Your blade, I want it. Now!"

The general lifted a pot-marked hand and brought out

his blade. As soon as Leona had it, she was back at Sid's side. She pointed the tip of the blade at the back of her neck and pushed the trigger button. Electricity stirred through the weapon, lighting up the tip and the queen pressed it into Sid's neck, releasing the pent-up voltage.

"No!" Ashlan screamed. "You'll kill her!"

"Hush, now Ash. You'll ruin the show," she said and squeezed.

The current surged from the blade into Sid's body. Her muscles tensed and froze and her blood began to boil. She could feel sweat coating every part of her. Heart racing, she tried to move but her body refused to respond. Her head dropped and she could feel the magic in her awaken. It growled and screamed, aching to get out. She tried to hold on, tried to calm down. She thought about the days in the jungle with Dalrak and the tricks he had taught her to control her power. She tried to slow her breathing but her lungs were moving on their own. Fast breaths, in and out. This is what the Qualin must have felt when Tazmin sacrificed their small bodies to Kartega. She couldn't hold on much longer. Sid cried out as the magic burst out of her. The lightline scorched against her wrists, burning through her flesh in response. She screamed. Loud enough to make the Starblades close to her jump back. Her body dropped with a thud; impotent.

The room fell silent. Ashlan stared at her, wide eyed and tear stained.

She was glowing.

"What is this?" He whispered. "What did you do to her?"

"Me? Oh, this is nothing I did," Leona said triumphantly. "I merely meant to punish her the way we punish every other rebel that refuses to cooperate. That blow should have killed her. It should have short-circuited her chip," she paused. "Unless, of course, she doesn't have one."

The queen bent over Sid's limp body, grabbed hold of the loose, sweat-soaked hair and pulled.

Everyone in the room gasped. Everyone but Tann who was no longer looking down. His dark eyes were wild with a fury Sid recognized all too well. He was plotting. *The fool. What in the muck does he think he's going to do here?*

"How?" Ashlan asked, "How is this possible?"

"I'm so glad you asked," Leona said. "You see, it seems that when the inhabitants were chipped, we missed one. Oh, it happened on a few occasions, of course, but we got them all in the end. Except this one here. Her parents did a decent enough job of hiding her, from what I'm told, but in the end we would have found her just the same. That is, if your father hadn't gotten involved."

"My father? What did my father have to do with this?"

"Well, he's the reason she got away! It's all very heroic, you see. He found this little creature and helped her parents hide her away from me. In the one place he knew I'd never think to look." She looked out of the large window at her side and pointed up. "I was so busy with keeping my precious Citizens safe that I never thought to look up. Clever little thing, your father was. He had this beast twirling around us in a ship all these years.

"He raised her, really. Protected her to the end. Died for her in that rebel attack."

"How? That was an accident?"

"Ash, don't be so daft! Do you really think it was an accident your father, *the general*, took such a simple job that day? Left his post here in the towers to chase down a few rebels?

No! No, he went there to warn them," she shot a disgusted look at Tann, "to warn his little group. It didn't do him much good in the end. These creatures are built for hatred. They attacked my Starblades like the blind force they are. And do you think any of them cared that he died for their pathetic cause?"

"They didn't kill the general!" Tann shouted. "They wouldn't do that! She's lying!"

Leona signaled and the Starblade nearest Tann rammed the tip of his blade into his back. Tann fell back to cradle the wound, eyes searching for Ashlan. Sid's heart broke for him as he realized that there was nothing left of Ashlan in the throne room. Tears flooded her face. She couldn't look at Ashlan, couldn't see the grief that must have drenched his expression. Couldn't face his loss. "I cared, Ash! I do care! I loved Colton! He was like a father to me!"

Ashlan was quiet for a moment. Slowly, he got up and looked down at her. "But he wasn't your father. He was mine. And he died for you. He died for you and you couldn't even tell me the truth."

"Ash! I'm sorry! I was going to! I was! But then the Al'iil got me and you came and I-"

"Stop. Just please stop," he looked away. "I trusted you, Sid. I trusted all of you."

"Please, Ash! Can't you see what she's doing? She's trying to make you hate me! Please!"

The queen laughed again, walked over to Ashlan and unfurled the lightline from his wrists. "I don't have to try. Seems to me, you've done the job quite well yourself."

"You're a monster!" Sid screamed.

She tried to get up but Abbot was at her side quickly. His boot raised and he let it slam into her back, knocking her back to the floor. Every bone in her body ached and she could taste the metallic flavor of blood on her lips. How did Leona find out about her? It couldn't have been Abbot; he had no knowledge of any of this. How did she know so much? How did she know everything?

"How?"

The queen turned back, "I'm sorry?"

"Who told you?"

"I would have found out sooner or later. Lucky for me, a few threats go a long way when it comes to dealing with vermin. All I had to do was push the right people and threaten the right rebels. Or should I say Freedom Runners." She turned to Tann, "Is that what you call yourselves now? I can't quite remember. I do believe that's the term your father used when he told me everything."

Tann's face dropped. She didn't need to look at him to know what he must be feeling. His father, his own father betrayed him. It wasn't something she could imagine. The only two fathers she'd had died protecting her. How would it feel to have your own family turn against you?

"You're lying," was all he said. His gaze shifted from Ashlan to land on his father's face. Pressing his side, he rearranged himself to crouch, his eyebrows raised in question.

"I'm sorry, son!" Edek exclaimed, "She threatened to kill you. I had to! Please understand that I had to!"

The queen gasped dramatically, "Oh, my! You two have so much to discuss it seems! Fear not, you'll have plenty of time to ask him about it in the holes."

"The holes?" Sid asked. "What's that?"

"Oh, they're these wonderful cages we have for the filthy

beasts that try to ruin our way of life here!" Kelyn squealed before the queen hushed her.

Cages? Holes? Sid's mind ran through the towers architecture to try and make sense of it. The empty floors in the Queen's Tower that Ashlan told her about. They weren't empty. They were prisons! All the talk of peace and living in unity and this entire time the queen had been imprisoning everyone who posed a threat to her own Citizens. Locking them up like animals to be held against their will. And from what she'd seen so far, likely tortured, or worse.

"Where's Dalrak?" She asked.

"Who? Oh yes, that strapping Al'iil you brought with you. You know, if they weren't such pointless creatures, I'd keep him as a personal pet."

"He's not pointless. And he's not a pet."

"You're right," Leona sighed. "Pets have a purpose and a master. Maybe when we're all done with you, I can work on breaking him to my liking. I could use someone so..." she paused, "vigorous around."

"You're disgusting!" Sid spat on the floor next to the queen, missing her gold-polished heels by a centimeter.

Leona stepped over her spit, draped an arm over Ashlan's shoulder and led him out of the room.

"What about her?" Sid heard him ask.

"Nothing for you to worry about. She is scheduled to be chipped in the morning in one of the domes. We'll telescreen the entire proceeding, make sure these Freedom Runners understand their place once and for all."

With that, the room fell into a hush. Sid let her head rest on the floor, her heart beat so slow she wasn't sure she was even alive anymore. It was over. In the morning, she would be chipped and bound to the domes. That is, if Leona let her leave in the first place. For all she knew, she would spend the rest of her life in one of the holes with all those who fought back. She would never again feel the cool air on her skin. Never see her friends. Never get to sail her ship through the air or watch the glow of Kartega from the safety of infinite space.

She heard the echo of boots around her. Vaguely heard Tann yell her name. Heard the scuffle of defiance as he fought back before the Starblades dragged him away.

Sid stayed on the floor until she too was dragged out of the throne room.

Her thoughts locked on the loathing in Ashlan's face when he found out the truth. *So this is what it's like to lose a friend.*

THIRTY-SEVEN

SEVEN HUNDRED AND TWENTY-FOUR. Seven hundred and twenty-four boulders lined the walls of the cylindrical hole Sid was thrown into. She had counted and recounted their brilliantly polished surfaces so many times that she was certain she could see the outline of her cage without even opening her eyes.

At least this time, her hands were free. Not that it was doing her much good. The thick stone around her acted as a shield, keeping her and her magic tucked far away and out of sight. Even if Sid managed to conjure enough power to flow through her, there was nowhere to direct it. She was entombed in rock. It was as if the holes were a burial site for those the queen wanted out of her sight. A memorial of everything that stood between her and the star's full surrender.

After being unconscious for what Sid assumed was several hours, she had woken up on the floor of the stone shaft. Her mind was dazed and she still had very little strength left after being electrocuted by Abbot's blade but she was aware enough to know there was no escaping the hole. The large boulders that made up the interior walls were polished so smoothly that there was nothing to grab hold of if she wanted to try climbing to the top. Though even if she was able to make the climb, she wasn't exactly keen on trying since the hole's glass ceiling sat nearly ten meters up. The only other access into her cage was through a thick steel wall. Unfortunately, there was no handle on the interior of the door and the guards did not bother opening it, choosing instead to torment her through the small slit in the center.

"Here's your last meal, traitor!" One of them yelled, tossing a rotten piece of soy bun at her feet. "Eat up!"

Sid cleared her dry throat but the air got trapped in her larynx and she ended up dry heaving instead. "I'm thirsty!" She yelled back. "I need water!"

"Traitors don't get water. Just like they don't get bathroom breaks. If you're thirsty, wait until you need to take a leak and solve your own problem!"

Boisterous laughter sounded on the other side of the door and she sank her back into the wall behind her. This was what Kartega had granted her in her final hours. This was what it thought she deserved.

She crouched next to the soy bun at her feet, soggy and lifeless and bruised. Just like her. How many days did it take for a bun to be this broken? How many hours of neglect and misuse? Did it try to fit in with the other buns only to be cast aside? Or did its mere existence anger the baker so much that they felt the need to let it simply wither into nothing? She sniffed its skin and tossed it against the wall. The bun flattened on impact and slid down the shiny stone until it splatted on the floor, dead. *If only it was that easy.*

The guards outside started talking again, some pointless

story about the domes she assumed. Until she heard one of them mention a rebel. Sid's ears perked up and she crawled closer to the opening in the door, careful not to step on the heels of her feet. Her own breathing was so loud that she could only make out every other word. She inhaled sharply, held her breath, and listened.

"More of these savages? Are you serious?" One of them asked. His voice was light and airy and Sid imagined what it would feel like to strangle him with her bare hands.

"Just caught today. Looks like we'll be pulling double shifts until this one here is taken care of." The second guard sighed. "If you ask me, just kill her already and get it over with. That way we won't need to keep throwing them in these stardamned holes and wasting my time."

"Oh, I don't know," the first guard said, "I don't mind this one so much. Too bad for the queen's eyes everywhere, I could think of a few things I could do with her before she's good and chipped like the rest of the beasts."

Sid's skin crawled and she held back a shudder. She could think of a few things she'd like to do to the mucking piece of garbage too. She pressed her ear to the cold metal and listened.

"So what are these new ones in for?"

"Same old charade. Some rebel garbage. Good thing they killed one on the spot or else we'd be stuck here till next week."

"They got one? Really?"

"Mucking straight they did. A high up one by the sounds of it."

"Not that angry one Kalvin told us about? The one with the bald head?"

"That's the one! Put up quite a fight, I hear. But you

know how these things are. They're as dumb as they are angry and they all get caught in the end."

Sweat poured over Sid in buckets. She fell away from the door, crawling back until she collapsed on the floor next to the foul-smelling bun. She couldn't move her arms or legs. Everything in her body shook but she couldn't feel the movement. There was only one Freedom Runner she'd known of with a shaven head and only one that was important enough to kill outright. Nyala. They had killed Nyala.

Tears welled in her eyes and she willed herself to hold them open, trying to contain the waterfall building in her which was itching to get out. Her eyes burned and when she couldn't hold them any longer, she blinked and let her world flow out of her.

Whatever magic was still in her sparked over her skin in small, pathetic bursts of power. She let it go. Let the magic leave her until she was nothing but an empty shell; a useless sack of skin on the floor.

Sid wailed. The guards yelled through the opening, ordering her to stop, unable to discern the depths of her grief. Unable to care even if they did. But she didn't hear them. All she heard was that Nyala was dead. Another person that cared for her, loved her even, dead because she wasn't strong enough to stop it. Because she was locked away in some hole while people, *her people*, died in the domes for simply wanting back what was theirs.

She felt like she was always locked away somewhere. In a ship, in a hut, in a hole. Always indisposed when the ones who were actually doing something were dying. She's the one that should be dead, not them. She was the coward; the reason for all of this. The girl who hid until everyone she loved was gone. There wouldn't be a chipping, Sid would make sure of it. In the morning, when it was her time to go, she would make certain that Leona would kill her. She didn't know how yet but it couldn't be that difficult. All she would have to do was feed on the queen's arrogance and pride, push her into ending her life.

Ending it once and for all.

HOURS PASSED before Sid heard the guards on the other side again. It was as though her dramatic display of emotion shocked them, like they hadn't been expecting a Domer to have any feelings at all. She could hear hushed tones and wondered if maybe the queen moved up the timeline and decided to chip her in the middle of the night. That didn't make sense. What would be the point? No one was awake and the entire purpose of the spectacle was to use her as a means of instilling fear in the Freedom Runners.

The voices got louder, loud enough that she didn't need to crawl back to the door to listen.

"I am your superior and you will let me speak with the prisoner. I will not ask again."

She knew that voice. The hard edges of it enveloped in a cocoon of jest and honesty; Ashlan.

Footsteps shuffled around, no doubt the guards getting out of the way for fear of losing their position. "Sid?" She heard him say on the other side. The sound was muffled by the weight of the metal but she could still make out the words. "Can you hear me?"

She said nothing.

"I know you can hear me, Sid."

"Go away, Ash." She cried.

"Not until you tell me why."

She sat up but stayed in her spot. "What?"

"Tell me why he did it, why he helped you."

"I don't know why. He was *your* dad. You figure it out."

"I'm trying to but I just don't get it. You were a random Domer. Why help a random Domer?"

Same old Ashlan, still carrying as much tact as a newborn frigger. All limbs and fluffy fur and wings that can't take flight. And words that work for nothing when it comes to getting someone to tell you what you want to hear.

"Did he ever talk about me?" He asked.

"No, Colton wasn't much of a talker."

"Ha!" He scoffed, "That's for sure. I guess he wasn't that different around you."

"What do you want, Ash?" She barked.

"I want to know why you lied to me. Why didn't you just tell me from the beginning?"

"Oh, tell you that I'm an un-chipped Domer that your dad's been hiding in a ship for fourteen years? That I came back to find him because that mucking ship almost killed me?" She yelled, then decided to lower her voice in case the guards were still nearby. "Or maybe I should have told you that I still had magic? Because I'm sure if I did you wouldn't go running back to Leona with the information just to get a higher ranking, right?"

"I wouldn't do that."

"Why not? You did it when she finally caught me. You did it when it mattered."

On the other side, Ashlan grew silent and she could hear his breathing speed up.

"Go away, Ash."

"I don't-"

"Go away! Go be with your people! You owe me nothing. We owe each other nothing."

"Sid, I-"

"I said go!" She screamed and tossed the bun against the door. The pastry had hardened from its time on the cold ground and sounded a sharp pang when it met the metal. She could hear Ashlan jump back on the other side. "I want nothing to do with you. Tomorrow I will be chipped and you will be free of me. Your life will go back to normal and you can forget we ever met each other. I don't want you here," she sighed. "Just let me have some peace in the last hours I have left."

She waited for him to rebut her, to keep arguing his point like he always did, but the boy outside was muted. Even his breathing had grown quiet to the point where she wondered if he was even there at all. Perhaps she just imagined him coming here? She was definitely hungry and thirsty enough to hallucinate. Maybe this was another trick her mind was playing on her like it did in the hut when she saw her twin of light? She had almost convinced herself that he was gone until she heard his steps recede.

He was leaving her. Again and this time forever.

THIRTY-EIGHT

THE BUN MADE for poor company and was left abandoned on the floor while Sid tried to run through her plan for
the morning. She'd already called the queen a monster and
while it had angered her, it hadn't been enough to make her
so incensed she'd wanted to kill Sid. She needed to hit a
nerve in Leona's stone heart. Trigger the queen enough to
push her over the edge. She hadn't the slightest clue what
she had to do or say to accomplish that and it was a fine line
between directing Leona's rage at herself and away from
some poor Domer who happened to be in the way.

She was playing out scenarios when the guards perked
up outside and spoke incoherently. Their tones were higher
than normal and she quickly fortified the entrance with her
body. Someone was coming to see her and from the sounds
of it, it was someone the guards feared.

"Thank you, gentlemen," the queen's indulgently civil
voice rang behind the door, "I'd like a moment with the girl."

She heard the sound of blades knocking once on the
ground and could picture the guards bowing awkwardly

before scurrying away. She hated them and their lackluster, pathetic way of serving. Even the droids the humans built had more character than those two.

When they left, Leona moved closer to the door.

"Are you awake?"

Sid kicked the metal enough to cause it to vibrate, hopeful the queen's cheek was pressed against it by some dumb luck.

"I'll take that as a yes," Leona said. "Starise is a few hours away."

"Great," Sid scowled.

"I wanted to come here to let you know that you have my word that no one else will get hurt as long as you cooperate with the procedure."

Procedure. She was talking about the chipping as though it was some trip to the physician for a routine diagnostic. It made Sid sick. "Your word isn't worth much these days."

"Tsk, tsk, tsk, that's not very cooperative, is it?"

"Do what you want, I don't care anymore."

"Interesting," the queen said and Sid could hear her smile on the other side. "How quickly the hero gives up."

"I'm not a hero. I didn't come here to save anyone. I came here for Colton and he's dead, so I'm done."

"Interesting," Leona said again.

"What is so stardamned interesting?" She yelled.

"Oh, nothing," Leona sighed and pressed the weight of her back on the door. "I just find it fascinating that the Domers are willing to die for someone who only came back to find one of *my* Citizens. Do they know that? Or did you lie to them like you lied to Colton's son?"

"No one should have died for me."

"So many already have; Colton included."

Tears burned her lids but she pushed them away. "I didn't ask him to do that."

"Oh, but he chose to do it. He chose you over me."

"So that's what this is about?" Sid scoffed, "Your bruised ego? Aren't you supposed to be above it all? Like a true queen?"

"I am a true queen, beast. I was Colton's queen and I am Ashlan's queen. But not yours because you're not like us, no matter how much you want to be. You're no one, nothing."

She stayed quiet. Not because she didn't have the right words but because in part, she agreed with the queen. She *was* nothing. Nothing important, nothing special, nothing to die for. In the morning, everyone would see that they had placed their hopes on a kid that didn't belong on Kartega and once they saw, she'd know they were free. Free to choose what they do next without holding their breath for some savior her parents promised. Free to either follow or revolt. She knew which one she wanted them to choose but she'd be stardamned if she was going to be the reason for the decision. In everything she'd learned in her lessons, nothing good ever came out of following a hero. Especially if that hero was someone like her.

"And I will not sacrifice my people's future for a nothing," Leona added.

"But you'd sacrifice the Domers? The Al'iil?"

"In a heartbeat!" Leona said, her voice ringing through the hole. "We are the only thing that matters. We saved this star. Without us, the Al'iil would have sucked it dry with their magic. Those savages."

"Kartega didn't ask for your saving. It was just fine before you got here."

"Where did you learn that word?"

"Didn't know it was a secret."

The queen grew silent for a brief moment before speaking again. "It isn't. It's simply," she paused, "antiquated."

"Just because you don't like a name, doesn't mean you can delete its identity."

"Oh, that is where you're mistaken," Leona grinned. "How many Domers do you know that still call themselves Kartegans? How many speak their native tongue? We dictate the order on this star and if we choose a name, it stays chosen."

Sid couldn't argue with that. Until she was taken by Tazmin and the Al'iil, she hadn't heard anyone refer to Neostar by its native name. It was as though it had been wiped from their memories, though she knew it hadn't been. The older generation knew the name, they just refused to speak it. How much fear did a person need to be exposed to before they forgot their true name? Sid didn't know the answer but she guessed it was a lot.

"What did you do to them? How did you make them this way?"

"Me?" Leona cried out, genuinely baffled. "*I* didn't do anything. You can thank my mother for that. The one thing she managed to do right."

"Your mother?"

"The original queen of Neostar, the creator of the entire facade, really. Her Circulum System is the reason we advanced as far as we did. If it wasn't for her brilliant mind orchestrating the ring, we'd never have had enough power for the technology we planned to build on this star. The system saved us all!"

"You mean the prison," Sid said quietly.

"Call it what you will but it worked. We had enough energy to build an entire world on this star. A world I won't let you or anyone else destroy!"

She hated the way Leona spoke about the ring. Like it was some mucking miracle. The humans didn't need it to live on Kartega, they wanted it for power and control. The queen's mother started this mess and here she was, acting as though they had brought salvation to the Kartegans by giving them a cozy little cage and fashionable collars. The worst part was that she believed all the nonsense. Sid could tell, in her core, Leona truly thought that the humans were on the right side of this.

"So you trapped them, robbed them of their magic and then what? Threatened to kill them if they disobeyed?"

Leona chuckled. "We didn't just threaten. Well, at least I didn't. Mother was always too weak for the task."

"You actually expect me to believe that you disobeyed the queen herself and did whatever foul things you wanted?"

"Oh, forgive me. I seem to forget I'm speaking to a savage. People like me don't disobey. We either agree or we do not and if we do not, we find a way to get our point across." Leona said. "Besides, mother was starting to get sentimental in her delicate age. It was best I dealt with her swiftly before she ruined everything we'd built here."

"She died of Amperfuge," Sid said in almost a question.

"She died because I willed it!" Leona howled. "Just like the rest of those beasts did when it was time to teach them a lesson about what happens when they disobey their queen!"

Sid's stomach turned and the image of Leona standing on a mountain of dead Domers rushed her thoughts. She was right, the queen *was* a monster. And she was the worst kind of monster; the kind that believes that what they've doing isn't wrong. "You killed innocent people to prove your point?" She asked, tears flowing freely down her filthy face. "Your own mother?"

"I killed useless creatures to save humanity. Mother was..." Leona paused and though Sid couldn't see her, she could feel the queen frown on the other side of the door. "Well, simply something that had to be done."

Sid turned the words over in her mouth before speaking. "From what Colton had taught me, humanity is kindness, not monstrous killings."

"Humanity is something you could never know anything about, beast!"

Leona's hiss pierced through the metal and she took a step back. The words rammed Sid right in the chest and impaled her heart. She might not know anything about being human but this wasn't what humans were like. Humans were like Colton, and Professor Cevil, and even Ashlan. Humans weren't this thing on the other side of the door that cared only for her own kind. *Muck, I'm more human than she is.*

The voice on the other side of the door grew still.

"I must prepare for the telescreens," the queen finally said. "Don't do anything rash tomorrow. Perhaps consider those friends of yours in their holes if any wild thoughts run through your tiny brain."

"Where-"

"Abbot!" Leona barked. Behind the door, boots shuffled. "Watch her closely."

She heard the whoosh and jingle of her gilded skirts and retreating steps. When the queen was gone and the guard's annoying laughter returned, Sid sank back against the wall and continued to plot for the morning. Leona's visit rattled her but it also brought a hint of assurance — she now knew the queen's weak spot. In the morning, she would use Leona's selfish need to save her own people against her. She would threaten the humans until the queen had no choice but to kill her where she stood.

THIRTY-NINE

"GENERAL," the squeaky guard said when they shuffled back into position.

"Soren," the general replied, "Clive, good to see you two again. I hope this one hasn't been giving you too much trouble."

"Oh, no! We can handle her!"

Their voices carried into the hole and Sid found herself rolling her eyes at every word. She couldn't believe she had to spend her last few hours listening to these fools small talk. She started to hum a tune in her head but was interrupted by Abbot's deep chuckle.

"I wouldn't be so sure. I've spent some time with her and she is a handful to say the least."

"I'd like to use *my* handful to break all your teeth," Sid muttered under her breath.

Abbot said something softly and she tip toed closer to overhear. The words sounded foreign to her and jumbled thoughts raced in her mind, threatening to overtake her sanity. She pressed her ear to the door and took a deep breath in, holding it against her rib cage.

"Oh, we couldn't!" One of the guards exclaimed, "The queen wouldn't approve."

"Please," Abbot said. "I insist."

"Are you sure, general? It gets spooky here after a while."

"Believe me, I've seen worse." Abbot replied and laughed again. "Consider it an order if anyone asks."

Feet trailed off outside, loud at first then softer and less pronounced. The guards were leaving! Abbot had sent them both away! The thought of spending time alone with him unnerved her to the core. No doubt he'd have questions, so many questions. She wasn't prepared to answer them. All Sid wanted was a few more quiet moments and maybe a chance to close her eyes. Why was it so hard to get that?

She leaned against the cool metal of the door, jumping back when a low hum sounded behind her. The door slid open and a fluorescent barrier stayed in its place; a previsionary measures in case the locks gave out. Sid stared at Abbot through the shield, his face contorted and his eyes as sharp as razors. He was oddly fit for someone his age, though she supposed that would be expected of a Citizen. Most of all, an NSO general. The old fool likely never had to spend days starving or locked away in a hole.

"Hello again, Sid." He said and grinned.

"What are you doing?"

"Just paying you a visit."

His hand slid across the scanner on the wall and the barrier disengaged. Abbot stepped into the hole. Slowly, like a predator taunting prey that's already been caught.

Panic filled her. She reached for her magic, fists white-knuckled and full of sweat. He sent the guards away. Not for their benefit but for his own. He was here to end her. She didn't know why or what she had done to instill such rage in the general but if he was here to end her life, she might have gotten a lucky break. There would be no need to try and trick the queen into killing her. Abbot would do the job just as well.

She took a step forward and raised her chin. "Get it over with."

"Oh, my!" Abbot snorted. "You really are fiery. Colton wasn't kidding."

As quickly as it had come, the panic dissipated, replaced by confusion and distress. Her brows cringed and she could taste the lack of understanding under her tongue. It tasted like the dusty pores of a red leaf.

"Colton? Colton told you about me?"

"Of course Colton told me about you! You think that mucker could pull off a stunt like that on his own? Stealing a kid is one thing, stealing an un-chipped kid and shooting her off into space is an operation. Operations need structure. Colton was more heart than head."

"Colton told *you* about *me*?" She wasn't sure if she was hallucinating or if he was simply toying with her before slicing her throat open with the point of his blade.

The general stepped forward, not by much, just a boot-sized worth but it was enough to send the hairs on the back of her smooth neck into a fluster. She backed up, her back pressing against the cold surface of the stone wall. With her hands still balled, Sid tried to will her magic to flow out. There were a few sparks jumping off her skin but she was still too weak to cause any real damage. Forget about the trick Dalrak taught her to weaponize the electricity, she'd be lucky if she could tickle Abbot into a laugh from where she stood.

But he might not know that. Sid tightened her lips and took a defensive stance.

"Relax, kid. I'm here to get you out," Abbot said. "And put those things away before you hurt yourself."

She shook her head.

"You're going to drain the little power you have left and I can't very well carry you out of here."

Sid shook her head again, this time desperately.

Abbot sighed and raised his hands in the air. "What's the number one rule, Sid?"

Her head swam. Those words — Colton's words — didn't seem right hanging off the general's lips. How had he gotten hold of them? Did Colton really tell him about her? Did he know this entire time? She didn't know what to do, what to say, how to act. She didn't know up from down anymore. Colton told someone about her. He trusted someone with information that could get him killed. *Did* get him killed in the end. He trusted Abbot. Not his son but Abbot; the new general.

"What's the number one rule?" Abbot repeated.

"Never use your magic. Especially if you're not alone," she whispered. "He told you? About the rule?"

"Told me? Ha! I made him give you that rule!" Abbot howled. "Half the reason you're alive is because of me. If it was up to Colton, he'd have dragged you back down here ages ago and stars know where we'd be then."

"Other than a hole in the Queen's Tower, you mean?"

"Ah! A sense of humor! Wonderful. I love a sense of humor on a rebel fugitive I'm about to break out," Abbot said dryly and she got the very distinct impression that there was nothing he liked about humor on anyone at all. "Now, let's go. We don't have all night."

"Abbot?" She asked and waited for him to face her. "Was he ever planning on bringing me back down?"

The question, though simple and honest, hung in the air like a pod drifting in zero gravity. Loaded with the weight of a thousand untried tears. She found the general's eyes and stared, waiting for the heartache to come.

"Sid," Abbot sighed. "Did you honestly think he'd keep you up there forever?"

She nodded which made the general smile.

"Yes, kid. He always planned on bringing you back down. He really cared about you, you know? Like you were his own. But it was hard."

"Why?"

"Because once he brought you down..." he waved a hand around the hole suggestively.

"Right. I'd start a revolution."

"So you understand why he waited so long," Abbot smiled again and this time she believed it. "He was keeping you safe. But you had to go and chase after him, didn't you?"

Sid laughed under her breath. "Couldn't help it."

The general moved to the door and she started to follow him but stopped short. "Wait!" She yelped.

"Now what?"

Their eyes met and she made sure to keep her head up. She'd once read somewhere that if you ever found yourself in a battle situation with someone who is larger and stronger than you, the way to show authority was with a straight face and a lack of blinking. Her eyes almost watered but she kept Abbot's gaze until she was sure he was listening to every word.

"I'm not leaving without my friends."

∿

"THIS IS A BAD IDEA, SID!" Abbot yelled.

His arm sliced through the air as he whipped the back of his blade against a Starblade's head. The boy's body twitched, then fell forward with loud thud, knocking his blade out of his hand. The weapon rolled across the floor, stopping when it bounced against the limp leg of the second guard Abbot had taken out.

They'd made their way to the fourth floor of the holes, leaving a stream of unconscious guards in their wake. Well, in Abbot's wake. Sid was still weak and useless and spent most of the time hiding behind the general as he cleared the path.

"We need to get out of here! Now!"

"We're almost there!" She hissed. "We can't leave without them."

She bent over to pick up the abandoned blade, twisting it around in her hands. "How do I turn this thing on?"

"You don't. Each blade is tailored to the guard and Starblade." Abbot nodded at the sleeping guard who looked almost peaceful if it wasn't for the large bump already swelling on his forehead. "You need his hand."

Sid's eyes darted from the guard to Abbot.

"Do you have a knife I can use?"

"What? No! Are you sure you're right in the head?" Abbot's face looked wild and frantic. "Just put his finger on the center console. Stars!"

"Oh," she said and followed the instruction. The blade lit up in her hand and though she was sure she was imagining it, it felt heavier somehow. As if the energy coursing through it weighed it down. Sid knew a thing or two about the heavy weight of magic. She smiled and got a better grip on the weapon. "This is nice!"

"Let's go. This way."

They stopped at a right turn and Abbot motioned for her to hang back while he took the first look around the corner. She wasn't sure why; with the blade in her hand, she felt invincible. Her renewed confidence was short lived when she tried to twirl the blade and follow the general only to stumble and nearly drop it on the floor. She caught the weapon by mere centimeters, exhaled briskly and decided to follow Abbot's orders after all.

The next corridor was free of guards. The general winked at her and they exchanged a smile of relief before marching forward. Dalrak's hole was a few doors down and she could already sense his agitation despite the layers of stone and aluminum between them.

Abbot swiped his palm in front of the lock console and she half expected the warrior to come charging toward them, furious and full of magic. Like an angry creature from one of Colton's stories. Instead, she found him crouched on the floor, his arms crossed and a tooth-filled grin on his face.

Of course. He knew it was her. He could feel her just like she could feel him.

"Thanks for ruining my surprise entrance, Dee. You're no fun!" She laughed and ran towards him.

His arms opened to greet her and she fell on her knees in front of him, rushing in for the embrace. Sid buried herself in his hard chest, tears streaming down her face in relief. He was alive. Her friend was well and alive. Dalrak tightened their embrace and she could feel the bones in her body tremble from his strength. It felt like a ship engine had fallen on her but she let him squeeze her tighter, happy to be back with someone she trusted. The warrior's magic surged under his skin and it didn't take long for his electricity to find hers. There, on the floor of a prison hole, their bodies were aglow with power. She closed her eyes and let his magic fill her to the brim, the strength returning to her like a wayward ship coming home to dock.

"Whatever that is, you need to hurry up," Abbot said sternly behind them.

The warrior, grinned against her forehead and she smiled.

Sid pressed her palms to his chest and got up, waiting until he followed. Her hands were tingling with renewed strength and she brought them up to her face. Energy swirled around her. Palpable and furious; fast and destructive. Her skin was brighter than ever and for the first time, she didn't care about the most important rule. She didn't care about any of it. There was no one else in this stardamned place like her and she was tired of trying to fit in. She didn't need to fit in. What she needed was to be different and fierce. She needed to be stronger than all of them. Stronger than the Freedom Runners, stronger than the queen and stronger than the ring itself.

"One down, one to go," she said to Abbot.

She was going free them. She was going to free them all.

FORTY

TEN THOUSAND VOLTS of electrically charged particles blasted into Sid's blood as she pulled the energy from the bottom two floors of the tower into her. The electricity crackled in the air, so loud that she couldn't even hear her own scream as she inhaled it. Her skin bubbled from the hit as the energy settled into her body and mingled with her own magic. She felt charged up. Not overloaded like her days spent with Tazmin. Instead, Sid felt like she had slept for days and ate a few large meals right after. She felt complete.

As soon as she'd drained the last of the power, the floors went dark. All doors slid open and the security system echoed a feeble alarm. Sid doubted it had ever been used before that very moment.

Red painted every surface; the glow of the emergency system lighting the way. Her own fervent glow was impossible to hide now and she walked proudly down the corridor to the towers exit with her friends and fourteen freed Domers in tow. Every few minutes, she glanced back to see

Edek trailing the group, his eyes darting away when he saw her watching. She wasn't comfortable with the idea of having him there but Tann refused to leave without his father, despite his actions against them. Sid understood him all too well. She still loved Colton despite his lies.

Citizens hid in darkened rooms and hallways as they passed. Some tried to set their droids and Droidhounds on the group but Sid and Dalrak shut them down without much effort. Sucking the energy out of a droid was child's play after shutting down all of the Queen's Tower floor by floor.

She knew it wouldn't be long until Leona made sense of their escape and restored power. The ring was good for times like this; an unlimited source of energy at the Domer's expense. She could see the warm glow of it outside the glass exit doors, so bright it almost overpowered the light of Jericho itself. So beautiful and frightening at the same time. An anomaly in every way.

They marched in silence through the city, not bothering to run. There was no one to run from really. The guards and Starblades were still in the towers, surrounding the queen in case of an attack, and the city was nothing but a boneyard of scared Citizens. Sid felt like all of Tower City was theirs. Back on the ship, she would have done anything to feel this way. Now, looking around at the cold, flawless streets, all she wanted was to get the muck out as soon as possible.

She looked back on the city when they had finally crossed the bridge. It felt smaller somehow, less wondrous. So different from what she saw in projections and telescreens and such a stark opposite to her own dreams. This wasn't the last time she would see it, of that she was certain, but something about this moment seemed finite. Like she was saying goodbye to an old friend.

Dalrak tugged at her suit and she followed him into the transport pod left over from that morning's worker shuttle. Sid pressed her nose to the glass, watching as the pod took flight. *This changes everything.*

"ASH?" She yelled out, pushing her way past Mannar and Lexia who were still lost in conversation with Tann. They hadn't seen him since he took off after her and the Freedom Runners crowded around him, poking and prodding and pulling him in for extended hugs. Many offered condolences for the loss, Nyala's death still flowing freely from their tear stained faces and Sid wondered how long it would be until her own heart healed, or if she would forever carry the death with her like a mark. Her own version of Kartegan symbols under her skin. Tann's discomfort was written all over his face, she'd have to make sure to tease him about this later. "Ash, is that you?"

The small flat was overrun with Domers and Sid had to flatten herself out just to squeeze through the bodies.

"Oh, hey, Sid!" Ashlan said, rubbing his neck. "How goes it?"

"How goes it? Seriously? What are you doing here?"

"Oh, you know. Fred wanted to see you so..." He smiled sheepishly.

"Fred? Fred's here?"

"Aha! Right over there, Dee's got him."

She looked over Ashlan's shoulder at the droid who, if she didn't know any better, looked like he was actually smiling. Sid waved and watched as Ashlan entered code into the screen to make the droid wave back. A nice enough gesture for someone who left her to rot in a hole.

"Why are you here?"

"Wow, straight to the point. Nice!"

"I'm not kidding around," she said and pulled him away from the crowd. "You need to leave."

Ashlan ripped his arm from her grip and pulled back. "I'm not going anywhere."

"Why? I lied to you, remember? I'm the reason your dad died!"

"And I'm the reason you got thrown in a hole so maybe we're even."

"That doesn't even begin to sound like even to me," she sighed.

"No, but I shouldn't have left you there. Just like you shouldn't have lied," he said. "I get why you did it, you know. I'm not a complete imbecile."

Could have fooled me!

"So that's why you came to see me?"

"Well, that and to tell you about Abbot. Surprise!" He threw his arms up but the awkwardness of the gesture made her squeamish. "Who knew dad told him everything."

"Right. Who knew," she said.

"Anyway, I'm not leaving. So looks like you're stuck with me again."

"Maybe I'm not the only one stuck with you," she smirked.

"What are you talking about now?" He followed her gaze to Tann who was still squirming out of an unwanted embrace. "Let's not, alright?"

"Sure," she nodded. "Have you talked to him? Since..."

"No. Nyala and him were close; she was like a second

mom to him," Ashlan said and looked at his boots. "I guess that's something we have in common now."

"Ash, I'm so sorry."

She reached for him but he shrugged her off. "It's fine. Don't start getting all emotional on me now. It's not a good look for you." He forced a smile and looked away, signaling for a change of topic.

Sid looked around the flat and stifled a laugh.

"What?" Ashlan asked.

"Nothing. Just this place. A Starblade, Freedom Runners and an Al'iil warrior. Sounds like a bad start to joke."

Ashlan rubbed the back of his neck again. "Doesn't seem that funny to me."

"Huh?"

"All these people, Sid," he said, "we're all here because of you, one way or another."

He wasn't wrong. If it wasn't for her, this flat would still be as empty as when she'd first seen it. A few Freedom Runners waiting for some magical girl to fall from the sky. Whether she liked it or not, this was her reality now. It wasn't perfect and it definitely wasn't what she thought she'd get when she finally made it down to the star, but somehow it was better. Because it was hers and it was as real as she could make it.

"We should talk," she said. "All of us. There isn't much time."

"Time for what?" Ashlan asked.

"To make everything right again."

CROSS-LEGGED, Sid sat on the single cot in the flat. Breathless.

"And you think you can do it?"

"Do I think I can persuade the Arcane to help us shut down the ring?" She asked with an exaggerated laugh. "Of course I don't! But I can try. Right, Dee?"

The warrior nodded and she could see some of the Freedom Runners exchange fearful glances. Despite his help in the escape of their loved ones, they still didn't trust the Al'iil. She couldn't blame them really; she still wasn't sure if she trusted Abbot, and he'd basically carried her out of there.

"Right now, I'm more worried about getting past the guards and Starblades without getting caught." She added.

"And the Magistras," Ashlan said.

"And the– wait, what?"

"You should be worried about them too," he continued. "They don't look like much but every lady in waiting is trained in the art of combat. They are the last level of protection for the queen in case of an attack."

"Wow."

"I can handle that part," he said and shot an assured look in Tann's direction that didn't go unnoticed by her.

"You'll handle the girls. Great," she scoffed.

"No, I meant I can get you through all of them."

Sid's eyes widened and from the corner of her eye, she could see Tann perk up with interest. *Well done, Starblade.*

"Did you forget about Fred already?"

"The droid? What about him?" Lexia asked.

"Droids. Plural," Ashlan said.

Ashlan, you brilliant stardamned mucker. "Yes! We use all the droids in the city! You think you can run that code?"

"I think I can try," he cracked his knuckles and flipped his hair. *Too far, Ash. Too far.*

"Good enough for me," she said. "Everyone else on board?"

"I don't think this is a good idea," Edek said from the back of the room.

"No one cares what you think, dad," Tann snapped and looked away. "Sid's leading this, take it or leave it."

Some of the others nodded in agreement, the rest were still trying to piece together their part in the coming days. She wished she could give them an answer but the truth was that no one had a true part in any of it. Not until she knew she could persuade the Arcane to help. She had a very rudimentary understanding of the Arcane in general, let alone how connected they were to the ring. Sid assumed it was symbiotic somehow, a more technologically advanced version of what the Al'iil did to exchange power with Kartega. Their magic was the key receptor for the ring which explained why the queen kept them under lock and key and protected at all times. Kill one and you kill the entire Circulum System. Without the Arcane, the city didn't exist. But did they care for Leona? Whose side were they on? All questions that Sid needed answers to and there was no one in the room that could help her get those answers. The domes were kept so isolated from the city and towers that any information on the Arcane was either hearsay or speculation based on stories parents told their children. Even Abbot knew nothing except where the Arcane resided in the Queen's Tower, which might have helped them strategically if not for the fact that strategy was the last thing Sid needed. What she needed most of all was hope. Hope that the

Arcane would help their cause. Hope that they cared enough for Kartega and its native population to choose the right side.

"So what do the rest of us do?" Mannar asked from the cot in the far end of the flat.

"We fight," Dalrak said.

A stifled hush lowered over them mixed with surprise from those that heard the warrior speak human for the first time. Even Ashlan looked confused by it and Sid couldn't help but laugh. She probably should have filled them in on Dalrak's hidden talent as soon as they were free of the holes.

Sid took a moment to run through their plan, as well as everything that was going to be at stake and every part of the possible consequences. The Freedom Runners stared at her, wide eyed and anticipatory — like they were waiting for her to stand up, raise a fist and yell a battle cry. Colton had told her of a telescreening from his home planet where a leader of a resisting army painted his face in blues to lead a charge. Should she be doing that? She looked down at her dirty hands and wondered if a filthy grey would inspire the same loyalty.

Her thoughts were still racing when Tann spoke up beside her. "When do we go?"

Nice, Tann. Straight and to the point. Very poetic.

"Starset. After the rotation is done."

The group dispersed. Some stayed behind but broke off into smaller groups, some went home to their families. Sid stayed on the cot, her legs nearly numb from the weight of her body on top of them and her eyes staring at nothing in particular. She felt a nudge at her side and turned to see Dalrak on the floor next to her.

"Lep ta il ta troken?" He asked.

"We fight, Dee. Now we fight."

FORTY-ONE

THE DOMES REEKED of Starblades and fear. Leona had spared no one as the NSO scoured the flats and marketplaces in the search of Sid and the rest of the escapees. Every nook and crevice of the domes was left vulnerable and open to the relentless disruption caused by armed men trampling through. Hiding the Freedom Runners had grown increasingly difficult. Despite Tann still having a lot of friends in the domes, it was only a matter of time before one of them got tired of sharing the minimal amount of food they earned or not being able to travel from dome to dome to see their loved ones. Tired enough to turn them all in. The queen cut off all food supplies into the domes and the effect was noticeably dreadful. People were angry and from what Sid had seen so far, anger fueled stupidity.

She pulled the hood of the tunic Lexia gave her over her eyes and ducked behind a shop tent, into the shadows of dank fabrics and further away from the commotion of the dome's center. If one could even call it a commotion these days. Since the NSO infestation, the dome's activity levels had gone down to a bare minimum. Sometimes, at night, it was so quiet that Sid wondered if Leona had wiped out all of the native population and she'd simply been missed, again. Even the Magic locations were non-operational; this many eyes on the streets was bad for business.

Heavy booted footsteps echoed on her right and she buried herself further in the tent's coverings until they passed. It could have been anyone but she wasn't about to test her luck to find out. She was already running late to meet Tann and the rest of the rebels, and getting into a confrontation with a Starblade was not on her list of things to do.

In the past few days that they'd spent hiding in the dome, they had nearly tripled the number of Domers eager to help with their plan to foil the queen and shut down the ring. Word was spreading fast that the Freedom Runners had a weapon that could change everything — despite Sid's protests when the rumor first started. She still wasn't comfortable with having to lead the rebels into an attack, and the added pressure of living up to the high expectations that had been dropped on her shoulders wasn't helping. Sid was many things but she certainly did not feel like any kind of weapon at the moment. Weapons don't hold their breath and hide behind dusty curtains.

She slid down the hall and hit the ground, crawling to the edge to make sure the coast is clear. She could see the flat they were meeting in today across the core and as soon as there was no one around, she made a run for it. It was more of a brisk walk really, running attracted too much attention.

Tann, Ashlan and Dalrak were already waiting for her inside with the rest of the growing number of Freedom Runners. Twenty-four in total; not nearly enough to take on the Starblades and queen's guard in one go. They would need to split up, strike from different angles and box the threats in. She looked around the room. None of the Domers that stared back looked like they'd be up for the task. Sid wasn't even sure she was up for it herself but at least she had magic.

"Where were you?" Tann asked.

"Taking in the scenery," she said and stuck her tongue out. "I went back to Magic."

"She isn't there, Sid. You need to give it up."

He was talking about Serryl. Sid had made it a point to check in at the club every few hours just in case she spotted the illusive owner. With all Magics shut down, there was no way to get a hold of Serryl and, as expected, the woman was impossible to track down. Sid's entire plan rested on Serryl's help so she continued to check in, despite the annoyed looks she got from the rest of the team when she returned.

"We need magic," she said decisively, "there's no winning this without it."

"Maybe we'll be fine on our own?" Someone asked from the back of the flat.

She looked at Dalrak who met her gaze and shook his head. "Seems like that's a big no."

"You don't know that!" Another voice, lighter this time. A girl about Sid's age with eyes so dark she had to look away. The girl was quite a bit shorter than Sid with hair long enough to touch her thighs, braided loosely across her back. But it was her face that drew Sid in. Pale with a deep scar running across her right eye. Sid tried not to think about what could have happened to cause the injury when the girl spoke up again. "Well?" She asked, her hands on her hips.

Starspit. They actually think they have a shot at this. No magic, no blades. The fools!

Eyes wild, she stepped forward. A few Domers instinctively stepped back but the rest held their position, eager to see what Sid would do next. Her gaze was still fixed on the girl when she waved her hand at Ashlan. "Thrust your blade," she ordered.

Ashlan recoiled at first but when she nodded approvingly, he pressed his finger to the blades center and activated the surge. The weapon glowed in his hand and he made his way to the girl. The rest of the group encircled her in a protective hub but Sid waved them off.

"Let her show me what she thinks she can do!"

The girl didn't shrink back, instead, she straightened her back and grinned straight at Ashlan. His footsteps quickened as he rushed to her, blade ready to strike. The girl raised her fists but Ashlan was quicker, more trained and much more powerful. He leapt in the air, pulling the blade behind him and thrusting it at the girl. She shrieked, covered her face with her hands and recoiled back into the crowd. In front of her, Ashlan landed with a loud thud, the blade's electric sparks just centimeters away from her tear-stained face.

"Now," Sid said with a grin, "attack me."

"Sid, this isn't going to-"

"Attack," she cut him off, "me."

Ashlan rolled his eyes and looked back at Tann who gave him a dumbfounded shrug. He turned to face her, blade at the ready, the tip shining bright. Ashlan pivoted on his heels, taking one last look at her as if beckoning her to change her mind. She didn't — wouldn't.

With a forceful grunt, Ashlan soared her way. The blade pulsated with energy and she could hear the electricity run through its core. The closer he got, the louder it became until she could hear nothing else but its powerful shriek. The crowd gasped but she could barely register their voices. Sid wasn't afraid, she wasn't even remotely bothered. Compared to what Tazmin and the queen had put her through, this was a walk in the stars. Right now, in this small flat full of Domers with a blade rushing for her throat, she was in control.

She took one step to the right and positioned herself in Ashlan's direct path.

His eyes were ablaze with concentration as he wielded the weapon, arm stretched out and ready to strike her dead. Sid's lips twitched and she pulled them into a knowing smile, raising her right hand to meet the tip of the blade. Two more steps and he would pierce her through. She closed her eyes, drenching her body in magic, and when she opened them again she was unrecognizable. The electricity sparked over her skin; a consuming yellow cocoon that burnt at her edges. More gasps sounded in the flat and people shuffled out of the way. Ashlan made his final move. The tip of the blade flashed past her hand and was just about to pierce her skin when she snapped her fingers shut. The overhead lights flickered and the blade vibrated in Ashlan's hand. He held strong, fighting the burn of the electricity exploding inside the weapon but she could see his grip was weakening. His fingers looked slick and shiny, covered in beads of sweat that threatened his position.

Heat rolled off the blade and it hummed with an electrical current so thick that the weapon shook his entire arm. Ashlan's eyes widened and she smirked before uncurling her fingers and reaching for the blade's power. She pulled it into her like she was swallowing a sharp breath. One minute the blade was full of power and the next it lay idly in Ashlan's grip like a dead snake.

"Great, now I have to fix the stardamned thing." Ashlan looked down at his weapon then back at Sid.

She smiled and turned her attention to the girl that was half hiding behind another Domer in the crowd. "Still think you don't need magic?"

The girl shook her head and hid further behind the man in front of her.

"Good, so we agree."

The girl nodded. "But what if we can't find Serryl in time?"

"Then we have to be ready to fight on our own. Between me and Dee, we can take on a good number of Starblades but the rest of you will need every resource you have. Keep training with the older Freedom Runners as often as you can."

"We switch locations every four hours. Train regularly in between," Tann said.

"I can help too," Ashlan added. "Teach you everything I've been taught so you know what to expect."

"Thank you," Tann said and she thought she noticed a glimmer of a smile in his eyes. The first one she'd seen in a long while.

"Great, me and Dee can help too," she looked for the warrior in the crowd but he wasn't in her sightline, though she could feel his energy somewhere in the flat. "Well, Dee can."

"So we just run from place to place and learn to fight?" The girl pressed.

"You have a better idea?" When the girl didn't answer, Sid looked to the rest of the crowd. "We're not running. We are waiting for the right time to make our move and until that time comes, we need to get stronger. The queen will defend the ring with anyone she can command and that's a lot more than what we have. So yes, we hide and learn to fight. We spread the word. We get more people. Then we move in and get the chipped free. Sound good?"

"Yes," the girl said.

"Great, now let's see how many of you can actually help us do that."

FORTY-TWO

"BE QUIET!" Tann whispered as they huddled behind the baskets of fruit in front of a small shop run by a widow and her daughter.

The crowd that gathered to witness Leona's first appearance in a dome grew by the minute and they used the excitement to sneak out of sight before someone recognized them. Sid peered over a pile of green pike fruit that had long started to rot and her stomach turned at the smell. Compared to the lush fruits she had munched on casually in the jungle, the selection the residents of the domes were provided with was nothing short of disappointment. Whatever deal Serryl had with the high priestess could surely be revisited to provide for better fruit. She sighed in annoyance at Tann and shot Ashlan a look of disgust as if to blame him for Tann's demanding tone. Dalrak crept closer to her and without looking his way, she could sense he was just as irritated as her.

"She can't hear us," she hissed back.

"No but they can," Tann whispered and she followed his gaze to the group of Starblades not far from them.

"I doubt they care about anything but her right now."

Starblades swarmed around the queen like a hive of misguided insects; a group of children waiting for mother's command. They stood in a semi-circle in the center of the dome, just steps away from the tent that once housed the liveliness of Magic. Sid couldn't help but smile at the inconvenience of it all. If the queen only knew the dark trades that had been happening right under her nose all these years. She raised her eyes over the top layer of fruit, hopeful to spot Serryl in the crowd but her luck was unendingly bad. Serryl had gone into deep hiding, or worse, run off altogether.

She ducked back down to face Tann. "What do you think this is about?"

"No clue," he said and she could see Ashlan shrug his shoulders in agreement.

"Why would she come to the domes now? She's never made a point of-"

"Shhhh," Tann said again.

Before she could scold him for his rudeness, a gasp escaped from the crowd and Sid looked up to see the ten Starblades part; their blades raised in unison to form a bridge. The crowd grew restless, shifting closer to the guards; all awaiting the queen. Children squirmed out of their mother's arms, giggling with joy as if the person about to greet them was anything but a prison warden. Sid could taste bile rise in her throat and pressed her nails into the soft ridges of her palm to keep from screaming. Her magic ignited. It was so raw and angry that she wasn't sure she could hold herself back. Electric sparks frayed behind her lids and she had to close her eyes to keep herself intact.

A hand squeezed her elbow and she felt another surge run through her; Dalrak.

The warrior tightened his grip and she let herself fall back a small amount, just enough to push her body into the steady weight of his presence. Her fingers uncurled, leaving small half-moons in her skin.

"Stuk lam," she said.

"You're welcome," the warrior whispered and smiled.

Her eyes met the parted wave of Starblades just in time to see the queen walk through. Each step slower than the first, as though she was trailing into a cold river on a hot day, testing the current. The crowd gasped again and this time, Sid could not fault them for their amazement. Leona's gold dress that hugged every curve of her long body sparkled in the light of the setting ring. With the light of Jericho behind her and the Circulum System making its decent, the layers of gilded fabric shone a cocktail of rainbow. Her hair, tightened into a high knot and braided with the same gold metal resembled a waterfall of light. If Sid was still the same girl she was back on the Arcturus, she'd be stupefied like the rest of them. Leona was ravishing. Not just in beauty alone; she looked like power in the shape of a woman, a queen in every way.

A woman next to Sid hushed a little boy that was getting louder with each step of the queen's dainty feet. Coming to a halt just ahead of the Starblades, the queen raised a hand and the entire dome silenced. Even the boy that couldn't stop squirming moments ago had gone slack in his mother's arms. Sid held in a breath, afraid to make a sound and draw attention to herself. She had almost turned blue when the queen finally cleared her throat and spoke.

"Greetings, my devoted workers!" She announced and Sid could almost hear her own eyes rolling. She turned to

Ashlan but he waved her off and continued to listen. "I am certain you are surprised to see me in your dome today. After all, it has been quite some time since I have come for a visit."

A visit! Sid was outraged at the queen's use of words. As though she was simply popping in for some pastry and a glass of water. Everyone knew she was here for one reason only, to find the escapees. To find her. She pulled her hood further over her face and slouched down, curling herself into a tight little ball.

"I will not insult you with long-winded explanations as to why I am here," the queen continued as if answering Sid's inner dialogue. "There are many more domes for me to visit and while I do so enjoy seeing each and every one of you, there is important business to discuss."

Starspitting liar!

Dalrak squeezed her elbow again as if urging her not to leap for the queen right there and then.

"As you all must know, my trusted Starblades have been paying their own visits to the domes in hopes of finding someone that is a danger to us all. Earlier this week, several fugitives escaped from our holdings and are yet to be found. Among them is a young woman that goes by the name of Sid." Leona took a long breath and shook her head, "Finding these rebels is a top priority. Not just for myself but for all of you. Do not be fooled by the rebel's tales and stories! She seeks nothing but the destruction of the peaceful life we have built for ourselves!

"My dear, departed mother has given her life to make sure we continue to coexist on this star and I will do everything in my power to uphold her great legacy. This girl, these fugitives, put all of us in danger and I will not abide while someone threatens my home. *Our* home!"

A few cheers rose from the crowd and Sid craned her neck to see who would be so foolish as to believe any of Leona's empty words. She knew that there were Domers that did not agree with the work of the Freedom Runners but even they couldn't be so daft as to fall for this. Leona was lying through her teeth, surely anyone could see it. She tucked her body closer to Dalrak, shielding her face in case any of the queen's sympathizers were nearby.

"In order to show just how serious I am, myself and the Neostar Order have agreed to offer a trade for anyone that is able to provide information on the traitor's whereabouts. Any worker that comes forward and helps me bring this defector to justice will be free of their duties to the star immediately. I will personally escort them to the towers where they will begin the process of becoming a Citizen."

More gasps fell from the crowd, this time, the shouts were loud and joyful. Sid looked to her friends who seemed just as bewildered as she was. The chance that Leona was telling the truth about this was slim at best but there was no telling what people might believe if they were desperate or hungry enough. She glanced at the boy near them who looked like he had not eaten a proper meal in days. His mother would probably let the queen float her off the star if it meant saving her child.

Murmurs drifted through the dome's core and Sid searched for an exit. They had to get out of here, make a run for it before someone pointed them out. But how? There was no way to leave without drawing attention to themselves. They were smack dab in the center of the dome, surrounded by Starblades. Anyone leaving now would surely be seen and apprehended.

"I ask you, my devoted workers, who has seen the girl?" Leona demanded, her voice rising to a shrill.

The crowd grew unsteady. Whispers and questions filled the air and people looked around to their friends and neighbors, quietly discussing their options. Sid's body tensed and she could feel Dalrak tighten next to her. All of them were thinking the same thing — get out before it's too late.

"Last chance," the queen cooed.

When no one stepped forward, Sid let herself breathe out. She looked at the woman next to her who met her eyes and smiled before turning back to Leona. Did she know who Sid was? Did all of them? Were they protecting her and the others or was she just imagining that someone might be truly on her side in this? Hoping that they had more able bodies to follow through with the plan. Her eyes raced, trying to find another ally, someone else that they could enlist after this pathetic show was over and done with.

The queen raised an arm just as Sid was scanning the front row. "Very well," she said coldly, "if a trade is not what you're looking for, perhaps another type of motivation will do." She tapped her polished fingers to the side of her head and two Starblades stepped past her and into the crowd.

Sid jerked upright but Dalrak caught her sleeve and pulled her back down with such force that she almost collapsed. She attempted to ease his grip but he held strong, pinning her in one spot. Sid peered over the baskets and watched in horror as the Starblades pointed their blades at the unprotected necks of two Domers and fired. Her eyes overflowed and she muffled a cry that threatened to break free. Her heart pounded in anger and fear and sorrow; every emotion she could muster beneath Dalrak's heavy hold. Her magic shoved and scratched at her skin, desperate for attention. Sid cried out and tried to force her way through but it was useless. The warrior was not letting her go.

The crowd in the dome mimicked her fury. Screams erupted around them, muffling her own cries. Children wailed and men and women rushed to the bodies of the two slain that lay flaccid on the ground, steps beyond the queen's feet. They pushed toward her, a mass of bodies and limbs, all wanting to punish the bringer of death. Before they could reach her, the Starblades formed a line and trained their weapons at the Domers. The glow of the blades pulsed in unison, making the line of defense look like a ship's runway; a beacon beckoning those eager to lose their lives.

A girl, barely old enough to walk, pierced through the crowd and was pulled back by a man mere moments before the tip of a blade punctured her chest.

The line of Starblades stepped forward as one and the mob shrank back.

Fear swallowed the dome in its entirety.

"There will be no more bargains," Leona said in a tone free of emotion. "Today, all of you decide what is more important, her life or your own." She turned to leave but whipped back to face the crowd, the heavy folds of her skirts sending a screeching ringing through the now silenced mob. "And if any of you cross paths with the traitor, give her a message for me. Tell her that all of this stops if she comes forward. She simply needs to make that choice."

FORTY-THREE

SID FOUND herself huddled in a stray shop tent long after the queen departed and the crowd dispersed. Peeking outside periodically, she couldn't believe how fast the dome returned to its usual activities. It seemed that only moments ago the Starblades carried off the bodies of the dead and she could already hear Domers arguing over produce prices and who carries the best frigger meat in the marketplace. A child's laughter sounded not too far off and Sid flinched. There should be tears and screaming. There should be an uproar. The whole stardamned sky should come crashing down with an angry thunder. Anything was better than life going on as though nothing had happened.

She didn't understand it, didn't understand any of them. Not the Domers whose mourning of their dead lasted shorter than a hiccup, not Ashlan and Tann; who were already coding fight plans in the dim light of the shop tent. Not even Dalrak, the simple image of whom made her wonder how she could be so connected to someone that belonged to Tazmin's deathly tribe.

As if on cue, the warrior bristled behind her, flexed his marked arms and peered through the tent's flaps over her shoulder. She wondered what they watched out for. Did it truly matter anymore? They all heard the queen's warning; surrender or more will die. How many more lives was she willing to sacrifice to save her own skin? Even if Leona killed only one person in each of the domes it was still too many people. Too many deaths to justify her own existence.

She was a fool to think they could end the separation between the star's residents and an even bigger fool to think *she* could be the one to lead the revolt. She was nothing more than a child playing with power she didn't understand. She wasn't like Leona or Tazmin, wasn't raised to believe in something so strongly they were willing to kill for it. It wasn't that long ago that she thought her true place was with Colton in the towers or that the queen was a savior sent to Kartega to correct its downward spiral. Muck, it wasn't that long ago that she didn't even know Kartega *was* Kartega.

Someone cleared their throat next to her and she looked up to see Tann hovering over her with a troubled expression on his face.

"You alright?" He asked.

"Do I look alright? How does someone stay alright after that?" She shouted and waved her hand in the general direction of where the killings had taken place. Everyone's eyes swung to her but she didn't care. "Are *you* alright?" She shook and tears welled in her eyes. It was wrong to take out her frustration on Tann but she couldn't help it. Besides, it was a stupid question to ask her, all things considering.

"Not really," he said, ignoring her outburst. "Want to talk about it?"

"Not really," she answered but he sat down beside her anyway.

"Let me guess," he mused, "you're thinking about turning yourself in."

"Wouldn't *you*? She's killing people, Tann! *Your* people!"

"*Our* people," he corrected her. "And she'd kill them regardless. Whether or not you give yourself up, our people are going to die. She either kills them outright or sucks them dry until they have no power left to fight at all."

"At least it'll give you a chance. I can bargain with her! I can-"

"We both know there's no bargaining with the mucking queen of Neostar. You think you're the first person to try that?"

She bit her bottom lip until she could taste iron on her tongue. "I can't just sit around and wait while more people die trying to protect me."

"Who says we're sitting around? We have a plan, remember? You sort of came up with it."

"And if it doesn't work?"

"It will," he said sharply.

"And if it doesn't?"

Tann's face darkened and his eyes looked somewhere beyond her. "Then we all die. But at least we die for the right reason."

"So let *me* die for the right reason, Tann! Why is it fine for all of you but not for me?"

From the corner of her vision, she could see Dalrak look their way, no doubt listening to every word they said. She checked on Ashlan to see if he was eavesdropping as well but if he was, he hid it well. His fingers toyed endlessly with the projection in front of him, moving holographic figures around the screened corridors of the towers.

"Because if you give yourself up, if you surrender without so much as a fight, that makes all of this pointless. Those two that died today, their deaths would be meaningless. Your parents' deaths would be meaningless. Nyala's death would be meaningless. Colton's death-" he stopped and lowered his voice. "His death would be meaningless. It would all be for nothing. Don't you get that?"

"I'm not some hero or some weapon. I don't know why all of you think that."

"No, you're not a hero, Sid," he whispered and she couldn't help but feel a tad slighted by the bluntness of his words. "But you are our excuse and sometimes that's better."

"Your excuse?"

"To do something, finally. To fight. To get our freedom back. Or at least to try."

"But why-"

"No, Sid. If you die, we give up. And it all goes back to how it was." He pointed to the draped ceiling of the tent, "The ring keeps turning and we keep giving. It would be like you never existed."

She thought about it. Not existing seemed to be a pretty good option at that moment. If she never existed, her parents would still be alive. Colton would still be alive. He'd be happy and he'd be with his son, both of them would have been so much better off if she hadn't been born at all. Even Dalrak would be free to live his oblivious life with the Al'iil and not be stuck on lookout in a fruit tent with the rest of them.

Tann tensed beside her and she turned to face him, meeting his gaze for the first time since that dreadful day she tried to kiss him. And what of him? And the Freedom Runners? And all the children born into the domes?

Crashing her pod on the star may not have turned out exactly how she had imagined but she did find her way. Maybe not to Colton and the towers as she had dreamed as a child, but to people who made her feel like she was worth more than hiding. Without even trying, she had found her own people. Not the Domers, or the Citizens, not the Al'iil; but all of them. She had found all of them.

And she'd be mucking crazy not try to and help them all now.

"I don't think I'd like not existing. I did it for too many years."

"Good, I wouldn't like it either," he said. "Neither would that one." He pointed to Ashlan and smiled before averting his gaze to the floor.

"Who? Ash? Oh, it's not me he's worried about," she blurted without thinking. She raised her hand to her mouth as if to shove the words back in but the damage was done and Tann was ogling her; flabbergasted and slack-jawed.

"What do you mean? Who?"

"No one. Nothing. I just meant that he's probably more worried about Fred and his blade than me."

"Oh," Tann said and she was sure she could hear disappointment in his tone.

"Unless, you're thinking it was someone else?" She raised an eyebrow.

He fumbled with the belt on his tunic, tightening and loosening it as if he was unsure of whether to disrobe or flee. "I mean, no one in particular. I was just wondering what you meant."

"No, you weren't," she said smugly.

She waited for him say something mean, to mock her somehow like he tended to do when he didn't like where the conversation was going. Instead, he turned his gaze to face her and lowered his voice until she could barely hear him. "Please don't tell him."

Not this again. Sid could almost laugh at the situation. She likely would have if she wasn't horrified thinking about the time she tried to force herself on Tann when he had no interest in her, or any girl, in that way. She wondered how he felt then. Was he as embarrassed as she was now? Was he repulsed? Did he laugh at her behind her back? He wouldn't do that, she was sure of it but the thought kept digging its filthy claws into her mind, forcing her cheeks to redden.

"I won't," she said, pulling up her suit collar to hide the maroon splotches traveling up her neck, "But take my word for it, you should probably say something to him."

"You think?" He asked, his eyebrows raised like he was begging a scolding mother for forgiveness after breaking her favorite multimeter. Or whatever it was that mothers favorited. Sid had no idea.

"Trust me," she said and nudged his side, "I know."

He smiled and she moved to wrap her arms around him when Dalrak jumped back from the tents flap.

"Someone here!" He yelled.

Within moments, Tann hopped to his feet and stepped in front of her. Ashlan dropped his projector and joined Dalrak by the tent's entrance, his blade ready and glowing. A light wind blew as the fabrics parted and Sid watched intently from in-between Tann's stoic legs as a slender, scantily clad figure stepped through. "Miss me, kids?"

"Serryl!" She shouted, pushing Tann aside and rushing to greet the club owner.

She was so happy that she almost threw her arms around the woman and kissed her cheek. Almost. The look on Serryl's face told her there was business to discuss and that was the only reason Magic's owner made this very dramatic appearance. "We've been looking everywhere for you!"

"So I hear," Serryl said in a monotone, yet playful tone. "Well, you found me. Care to tell me why?"

FORTY-FOUR

TEN ON THE right and six in front. Sid counted off the Starblades as they marched past their hiding spot in a supply cage just under the blade charging room. Each step outside the frosted glass doors sent shivers down the back of her arms. They had one shot at making this work and she was starting to doubt that their plan was sound enough to withstand the security measures in the towers. The queen was no fool; after their escape, the corridors were full to the brim with Starblades. She even noticed a few of the queen's own guards passing through though they did not linger, likely eager to get back to their post closer to Leona.

The sound of metal on metal startled her and she turned back to see the droid remove a screw from the ceiling grate.

"Shhh!" She hissed, "There's two of them just down the corridor!"

The droid looked at her with empty, glowing eyes and continued his business.

"He has to get the grate off, or we're here for nothing," Ashlan said.

"He's going to get us all killed if he doesn't keep it down," she barked. "And since when is he a 'he' to you?"

Ashlan shook his head and went back to helping the droid with the grate.

More footsteps sounded outside the doors and she grew still, her magic at the ready in case of an attack. The plan had to work, it just had to! They simply needed to stay hidden long enough for the droid to get the vent open. Once the coast was clear, they could sneak into the blade charging room undetected and take the weapons they needed to arm their group. Carrying out dozens of concealed weapons while staying hidden would prove to be difficult but it was the only way to give them enough leverage to attack. She had to trust in the plan.

Another clank sounded behind her and she cringed. *It's fine. We're fine.*

Clank!

"Stardamnit, Fred!"

Boots shuffled in the corridor, closer this time, and everyone froze. Even the droid stopped moving though she was sure Ashlan's fingers on his controls had something to do with it. They waited, barely breathing, until the steps retreated.

Sid sighed in relief. "We're cutting it close."

"Almost there," Abbot's gruff voice echoed in the room, startling her. She had almost forgotten he was there.

"You think this will work?" She asked the general. Or ex-general, as she imagined Leona placed a warrant for his arrest like the rest of them.

"It will," he said. "And if it doesn't, you have me as a distraction."

"That's not the only reason you're here, you know?" She

tried to smile but the gesture fell flat. Using Abbot as a distraction in case things went wrong was the main reason he was here. That, and his innate knowledge of entry points into secured rooms without being detected. Still, she hated hearing the words fall from his lips. Like he had sacrificed himself already. "It won't come to that," she added. "The plan will work."

Abbot smiled and placed a hand on her shoulder. "Why don't you go help Ash. I can take over here for now."

He didn't need to tell her twice. Sid was relieved to leave her post, the anxiety from replaying different scenarios in which they could die was not helping her nerves at the moment.

Without hesitation, she made way for him by the doors and crawled to the back of the room where Ashlan was holding a spare tunic over the droid's body while it drilled, hiding its glowing metal frame. Another screw fell away from the grate and she caught it before it hit the floor, winking at Ashlan. He cracked a smile and from where she stood, it almost seemed like he meant it. Though she couldn't imagine what there was to smile about.

"Is that a Starblade thing?" She asked.

"What?"

"Being overly confident in petrifying situations."

She heard a light chuckle from Abbot by the doors and was glad to find someone else found Ashlan's attitude infuriating.

"Relax, Sid. This will work," Ashlan said, shooting a side glance in Abbot's direction.

"Excuse me for being on edge. We're only trying to break into a weapons facility in the most guarded Tower in the city while being hunted like fugitives." She rolled her eyes, "But you're right, I should relax!"

She caught another screw and tucked it into her suit pocket.

"Incoming," Abbot whispered and they froze.

Her breath hitched in her throat as they cowered while a group of Starblades gathered outside the room. She could hear their muffled chatting just outside the doors, so close that she could almost make out words they were saying. Too close. She let the hum of her magic increase, raising her hands in defense. If any of them decided to come in, she would have under a second to blast them with enough current to knock them out, leaving their group mere moments to attempt an escape. Her hands started to shake with the power gathering at her fingertips and she pumped them open and shut before going back to her original position. She caught Ashlan's glare and the shake of his head, urging her to keep it together.

At the foot of the doors, Abbot reached slowly for his blade, keeping his finger next to the trigger but not yet pulling it out.

They waited in silence until a laugh sounded in the corridor and the group of Starblades walked away.

"We need to hurry," Abbot said. "This isn't safe."

"You think?" She scoffed and nudged Ashlan to hurry the droid. "Can you speed him up?"

Ashlan's stare burned through her and she could almost taste his annoyance on her tongue. "Think you can do better?" He asked and shoved his projector toward her.

She shook her head, "I know I could. But then what would you be doing?"

He chuckled but pulled the projector back, tapping

another set of codes. The droid's finger whirred only slightly faster but he raised his second arm, using it to begin removing the screws on the opposite end. "There," Ashlan said. "Happy?"

"Ecstatic."

When the last of the screws fell from the grate, the droid tugged down to pull off a piece large enough for one person to squeeze through and the three of them sighed audibly through clenched jaws. At least one thing went smoothly since they'd got here. So much rested on them getting the blades out of the city. Her magic was strong, so was Dalrak's, but it was still the only thing they had going for them. That and the small amount of magic they were able to harness from Serryl's supply pipes. It wasn't much but it gave those that were weak a fighting chance. Though Sid knew that teaching them how to wield power that she had spent her entire life trying to understand in a few days was a pointless task. So far, all she'd managed to do was teach the younger rebels to use their electricity to intimidate an opponent. A big magic show with very little result, but one she hoped would be enough to distract their opponents long enough for an attack. Still, for all the training the Freedom Runners had had over the years, it was nothing compared to the brute force of the queen's army. As Ashlan mentioned, even her ladies in waiting had full knowledge of battle. And what did they have? A few dozen Domers. Sid was still wondering if they'd made a mistake coming here when Ashlan gestured for the droid to hoist him into the ceiling vent.

"Where do you think you're going?" She caught Ashlan's pant leg before he could disappear out of sight.

"To get the blades, obviously," he tugged his leg away from her grip and pulled himself up into the vent. His body retreated into the darkness of the ceiling and Sid didn't waste time before hopping up on the droid's already outstretched arms and following him.

"Ash," she hissed, squeezing her body as low to the metal tubing they were in as possible. The mobility in the vents was minimal at best and she pushed the sides of her boots against the walls to slide forward. Surprisingly, despite his large mass, Ashlan was making his way forward much faster than her. "Wait up!" she hissed, "I don't know where I'm going!"

"Then you should have stayed back," he whispered, not bothering to slow down.

She cussed under her breath and pushed forward. There was no way she was letting the fool prove her wrong. This was *her* plan and she wasn't about to sit around while he took all the risk. The nerve!

Sid pushed forward on her heels, sliding her body like a snake along the cold, smooth surface. Once she got the hang of it, it was surprisingly easy to accumulate speed and she was caught up with Ashlan in no time. She craned her neck awkwardly to face him and nodded to the grate above his head.

"So how do we get this one off?" She sneered.

Not bothering to respond, Ashlan pushed carefully up and slid the grate cover over, smiling at her open mouth. "We push," he chuckled and poked his head out on the other side.

When he was certain the cost was clear, he pulled himself through the hole and motioned for her to follow.

"I take it you've done this before?" She asked, taking note of the unhinged grate at her feet and his eerily fast way of getting around the vents.

"When I was a kid, I used to want to see everything in

the towers. My dad wasn't so keen on the idea so I found another way to get around. This was one of my favorite places to come so I was hoping no one would have bothered to close up the grate."

"And if they had?" She asked wide-eyed.

"Plan B?"

"There is no Plan B!" She huffed.

"Good thing it was open then," he noted with a grin and headed to the charging walls. "Let's get what we need and get the muck out of here. This place gets serious foot traffic during the day."

Not waiting for her to respond, Ashlan started to work on collecting blades from their stations. She followed his lead, speedily snapping out only the blades with the highest charge. They could each push four blades through the vent without straining and while Ashlan's original calculations left them enough time for the extra trips needed to gather the weapons, she was trying to move as fast as possible. When the first dozen blades were safely deposited on the floor, Sid ripped off the ragged tunic she had tied over her suit and threw it into the vent, before proceeding to pile the four blades quietly into it. Without waiting for Ashlan to do the same, she scurried into the vent and crawled back to the entrance point where the droid's waiting arms were outstretched in anticipation.

Sid dropped her pile and crawled backward, poking her head out of the vent to let Ashlan know she was ready for the next load.

After a few repeated trips, she breathlessly pulled herself onto the floor of the charging station.

"It's your turn, I need a break," she whispered in between breaths.

Ashlan nodded, pushing a set of blades through the grate opening and disappearing into the silent darkness of the vent. When she could no longer hear the quiet whoosh of his pant legs, she sat next to the weapon pile, staring at it in earnest disbelief.

This is actually going to work!

She couldn't believe it. The more they went over the plan before coming here, the more terrified she had become. So many things could go wrong, but Ashlan had assured her that they could do this and stardamnit, she hated when he was right.

Sid could hear the familiar scuffle of fabric come into earshot and smiled; two more trips and they'd be out of this place. Ashlan's messy head of hair started to poke through the grate when the door opposite her slid open. She didn't waste time, using all her vigor to shove him back into the vent. "Stay down!"

Sid froze and waited for the increasingly speedy footsteps to approach her. Magic rushed from her and her body glowed as brightly as ever, drowning out the blue light of the blades around her. Beads of sweat poured down her neck and her short hair clung to them for dear life. She crouched over the weapons like a mother protecting her young, not letting anyone come between them.

I should have known it was too easy! This is never going to work! We're done for! We're—

"Professor Cevil?"

The old man nearly tripped over her in his stupor. When he finally looked over his projector, his eyes narrowed, darting between Sid and the pile of weapons at her feet.

"Miss Sid?" He asked, then gesturing to the blades, "What's the meaning of this?"

"This..." she struggled for an excuse, "I'm checking the weapons. To make sure they are fully functional in case of an attack."

"An attack? What attack?" The professor asked, his eyes landing on the open grate.

She caught his gaze, begging him not to do anything with her eyes. "Professor, please, you need to let me finish."

"Nonsense! You expect me to believe you are here on official duty?" He tapped his wrinkled fingers into the projector and turned it around to face her. Sid's own face reflected back to her with capture warnings across the top and bottom; the queen's telescreen warning frozen on the screen. "I am not as clueless as you seem to believe me to be. This is treason!"

"Professor! Please, You don't understand!" She screamed, stumbling toward him.

The old man swung the projector over, his fingers starting to tap a code. She had no doubt he was sending an alarm out to every armed man in the vicinity. "I understand it all too well, Miss Sid. I know what you are. You're glowing brighter than Jericho, for star's sake!"

Sid looked down at her arms, realizing she had no choice. All that magic, all that power — it was the only way to make him stop. She leaned her weight on her right leg and pushed her hands together. The professor betrayed her, she should hate him, want to kill him even, but she felt nothing of the sort. He did exactly what she expected him to do and while she had to stop him from calling the Starblades, she didn't want to see him dead. She most definitely didn't want to see him dead by her own hand. He had been kind to her at one point when she needed someone most, and she had to repay the favor.

She pressed her fists tighter into one another, calling on the current running through the projector in his hands. With one pull of her hands, a shot of electricity sparked over the hologram and into the professor's hands. He yelped, dropping the interface box and shaking his hands which Sid imagined were burning hot right then. His eyes met hers in confusion and she looked away, her gaze running over the charge stations on either side of him.

Her hands shot out and she grasped at the tendrils of energy on the surface of the station glass, pulling it out from where it was contained. Blue sparks of electricity danced at the edges of the glass, twirling in tight circles as if waiting for her instruction. She flipped her palms. "I'm sorry," she whispered and slapped her hands together, letting the currents on either side of the professor collide.

Cevil went down instantaneously, his body collapsing on the floor in front of her. She crawled over to him, checking to make sure he was still breathing. When she found a pulse and heard his jagged breath, she sighed and crawled back to the grate.

"You can come out now," she said and watched as Ashlan popped up from the vent.

He looked at the professor's body then to the char marks across the glass cases. "How long will he be out?"

"Not sure, we'd better hurry," Sid said and started to lower the remaining blades into the vent. "Ash?"

"Yes?"

"Do you think Dee and Tann had better luck in the jungle?"

Ashlan looked from Cevil's body to the blades to her, "Compared to this, gathering a bunch of Tecken sounds like a breeze."

FORTY-FIVE

THE TALL, densely packed grasses that lined the jungle's edges ebbed and flowed, revealing glimpses of the ring's light over the horizon. Sid watched the movement, squinting each time a larger opening formed to see the city's bridge in the distance. Its glittering shape, once leaving her in awe was nothing more than a nuisance now. A bushel of grass moved in the wind and she counted five more Starblades on the bridge, bringing the total to twenty-seven. Too many.

"Looks like the ring is almost through," Tann noted beside her. "Should be another hour or so."

"Should be," she sighed.

"Worried?"

She tore her gaze from the bridge and looked at him. "You're not?"

"Sure. But that doesn't help, does it? We can do it. Just have to get into the city, then the plan is solid."

"There's too many of them on the bridge. We didn't account for this many," she said, keeping her voice low. The last thing she wanted was for some of the younger fighters to overhear and get spooked.

"The Tecken will help," Tann smiled reassuringly, "and Serryl gathered more groups from the other domes. People with loyalties to the club, all powered up and ready to go."

Her eyes barely grazed the outline of people behind her. She listened to the chatter, periodically interrupted by the echoing moan of the Tecken herd and sighed. "It's not real magic, Tann. We both know that. Whatever Serryl pumped them full of is just for show."

"I know. But it's all we have now. *This* is the only army you have."

She wanted to laugh in his face. An army. These kids and a few large beasts! This wasn't an army and she wasn't some general. She hated that they kept asking for her advice, her thoughts, her plans. *Don't get killed!* She wanted to shout at them, *that's the plan!* Instead, she asked Abbot for advice on how to lead them. She trained with Dalrak every waking moment to get her own power in check. She did everything she could to keep the illusion going and their spirits high. If they were all going to die, they should do it without fear. That's what Tann wanted her to believe but she had doubts upon doubts invading every nook and cranny of her body.

Maybe fear is what they needed to survive this.

Another low groan sounded in the distance. "I should say something," she said in more of a question than a statement. When Tann nodded in agreement, she stepped through the jungle's flora and made her way to her militia, leaving the glitter of the bridge behind her.

BODIES FILLED every empty spot in the small jungle clearing they found themselves in. More people showed up to fight than Sid had hoped for and she was told that Serryl was to return shortly with another round of Domers all willing to side with them. The small army should have made her pleased but all Sid could feel was remorse and guilt. She thought back to her days on the ship, orbiting the same people that now crowded on trunks and boulders around her, the same people she hid from for all these years. She wondered if Colton kept her away because of this very moment. If he knew she would end up in this tiny clearing in the middle of the wilderness about to lead a group of untrained fighters to their deaths. What would she do if things didn't go like they had planned tonight? The thought of dying at the hands of the queen did not mean much to her but looking over the anticipant faces of the group, could she be just as careless with their lives as she was with her own? She couldn't; not by a long shot.

The thought left her speechless. Not just without words but entirely dumbfounded. They were looking for her guidance and she didn't have the heart to tell them just how misguided they were. She had no words of fight ready, no encouraging tales to keep their spirits afloat. She'd never been in a fight and now she had somehow landed herself in the middle of this mess. No, not landed — orchestrated. She chose to be in this clearing, chose these people as her own.

Great job, Sid. Way to mucking go.

"Is she alright?" Tann whispered to Ashlan behind her.

"Want me to zap her with my blade, see if she moves?"

Sid turned to see the two of them chuckling, their arms so close they could almost touch. She wondered how nervous each of them was thinking of the closeness to the other. The fools were circling each other like a hungry Tecken herd and no one could so much as make the first move. If only Ashlan had the same gutsy foolishness that she was made of. *Grab his face!* She wanted to shout. *Kiss him!* "Keep laughing and I'll zap you both myself," she hissed instead.

A sheet of ivy parted next to her and Dalrak's sharp face poked through. He pushed the plant out of his way with ease and came to stand beside her. Sid immediately relaxed. The warm spark of his magic muffled her guilty thoughts and she found herself standing a little taller.

"Do not worry," he grunted.

"Easy for you to say," she scoffed, "they're not all here to follow *you*."

"Or you," he smirked and nodded to her glowing skin.

"Right."

Ashlan and Tann whispered something she couldn't hear and exploded into a harmonious low cackle and she shot them a crossed glance before stepping into the circle formed by the crowd. She smiled when Dalrak followed her sneer with a raised fist, making the two stop their laughing abruptly.

"I am not someone you should follow," she started.

"That's a good start," Ashlan said behind her but she pretended not to hear him.

"I'm just a girl, a kid, really. None of you even knew me until I crashed on this star not long ago," she continued. "When I was up there," she pointed to the sky, remembering her ship, "I thought this place was magical. I thought the towers were the only thing I wanted and I thought the queen was a savior to you all."

A few throats cleared in the group.

"I am here to tell you how wrong I was. Not because of

what I thought, it was the only thing I knew so how could you blame me? I was wrong to think that anything could be magical that included me hiding who I truly was. I was wrong to think that if I hid who I was, that I could be better somehow. That I could wear the fine clothes and eat the wonderful food and be someone that I really wasn't. That I could be anyone other than me.

Someone I cared about deeply once told me a rule — a rule I had to follow no matter what the cost. To hide my magic and stay in the shadows. And as much as I loved that person, as much as I wish he was here today, I am here to tell you that he was wrong! You should never hide who you are!"

Sid looked around, raising her hands over her head. "So I am not someone you should follow. *This,*" she shouted and sank two bolts of electricity into the ground, "is what you should be after! This is the only thing you should be fighting for tonight! Because this power, this magic, is what you are. And you should never hide it. And it should never be taken away from you. Tonight, you get back what is yours! You get back your star, you get back your magic, and you get back your freedom!"

There was silence all around and she wondered if she went too far with the yelling when a loud cheer sounded at the back. She looked over the gathering to Serryl whistling loudly with over twenty more fighters at her back. The rest of the group joined in and soon, the entire clearing was filled with yelps and whistles and applause. She could even hear a few people chanting her name and the blood rushed to her cheeks instantaneously. Sid looked back to Dalrak and shrugged. He shrugged back, grinning like a wild man.

She turned. "Not bad for a rough start," she said slyly and knocked an elbow into Ashlan's side, making him collapse onto Tann's wide chest. The flustered exchanges that followed were muted by the sound of her own heart beating madly.

The ring's glow had set, replaced only by the lights of Tower City in the distance.

This was it. Their time had come.

FORTY-SIX

"ASH! WATCH OUT!" Sid yelled as she charged atop her beast toward the group of Starblades ahead of her. Her body was a blinding ball of light and she straddled the beast with both thighs, squeezing as she wielded the magic in the direction of the guards' ready weapons.

To her left, Ashlan turned on his heels and knocked the back of his blade on the temple of a Starblade that raced his way, turning quickly around to rush the tip of his weapon into the man's shoulder. The Starblade hunched over, blood dripping from his wound as he tried to scramble for his weapon. He was about to grasp hold of it when Tann knocked it out of his reach and thrust his boot into the Starblade's cheek, knocking him unconscious.

"You alright?" He asked Ashlan and waited for him to nod. "Good, you had me worried for a minute."

Ashlan's eyebrows lifted in surprise but he quickly regained composure, just in time to run his blade through the leg of the Starblade charging at Tann from behind. "Right back at you. We're moving in from the left!" He yelled to Sid, "You and Dee take the right! Center them to the gates!"

She followed his lead, letting out a loud whistle for Dalrak to follow.

Pressing the edge of her boots into her beast's sides, she charged to the right, imploding the blades of those she passed and letting the warrior knock them out once their weapons were useless.

They moved quickly, leaving a trail of sleeping Starblades in their wake. Sid was clear in her instructions, there was to be no killing tonight. A rule not everyone agreed with but she hoped would listen to regardless. Behind her, a roar of beasts sounded and she turned to see the herd charge forward. Dust rose on the bridge, flying like a tidal wave through the dim light of night.

Shrieks and yells rose from the Starblades that scurried away from the incoming herd. Some managed to jump out of the way but some were too late, their limbs trampled by the weight of the beasts' heavy footfalls. Sid heard the cracking of bones near her and grimaced, choosing to concentrate on holding her magic over the energy of the blades the guards held. Her body was inhaling their currents, lighting up her skin in a cacophony of colors.

In front of her, she could see the gates to the city begin to close and her eyes quickly found the source. A young Starblade, about her own age, was scrambling to input a lockdown code into the system lock behind the group they had cornered in the center of the bridge.

"Dee! They're shutting down! Get to the gate!" She yelled.

The warrior leapt from behind her, his large legs stomping past the crouching Starblades. He slid to a stop next to the Starblade and without hesitation, crashed his elbow into the back of the boy's head. The Starblade crumpled to the ground with a thud, air escaping his lungs in a loud exhale as he fell. Not bothering to check for a pulse, Dalrak stepped over the limp body and pressed his hand to the control panel. From where she sat atop her beast, Sid could see his body shake as he sent a rush of magic into the console. Sparks flew from his hand and a sharp screech echoed over the bridge. She closed her eyes, trying to shut out the sound without losing her hold on the energy of the weapons. When she looked up again, the warrior stood tall, grinning in her direction, a charred console behind him.

"Thank you!" She yelled and the warrior nodded, moving back into formation behind the Starblades.

The herd behind her was restless, stomping their hind legs into the flatness of the bridge. Each stomp sent shivers down her spine as she felt her own beast twist beneath her weight, eager to charge forward. She looked in Tann's direction, his back turned to her as he held a Starblade by the throat, wrestling his blade away. Ashlan was not far from him, his own blade aimed at a group of Starblades kneeling before him.

The protectors of the bridge were surrounded. Weaponless and overpowered.

One of the beasts took a long stride forward and she could hear a yelp sound from the back. They were afraid. She should be happy; this was what they came here to do. They took the bridge and no one died, she should feel something akin to relief right now. Instead, Sid thought only of Edek.

Fear made people do foolish things.

She felt her beast's eagerness to charge and pressed her

heels into its back. Her hands stretched out in each direction as she grasped hold of the magic of the abandoned blades on the bridge. With a deep breath in, she closed her eyes and called their energy to her, swallowing the currents. One by one, the metal of the blades magnetized and she yanked them to her. The scrape of metal on metal rang in her ears as she pulled harder on their currents until all of the blades lay in a pile at the feet of her beast. Sid opened her eyes to find nothing but the awe-struck faces of the surrendered Starblades, their gazes shifting between her and their blades uncomfortably.

Slowly, she climbed off the beasts back and came to stand in front of them.

"No one will get hurt if you do as we say," she said, hoping it was enough to convince them.

When no one moved, she nodded to Tann who raised two fingers to his lips and let out a whistle. From behind them, Serryl stepped through the wall of beasts, followed by a group of Freedom Runners. Each person held a blade in one hand, charged and ready to strike while wielding a current of electricity in the other. Their faces were nothing like those Sid had grown accustomed to, no longer questioning every move and fearful of the outcome. They were hungry and strong. They were warriors.

Sid noted the looks of shock that spread through the Starblades. *It's actually working!*

"Leona held us captive for too long!" Sid yelled over them. "We don't want to hurt you but if anyone tries to stop us," she nodded to the graveyard of blades to her left, "you'll meet the same end as your weapons."

The Starblades exchanged looks but not one dared to move.

"Time to go!" she shouted. "If anyone so much as moves, blast them!"

With a reluctant smile, she patted the back of her beast.

"And you can eat them," she said loud enough for the Starblades to hear. When they recoiled away from her, she grinned and charged past them and into the city, her team on her heels.

The bright lights that dominated the streets of Tower City made it nearly impossible to imagine that night had swallowed the star. From the corner of her eye, she could see discomfort wash over Dalrak's face, his large, savage body sticking out amongst the glass and clean lines of the city; an imposter in its midst. She reached for his hand, giving him a jolt of magic to bring his attention to her. "Don't worry, Dee," she whispered, "I got this."

As they moved through the streets, Sid basked in the electric surge of the city, letting its power cradle her in its warmth. Step by step, she breathed it in, turning off the life around them light by light until they were consumed in darkness.

Until the only glow in Tower City were their blades and Sid herself.

FORTY-SEVEN

SID PRESSED her back into Dalrak's and fired an energy burst at the two Starblades charging toward them. From the grunts at her back, she assumed the warrior had done the same. As two Starblades went down, two more ran down the corridor in their direction. It was as if they were multiplying each time. She knew the Queen's Tower was drowning in armed men but at this point, she thought they would have at least gotten most of them. Three more heads whipped up and she wiped the cool sweat on her brow before firing again. If it wasn't for the energy she was feeding on from their blades, she'd be drained by now. She felt an elbow nudge at her side, Dalrak checking to see if she was fine, and flooded the warrior with her magic to get him to back off. He'd been glued to her side ever since they stepped into the city and she was starting to get annoyed by it. She was fine. Better than fine, she felt invincible. Why did Colton stop her from using her magic? It made her so much stronger!

"How much longer, Ash?" She yelled out, not taking her eyes off her next targets.

To her left, Ashlan was furiously running code and has been since they pushed through to the throne room doors. There were no guards in sight but she could hear commotion behind the shatterproof, frosted glass. She knew Leona was on the other side of the doors with her guards and Magistras and they were going to get to them. She was going to get to her.

"Ash! How long?" She shouted again.

"Almost there!" He yelled back, slightly breathless. "Just hold them off!"

"What the muck do you think we're doing over here? Having lunch?"

She shot two more energy bursts back to back, knocking her opponents off their feet and landing them squarely in the pile of bodies starting to form at the corridor barrier. Two more Starblades emerged and tried to drag some of their incapacitated teammates into the dark but she managed to knock them out before they succeeded.

"Tann! Get Serryl and the rest and starting defending the corridors! We need to get the entrances closed off!"

A scurry of feet ran past her, blades at the ready. Tann and the Freedom Runners rushed toward the small pile of unconscious Starblades and crouched, using the bodies as a barrier between them and the army charging from the darkness.

"Not yet!" Dalrak commanded in a guttural tone.

Sid trailed the magic to her fingers, readying her attack for his command. She could see Starblades begin to reappear from behind the wall of bodies, their blades glowing a familiar blue in the dark. Tann and Serryl looked her way, worry in their eyes but no one dared to move. "Dee? They're coming through," she said through clenched teeth.

"Not," the warrior repeated, "yet."

She rolled her eyes. His 'man of few words' act was another thing that was starting to get annoying.

When two of the Starblades she could see easily pulled apart the limbs of their fallen and stepped through, her body temperature rose past discomfort to utter fear. Sweat gathered over her lip, and under her arms, and in every crevice really. "Dee!" She hissed but the warrior said nothing.

Her hands shook and she could imagine the fear running through Tann and the rest at the front, so close to the blade tips of the Starblades.

Finally, when she almost lost consciousness herself, Dalrak lifted his shaking muscled arms.

"Now!" He yelled.

The Freedom Runners did not hesitate, flinging their blades forward at the incoming army. Unexpected yells rose over them as dozens of Starblades fell over the bodies, bloody puncture wounds covering their skin. They scrambled on the ground, some trying to regain control of the blades they lost and some simply orienting themselves to pinpoint the attack.

"Our turn," Dalrak said quietly and she nodded and released her bridled magic.

Bursts of energy exploded from her and the warrior, flowing from them to the confused Starblades in waves of energy and heat. When her magic reached them, she used one hand to pulse the electricity into their bodies and the other to drag their blades to her. There were more screams, followed by loud pangs as the emergency lights on the walls burst one by one.

"Aaaaah!" Sid shouted as the blades screeched across the metal tile floor and collided with her boots.

She stood breathless, her eyes feeling raw and heavy in

her lids and though she couldn't see herself, she knew they glowed wildly. At her back, Dalrak's tensed muscles shifted as he relaxed, dropping his arms to his side. The silence around them did not last long before the Freedom Runners started to move from their positions. Some pushed the unconscious bodies of Starblades off them while others rested against walls and columns, eager to catch their breath.

Sid looked around her, awe struck.

"Well, that was different," Ashlan said and she jerked her head to face him.

"Please tell me you're almost done," she begged, "it won't be long until more come. We need to get inside."

"Oh, I was done a while back," he smirked.

"You wha-" she started but was interrupted by a loud, repetitive clang from the corridor facing Dalrak.

Her back stiffened and she stood alert, eyes squinting to see into the darkness. There was a glimmer of light at the far end of the corridor and Sid tried to peer further in. Her eyes adjusted to the light, pupils shifting from a thin line to a thick mass, focusing on the growing blue glow ahead. Sid threw the balance of her weight onto her right heel and cocked a hip out, resting her hand on it.

"Here they come," she said, beaming a smile in Dalrak's direction.

The blue light intensified and took the form of strong, metal limbs as one by one, the army of droids Ashlan had taken command of marched forward. Their steps shook the vast hall, banging and clanging as their heavy legs landed on the floor. Sid tried to count them as they approached and stood side by side in front of the throne room doors. One, two, five, fourteen. She stopped counting when she realized that there were more droids than people in the hall.

The queen doesn't stand a chance!

"Ready?" She asked.

Ashlan smiled and looked at Tann before shifting his gaze back to her. "You bet." His index finger tapped on the screen and the droids took one collective step forward, arms interlocking and metal bodies tightly clenched together. "Are you?"

Hands in pockets, she squeezed through the wall of droids, careful not to let her magic interfere with their currents. Without hesitation, she placed a palm on the lock screen and waited.

"UNIDENTIFIED HANDPRINT," a robotic voice screamed as the lock screen buzzed, trying to recognize her touch. "CLEARANCE NOT ADMITTED. PLEASE REMOVE PALM AND STEP AWAY IMMEDIATELY. GUARDS HAVE BEEN CALLED TO SECURE THE AREA."

Sid laughed, thinking of the guards cowering with Leona behind the doors. *No kidding!*

A quick burst of her magic into the screen and the box huffed and hissed under her touch before the screen went dark. A light smoke rose from the fried lock screen and Sid flung her hand out of the way, wiping the singed skin on her suit's pant leg.

"Did it work?" Serryl asked from behind the droid wall.

She nodded, "Give it a minute."

A spark flew from the box and she jumped back, her back colliding with the droid behind her. She laughed at her own, foolish fear and straightened up, eyes widening as the throne room doors slid open, revealing a row of the queen's guards with blades pointing forward.

Sid shot a glance at Dalrak, whose hand was already

pressed onto the emergency fail-safe at the far end of the hall. He grunted and sent a shock into the small, metal casing. Alarms rang out immediately and the flashing, red emergency lights screamed over their heads. She noted the guards falter, adjusting their eyes to the jarring light and sound. Slinking away to get behind the droids, she joined Ashlan by his side. Within moments, he was typing in code, making the droids come to life.

In unison, their metal army marched forward, their bodies never swaying from the path.

It was difficult to see past their large bodies but she could hear the clang of blades on metal, followed by screams and shouts as the droid army walked forward — unencumbered.

The queen's guards fought them valiantly but Sid knew it was a fruitless task. With the lights interfering with their line of sight and the screeching sound of alarms, the guards could do nothing but throw aimless jabs at the unstoppable metal shield pushing its way through them. Some tried to get around the droids but their attempts were unsuccessful. When the droid line reached a third of the way into the throne room, Ashlan entered another sequence and they began to taper in, forming a circle around the guards and closing them in. One guard realized what was happening and dropped his place in line, escaping the hold of the droids and rushing straight for Sid. She was about to hit him with a blast when Serryl pushed past her, striking her blade into the guard's shoulder and knocking him to the ground. The club owner raised her blade, ready to deliver the final blow.

"No! Don't kill him!" Sid yelled.

Ahead, the droids had successfully fenced the guards in. A prison cell built of metal bodies and unyielding limbs.

Serryl threw her blade down and Sid tightened her eyes

shut, looking away. She heard a scream, followed by whimpers. She looked up to see the guard hunched on the floor, holding his leg, Serryl's blade sticking out of it defiantly. Blood flowed from his leg, covering the floor in a deep maroon and leaving a tang of iron in the air. He screamed over and over, dulling the pain before his eyes closed and his body fell, blonde hair getting soaked in the blood of blood that made its way to his shoulders.

Slowly, the club owner walked away, knocking Sid to the side with her shoulder. "Sooner or later," she said, "you'll have to kill. Time to grow up, kid!"

There was no time to retort. Before she could say one word, a strong hand pulled her back, swinging her around just as a sharp knife flew past her. The blade nicked her shoulder and she yelped, pressing a hand against the gash. She looked back at the knife that lay on the floor then turned, facing the Magistra that had thrown it head on.

The girl was younger than Sid but the anger and hatred aged her bright features. Her eyes were bloodshot and feral, and her red hair hung in sweat-drenched pieces over her face, making her look like a fire that'd been put out. She curled her bottom lip, reached back, and pulled the largest sword Sid had ever seen from her skirts. Pointing the sword at Sid, the Magistra ran. Leaping over the body of the guard on the floor, she charged for Sid, a violent scream on her lips.

Behind her, twelve more Magistras emerged, running faster than a breath of air; swords swinging and clashing.

"Here we go!" Ashlan yelled and dropped the projector. Wielding his own blade, he ran forward.

Sid dropped her hand from her shoulder and followed; Dalrak, Tann and the Freedom Runners close behind her. They met the swords of the Magistras with their blades, slashing and ducking as they fought with all the strength they could master. Ashlan had taught them well and they held the attack.

The girl that met Sid's gaze pushed her way through the crowd, her sword unrelenting. She raised her skirts, revealing muscular legs and kicked her way past the Freedom Runners at her side, her eyes never leaving Sid.

Oh, sweet star, she's coming for me.

In a split second, Sid collected the power in her and ran forward, blasting bursts of electricity at the girl. Sid was quick, but the Magistra was quicker, ducking and rolling off the blasts with her sword. She soared through the air, yelling out what Sid could only describe as a battle cry, her sword raised above her head. The girl's gem-covered heel dug with full force into Sid's clavicle and she fell onto her back, holding her throat and trying to breathe. Her breath felt like it was trapped somewhere between her stomach and chest and she wheezed whatever air she could muster into her lungs with difficulty.

When Sid finally got a breath in, she felt the sharpened tip of the Magistra's sword along her jaw and looked up slowly and carefully. The girl stood above her, fierce and unyielding, colder than the cosmos void.

Sid tried to move, tried to use her magic but the girl had her pinned. She needed to get her distracted, at least long enough for her to use her magic and get control of the sword. Why in the star's name did she not let Ashlan give her a weapon? It was a stupid move and she was about to pay for it with her life. She was about to–

The girl raised her sword and whipped her arm down.

Sid closed her eyes then forced them open again. If she was going to die, she refused to do it blindly. She watched the edge of the blade reflect the red hue of the emergency lights as it ripped through the air toward her. Watched it pick up speed and rush, rush, rush to her neck. Watched as a blade tore its way through the girl's arm. Heard her screams of terror and felt the blood that sprayed from her dismembered forearm land in blotches over her face and hair.

Her body reeled with horror as she saw the Magistra try to stop the blood flowing from her wound. Everything seemed to slow around her. The sounds of the battle disappeared into mindless echoes and all Sid could hear were the footsteps coming toward the injured girl. Footsteps followed by the scrape of metal on the floor, a sword dragging.

She looked over to see Serryl approaching, raising the sword she no doubt took from the body of another Magistra she had killed.

"Nooooo!" Sid yelled but she was too late.

Serryl's sword tore through the air and sliced the girls head clean off.

Bile rose in her throat and she could no longer hold down the contents of her stomach. She turned away from the sight in front of her and wretched. When she was done choking up that morning's meal, she wiped her mouth and face with the sleeve of her suit and turned to look at Serryl.

"Why?" She asked with a sob.

The club owner didn't answer her question. Instead, she outstretched her arm, helping Sid get back on her feet. "Next time, you're on your own," she said and rushed back into the clash of weapons.

Someone called her name, the voice vaguely familiar, Dalrak perhaps, and she tried to find the source of it. Her eyes shot from side to side but all she saw were blurs of bodies and blood, so much blood. No one was supposed to die. That was her only rule and they broke it. Worse, she was the reason for the deaths. How could she believe that there would be no consequences? It was a foolish hope, the hope of a child who knew nothing of what these people had been through. Knew nothing of how deeply Leona's control resonated on the star. She underestimated the Magistras, they all did. These weren't just girls, waiting on the queen day and night. They were fighters. They were killing machines. And more than half of them were dead.

She took a step back, legs shaking and cold sweat running down the backs of her thighs. Then another and another until her back hit the cool wall behind her. Her breaths came in pieces, small ragged slips of air that barely filled her lungs. Sid stood against the wall, panting and digging her nails into her muddy palms. She heard her name again but didn't bother to look up.

Instead, she filled her lungs, shut her eyes, and screamed.

Her yell rushed through the throne room, spilling her magic in its wake. The current that escaped her took no prisoners, rolling through the entire tower and blasting it to pieces. Lights shattered, machines died on impact, and every glass pane burst into a million pieces. The Queen's Tower rained glass. Broken panes flew from every floor, showering the ground of the city below in a hail of knife-like shards. The Citizens that hadn't already been hiding in their quarters ran for shelter, dodging the panes of glass that threatened to slice them in half. The city was in chaos.

The scream passed through Sid, dangling on her lips like it was standing on the edge of a cliff, contemplating the jump. She took a deep breath and opened her eyes.

No one moved. It was as though they had been frozen in time, watching her with wide eyes and open mouths.

The Freedom Runners had the Magistras surrounded but she could see their blades were down. Ashlan and Tann held a girl each, arms tied behind their backs and they nodded in her direction before stepping away. The girls scattered, holding each other and running out of the throne room.

Behind them, Dalrak loosened his grip, letting two more Magistras escape.

She looked over the room, eyes landing on the tomb of droids around the guards. Though still in formation, their blue glow was gone and she could see their heads hung in off mode.

Did I... she thought, *did I shut the whole tower down?*

"How?" Was all she could mutter out loud. Her voice trembled but she regained her composure when the slow sound of clapping rose from the other end of the room.

"Well, isn't this something?" Leona sang, moving slowly around the droids. Her long skirts dragged on the floor, smearing blood with each step she took. "Perhaps I underestimated you."

"You think?" Tann shouted but she ignored him.

"We've known each other for such a short time, Sid. As I recall, it was right here in this room that we first met. I so cherish that moment."

"The room where you killed someone I knew as a child," Sid hissed.

"Yes, well, an unfortunate situation, though I do believe you should thank me."

"Thank you? For what?"

"If we didn't meet under those dire circumstances, we might not be here right now." She smiled and Sid's stomach turned. "And I might not know just how powerful you truly are. Colton was right to hide you; you just never know who you might meet."

"He hid me from you!"

Leona looked around the room, her eyes scanning over the bodies. "Are you quite certain about that?"

Sid's head was still spinning but she wasn't about to let the sadist get in her head. They came here for a reason. Did it play out the exact way she was hoping? No. But did they get through the guards, Starblades and Magistras? They sure did! A feat that days ago, Sid never would have imagined to be possible for them.

"Are you going to make this hard?" She asked.

"Not at all," Leona said coyly and raised her arms dramatically, "I am at your command."

The queen's words were filled with trickery and untruths but what choice did they have? She was the only thing standing between them and the Arcane, the only thing in the way of their freedom. Sid waved Dalrak over and tossed a lightline his way. Once the queen was restrained, he pulled on the line to drag her to Sid. She squirmed, clearly annoyed by the maneuver. Even without the electrical current running through the lightline, the wire cut through her skin with each strong pull from the warrior. When they reached her, Dalrak pushed the queen forward to face Sid.

"Take me to the Arcane," Sid said, "now."

Leona's lips curled as she half-bowed with a smirk, "Anything for you, Sid."

FORTY-EIGHT

THE VAULTED, glass ceiling of the tower was nearly in pieces and Sid found herself dodging around broken glass which seemed to have shattered across every part of the dark, steel floor. She jumped over another large piece, careful not to step on the etchings that spanned from the center of the room all the way to the edges. Something about the markings felt familiar and she felt stupid for not recognizing them sooner. They were the same marks Dalrak and the Al'iil had over their bodies. Except these were intricately stacked and positioned, making her wonder if someone had spent a little too much time figuring out the pattern. From what she knew of the beliefs of the Al'iil, precision was not the thing that made them feel connected to Kartega. The light of the moons danced across the room, drenching the shards of glass in a silver gleam that made the destruction Sid had caused look almost beautiful.

She glanced over the detailed metalwork that formed the arches above them. Of course, the attention to detail must have been a human thing.

It seemed the queen read her expression because she jerked herself away from Dalrak's hold and ran to walk by Sid's side.

"Beautiful, isn't it?" She asked.

"It's something alright," Sid noted, hating the fact that she did find the place beautiful.

Leona waved a hand in front of three tiers of metallic rings, all with the same intricate designs and arranged in cascading order to the open ceiling above. A chandelier of sorts except there was no source of light within it. "It's the one thing my mother actually got right."

"So what do all of these mean?"

The queen shrugged, looking away from her. "I wish I could tell you. I would ask your large friend though, seems to me he is the closest to these symbols out of all of us."

"Forget it! I'll just the Arcane."

Sid glanced back at Dalrak, who looked to be as intrigued by the signs as her. His usually straight stance was replaced by an uncomfortable hunch as he studied the lines and circles that covered the top floor of the Queen's Tower. His lips were moving slowly, trying to read the symbols. Every once in a while, he shook his head in frustration, making Sid realize he'd be no help at all. He was as clueless as Leona when it came to the meaning behind them. In front of them, Ashlan and Tann ran ahead to take in the details of the domed space. Ashlan tapped Tann's shoulder periodically, pausing to point up at something new they'd discovered and Sid wished she could be as excited as they were about this place. All she felt were knots in her stomach and a lingering scream in her throat. Something about the place felt haunting, like it was built on death itself.

"Might want to get on with it, kid!" Serryl shouted from

the intricately decorated entrance doorway. She had hung back to stand watch in case more guards showed up. Though Sid doubted that to be the case. Whatever her magic did to the tower, it wreaked enough havoc to keep them safely out of reach. The elevators were all down and Dalrak tripped every lock as they passed through to make sure no one else could follow. For better or worse, they were alone.

She saw Leona start to smile from her peripheral and turned to glare at the queen. She was captured and it was over for her. Soon, they would have all the answers they sought to help them shut down the ring and free the domes for good. What in the star did she have to smile about?

"What are you grinning about?"

"You'll see, darling," the queen smirked, venom coating the words. "You'll see."

"Enough games! Where are they? Where are the Arcane?"

Leona's smile deepened and she pointed her lacquered, jewel covered fingers to a dark doorway on the other side of the room.

"I don't see anything! Where are they?" Sid roared impatiently.

"Ladies!" The queen beckoned, "Don't be shy. Come on out. Your queen demands it!"

There was a rustle of metal from the darkness ahead and Sid followed the sound, starting to walk toward it. Behind her, Dalrak jumped forward, grabbing her elbow and pulling her back. His other hand glowed with magic as he stood defensively by her. Ashlan and Tann stopped their chatter and joined them, blades powered up.

She wrestled her arm away from the warrior and gave him a look that told him not to worry. These were the

Arcane. Natives of Kartega just like them. They had nothing to fear from them. They would jump at the chance to free their people; she was sure of it!

Sid could taste all the answers she needed on the base of her tongue and smiled, waiting as the sound of metal got louder and louder until it was nearly in view. So close she could hear the mix of small footsteps that were entwined in it.

"They're here!" She yelled and bolted forward. She was halfway to the sound, right in the middle of the room, her head directly under the dim glow of night that trickled in over the chandelier above. The warm glow of her body pulsed, casting shadows on the walls that danced slightly when she took a breath. "You can come out. We won't hurt you. I'm here to help."

At the sound of her voice, the footsteps slowed but didn't stop, and soon she could see a figure emerge from the dark doorway. Sid strained her eyes to make out who it was when another figure emerged, then another. She stood as still as she could, trying her best not to startle the people coming forth to meet her. When the figures were close enough to see clearly, she looked over them and gasped, understanding the sound of the metal. Before her stood three women, pale and thin in gold, chain-link gowns that trailed to the doorway from which they'd appeared. Sid's mouth dropped open when she realized that the women were chained by their own dresses. Their bodies covered from neck to toe in metal that was so heavy, she could hear their skin burn under it in agony. The women's heads were shaved and there was no life or light in their eyes. They were barren of existence, stripped of anything a person might process to be rendered alive. The women walked closer, their fogged eyes never blinking, eyes that bore a similar shape to hers. Wide, with thin long pupils down the center. Domer eyes.

Sid studied their faces, trying to find some hint that the women were conscious, that they knew where they were. Some hint that she could talk to them, ask them for their help. Tears and bile rose within her when her gaze settled on their mouths. *No! No! No!* She shouted in her head. The Arcane couldn't help them. They couldn't tell them how to shut the ring down or guide them in the right direction. They couldn't tell her anything at all. She stared in horror at the women in front of her, each one with nothing but a layer of skin where her mouth should be.

"What the muck is this?" She shouted, her eyes burning through the queen who was now laughing uncontrollably.

"Whatever do you mean?" She asked and tried to stifle another laugh, unsuccessfully. "You wanted to meet your precious Arcane, and now you've met them. Don't tell me? You're not impressed."

"What did you do to them?"

"I'm sorry, do to them?"

"Yes! Where are their mouths?"

Sid was furious. She was sad and disgusted but mostly, she was furious. She should have known better that Leona wouldn't just lead them to the Arcane so easily. Of course she brought them here! Why wouldn't she? From the moment they'd seized her tower, she didn't do anything to fight back. The Starblades, the guards, the Magistras — it was all just a game to her. A game she knew she would win because even if Sid got through to the Arcane, she couldn't get them on her side. How do you convince someone to hear your point of view when they're not even alive enough to understand you? The Arcane weren't the women she heard stories of, the brave three that chose to give up their lives and magic for the ring. They were nothing but sacks of bones and helplessness. Prisoners of their own bodies.

Sid reached over to cup the face of the woman closest to her and gulped when she didn't recoil at the touch. She simply swayed slightly from side to side, in unison to the other women, their metal dress prisons ringing lightly like some eerie lullaby. "Where are their mouths, Leona?" She said sternly, never taking her mind off the Arcane.

"Oh, they're in there somewhere, I'm sure. After my mother died, they spent so much time shrieking and crying. I never understood why but it was quite bothersome. It made coming here unbearable. All that noise."

"What did you do?"

"I did nothing, of course. I simply had the scientists find some way to make the screaming stop. You know, this is one of my favorite places in the city. This room is the only place I loved as a child. It was so peaceful. I loved spending time here and believe it or not, the ladies loved seeing me. They used to spend hours on end telling me stories. About my mother; about the ring. They just knew so much." The queen walked over and ran a finger across the chain-link of one of the Arcane. "I couldn't very well have them spill all their secrets to anyone who would listen."

"So you, what? Chained them up and shut them up?" Sid yelled.

"What else would you have me do? They threatened to leave, to shut the ring down and just leave. I couldn't have that. I had to protect the Citizens!"

"You turned them into," She couldn't say the words, "into-"

"Oh, stop your babbling!" Leona snapped, tugging at the

woman's dress and making her buckle back. The queen twisted her head, revealing the scar of her chip and Sid noticed that the Arcanes' chips were glowing a bright blue. "I turned them into the keys they are. Nothing less, nothing more."

"They're not keys," she spat. "They're people!"

The queen chuckled and let go of the woman's head, "Not anymore."

Sid jumped at Leona. Her hands wrapped around the queen's throat as she pushed her back. The queen stumbled and reached for Sid's fingers, clawing at them with her perfectly manicured nails. Scratches covered Sid's hands but she didn't care. She wanted this monster gone. She wanted her dead.

Magic danced its way to her palms and she squeezed, letting the current jump into Leona's body. As her body convulsed under Sid's grasp, she smiled, noticing for the first time a hint of fear in the queen's eyes. *I will end you!*

"Sid! No!"

Someone grabbed her arm and pulled but she didn't budge. She kept squeezing, watching as Leona's face turned blue, as her eyes started to bulge out uncomfortably far. Another grip tightened around her and whoever had her pulled her arms apart. They dragged her back, back, back. So far that she couldn't reach the queen, couldn't finish what she started.

"Nooooo!" She screamed as Leona's body fell to the floor. Unconscious but breathing, "She needs to die! She needs to pay for what she did!"

"Not by your hand," Dalrak said and wrapped his arms around her.

"Then by whose?" She yelled, choking on her own spit and tears. "Yours? Theirs? Who will make her pay for this?"

The warrior didn't answer at first but his grip lessened, just enough for her to slide out. "Kir solkita, Sid," He said quietly. "Another way."

"There is no other way, Dee. We're done for. They were our only hope."

She searched his eyes but they were as empty as her own. No, this was wrong. She wouldn't stop! She couldn't! They came this far and they could still figure this out. She just needed a minute to think. Sure, the Arcane were barely breathing but that didn't mean she couldn't persuade them to help. Maybe if she talked to them. Or brought the Freedom Runners. Muck! She could show them the rest of the domes if that's what it took. She had to wake them up! She had to!

Dalrak had grown silent. *Why is he always a mute when I need answers?* She needed to tell him that there was still hope. That she would come up with a plan and they would pull this off. She needed all of them to hear it and believe her. To believe *in* her. Sid turned to face him and the others and froze.

They weren't alone in the room anymore.

FORTY-NINE

"WHAT ARE YOU DOING HERE?" Sid yelled at the impostor.

"One must always follow the path of Kartega, Stardaughter," Tazmin said calmly as ten warriors moved forward to stand beside her. "She has led me here to you."

The high priestess's eyes landed on Dalrak and she sneered. When she was done counting off the people in the room, her gaze landed on the Arcane. "Oh, sisters, you have chosen poorly indeed."

"They didn't choose anything! She made them this way!" Sid yelled and pointed to Leona's slumped form on the ground. "Help me! We can end this together!"

"Help you, Stardaughter?" Tazmin asked. "It wasn't long ago that I was asking for your help myself. Kartega was asking for your help and you chose to run." She sneaked a glance at Dalrak again but he looked away.

"Kartega does not want what you want!" Sid screamed. "Help us, Tazmin!"

The priestess's shoulders dropped and Sid's heart

swelled. With her help, they had a shot at getting through to the Arcane. And if that didn't work, the magic the priestess and the warriors could bring might be enough to take hold of Leona's following for good. Her lips curled upward and froze.

"Sil gecko rohan!" Tazmin belted to her warriors.

One by one they moved in, the magic in them bursting out in tendrils of light. The two warriors on the priestess's left charged first, blasting two perfectly aimed surges of electricity at Tann and Ashlan. *They're not here to help. They're here to kill. Stars help us.*

"Tann! Ash! Duck!" She yelled and ran for them, palms out to greet the warrior's magic.

Her hands reached for their magic with her own, grabbing hold of the tips of their bursts with electric currents and dragging them toward her. Arms shaking, she pulled their magic in, breathing through clenched teeth to control it. Spit bubbles flew from her lips as she pushed air in and out, trying to keep hold of the surge of power hurtling through her body. The added energy made her head pound and she had a flashing memory of laying on the filthy ground in Tazmin's hut, swollen with magic and electricity.

"Sid!" Ashlan yelled from behind her.

"I'm fine! Can you all handle the warriors?" She shouted back as another bolt of magic rushed by her, hitting the back wall. "Serryl, you need to stay with the Arcane!"

"What are you going to do?" Serryl hissed and ran to the chained women.

"I'm going for the priestess!"

She took off. Her legs pumping fast as she ran straight for Tazmin. She reached the spot where the queen's body lay, serene and peaceful, as though she wasn't responsible for the enslavement and murder of everyone on the star. For a moment, Sid considered pulling her out of the path of destruction but the thought passed quickly. Sid leapt into the air, jumping over her and barely missing her plump hip with her boot.

Ahead of her, Tazmin stood calmly. Unencumbered and looking quite a bit bored. The symbols on her body pulsed with light but it was nothing compared to the glow Sid was giving off. *She's not even trying!*

Sid skidded to a halt ten steps in front of the priestess and glanced back to her team. Tann and Ashlan were surrounded, six warriors stood around them, hands outstretched and a hurricane of magic dancing at their fingertips. She saw one reach out to grab ahold of Tann's body, pulling him like he weighed no more than a drop of water. She attempted to yell for Dalrak's help but quickly noticed him fighting off two warriors himself. He held his ground but she could see his movements were strained; he was losing energy. And fast. In the center of the room, Serryl flashed her teeth at the approaching warriors. She seemed confident but Sid knew that if they got too close, they'd rip her apart without even trying. The sword she swapped her blade for was nothing but a toy when compared to the raw, unbridled power the warriors had been trained to use.

"Why are you doing this, Tazmin? We're on the same side!"

"I am on the side of Kartega," Tazmin glowered, "I choose no other side than that."

"And you think this is what the star wants? For you to kill the people trying to help everyone?"

Tazmin smiled.

"We're not your target, are we?" Sid asked, her eyes

widening in fear as she realized why the Al'iil had decided to make an appearance. "You're going to kill everyone in the city like you planned."

"Kartega would like to thank you for leading the path to salvation."

"You don't speak for Kartega!" Sid yelled. "You're insane!"

"I had hoped our lessons would have taken some hold on you but it seems you refuse to see the true path that you have been put on."

"What lessons? All you did was try to turn me into a magic bomb for your own misguided use!"

"There were many things to learn in your time with us, Stardaughter," Tazmin said. "I am surprised you missed the most important lesson of all."

"And what's that?"

"The death of the few do not outweigh the lives of the many."

Sid's thoughts rushed through her, jumbled in the memories of the Al'iil camp she had tried to bury deep inside. The pain she had suffered there. The hope she'd lost. Her mind raced as pictures of moments flashed, landing on the Qualin in the jungle. The first time she realized that the Al'iil were not the answer to her problems. That they were all mad and that Tazmin was a self-guided killer masquerading as a leader.

"Only someone who is blind would think that! This is not what Kartega wants, Tazmin!" She yelled.

The high priestess placed the back of her hand on her forehead and closed her eyes. As she did so, the symbols on her body glistened, as if suddenly turned on. "Thank you,

Stardaughter." Was all she said before she pounced forward and shot a burst of magic directly into Sid's chest.

The magic burned as it collided with her body and the force knocked her back. She tried to keep her balance but her feet tangled and she dropped to the floor with a loud thud. Sid could feel the familiar ache of the priestess's magic on her, the sickly sweet taste she got in her mouth when it entered her system. Brushing her palms furiously over the charred spot on her suit where the magic hit her, she scrambled to her feet.

Tazmin was already moving closer to her, readying for another hit.

Trying not to look weak, she straightened up, fighting the vertigo that threatened to overtake her. She shot a charge at the priestess, then another, followed by a third. The priestess blocked each one easily, trapping the electricity in a loop of blasts that dissipated Sid's magic like she had blown out a small fire. Tazmin's body, that seemed so relaxed before, was now glowing intensely and the thick muscles in her legs and neck bulged as she ran for Sid. She shot her hands forward, grabbing hold of the magic Sid had stored in the veins of her legs and pulled.

Within moments, Sid was on the ground again, her head pounding from the hit it had taken when she fell. She reached up to touch the back of her head and pulled away a wet palm. Blood.

Still holding her head, she jumped back to her feet.

"I will give you this, Stardaughter. You don't give up easily," Tazmin smirked and threw a blast of energy at Sid's shoulder.

It hit her with such strength that she was spun almost all the way around. She looked to Dalrak who was still holding off the warriors around him. He was close to her, so close she wanted to reach out and pull him in. Fifteen steps, maybe twenty. She could make a run for him, unite her magic with his. Strengthen them both. But she needed to get away from Tazmin and her wrath first.

It was then that Sid noticed the figures behind Tazmin. Uniforms of blue and bright, silken dresses; torn and covered in bloody rips. The guards and some of the Magistras rushed into the room, weapons in hand. Among them she spotted Abbot and sighed in relief. At least she didn't lose someone else she cared for today.

Fear and relief flooded Sid's mind. Whatever Tazmin and the warriors did when following them must have cleared enough of a path for the queen's guard to get through. She wasn't certain they were there to help but at least it gave her a chance to get Tazmin's attention off her until she was able to recharge. If she could just preoccupy the priestess for a few moments while she scurried away, she could make it to Dalrak.

"It's the Al'iil!" She shouted, with somewhat truthful fear coating her words. "They've broken through!"

Tazmin looked at her like she had lost her mind then followed her gaze to the doorway. Sid could see her anger boiling under her skin, her magic in turmoil once her eyes landed on Leona's puppets. The same people she had despised for so many years. The people she wanted dead and gone.

The guards and Magistras stood dumbfounded and Sid wanted to walk over and slap each one of them individually, then maybe all of them as a group. *What the muck are they waiting for?*

She pointed an index finger at Leona's body. "Protect your queen, you fools!" She yelled.

That seemed to do the trick. Her words stunned them into action and they hurried for Tazmin, blades and swords slashing through the air. Sid had gotten her chance. As soon as the priestess turned her back, she took off. Her calf muscles felt like they were going to tear through her boots but she breathed through the pain, her attention only on the back of the warrior crouching over Dalrak's form. His hands were twisted against Dalrak's neck, twisting and electrocuting at the same time. Sid's stomach turned as she jumped in the air and leapt onto the warriors back. Her fingers latched around his forehead and travelled down, finding his eyes. With a guttural scream, she pressed into his eye sockets, making the warrior fall back from Dalrak in agony. He was clawing at her hands, trying to loosen her grip and relieve the pressure. Slashing and jerking, his body wriggled above her and crushed her with its weight. He was going to pummel her to death if she didn't move. Sid took a breath, tightening the grip of her legs around his waist and shot a burst of electricity from her hands, straight into the warrior's eyes.

A yell left him that echoed all through the room. She let him go, watching in horror as he flipped to his hands and knees, feeling the ground for something resembling his weapon. "Kehen!" He yelled, blood and pus oozing from the holes where his eyes has once been.

The warrior turned to her and his hands shot out, ready to blast. Sid fought for her magic — draining fast now — trying to gather any semblance of energy to block the attack. Suddenly, the warrior's body twitched. Slightly at first, then with such force he began to rise from the floor. It was as though something had gripped him by the neck and was pulling him into the air. His body shook and sparked and over his shoulder she could see the bright yellow glow of Dalrak's magic holding tight. It threw shock after shock into the warrior's body until his head slumped over his shoulders, his once glowing skin now charred beyond recognition. Dalrak dropped his magic and the warriors body dropped with it, hitting the floor lifelessly.

"Good?" He asked and she nodded, jumping to her feet.

She ran to him, averting her eyes from the body on the floor. Not far behind lay the second warrior Dalrak fought, his head twisted at an unnatural angle and his eyes as blank as starlight. "I could use a charge," she said and held out her hands.

Dalrak grabbed hold of her small palms, obliterating them from view with his own. Just touching him made her feel like she was stronger and when he let his magic roll over her, her entire body shook with elation. Every cell in her swelled as she fed on his power. She felt like she had just woken up from a two-day nap after not sleeping for a year. Her magic screamed, bashing against the confines of her skin. She let some of it free, signaling for Dalrak to stop. The warrior let go and smiled.

In a second, his lips turned downward and he swung her around to face the doorway where most of the Freedom Runners started to pile in.

"No!" She yelled. "Why are they here?"

It wasn't that they couldn't use the help. They were low on numbers and even with the guards and Magistras helping, the high priestess and her warriors were flicking them off like dirt on their feet. She could already see five guards and a Magistra on the floor, eyes rolled in the back of their heads. The girl looked familiar and it didn't take Sid long to recognize Kelyn, her once stoic face now darkened with burn marks down her cheeks and neck. These were trained fighters and even they couldn't stand against the Al'iil. The Freedom Runners didn't stand a chance. Sid had to do something.

A warrior headed for her and she turned to Dalrak with questioning eyes.

"Go," he said, stepping in front of her and blasting a bolt of energy at the attacker.

Without turning back, she ran. Past Tann and Ashlan who were fighting back to back with two warriors each on their sides. They worked in tandem, each one picking up where the other left off, slicing their blades through the air to block the attacks. One of the warriors charged forward and Tann nudged Ashlan in the ribs to signal him. On cue, Ashlan spun around Tann's side, vaulted in the air and delivered a high kick to the side of the warrior's skull. As the massive man stumbled to the side, Tann swung his blade, puncturing a hole in his abdomen. The warrior crouched, holding on to his bleeding stomach and the two got back into formation, their backs tightly pressed against each other.

Wow! These two are good together! Sid noted but kept running.

She slipped through the crowd, ducking and turning as she made her way through the room. The once peaceful place was a battlefield. Shouts swept the room and weapons clashed as a staggering amount of magic rifled through the air. She ran blindly, not checking to see who she was passing. Guard, warrior, Magistra, Freedom Runner — they were all the same to her now. Just people getting slaughtered for no reason at all.

"Tazmin!" She yelled when she finally reached the priestess.

The high priestess turned to face her, her body glowing so vividly that Sid had to look away. The crazed look in the priestess's eyes scared her but she stood tall before her. Trying to regain some composure in her words.

"This has to end," she said. Begged it, really. "We have to end this!"

The priestess cocked her head like a beast trying to understand a command. She smiled, her expression wild and sinister, and rushed forward, magic bellowing from her, surrounding her body in a wave of electricity. She was almost in front of Sid, her body so hot that Sid could smell the energy. She stumbled back, tripping over her own two feet and fell. As Tazmin hovered over her, Sid closed her eyes. Shut them so tightly her brain hurt. *Now I die,* she thought and waited. When nothing happened, she flung her eyes open just in time to see Dalrak step in between her and the priestess.

"Move!" Tazmin roared but Dalrak held his place. "Move or die!"

When he didn't shift, she saw the high priestess swirl around to his side, forcing an energy blast at Sid's face.

One step was all it took.

One step and Dalrak blocked the blast with his abdomen. His body reeled back and landed on Sid.

"Noooooo!" She yelled, cradling the warrior in her arms. "No! What did you do?"

Tazmin stopped, her eyes darkening as she lowered her gaze to the bleeding wound in Dalrak's stomach. She stepped closer to him but Sid wrapped her arms around his chest protectively, trying to move away from the priestess.

The warrior was too heavy for her to carry and his unconscious body made distributing his weight impossible. Her feet kicked out from under her and she landed hard on her bottom.

"Leave him alone!" She yelled as the priestess crouched over them.

Tazmin's hands reached for Dalrak's wound and she tried to slap them away. Tears streamed down her face, leaving a trail of clean skin on an otherwise filthy canvas. The priestess looked at her and Sid paused, registering the fear in her eyes.

She waited for her to say something and for a long while she thought she never would. As though Tazmin has gone mute from the act of hurting one of her own. A cry sounded somewhere behind them followed by the slashing of a sword across flesh. Sid refused to turn her gaze though everything in her screamed to look away. She raised her chin and cradled her arms tighter around Dalrak's neck. Tears streamed down her face and she choked on sobs that barely left her lips as Tazmin lowered herself to her knees over them.

The high priestess pressed her palm into Dalrak's stomach, stopping the bleeding. "We need to end this. Now."

FIFTY

THE ROOM that held the Arcane prisoner was covered in bodies and the smell of blood and charred flesh wafted through, turning Sid's stomach each time she inhaled.

She looked over the destruction they had caused. Heaps of death surrounded her and she tripped over limbs as she stumbled through the room. People glared her way, some wounded and others still holding up their weapons in anticipation. Tazmin walked beside her, holding up her hand to every warrior they passed, urging them not to attack. Some dropped their weapons at her command, others stayed vigilant in their doubt, looking to Sid periodically and muttering in Kartegan. Only three Magistras had survived and they huddled behind a group of guards, trying to nurse Leona back to life. Sid knew it would be some time before the queen regained consciousness and she resented the moment it would happen. If she was to kill, she should have quenched her anger with the queen. She took solace in the fact that there was still time and with Leona's mouth shut for the time being, they at least stood a chance of getting control of the situation.

By the time they reached where Serryl, Tann and Ashlan stood, her legs were exhausted from having to wade through bodies. What had they done? What had *she* done? Surely this was enough to wake the Arcane from their slumber!

She was very aware of Tazmin's magic vibrating behind her and felt some relief in knowing the high priestess had abandoned her crusade, at least for the time being. Sid still couldn't trust her but the high priestess's magic was stronger than anything she'd seen. They could use that kind of power when they finally shut the ring down. People would need structure in the new world they were about to create and if she had to choose, Tazmin was the least unstable leader for the star's residents.

Sid let herself smile, despite the tears that still flowed freely down her face.

"Where are they?" Sid asked when she realized she couldn't see the women near Serryl. "Where are the Arcane?"

Tann and Ashlan exchanged glances and her stomach dropped as Serryl stepped aside, revealing the three women on the floor, blood pouring from their sliced throats. The body of a Magistra lay behind them, a blade-sized hole in her chest.

"I'm sorry," Serryl said. "I was too late."

Sid couldn't feel herself fall. Her knees hit the floor, almost shattering her bones to pieces. Arms cradled her on either side and her gaze trailed over Dalrak's markings as he squeezed himself against her. The cold wet of his wound pressed against her suit and she could feel the blood soak into the fabric. She wanted to push him away, to help him be strong like he had helped her so many times. To heal his wounds. But her limbs refused to budge. Her chest rose and fell sporadically as her body tried to regain composure. Her head ached, her entire being ached. Everything they'd gone through, all the people that had died to get them here, it was for nothing. The Arcane were dead and they had no way to turn the ring off. All those people in the domes would never be free. And the Citizens? What of them? Would they go on living their life under the guidance of a power-hungry lunatic? She couldn't let that happen. If she couldn't turn off the ring then she would at least turn off the source of this star's poison. She would kill Leona. If these three women wouldn't be able to help...

A thought pinched the back of her ears and she squirmed under Dalrak's firm hold. *Three! That's it!*

"Three!" She shouted and looked up, "I got it!"

Tazmin cleared a path for her, confused. She looked over to Tann and Ashlan who only shrugged. Sid knew she was starting to sound like she'd lost it but she didn't care. As soon as she was on her feet, she rushed to the Arcane, inspecting the still glowing chips at the back of their necks.

"Sid? What's going on?" Ashlan asked and approached her slowly, his arms up in surrender. "What three?"

"Ash! Your dad!"

"What?"

"He said something the last time I talked to him before my ship went to muck. I didn't get it then but I get it now! I think he knew, Ash!"

"Knew what?"

"That this is where I'd end up!"

"That doesn't make any sense." Ashlan took a few more

awkward steps toward her, "Why don't you let them go and we can try to figure out another way to end this."

"I *have* figured it out! Well, I didn't. Colton did."

"My dad?" He looked back at Tann and shook his head. "My dad figured this out?"

"Look," she said, continuing to inspect the chips, "I know this sounds mad but the last time he talked he said I needed all three. I had no idea what he meant but now I do!"

"Alright..."

"The chips, Ash! I need all three!" She pointed to the necks of the Arcane. "The chips are part of the key right?"

Ashlan nodded.

"And you need all three to have control over the ring?"

Another nod.

"So all I need is these three chips. Not the Arcane, just these."

Ashlan looked from her to the chips to the rest of the group. "In theory, yes, that's what you need. But where do you suppose you're going to get three un-chipped Domers to volunteer? Tann and Serryl are already chipped and the priestess is useless!" Tazmin grunted and Ashlan shook his hands apologetically. "I'm sorry but since you and your tribe ripped your chips out, you pretty much destroyed any chance of going through the process again. The neurons are fried."

"I don't need three volunteers, Ash."

"Huh?" He looked from her crazed expression to the glowing chips. "No! Absolutely not! Are you crazy?"

"Can someone fill me in?" Serryl asked.

"She wants to put all three chips in herself. I'm not wrong, am I? That's your big plan here?"

She nodded. "It's the only plan. It was the only plan

from the start, I think. We just didn't know it. Colton did though and he made sure to warn me. I have to do this, Ash, for everyone. I'm the only one who can."

"But you could die. No one had ever been secured to more than one chip. It could suck your energy dry. It could kill you!"

At those words, Tann perked up and started at her. She threw her hand up to stop him and smiled. "Calm down, I'll be fine."

"We don't know that," Tann said.

"We're about to find out," she smirked and placed her hand on the back of the neck of the Arcane in front of her. Her magic grabbed hold of the metal, magnetizing and pulling on its strings until she ripped it out. "I'm sorry," she said and patted the exit wound on the back of the dead woman's neck. "You can rest now."

Shouts of shock rose from her team members as Sid pulled out the screwdriver from her pocket and shoved its rough tip into the back of her neck. Blood poured from the wound as soon as she opened it and she dropped to her knees, wheezing. Ashlan rushed to her side, holding her up with one hand and trying to stop the bleeding with the other. Her hand trembled as she raised it to him, the small, bloody chip in her palm. "Put it in! Do it now!" She yelled.

Ashlan's face scrunched and he shook his head no. "Now, Ash!"

His eyes were wild, fear and fury gathered behind the irises. He let go of her neck, letting the blood flow freely down her shoulders. Grabbing the chip, he looked at her one more time before shoving the device into her neck. Her body tingled for a brief moment before the sensation of burning encapsulated her. She felt like every blood cell in her veins was set alight. Her magic rushed from end to end, swirling in panic and commotion. Sid wanted to scream. She wanted to reach back and claw the stardamned thing right out. Instead, she dropped to her hands and knees and breathed deeply. "Get the rest before it's too late!"

"We got it!" Tann shouted, "Serryl! Use your blade!"

The two ran to the Arcane. With a quick swipe of their blades, they sliced the backs of their necks and pulled out the chips. The absence of the blue glow from the chips made the bodies look like mauled cadavers, cold and hopeless. They ran to her, holding out the chips to Ashlan who grunted in disapproval before inserting them into Sid's neck one by one.

If one chip was pain, three were an unspeakable torture. Her magic riled in her, defying the foreign objects and trying to push them out. Sid's back curved and she punched into the floor to keep from screaming. Beating it until the skin on her knuckles ripped and bled.

"Now what?" Ashlan screamed.

She unclenched her fist and pressed her hand on the back of her neck. *Please work.*

"Get me a cloth!" Tazmin yelled, kneeling beside her. "Breathe, Stardaughter."

Sid nodded, taking deep breaths and trying to calm her racing mind. With each breath, she regained control of a small part of her magic. She willed it to still. Commanded it to listen. Everything around her flowed. Her vision blurred and she tried to focus her eyes but all she could see was magic. Its glow surrounded her, sparkling and bright, like a fuse on fire. She felt hands on her neck then something rough, a fabric of some sort. Tazmin wrapped the belt of Tann's tunic three times around her neck and tightened it, stopping the blood flow.

"How long until we know if it worked?"

Something yanked at the back of her brain and she fell backward. Her body shook and she could hear the clamor of her team around her. Could see them bending over her, holding her limbs to steady her writhing form. The magic grabbed hold of the chips, a wave of electricity binding into the microns of the devices. It pulsed its power into them, pushing and pulling until it inhaled them. Until it trapped them entirely in its hold. Her body stilled and her limbs dropped to the floor on either side, feet collapsing out and hands outstretched. Sid lay there, for how long she couldn't tell, before she finally raised herself half up on her forearms.

"Do you think it worked?" She asked no one in particular.

"I believe so, Stardaughter," Tazmin answered and searched the floor for something.

The high priestess grabbed hold of a large piece of glass that had shattered from the ceiling, bringing it up to Sid's face. It wasn't the most reflective surface but it was enough for her to see her own shape clearly. She stared in awe at herself, taking in the new form of her body.

The warm glow of magic that had once surrounded her was a bright blue, the color of energy and power; the color of weapons. She shone bright enough to light half the room. Though that wasn't the part that shocked her most. What Sid had the most trouble accepting were her eyes. The eyes she once tried so hard to hide were pure white, her pupils gone entirely. She looked like someone had slapped two ship headlights into her skull and turned them to full power. She reached for her head, her fingers finding the musty goggles with ease and snapped them into place.

Smiling sheepishly, she looked at the rest of her team, all

covered in sweat and blood. "So," she asked with an awkward chuckle, "who wants to shut the ring down?"

"Sid," Ashlan said, gawking at her, "you're-"

"We have a problem!" Serryl shouted over him.

"What now?" Tann asked.

The bar owner pointed to the doorway. "The queen, she's gone."

FIFTY-ONE

"WHERE DID SHE GO?" Sid asked, adrenaline still pumping through her.

"The Magistras are gone too," Ashlan said. "They must have carried her off."

Sid fought her initial instinct to chase after the queen as she looked around the room and counted off the people left standing. Eight warriors, seventeen guards and twenty Freedom Runners. Ninety eyes and they all watched her every move.

Saliva gathered under her tongue and her teeth felt hairy and thick. She looked to Tazmin for help but the priestess only flipped the palm of her hand and nudged her forward. Whatever she had to say to these people, she was on her own figuring it out. *Great!*

Sid cleared her throat which did nothing for her dry throat. If anything, it only made her feel even more nauseous.

"Uhm, hello," She said and reached for the back of her

neck, dropping her hand when she touched the rough fabric of Tann's tunic belt still tied there. "Right. Hi, I'm Sid."

"We know that," Ashlan whispered under his breath and she shot him a side glance that seemed to seemed to silence him.

"I'm sure you all have some questions so instead of doing some big speech about why you shouldn't kill me right now, how about I let you ask them?"

"Maybe don't encourage them to *kill* you?" Ashlan whispered again.

"Shut," she hissed, "up."

"So you're turning the ring off?" One of the guards yelled front the back of the group.

"That's the plan, yes," She said.

"Won't that break the star or something?" The same guard, louder this time.

"The star was never broken in the first place. The ring was built to syphon power. To run machinery and build the city. It came at the expense of all of these people," she pointed to the Freedom Runners, "that's not a star I want to live on and neither should you. It's wrong."

"Sol tukti berros Kartega?" One of the warriors yelled out.

"How will I feed Kartega?" She repeated for everyone in the room that couldn't understand. "I won't. I have no intention on growing my magic. I just want everyone to be able to live however they choose. You can choose what you do and you can do it on your own terms without someone telling you otherwise. That sound good?"

He nodded and exchanged looks with Tazmin who seemed satisfied as well, a fact that hasn't yet stopped surprising Sid.

"What's Kartega?" Someone yelled out.

"It's the name your grandparents and their parents and everyone before them had for Neostar. Before the humans came."

"Are you extra strong now?" A girl asked, one of the younger Freedom Runners in the group.

Sid thought about her question, not sure how to answer. "You mean because of the chips?" She tapped the back of her neck and cringed a little from the shock the devices gave off. "It's odd. I don't feel stronger, just different. Like my magic has an extra kick and a few more volts. Does that make sense?"

"Well, yes!" Serryl chuckled, "You've gotten some serious juice from the ring, I'm sure!"

"I guess. I didn't think of it that way," she nodded.

"Did it hurt?" The same girl asked with some worry.

"Like dropping half a motor on your toes!" She chuckled. The girl seemed to be confused. "Yes, it hurt." She corrected and rolled her eyes, though without visible pupils and her goggles on, her agitation was lost on the girl. *Kids these days!*

People seemed to grow less restless, most of them stopped fidgeting and a few even dropped their weapons. Even some of the warriors relaxed, their shoulders no longer grazing their earlobes. She looked at them. Not to see their expressions but to really look at them. To memorize each person that had filled the room on this very important night, the night the domes would become free. In her mind, she saw Colton smiling. Remembered his face when she said something particularly clever or funny. She thought of the way his nose scrunched when he grinned at her from the screen, telling her she'd done well. She hoped that wherever he was now, his nose was scrunched so tightly it hurt.

Sid thought of her parents too. Trying to picture them standing by her and squeezing a hand each, telling her it would all be alright. She still had no inclination of what they looked like and her first line of business after she shut the ring down would be to get someone to draw her a picture of the people that gave her life. She needed something to remember them by that wasn't the clouded shapes of people she now held close to her heart.

A loud cough jarred her attention back to the group and she looked up to see a guard standing up and pointing. His finger trailed straight to the horizon where a dim light was starting to shine through the darkness.

"If you're going to shut the mucking thing off, this might be a good time," he said. "Or your chipped friends here get zapped for missing check in."

Sid's orbit of dreams shattered into pieces. She had mere moments to shut the ring down or risk losing every single Freedom Runner not in their domes at Starise.

"What do I do? What do I do?" She yelled, hoping someone could guide her. "I don't know how this thing even works!"

Worried chatter spread over the crowd of people, all of them rising in panic. Some questioned staying and debated making a run back for the domes, others just negated everything that was said and told them to give up. The voices overlapped until she couldn't make out any words at all, until her brain was swimming in her skull and she had nothing but the low hum of magic rocking at the back of her neck.

A hand gripped her and she turned to see a pale Dalrak holding onto to her. His energy had drained so much she could barely feel him near her.

"Dee! What are you doing?" She screeched, "You should be resting!"

"Think it through," he said.

She sunk to her knees, pulling him down with her until they crouched on the floor, their foreheads pressed tightly together. "I don't know, Dee. I don't know how this works. I'm not a scientist," she wailed.

"You're a mechanic. A stubborn mechanic."

"I'm going to let that last one go for now," she noted. "What are you getting at?"

"Think like a ship, Sid." He said.

"Like a ship? Dee, what in the stardamned-" she stopped. "Oh! Like a ship!"

She clapped her hands cheerfully and the quick movement made the warrior lose his balance and almost topple her to the floor. "Sorry! But yes! That's brilliant! It's all in the threes!"

"There she goes with the threes again," Ashlan joked and she swore she heard his eyes roll.

"It is the threes! Always the threes!" She yelled defensively, sticking her tongue out at him. "There are three keys? Why?"

Ashlan shrugged his shoulders.

"Exactly! You have no idea! But you know who would know?" She asked. "Someone who spent her whole life fixing a ship!"

"And?"

"And ships need energy! And in order to have energy, they need three things. A harvester, a place to store it and a processing unit to redistribute it. Three things, three keys!" She yelped in excitement. "Each one of the chips controls a piece but it's the three that make the ring keep going. You shut down one and it's system failure!"

"I'm not a mechanic," Ashlan said, "but that sounds like a bad thing."

"It is," she said, thinking for a moment before tapping a fingertip to her neck. "That's why I have to shut down all three."

She had a feeling Ashlan was going to fight her on this but she couldn't doubt herself now. There wasn't much time left, the ring had already passed twenty of the furthest situated domes. It wasn't long before it reached the resident domes of everyone in the room. Their death would be on her shoulders for the rest of her life. She couldn't let anyone else die for her actions. Sid knew the risks, went into this knowing them. She knew that she might have to die to save them all and this was her chance to prove it.

She ripped off her goggles, her white eyes reflected the yellow glow of the rising ring, and reached for the electrical hum of the Circulum System. Homing in on the flow of energy circling through it. As soon as she grasped it, her entire body ached. There was a small pinch on her neck and her magic rushed to the spot, magnetized by its pull.

"I've got the first one!" She yelled and kept reaching.

Each blood cell in her veins was on fire as she searched for the energy in the other two chips. The second one she needed was the storage system; that had to be the blade charging station. It was the one place that had the highest energy source in all of Tower City. When she could finally feel the power of the chip in her grasp, she tightened her magic around it, sending her power to search for the third. Figuring out the processing unit was easy. All she had to do was imagine the domes as though she was viewing them from her ship's observation deck. The tubes that fed the domes led back to the city and they all met in one place. Right under the bridge. That had to be the processing center! It would explain why it was so heavily guarded. *Clever move, Leona! Guarding the one thing that held all the magic right under everyone's noses.*

Sid's blood overflowed under her skin and she could see her veins begin to glow in such an intensity of blue that she looked like a piece of a river on a brightly lit day. It didn't matter, she almost had it!

With a final push, she grabbed hold of the last chip, threw her arms over her head and expelled the energy of all three chips outward.

The burst of light was so acute, it shot up like a tube of lightning, destroying anything still left in its path. It burnt through the air, flew past the dark clouds of the dimly lit night, and burst into the atmosphere. As the last of the energy left her body, the ring's light went out faster than an engine being turned off. Sid screamed and toppled to the floor, collapsing onto her stomach with her arms stretched to either side.

Murmurs swept over everyone who watched in awe as she lay on the floor, barely breathing but mostly alive.

"Sid?" Ashlan dropped to his knees next to her with Tann right behind him. "Sid, are you alright?"

She croaked a mumbled 'fine' and raised herself onto her elbows. Her eyes, though curtained in dark circles, were back to their usual self. Just as pale but with feline pupils running down the center; Colton's favorite.

"I did it?" She asked.

"You did it, kid," Abbot said. "But you might want to come take a look at this."

She let Ashlan and Tann help her to her feet, glanced over to Dalrak to make sure he was still conscious, and walked on shaking legs to the general. His back was turned to her and he stood so close to the edge of shattered glass that she feared a slight wind might rip him over the side and toss him off the tower. When she joined his side, she used one of the metal frames to steady herself, ignoring the broken glass that stuck out and tore at her skin. Her eyes looked down as she followed his watchful gaze to the streets of Tower City.

Streets that were littered with angry Domers tearing through it and killing anyone in sight.

FIFTY-TWO

FOR THE FIRST time in decades, magic had entered Tower City. On any other day, Sid would have been glad to witness such an occasion, to see the city wake up for the first time and embrace the wonder of Kartega. On this particular morning, she felt nothing but dread and disgust as she watched thousands of Domers rush the streets. Their faces, rabid and irate, turned from side to side — in search of victims. Their magic had just begun to wake up, still weak in its infancy, but their sheer numbers were enough to trample the Citizens to oblivion.

She had freed them and this was the result.

Her eyes squinted to focus from the top floor of the Queen's Tower. Somewhere below, she saw a flash of electricity followed by two more, all directed at the same spot. In mere seconds, whatever the bursts of magic had hit erupted into flames, spreading quickly through the street. She watched as projections flickered and died, the poles that held them toppling over with loud clangs. New magic or not, the Domers were getting the hang of it fast. It took Sid months to figure out how to channel her energy to create electrical bursts. Granted, she was practicing out of necessity in dark corners of her ship without an unbridled rage fueling her motives.

"Well, this can't be good," Serryl said, tipping over the edge to get a better view of the streets. "They're going to burn the star down at this pace."

"I know," she agreed. "This wasn't supposed to happen."

Serryl let out a half laugh, "Ha! Kid, this is exactly what was going to happen. They're mad and they have every right to be."

"They don't have every right to destroy this place. Or hurt the Citizens."

"They think they do," the club owner said, "that's probably worse. And they have their power back which I have to admit," she smiled and let a few electrical sparks dance from palm to palm, "is so much better than the garbage I was swindling at Magic."

Sid's head whirled in the direction of a scream coming from a transit pod docked on one of the streets near the gardens. For a moment, she thought she saw a light turn on but soon realized that it was just more fire. Someone had blasted at one of the trees and the flames were eating through the beautiful foliage like hungry beasts.

"No!" She yelled, reaching over as if she could do anything from where she stood. She nearly tripped over the edge but caught hold of the metal bar next to her just in time to regain her balance. "They're destroying everything!"

"Have any big plans?" Serryl asked.

Sid shook her head, dumbfounded. Who could plan for something like this?

"They need a priestess," Tazmin said over her shoulder, her long hair barely fussed. "They need guidance."

"Oh, no!" Sid yelled. "You are not going to start your mind control right now! They are not the Al'iil! They're just mad. And scared. And really, really strong," She added as she watched a Domer magnetize the side of the transit pod and topple it to the side.

"Not me, Stardaughter."

"Oh," Sid said. "Who? Me? No, no, no! I'm not really the leading type. I'm more of the lets figure stuff out and I'll help out type."

The high priestess stepped aside, revealing the large group that watched Sid with eager eyes. "Tell that to them."

This was a disaster. According to Serryl, she should have anticipated this outcome once they shut the ring down. She didn't. Yet another failure to add to her growing list and why would the priestess think that anyone could possibly need her? All she did was make decisions based on zero factual evidence and follow them through with all the swagger of a rusted satellite. She had no right to tell these people what they should or shouldn't do. *She* wasn't the one that was held prisoner and sucked dry of her magic her entire life. *She* wasn't the one forced to live in tiresome conditions and sent to work to keep the Citizens perfectly content in their glass city. They were Domers; the people who were here first.

Except she knew how they felt. She knew it because she felt the same betrayal when she found out that Colton had known about her parents and who she truly was. Felt it so deep in her bones she could set the entire star ablaze. What's a few gardens compared to that rage?

Sid knew exactly how they felt because she was them. Maybe without the chips or the domes but the hatred in her was just as strong at one point. So what changed? What changed her that could help change them now?

She glanced around the room, smiling when she noticed a guard and a Freedom Runner chatting like they were on the same side of this war. Smiled harder when she caught view of two guards help Dalrak sit up and applied nanite cloths to his wound.

This was it. This was what changed her.

It was them.

All of them.

Not the Citizens, or the Freedom Runners, or the Al'iil. It was every single person that lived on Kartega and breathed its air. It was everyone who went to bed gazing up at its moons and woke up with the light of Jericho shining down on them. *They* changed her. And if they could change her, then she was sure going to try to change them.

"Uhm, magic girl?" Tann asked, jarring her back to the room. "We kind of need a plan."

"I have a plan," she said. "And don't call me that. Every girl is magic girl now."

Abbot patted Tann's shoulder in solidarity and walked past her to the doorway. As he passed, people looked up from where they were, wondering why he would be leaving at an urgent time such as this. Sid was actually wondering that herself.

"Where are you going, general?" She shouted after him.

"To the telebox. I'm assuming you'll be broadcasting soon?"

She looked from Tann to the general in surprise. "How did you know that?"

"Because," Abbot said dryly and cocked an eyebrow, "it's what Colton would have done."

~~~

THE TELEBOX WAS MUCH SMALLER than Sid had expected. From the telescreens that Sid had seen of the queen projected over the domes and city, it always looked like she was casually relaxing in a rooftop garden. This place was more of a closet than a garden, it was barely large enough to be called a room.

Abbot ran his palm over an interface box implanted in the wall and the room came to life. Lights flickered on from every angle and a projection of a garden with a magnificent sky filled the space.

That's more like it! Sid thought and walked through a hanging vine.

The projection froze as her figure moved through it, coming alive again as soon as she had crossed into a clear area. Sid turned to the others, spotting a small red dot on the far end of the wall in front of her. "I talk to this thing?" She asked.

"Yes," Abbot said. "You talk to that thing."

Though the general was not great with humor or any light-heartedness, she was sure she saw him crack a smile. Perhaps it was at her expense but a smile is a smile and she was willing to take a win where she could. Smiling back at him, she straightened herself up and shook off her nerves.

"So what do I say?" She asked.

"Whatever you came here to say," Serryl scoffed. "This was *your* plan, remember?"

"Right, of course. Right." She bit her bottom lip until it started to swell. "This is much harder than she made it look, you know."

"Just pretend you're talking to me," Ashlan yelled out from the back.

"Actually," she said, "all of you standing there and staring makes this a lot worse. Could you maybe...?"

Tann, Ashlan and Serryl exchanged glances and shrugged, not bothering to step away. She was about to blast them with a good dose of energy when Abbot shooed them off. Urging them to leave as soon as possible for the sake of the star itself. *Whoa,* she smirked. *This guy is good!*

When the group was finally out of the room, he turned his attention back to her. "Ready?" He asked and smiled when she nodded yes. He tapped something into the small screen under the red dot and it changed to a bright blue.

"Oh, Sid?" He asked and she gazed up from her fingers, "Not the goggles."

She touched her face, realizing that at some point, she'd taken to wearing them again. With another nod, she slid the goggles off her eyes and snapped them in place on her head. Her eyes shone, even in the brightness of the garden projection. It was as though, turned on or off, the chips were magnifying her magic simply by existing inside her. It would be some time until she was able to get used to power this strong but she already felt like she was complete now that she had hold of it.

Abbot held up a finger, tapped something else and abruptly dropped his hand. The garden around her flourished, suddenly coming to life. Leaves rustled next to her in simulated wind and she jerked her gaze from the projection to the blue dot, quickly forgetting everything she was supposed to say.

"Forget it," she said.

"You're live," Abbot whispered and she stared wide-eyed at the dot, mortified.

"Uhm, hello there," she started. "I'm sorry, I'm not very good at this. You're probably used to seeing the queen up here and she is definitely much better at this talking thing. Actually, let's not call her that anymore. I guess she might be just Leona now. Is that how this works?"

She looked to Abbot but he shrugged and moved his finger in the air, urging her to move on.

"Right. Well, *Leona*," she emphasized the name and looked at Abbot with a grin, "she was always very good at talking, wasn't she? I don't know if many of you know this, but I grew up on a ship. A really great ship actually. Not really, it was a piece of junk. But the point is, I only knew things about your star," she paused, "*our* star from what I saw on telescreens. And what I saw was Leona. And she was beautiful. I mean, I used to watch her for hours, just picturing the day I would meet her. And then I did and she was not at all the person I thought she would be. She was cruel and vicious and the more I got to know her, the worse she became. Because that's what happens. You idolize people and then you meet them and they're not that person at all. I felt the same way when I met the Domers. Again, we should think of a better name," she sighed. "And when I got captured by the Al'iil. Everyone turns out to be so different.

You're probably wondering why I'm babbling about this when all you want to do is fight each other. I'm kind of wondering that myself. I should just let you, right? Because you deserve it. Because you can finally do whatever it is you want to do without someone telling you what to wear, or what to eat, or what time to return home. But you have your freedom now!" She shouted, "You are free! Is this what you want to do with it? Because I can tell you — no, I can promise you — that the people you want to hurt so badly might not be who you think they are. They might surprise you in the end like all of you surprised me. Like I'm hoping I surprised you just now."

In her peripheral, she could see Abbot beam and hoped the people on the streets had some of the same sentiment.

"So it might be hard to stop fighting. It might be hard not to be angry but trust me, you have to. It's the only way to-"

The lights flickered again and the blue dot turned dark. The garden around her flashed momentarily before disappearing.

"Abbot! What happened?" She yelled as the rest of the group ran back into the room.

"It's the queen," he cleared his throat, "Leona. She shut you down."

"How? How can she do that?"

He fumbled with the screen on the wall, tapping a few sequences of code. His fingers froze as did his expression.

"What's happening, Abbot?"

He flicked his fingers and expanded the screen for all of them to see. "She's screening herself."

On the screen in front of them, Leona sat in the middle of a lushly cushioned, levitating bed. The color seemed to have returned to her face but Sid could still see the charred marks of her fingers on her throat. She looked serene; serene and absolutely evil.

"That was truly lovely. The girl learns quite well from her superiors it seems," she sang on the projection. "My darling Citizens, fear not. Your queen is very much alive and well. I will not abandon you in this time of need. It looks as though our savages have escaped and while you may be fearful, I urge you to find courage. Today, we fight for what we have built. We fight for what my mother has built. We fight for Neostar!"

"What the muck is she doing?" Sid asked.

On the screen, Leona smiled. "The savages on our streets must be put down! Stand with me and fight for what is yours! Arm yourselves and kill anyone that threatens our survival. We are Citizens! We are the chosen! We are human!" She shouted. "Take arms and show them why they should fear us! We have weapons for anyone who is going to stand by my side to rid our star of this scourge. But know this, if you are not with me, you are against me. And anyone against me pays the price."

The screen flew across the room to four guards, tied together with lightlines and bound at their hands and feet. A Magistra stood next to them, a sword in each hand. She was young and beautiful though blood covered her silky brown hair. Sid immediately recognized her as one of the girls that huddled over Leona's body in the aftermath of the Arcane attacks. Before the guards had a chance to take another breath, she lifted her swords and sliced. One time, two, three, four. Each slice rushed through the air and cut though the guards throats so quickly that Sid did not have a chance to cry out. The last guard's head fell back, revealing a thick gash across his neck, blood pouring from it like a fountain.

"Time to decide, my darlings," Leona said off screen as the projection faded to black.

FIFTY-THREE

"I'M GOING TO KILL HER!" Sid roared, ripping through the telebox to get past them. "I'm going to burn her where she stands! Sits. Whatever!"

She tore past Ashlan and Tann. A shock of magic escaped her when she passed and Tann jumped back from the burn, rubbing his arm repeatedly to alleviate the pain. Her feet clanked on the floor as she walked and sent echoes of angered steps down the corridor leading away from the telebox. The emergency lights were still on in some sections of the tower and she was pleasantly surprised to see how far her power could reach. Maybe she didn't need to even get close to Leona? Maybe she could shut her down from right where she stood? No, that wouldn't do. She needed to be there. *Wanted* to be there. She wanted to see the look on her face when her power grabbed hold of her neck and squeezed. Wanted to smell the sour scent of her flesh as it burned under her hold.

She will end her.

The faster she walked, the louder her anger became,

until the only thing left in her vision was the goal of killing the queen before she did any more damage. Choking the life right out of her before she undid everything Sid had fought so hard to accomplish. She could see it so clearly, could almost touch it with her fingers. Dangling right in front of her like a trail of light left by a dying star.

"Where are you going?" Ashlan yelled, running after her. She could hear more hurried steps behind him, the rest of their group struggling to catch up.

They kept a good distance and as she caught glimpses of her reflection walking past the red-lit glass of the corridors, she understood why. She could barely see herself under the blanket of magic she had become cocooned in. It was like Sid was gone and the only thing left was an aura of lighting and electricity swirling madly around. If it wasn't for her goggles sitting prominently on her head, she never would have recognized herself.

"I'm going to find that monster!" She yelled back and stomped forward. "You saw the screen, she's in a bedroom. Probably her own. The coward!"

"Sid!" He ran next to her and tried to grab her arm but yanked it back with a shriek as his skin collided with her magic. "Ouch! Sid! Stop!"

Her body vibrated and she dug her heels into the floor. Her face swung around, turning to face him, eyes a pure white. "Why, Ash? Why should I stop? She's ruining everything!"

"Fine but please just listen to me for a minute," he sighed. "I just want to talk to you."

"You have two minutes. Then she's dead."

Ashlan took in a breath and glanced at Tann for assurance. When did they get this close? Was this a thing now? If it was, Sid hated it. She didn't want more people teaming up against her. Every time things became difficult or unbearable, they ran to her for answers. Pushed her to make decisions and basically begged her to choose for them. And now what? She was finally taking a stand against the queen and they simply couldn't let her go? Didn't they see she was doing this for them? Everything was for them!

She stared at Ashlan, annoyed.

"First of all, the new look," he waved a hand over her, "it's unnerving. Second of all, running off to kill the queen is probably the stupidest thing I've ever heard you say. And you've said some pretty garbage things before."

"If this is supposed to make me change my mind, it's not working." She rolled her eyes and turned.

"What exactly are you hoping to accomplish by killing her?"

"Uhm, I'm hoping to make her dead. I thought that was obvious."

The others had caught up with them and she could hear a few whispers pass their lips. They kept a good enough distance and she wondered if they were afraid that she might get mad enough to explode. She certainly looked like an oxidizer shaped like a girl; one wrong move and she could go boom without thinking.

"And what's going to happen when you get there and she's hiding behind armed Citizens? You going to kill them too?"

Sid turned back slowly. *Would I?*

"Haven't thought about that, have you?"

She shook her head. "She needs to be stopped, Ash."

"Sure, tell me this though," he quizzed, "what happens if you get there and things don't go your way?"

"What do you mean?" She asked. She was genuinely interested and she could see the rest of the group was starting to lean in, eager to see her response. They seemed just as interested as her.

"I mean, what happens if you don't kill her?"

"That's not possible," she said with assurance.

"Look at yourself, Sid! Anything is possible."

"Fine, so I don't kill her. I'll figure something out."

He shifted his weight form foot to foot. "Right. And if she gets hold of you before you do *figure something out?*"

"I'm not afraid to die, Ash."

"You really are dumb sometimes, aren't you?" He raised his voice. "I thought my dad taught you better!"

Her body convulsed and the bolts of magic sparked. "Excuse me?" She yelled back.

"If you die, she gets the chips!" He shouted in her face, spraying stray spit across her cheeks. "She gets the ring, Sid! She gets all of it!"

Well, he's not wrong.

The whispers behind them quieted but she could still feel all eyes on her. The way they watched her made her feel uncomfortable, like she was a creature on display. Sid thought back to her first day in this tower with Ashlan, of the way she felt looking at the portrait of the queen's mother. *Stardaughter! I'm the painting now, aren't I?*

Her hand reached for the back of her neck instinctively, to check if the chips were still there. She wondered if this is what it felt like for the Domers that got chipped first. To constantly be checking themselves, making sure they were still chipped. Fondling their skin to see if they were still someone other than who they were meant to be. Some halfway version of themselves; free to breathe and live but not really free. It's how she felt right now, standing in the corridor with her magic so exposed. Like she didn't have a choice at all. If only Ashlan and the rest of them could understand it. Getting fitted with the chips didn't mean she was stronger now, it only meant that she was trapped. There was nowhere she could go that didn't put her in danger, not until the source of the danger was wiped off the star.

She bit her lower lip and turned from him.

"Sid!" Ashlan yelled after her, "Stop!"

"No!"

"What if you die, Sid?" He shouted.

"Guess I'll have to try not to!"

She picked up her pace, running through the corridor and trying to get as far away from him and the guilt that was crawling under her skin. If she could just round the corner fast enough, she might have a shot at losing him. She could still hear his steps behind her, keeping in sync with her own. "Stay back, Ash!" She yelled and let a burst of lighting shoot behind her. She heard his steps falter and turned to see he swerved to avoid the hit, running faster now to make up for the distance between them. "I mean it!"

Another bolt of lightning burst through the air and catapulted past Ashlan's shoulder. He was quick but she was quicker, her magic grazing his skin just enough to hurt but not enough to cause any real damage. It pushed him hard, faltering his run and knocking him to the floor.

Ashlan cursed under his breath and stumbled to get back on his feet.

Relief washed over her and she realized that this was her only chance to get away. She pumped her legs, tearing the muscle in them with each accelerated jump. Her reflection blurred until she looked like nothing but a blue and yellow streak of light across the corridor. Sid rounded the next corner, skidding across the floor to make the turn. Her eyes looked ahead and she dug her heels in.

It was too late.

A blade whirled through the air, twisting as it picked up speed mid-flight. Its sharp, electrified tip pointed directly at her chest.

Sid tried to swerve out of the way but she wasn't quick enough and the blade hit her square in the shoulder and pushed her back. She screamed, one hand outstretched forward as she flew back and one clutching the blade that protruded from her skin. Her eyes fluttered and she was sure she was about to throw up.

Her back hit the floor first, followed by her arm. When her shoulder collided with the floor, she screamed again, rolling over to the side to mask the pain. Tears welled in her eyes and her mouth felt so dry that she couldn't close it. She could barely breathe.

Something like footsteps and voices approached her but she couldn't pick out one sound from another. The room faded to a buzzing around her and she let herself go, surrendering to the dark.

FIFTY-FOUR

SID'S EYES fluttered open to small slits and she could feel the sticky goop of sleep on her long lashes. She wanted to move but her body felt weightless. Panic rose in her as she realized her feet weren't touching the ground. It was as though her entire body was floating, neither in one place nor another. She wiggled her fingers and toes, relieved to find some feeling there. She was weak and tired, drifting in and out of sleep for what seemed like hours.

Sid's head rolled back and she let herself relax. Eyes shutting.

Some time had passed before she opened them again, pulling up her head to find that she was still nothing but air. Something moved under her back and she jerked up. At least she thought she did. Instead, she just let her head tilt to the side and strained her vision to get an idea of what was happening around her. Something gripped her gently, cradling her so her arms lay folded across her chest and her legs dangled back and forth. She was mobile. Someone was holding her and they were walking, slowly but with determination. Whoever held her squeezed her shoulders and she felt them take a sudden turn. Her body bucked with the movement and she felt a sharp pain in her shoulder and cried out. The words were not real, none of this was. It couldn't be.

Her eyelids grew heavy and she tried to fight the need to sleep without much luck.

When she finally awoke, Sid found herself stretched atop a flat surface. It felt oddly familiar, like a distant memory she had long since forgotten. Her hands scanned her body for restraints but she found nothing of the sort. Instead, all she felt was the soft fabric of a space suit that fit snugly on her body. Not her own, but an NSO issued one as she noted, counting off the similarities to the one she'd worn on her own ship. She'd grown through so many of those suits that she'd recognize one anywhere. She sat up slowly, carefully inspecting her surroundings. Metal grated floors, low vaulted ceilings and a ship-compliant sleeping bag under her. She was on a stardamned ship!

Sid fumbled for a moment before swinging her legs over the edge of the sleeping bag and pushing up to stand. As soon as she put pressure on her left arm, a numbing pain shot from her shoulder and she fell back down with a scream. Memories rushed back to her. The corridor in the Queen's Tower. Running like she was being chased. The blade flying through the air toward her.

She turned to look at her side, seeing the bandaged wound between her shoulder blade and left arm. She carefully peeled the edges of the nanite threaded cloth to see the extent of the wound.

"Stop picking at it!" A voice sounded from the doorway behind her and she turned to see Ashlan. He leaned casually on the silver doorframe, his hair a tousled mess and his eyes blood-shot. *Had he been crying?* She wondered but thought better than to probe for information, her head still spun uncontrollably and she couldn't be bothered to process his emotions on top of her own at the moment.

"Where are we?" She asked instead, her mind still groggy with sleep. "Are we on a ship?"

He nodded. "We're on *the* ship."

"As in…" she trailed off.

"You got it. The original human ships that brought my people here."

"But…? Why…? How…?" She hiccupped, her mind racing at the possibilities. "How did you find it?"

"Me? Oh, I found nothing," he smiled. "This was all Abbot. Pays to be the general, I guess."

She felt for the sleeping bag under her and used her right hand to push herself up. Ashlan bolted over to her, gesturing for her to use his broad shoulder to lean on when she stood. Her legs were liquid but she took a staggered step to the doors. She was on the original ship! Nothing was going to stop her from getting a grand tour.

"How did we get here? What happened?" She asked as they slowly walked together. Her eyes danced from side to side, inspecting each section they passed. The ship was old, built with antiquated technology but most of it looked very much like what she'd been used to on the Arcturus and it made her wonder if her own ship was one of the originals as well. It would make sense that Colton would put her on a ship no one would miss or look for.

"Well, the short story is you got a little crazy," Ashlan said.

"And the long story?"

"A guard pierced a blade through your shoulder, thinking you were going to kill him. We got to you in time to pull the blade out. When we regrouped with the rest, everyone was looking for a way off the star when Abbot mentioned the original fleet of ships. Seemed like a good idea at the time."

"It was a good idea," she thought, remembering her own plan to find them.

"Anyway, it was a long walk through the jungle. A very long walk! Dalrak carried you the whole way. Tann and I offered to help but he refused to let go," Ashlan's lips curled up. "If you ask me, that one has a bit of a crush on you."

"Stop it!" She laughed and sent her elbow into his side.

He jerked a bit but kept walking. "You were really out of it, Sid. We thought you'd die. As soon as we found the ship, we patched you up but we had no idea if you'd make it or not. Dalrak and Tazmin tried to feed you their magic but your body just wouldn't take hold."

"Sweet stars, you were worried about me!" She teased.

"We all were," Ashlan said. The smile on his face faded and was replaced by something dark and melancholy.

"I'm fine! See?" She said and formed a small burst of magic with her good hand. "Almost back to normal!"

They reached a fork in the corridors and she stopped short. "So who else is here? Beside you and Dalrak."

"Oh, you know. The whole team!" He smiled, "Serryl, Tann, Abbot." Sid noted the way his lips pursed when he mentioned Tann's name, "And Tazmin."

"Tazmin? Seriously?"

"I know. We were shocked too. I think you made an impression."

"Or she's just waiting for the best time to finish me off."

"I don't think so," Ashlan said. "She had a pretty intense conversation with Dee while you were out. I think he convinced her. Weird he can speak human by the way."

Sid laughed, remembering the shock on Ashlan's face when Dalrak first spoke his language in the domes. "Yeah, he's full of surprises. Wait," she chirped, "Abbot is here? What about Sylva?"

"The general's wife is a pretty amazing woman. She'd wait for him no matter how long it would take."

"But isn't he worried about leaving her there alone?"

Now it was Ashlan's turn to laugh. "Trust me, Sylva can take of herself. Like I said, she's amazing."

She took a deep breath in, quieting her thoughts for a moment. "And Leona?" She asked, rubbing her sore shoulder.

"She's not a priority right now, Sid. That's what I was trying to tell you before but you were so mad! It was like there was no sense talking to you. You couldn't even hear me."

"I heard you," she said. "And I understand." She touched the back of her neck where the wound from the chips was slowly closing up. "We can't let her get me."

"Good," Ashlan nodded. "There's just one small problem..."

"What now?"

"We kind of need you to get this thing running."

"TANN! CHECK THE THERMAL CONTROLS!" She yelled from the command chair.

Next to her, Tann stared blankly at the motherboard,

trying to discern what each switch and button did. The controls on the original ships were manual and unless you'd spent most of your life learning how to operate them, it likely looked like a jumbled mess.

"The blinking orange light!" She shouted, pointing to a spot on his left.

Tann pushed the button, reading the display in front of him. "Heat levels are critical!" He yelled in a panic. "What does that mean? What do I do?"

"Isolate the thrusters from the main circuit! The switch on your right, the small one next to the display."

Following her instruction, Tann flipped the switch and turned his attention to the display again. His eyes ran over the flashing numbers. "We're good! It's coming down!"

"Good," she sighed loudly. "Tell me when it's in the green. Ash, what's the status of the spherical thrusters?"

"Up and running," Ashlan noted to her right. "But FTL's are down."

"That's fine," she said considering the possibilities, "we just need to get this thing up. We can worry about that when we're in orbit."

She looked out of the observation window at the graveyard of ships scattered across the massive jungle clearing and wondered if the Al'iil ever found their way here. She'd have to ask Tazmin about it later. Her first priority was to get all of them off the star safely.

She checked the controls one last time before preparing for lift off. "Everyone strapped in?" She yelled over her shoulder, not waiting for a response. "Time to go!"

SID WATCHED the star get smaller and smaller in the large panes of the observation windows. The place that brought her so much joy and grief was nothing more than a red dot now, floating peacefully in space. The ship bucked a little and she placed a hand on the back of the command chair to steady herself. It was going to be a rough ride for a little while but she had no doubt they were safe for the rest of their journey. If only she knew where they were going.

Next to her, Ashlan looked just as grim and she cast a smile in his direction.

"So," he said. "Any plans on where we're flying this thing?"

She thought about it for a moment then breathed out deeply. "We need to get to my ship. We can dock there, repair the damages remotely and figure out a plan. This thing wasn't meant for long travels."

"You think we can do that?"

"Sure! I've fixed that rusted piece of junk with next to nothing for years. With whatever we have on this ship, we should be good for a while."

"Oh! Forgot to tell you before!" He exclaimed excitedly. "We found some droids in the engine rooms. They look old and beat up but maybe we can use them."

"Seriously? That great news! I'm sure you can figure it out, droid doctor." She punched his shoulder with a chuckle and winced. Her own shoulder was still throbbing despite the nanites that had started working on repairing her skin cells. "Ash?"

"Hmm?"

"What do you think Leona's doing right now?"

He laughed, "Probably kicking herself for letting you get away."

"I'm serious," she frowned. "Do you think she's waging war?"

"I wouldn't put it past her. You heard her screening. Anyone not with her is against her."

Sid glanced back to the star, ringless and alone, thinking of the horror it must be enduring. She wondered if more of the Al'iil came and how many of the people they left in the tower were still alive. She thought about the domes and what would happen to them now that the queen had waged civil war. How many would turn against their own just to survive? She thought that by shutting down the ring, she was helping everyone but maybe all she did was cause chaos. Though sometimes, a little chaos was necessary to unshackle an entire star. Ashlan was right to get her away. The best thing she could do for Kartega was to leave and come back when they had a plan that was well thought out. One that benefited everyone. She just needed some time to think and what better way to do that than to go back to the one place where she did her best thinking; the one place that felt like home.

"Think we can telescreen to the star from here?" She asked.

"You tell me," Ashland said.

"I think so."

"What are you going to tell them."

She looked down at her hands, still shaking from takeoff and the culmination of her life until that point.

"That they're not alone. That we're coming back and to try not to destroy the star before we get there," she smiled. "And that I'm coming back for the queen."

The ship shook again and she let the vibration run through her body. Her magic jumped at the impact, ready for attack at any point. She took a deep breath and let it flow through her, feeling every single spark of electricity in her veins.

She was coming back for them. Coming back to Kartega. And this time, she wasn't alone.

THANKS FOR READING!

I would love it if you could leave a short review of the book to let me know what you thought. You can post your review at any of the sites below and I hope you know how much I appreciate you doing this!

https://www.amazon.com/dp/B0852QNPWY

https://www.goodreads.com/book/show/51627107-kartega

If you want to hear more about my books or be the first to receive news on sales and giveaways, sign up for the newsletter!

https://www.ansage.ca/newsletter-1

A.N. SAGE

KARTEGA 2.0

A STAR REBORN

KARTEGA 2.0: A STAR REBORN, BOOK 2 OF THE KARTEGA CHRONICLES

Letting her escape was the biggest mistake they made...

After barely escaping Kartega with their lives, Sid and her friends find themselves hiding on the Arcturus in an endless loop of counted days. Between fixing the rust bucket of a ship they live in, struggling to contain the numbing magic of the keys implanted in her neck and fighting her growing feelings for the brooding warrior on board — Sid has her days full. As days turn into weeks, Sid grapples with the possibility of returning back to the star, the place she'd like to one day call her home.

But how could she ever find her way back without jeopardizing everything they've fought so valiantly to achieve?

While Sid tumbles through space, the vicious and bloodthirsty queen takes control of Kartega once more. As the domes fall under attack, no one is safe from the queens wrath. With supplies running low and time running out, Sid must decide if she will stay in hiding or risk everything to return to Kartega and save the domes from destruction.

What began as a rescue mission becomes a fight for freedom and Sid finds herself, yet again, in the center of an epic battle for control of the star.

Unfortunately for Sid, sometimes when you wish to find where you belong, you get exactly what you wish for...

BUY ON AMAZON NOW!

https://amzn.to/2ZhT7yR

ALSO BY A. N. SAGE

Kartgega 2.0: A Star Reborn- Kartega Chronicles Book 2

https://amzn.to/2ZhT7yR

AetherBorn- AetherBorn Saga Book 1

https://amzn.to/31tCAdB

AetherQueen- AetherBorn Saga Book 2

https://amzn.to/38mMGyJ

AetherBlood- AetherBorn Saga Book 3

https://amzn.to/2VuUxov

AetherWars- AetherBorn Saga Book 4

https://amzn.to/3gcuFWy

AetherBorn- The Complete Saga Box Set

https://amzn.to/3ifXog6

ABOUT THE AUTHOR

A.N. Sage has spent most of her life waiting to meet a witch, vampire, or at least get haunted by a ghost. In between failed seances and many questionable outfit choices, she has developed a keen eye for the extra-ordinary.

Since chasing the supernatural does not pay the bills, she dabbled in creative entrepreneurship, marketing and retail management. A.N. spends her free time reading and binge-watching television shows in her pajamas.

Currently, she resides in Toronto, Canada with her husband who is not a creature of the night.

A.N. Sage is a Scorpio and a massive advocate of leggings for pants.

For more books and updates:
www.ansage.ca

Connect on social media:
Facebook Group:
https://www.facebook.com/
groups/945090619339423/
Instagram:
instagram.com/a.n.sage/
Twitter:

twitter.com/ANsageWrites

Facebook:

facebook.com/ansagewrites

Pinterest:

pinterest.ca/ansagewrites

Goodreads:

goodreads.com/author/show/18901100.Alexis_N_Sage

Amazon:

amazon.com/author/a.n.sage